WORLDWIDE
MEDIA BOOK 2

HEART
CRIMES

SANDY
J MCNEILL

Book Cover Design by Giessel Design

Edited and Proofed by Represent Publishing

Interior Design and Formatting by Sandy J Mcneill

To my personal spider slayer, kiss keeper and smile bringer.
For always reminding me to write what I want, how I want and when
I want.

For anyone who has ever left a job, a relationship, your home. Only to find the grass isn't greener... Look closely at the new shoots. It actually is.

Author's Note

Dear Reader

Heart Crimes is Book Two in The Worldwide Media Duology. It can be read as a standalone, however there are a few references to some storylines from Book One.

If you intend to read both books, it is recommended you read *Remains of our Souls* first.

Please note there may be subject matter which may be upsetting to some.

Familial demise, stalking and violence are mentioned.

I hope you enjoy Miles and Cara's story.

With love

S.J

BLURB

♥

Doctor Cara Braithwaite lived for the pulse of the operating room until one fateful mistake shattered her confidence. The weight of a patient's life lost propelled her to abandon her ambitions and familiar life. Presented with a new opportunity to rewrite a difficult experience far from the bosom of home, she moves to Seattle, where fate leads her to cross paths with divorced single father and reluctant heartthrob Miles Masterson.

Their connection ignites a sensual and fiery romance, but an ominous shadow emerges around Cara, and unresolved complexities from Miles' previous relationship cast a dark cloud over their budding romance.

Can they confront the intricacies of past lives, present passions and future expectations? Will they come out on the other side unscathed?

Told in dual point of view, *Heart Crimes* will break your heart and shatter your soul yet somehow put it back together again piece by piece. It will make you realise second chances come in all guises.

♥

London , England

Prologue

♥

"Doctor Braithwaite, I leave the operating room for a split second and the patient is bleeding like a pig. Out of my way now," Edwin Frost spat, as he jostled his way back to the operating table. "Clamps." Incandescent with rage, he held out his famously steady left hand at the scrub nurse, having returned to the operating room after he unceremoniously left, only to return fifteen minutes later. "I said, pass me the goddamn clamps!"

"Mister Frost, it's the circ. I'm not sure how this happened." I floundered and glanced nervously at him while I clamped the artery to stem the bleeding. It was all in vain as the blood continued to spurt angrily from George Templeton's open chest cavity onto my clear goggles and my OR blues and sputtered angrily onto the once white, vinyl floor.

Despite my best efforts the patient wouldn't stop bleeding.

"The name is Sir Frost," he retorted icily. "Not sure how this happened? Right coronary artery. Left coronary artery and the circumflex going AROUND here," he stressed.

He had spent many years educating, embarrassing and deriding all in the same breath. This time he needed to be sure, after four years of additional cardiology training, I remained up to date with basic heart anatomy.

"It's hard to believe in only a couple of years you'll be leading your own surgical team. Heaven help us all," he snickered, making a melodramatic praying motion with his palms. Every moment with him was a teaching moment, and each time he did it with derision.

My stomach clenched as I breathed deeply behind my surgical mask. I worked hard to ignore his diatribe while I worked on the patient.

"We've stemmed the bleeding right there," I exclaimed in relief a minute later, coupled with my own internal celebration, after I clamped the bleeder. I spoke too soon. The jet of blood started again, this time worse than before.

"Obviously not. This patient was ill-prepared for surgery, and that's on you Doctor Braithwaite." Gone was Sir Frost, my all-knowing medical supervisor. In his place stood a man who had lost fifty-four years of cumulative cool and calm under pressure.

"This was emergency surgery. There wasn't enough time for a more thorough workup," I returned, head held high but feeling marginally more significant than a gnat. Despite confidence in myself, and in my capabilities as a surgeon, I despised confrontation at all costs.

"Still not good enough," he muttered under his breath with biting scorn.

"His bloodwork was fine. Respectfully, Sir Frost, you gave me permission to proceed. In fact you chaired the meeting yesterday when I presented this case," I said, almost to myself, while the merciless blood loss continued.

He continued to berate and belittle me while I fought to repair the damaged artery. "Now isn't the time for a soliloquy. We're losing him. I've often wondered how you got here. Young and daft with nothing but big hair and even bigger tits. Truth be told, you belong on some runway or film set, perhaps one of those brothels in Soho," he mumbled, shaking his head.

The sting of tears pricked the back of my eyes, and I was quick to blink them away.

I couldn't lose my concentration, not while in the throes of life and death. I was used to the misogyny at work, the cardiology boys' club was famous for it. But today, while under immense pressure, on the precipice of losing a patient and within earshot of my colleagues, it felt worse than usual. I wanted to storm out of the OR with some of my dignity, but I owed it to the patient to stay and do everything I could to save him.

The operating room was a hive of activity. Nurses, theatre techs, all working hard to save George's life. The medical students who observed and took notes at the viewing window magnified the petri dish feeling in the room. The bright white overhead light illuminated the colour and life leaving the patient's body. It highlighted his open chest cavity and his irregular, painfully slow heartbeat.

An ominous alarm sounded again on the anaesthetist's Boyle's machine.

"He's crashing, people. Call for a secondary operating room team, and activate the massive blood transfusion protocol," yelled Doctor Harrison, the anaesthetist. Also eminent, in his own right.

"You hadn't done that already? I'm dealing with amateurs," complained Sir Frost, more infuriated. Although it was my hand which caused damage to the patient, he was ultimately the man in charge.

"Frost, don't take that tone with me, or anyone else here. In your absence Braithwaite tried everything to save this man. You're the knight, ride in on your white horse, play the god which you believe yourself to be and help her." The small amount of skin visible underneath Doctor Harrison's surgical mask turned red as he stood up to Edwin Frost: Cardiothoracic Surgeon Extraordinaire, a twenty-first century knight, my medical supervisor and the man who could make or break my career.

Seattle, Washington

Twelve Months Later

Chapter One

♥

Miles

I enjoyed my work running Worldwide Media – one of the biggest and oldest media corporations in the world – alongside my older brother, Michael, the CEO. The unanimous vote by the board to appoint me to chief operating officer eighteen months prior came as a surprise. Although I was born into the Worldwide Media family, it was never guaranteed I would be a part of it, or its C-Suite.

Over the years I proved my worth and learned all the moving parts of the business. Acquisitions, however, were my strongest suit. My father, the previous CEO, sent me to my first cut-throat negotiation at twenty-four years old, just out of law school. I soon discovered brokering and bargaining came naturally to me.

It was the endless monotony of meetings, like the one I was in, that made a good work day unbearable. The quarterly mandatory meeting hosted by the research and development team. My eyes glazed over while I stared past the projector and its predictable spreadsheets, which I had perused the night before, energised after a gruelling session with my personal trainer.

From the spreadsheets and Greg Benedict, lead data scientist, nothing had changed in the last three months with the challenges facing print media. My father never let that plague him; Michael and I didn't either. We grew and advanced the business a thousand other ways in tune with our times, and that ensured Worldwide Media maintained its status as a titan in the industry. Greg needed to be moved along.

"Greg, these aren't different from the insights you presented three months ago. Do you have anything else?"

"Ahh, yes. In that case we'll proceed to slide six. In fact, let's skip over to, umm, slide nine." Which was still much of the same thing.

Greg, who was from a different time, was fixated on newspapers not selling at the street corners. What he wasn't privy to yet was the record-breaking half yearly profit that would be announced publicly the following day.

Past Greg was the Seattle skyline, which beckoned me outdoors to enjoy hiking, climbing, camping and just being. The simplicity, peace and clarity offered by the fresh, crisp mountain air was what I lived for, with the little leisure time I had. I even craved the burn in my muscles, achieved only after a day spent hiking.

I should have skipped the meeting. It hadn't added value to my work day.

My reverie was interrupted when my new assistant, Alistair, strode purposefully towards me and whispered in my ear. Without wasting time, I made the perfunctory apologies and left.

Of all the excuses in the world to leave, the worst one imaginable came up. During my short stint as COO, I had never left work for a family emergency. My family life hadn't been smooth sailing, but finally it was under some measure of control.

I found myself inside the express elevator, which took me down to the subterranean parking lot at One Worldwide HQ. Adrenaline in overdrive, I remembered little of the drive to the hospital at speeds I had never tried and never imagined the DB12 could reach. Downtown traffic in the early afternoon was surprisingly manageable.

As I drove through the city streets and the worst thoughts swirled in my mind, my hope was that the emergency room visit wasn't serious and my mother was overreacting. She was fiercely protective of my daughter, Maxie, who already knew too much sorrow and sadness in her young life. What could have happened to send her to the ER? The last time I had rushed to a hospital, I lost half of what was my whole world, my younger daughter. I couldn't take another crushing loss, not when being a single father was finally getting easier.

A car pulled out of a parking spot just as I arrived and I smoothly replaced it. Filled with dread, I hurriedly walked towards the entrance. The automatic doors opened, and I entered the mayhem and chaos that was the downtown children's hospital.

Hospitals are known to be cold and sterile. The children's hospital was one for two – it was freezing cold. Its sterility remained highly questionable, as rows of sick children filled the vast space, some hidden by disposable partitions.

I walked past a stretcher where an unaffected teenager, too cool for school, stared down into his phone with his left arm in a makeshift sling. Opposite him sat a frazzled woman with a screaming toddler, and so it continued stretcher after stretcher.

With apprehension, my eyes scanned the row of stretchers with children of varying ages, in varying states of distress, with their equally afflicted parents next to them.

It had become a different kind of Tuesday for me.

"Help you?" A nurse in multicoloured scrubs asked noncommittally as she strode opposite me, in a hurry but seemed to recognize the dazed and dread-filled look on my face. As soon as she asked, my eyes caught a glimpse of my mother in her smart signature Chanel suit, out of place and sitting in a chair next to a stretcher.

"Don't worry, I've just seen my mother." I walked towards her. Somehow she was in the quietest corner of the emergency room where even as I approached, it became more tranquil.

I arrived at the stretcher and took a fortifying breath.

"What happened to her?" I blinked in disbelief as my eyes took in the angry red lump on Maxie's forehead and a repaired split, which she didn't have in the morning when I had driven her to school.

"She slipped on one of the other kids' spilt juice and hit her head. Her school tried to call you before they called me." My mother weighed each word she spoke, perhaps stuck between telling me everything and sparing me every detail.

"Juice? They did? I didn't get any calls," I grunted. I pulled out my phone and stared at its screen – six missed calls. All unanswered while my phone was on Alistair's desk for his attention. My intuition about him was right; he was too green. Next time I would hire an assistant using my head, not my heart.

"You look stunned. Relax, she's okay." She smiled reassuringly. I wasn't at ease. I could hear my heart pounding in my ears.

"She doesn't look it, and she never naps during the day." My gaze was focused on her head. It was unnerving. I had never seen it like that before.

"I know. It's that egg-shaped lump on her forehead and that cut, which the most charming paediatrician has glued shut—"

"Glue? No stitches?" I interrupted.

My mother was personable and could easily find charm in a rock. This time, she found it in the humdrum and tedium of the emergency room. I moved closer and peered at Maxie. The lump looked sore, with what looked like its own heartbeat. A dull thud started in my own head.

"No, son. She said the glue wouldn't leave any scarring, which could bother Maxie when she was older," she chuckled. Anyone who knew my mother was lucky to. Without trying she made the world right, no matter how bleak the outlook.

"Thanks, Mom. I don't know what we would both do without you." I momentarily shifted my gaze from Maxie to her.

"That's what grandmas are for. It's all in the manual." She said, trying to reassure me with her long-standing joke.

"Why is she in this hospital and not on Mercer Island?" I pressed again, worried this was more serious than my mother was letting on.

"They were here in the city on their field trip to Chihuly Garden and Glass when she slipped. This is the closest hospital," she added, still working overtime to try and convince me Maxie was fine.

"That was today," I remembered, shaking my head. How could I forget? I had signed the permission slip. Maybe I hadn't got to grips with being a single father as much as I thought.

When she heard my voice Maxie stirred and spoke in a sleepy voice.

"Daddy," she called, arms outstretched. I leaned into her delicate embrace and my worries started to melt away. I exhaled, and the tension that had built up since leaving work left my body.

"How are you?" I held her close. Green apple hair conditioner filled my nostrils, calmed me, and reminded me she was there with me. I hadn't lost her too. While I held her, I promised myself I wouldn't lose her, I couldn't lose her. She was my world and all I had left.

"I'm so happy, Daddy." She smiled as she hesitantly touched her lumpy forehead and grimaced.

"Does your head hurt?"

"Only when I touch it." She spoke with a lisp while the tears filled her eyes, which she bravely blinked away and let her toothless grin fill her face instead.

"Try not to touch it too much. Why are you so happy?"

"I remember you," she said, and her smile became wider.

"Why would you forget me, beautiful girl?" Puzzled, I perched on her stretcher.

"When Uncle Mickey hit his head, he woke up and didn't remember us. I was scared I would forget too."

He was back to his normal self, but I realised Maxie was still affected by her uncle's injury two and a half years ago if that was her first thought when she hit her head. Fleetingly I wondered how she would feel when she was old enough to understand what happened in Istanbul. How would I explain the bombing to her? It wasn't the time to let my heart break again. But I couldn't wait too long to tell her. It had been international news and any one of the kids at school could bring it up.

"That was different. Your uncle's always had a soft head. You, on the other hand, have a tough nut." I smiled and sat her up next to me.

She giggled and the relief I felt made me forget where I was, and I relaxed into her pillow. Losing a child made me overly cautious. I wouldn't know what to do with myself if I lost Maxie too.

"I need the bathroom," she announced. She had the knack of skipping from one topic to the next and back again. It was enough to make anyone's head spin.

"I'll come with you." I quickly volunteered, making to get up.

"I'm not a baby, and you can't go inside the girls' bathroom," she chided in a grown up way. Her mother's absence, followed by her sister's death, forced her to grow up far quicker than she needed to.

"Mom, should she be walking around?" I hoped she would be the voice of reason and repeat the doctor's orders.

"Go ahead, Maxie. We'll be here. Remember to wash your hands."

After Maxie left the two of us alone, she turned to me with kindness in her eyes. "Son, you can't wrap her up in cotton wool forever. You and your brothers hit your heads more times than I care to remember, and you turned out fine. Give her a little freedom and room to grow," she continued to whisper with compassion in her eyes.

She understood what I had been through; she had lost her first born son too soon.

It was two years since we lost Laila, and when it was needed she held my hand through my loss. I wondered who had held hers years ago and, more recently, while she navigated life after another loss.

"She's seven. How much freedom does she need?"

"Enough to go to the bathroom by herself. We can see the bathroom door from here. Don't coddle her. You don't want a spoiled princess on your hands." She continued the speech while Maxie was in the bathroom. My mother and I had always been close, and when it came to some matters of raising Maxie, I leaned on her maybe more than I should.

In no time, Maxie returned to her spot in the emergency room. "All done. Can I go back to the glasshouse for the blowing? It's such fun." The visit to the bathroom had invigorated her, but I didn't have the heart to tell her she wouldn't return to join her class on the field trip.

"Let's check in with your doctor first." Mom smiled at Maxie and looked around.

I stood up and looked past the nurses' station, across the ER. In a sea of blue scrubs and dozens of other pairs of eyes, mine locked onto a pair of almond-shaped green ones. She stole my breath and I couldn't look away. Neither did she. Instead she walked towards me, smiling. In an ordinary pair of blue scrubs, she was still a vision with a confident spring in her step, and I couldn't stop staring.

When she arrived at Maxie's bedside, she spoke gently to her. For a person so young, she radiated a sense of calm assurance that even put *me* at ease. It became clear why my mother was charmed.

"How's your head, Lady Maxie? I saw you take a trip to the bathroom." They smiled at each other. Hers was a polished British accent. From the time I spent there, I recognised it to be from the south of England. *But why do I care so much?*

"Doctor Cara, my head hurts when I touch it." Surprisingly, my mature-beyond-her-years Maxie became seven years old and allowed herself to be vulnerable with this woman. The woman who took Maxie's hand and spoke gently to her. I wondered if she was as kind to all her patients.

"It will hurt a little, but that should soon go away. Do you feel woozy or queasy?" she asked and let go of Maxie's hand as she checked some things off on the tablet fixed on the wall at the bedside.

"No." Maxie shook her head gently.

"Good. I think it's time you took your nan home," she hinted, beaming. *I have never seen a woman so beautiful.*

"My nan?" Maxie asked, confused.

"Yes, your nan. What do you call this lovely lady with you?" she asked as she smiled at my mother, who seemed as dazzled by her as Maxie and I were.

"I call her Grandma," Maxie said, matter-of-fact.

She laughed softly before she continued. "Okay then, will you take Grandma home? No driving for the next two days," she whispered and shook her head playfully.

"I can't drive. I'm seven." It was Maxie's turn to giggle.

The doctor turned her enticing gaze, focused on my eyes and spoke to me for the first time.

"Hi, I'm Cara Braithwaite, Maxie's doctor." Like a fly caught in a spider's web, I was ensnared in the depths and mystique of her green eyes.

I didn't know if it was the accent or her, but I was speechless. Everything around me became deathly still and silent. She was all I saw and heard.

Even in the scrubs she wore, it was clear her sculpted body was well-proportioned and begging for attention. Her caramel brown hair was up in what I once heard called an artfully messy bun. She had it up, away from her long slender neck, where a lone beauty spot took pride of place in the centre. I briefly wondered about the average kiss count needed to cover all of it. In the hollow of her neck rested a delicate platinum-coloured necklace where a teardrop shaped sapphire hung. My eyes stopped there and I imagined how she would smell. All I had to do was get close enough to breathe all of her in.

After all her elegant details were slowly catalogued, stored and safely locked away in my mind, my conclusion was that she didn't belong in the chaos and commotion of the emergency room. Anywhere but there.

Not to be caught staring, I looked up at her face instead, where our eyes met. Overwhelmed, I worked hard to regain my composure. Gradually, my mind returned to the right focus.

Maxie.

The reason I was in the downtown hospital, where all the noise and hubbub returned too.

"This is Miles, Maxie's dad," Mom announced with a quick glance at me. I hoped she didn't recognise the internal storm that raged within me.

"Hi, Miles. We've done some imaging, a CT, and everything looks good. Although, Maxie has suffered a concussion," she said quietly. I guessed so Maxie wouldn't overhear.

"A concussion?" I was in disbelief. In my ignorance I associated concussions with high impact accidents and rough sport. Never with anything that would involve my Maxie.

"It's a mild one. She should make a quick recovery. If she starts to vomit, loses consciousness, or even becomes confused, bring her straight back. Calpol should work for the headache." Her gentle tone was reassuring and, again, put me at ease.

"Calpol? Is that some type of anodyne? I'm not familiar with it."

Maxie had her fair share of colds and sore throats, and I was sure a headache would also fall within my limited purview, but the recommendation was new to me.

"Sorry, I meant Tylenol. Force of habit," she admitted with a light chuckle. Her laugh sounded like a melody, one I needed to hear on repeat. Her alluring smile made me smile too.

It had definitely become a different kind of Tuesday.

"I suppose Calpol is what they give kids in ... ?" Instinctively my ear went closer to her, where I caught a hint of vanilla. I took a deep breath, which I hoped she didn't notice. I already knew where she was from, but I needed to be around her for as long as possible and hear her talk about anything, including Calpol.

"London. Well, that's what it's called in most of Europe, really," she explained as she looked me over, without being obvious.

Was it my imagination, or had she noticed me too?

It took everything in me to respond to her. All I could do was drink her in. Her voice, her smile, her body. That vanilla scent. Even the Briticisms she unwittingly dropped into conversation which I had to think twice to understand. I needed to stop leering. She was working, and I was there for Maxie's injury.

I wrestled with my thoughts, trying hard to say something, except what I really wanted to say.

"You're a long way from home. You were there for Maxie, and I appreciate that."

"She's a pleasant girl, wise beyond her years." Her eyes lit up, accompanied by another flash of her dazzling white smile.

In the few minutes I was around her, she was kind, funny and genuine. She was different from the women I crossed paths with in the last few years during my half-hearted attempts at dating. I was entranced, and I had to do everything in my power to see her again. But how? My mother was standing a few feet away, possibly listening in, and Cara Braithwaite was Maxie's doctor. Normally self-assured, my cheeks heated, as did the rest of my body, while I imagined how she would look without the scrubs on. Or anything else. This wasn't the right time nor the place for those thoughts. I had been alone for too long.

"Come on, Nan, let's go. Can I call you Nan, Grandma? I think I like it," Maxie piped up, laughing.

"Nan's fine, darling. Let's get your raincoat on to go outside," Mom insisted with a smile and snuck another look at the doctor. She got Maxie's things together, and as Doctor Braithwaite turned to walk away, I didn't think twice and followed her. This was my one chance to impress her.

"Doctor Braithwaite, will Maxie require follow up?" I realised I had to be the only parent yearning for a repeat consultation with a paediatrician.

"Ordinarily no, but if you're concerned about her condition, take her to her usual paediatrician, or bring her to me. For my sins, I have clinic days at a paediatric practice nearby. You can give her mother my card if she needs it." She flashed another smile at me while she felt around in her pocket, wrote a number down, then held her card out towards me.

"Her mother won't need it. She's out of the picture, but I'll take it anyway. Just in case." I fought hard to keep the huge smile threatening to break out at bay.

Her roundabout way of bringing Maxie's mother into the conversation was a stroke of genius. Could she indirectly have been asking if I was attached, or was that what any doctor would say? Even my perception at social cues was askew. We both smiled as I took her card from her outstretched hand, and it felt like a major victory.

I followed Maxie and my mother towards the exit, my heart pounding, coupled with a feeling of accomplishment. I would see her again. No acquisition had ever made me feel like a winner as much as I did then.

Chapter Two

♥

Cara

I surprised myself and gave a patient my personal number. Doctors do it sometimes, but there was a reason I gave it this time. I'd never had a problem attracting male attention, but this was different. His was the right kind of attention. Miles Masterson looked at me in a way no one ever had, as if he wanted to see more of me, maybe the real me.

He was handsome, and underneath the suit he wore it was easy to see he was built solid. He even looked like he had stepped out of a dream I may have had a time or two. I hadn't noticed a man in a long time, not in a way that awakened something. The emergency room was hardly the place for the thoughts racing through my mind.

I could never drown the constant beeping of the machines, the endless chatter of my colleagues and the occasional child's cry. Despite the challenges, it was my job and where I thrived. Could three years of living the single life, without a man's touch, make me feel this way? He wasn't the first man I'd seen in the last three years, but he was the first one who made me lose my mind and made my thoughts wander in the middle of a workday. Out of the blue, I was tied up in knots.

After my arrival in Seattle eight weeks ago, I lived with my brother, Dean, and his family for three of those until he showed me around a group of four reimagined townhouses in Queen Anne, only a five minute walk from his family home. I jumped at the chance of leasing a newly renovated townhouse, with a bespoke kitchen straight out of my brother's imagination. A skilled carpenter who left London ten years ago for love, after a chance meeting with Charlie. His business flourished, and they built custom kitchens, laundry rooms and mud-rooms in homes up and down the Pacific Northwest.

My townhouse, nestled in a quiet downtown neighbourhood, was my sanctuary from the bustling urban streets. My transition to rainy downtown Seattle was marked by a sense of rejuvenation. The city's misty embrace seemed to wrap around me inviting me into its unique rhythm.

After the long shift and a quick detour home to freshen up, I was on my way to meet a school friend I kept in touch with over the years. I approached the restaurant, the funky Pink Door, and saw Izzy in a seat at the window. As soon as she laid eyes on me, she squealed. I couldn't help myself as I squealed just as loudly as she did. When we held each other in a tight embrace, the years we were apart seemed to disappear.

"Izzy, you haven't changed a bit," I shrilled as she did a dramatic pirouette in the tiny space between our table and the next, drawing curious glances from other restaurant patrons.

"Neither have you, Braithwaite. You're still the prettiest flower in the bunch. I can't believe we are both here in the Emerald City. I'm sorry you arrived while I was travelling. I would have loved to see you straight away." We both couldn't help the excited chatter as we held hands, then sat down.

"Don't worry, Izzy. We're here now. You're gorgeous too. That bob works well with your bone structure, and the colour is amazing."

"Really? I was worried it was giving off some schoolmarm vibes. It's low maintenance and fuss free. Perfect for early mornings and late nights."

"Domme maybe, not schoolmarm." Izzy was gorgeous, and she knew it. That didn't stop her fishing for compliments wherever she could get them.

"That magically explains the failures that were my last two dates." We both became teenage girls again and giggled.

In between talking, I stole glances around the Pink Door, appreciating its relaxed ambience. "This restaurant has a great vibe. What's good here? I'm starving." I scanned the menu half-heartedly, preferring to catch up with Izzy instead.

"What Italian menu isn't good? Wait til you see the trapeze artist."

"In a restaurant!" I exclaimed, wide eyed.

"They don't make restaurants like this in Mother England," she remarked as she looked around too.

"No, they do not. Right, I'll get the linguine with the clams," I said after a cursory glance at the menu.

"Good choice, I'll have the same. Cocktails too. My shift doesn't start until midday tomorrow," she added with wide eyes and an enthusiastic nod.

We ordered, and while we waited she spoke, a little subdued. "How are you? I read the transcripts from that god-awful hearing. The bollocking you got from the General Medical Council must have been the stuff of nightmares." She sighed and stretched out both her hands across the table to hold mine. She had always been tactile.

I laughed softly. "*Enfant terrible*. You're still as vulgar as ever. I'm trying to put it behind me. Although I still think about it sometimes. All the things I could have done better, all the ways I could have done things differently. Who knows, he might still be alive now." Overwhelmed by that memory, I took in the eclectic mix of patrons filing in.

I'd always enjoyed people-watching and imagining their stories. Were they happy? In love? Like me, did they chop and slice their breakfast fruit with surgical precision? The place was crawling with good-looking, clean-cut men, but only one crossed my mind just at that time.

"You can't keep doing that to yourself. I don't mean to sound callous, but we're in the business of life and death. It was bound to happen sometime, you didn't know when. No doctor ever does." She took a sip of her charred chilli and orange cocktail. She seemed to love it, and I made a mental note to order it next.

"You're right, and I know it too. My mind is independent of me and likes to overthink, even when it knows not to," I said, as if I were repeating a helpful mantra.

"Was your last medical supervisor in London an actual knight?" She tactfully changed the subject but failed to pivot far enough from its gloom.

"Yes, he was." I sighed and groaned as memories of Sir Frost came flooding back.

"How does a cardiac surgeon become a knight? That must have been something," she giggled.

"You have no idea," I added with an eye roll. "We all had to address him properly, otherwise there would be hell to pay. He was bestowed the title, you know, the MBE for his services to sciences. He was good at what he did, I guess." I shrugged.

"You don't sound convincing at all." Her tone became serious; the look on my face must have shown how life had been under the tutelage of Sir Frost.

"If you really must know, he was a misogynist, who belittled me and other female doctors at every chance he got. He described our body parts in painful and elaborate detail and picked apart our intellect and surgical skills." I let it all out. Izzy was good company and I was ready to vent.

"Nobody thought to report him? Get him turfed out?" She sounded surprised, but she should've known better. I was sure she must have seen or heard something vaguely similar anywhere she had worked.

"In hindsight, I see your logic. Back then, being accepted onto his registrar program proved what a promising surgeon you were. Why rock the boat by complaining about the knight's teaching style. I couldn't stay, not after the fiasco with that patient." I sighed dejectedly and took a long sip of my cocktail.

We were both quiet for a while. She searched my face while I searched for a server to bring another cocktail. The purging called for more social lubrication or drowning of sorrows, perhaps both.

"I'm sorry you went through that hell. I'm relieved you're out of there. How's this place treating you anyway? Have you settled in?" She asked the same question with the same look she had sixteen years ago when we both started at Stowe School – home of the Stoics.

She was a scholarship kid, and I was a lonely, trepid orphan enrolled on compassionate grounds. We were both longing to fit in at our elitist school. She was thirteen years old, small and timid. Now she had come into her own and was a firecracker.

"The rain and coffee are both living up to their reputation. Are you still enjoying endocrinology?" I was starting to become inarticulate, the cocktails getting to my head. I had to slow down.

"Same old chaos. Repeat after me: B.U.R.N.O.U.T."

"Could it be time for a change?"

"I'm not sure what I would change to. I believe I'm stuck in a rut. Have you explored much?"

"Some hiking, not as much as I want to. Washington State is much bigger than I realised. And who knew Seattle was wetter than London? I've been around Pike Place Market with its fish tossing. Paid a visit to the gum wall; I had to see it to believe it." I had enjoyed plenty of tourist bucket list items. I still had plenty I wanted to see and do. All I needed was time to do it.

"Yes, the infamous gum wall. A testament to both art and dental hygiene," she laughed raucously.

"So, dish. What's the latest gossip from Izzyland?" Without a social life to speak of, living vicariously through Izzy would have to do.

"Do you remember Liam Hughes?"

"Can't say I do. He must have been forgettable."

"He was when we were at Stowe, two years ahead of us. Anyway, he started at St Mark's in orthopaedics."

"Hang on a minute, three Stoics, in Seattle, at the same time. What's his story? How did he get here?"

"Like me, he did the Semester Abroad Program here, returned to England, but he found the working conditions difficult, and he returned to Seattle as soon as he could."

Pursing my lips, I shook my head. "All this time I thought this doctor life was easier on the boys."

"Only marginally, Braithwaite. He, too, has some war stories and war wounds from the medical battlefield. He's also become Doctor

Tall, Dark and Disarmingly Charming. But you know the golden rule – don't dip your stethoscope in the company ink."

"Yes, that never ends well." I had my own cautionary tale of a workplace romantic entanglement. It made the rest of my interventional cardiology rotation long and unbearable. That was three years ago, and the last time I made any attempts at dating.

"Enough about my workplace crush. Any potential love interests at your new gig? I still can't believe you're required to split your time between two places; how hard could it be to transition from adult cardiology to paediatrics?"

"Working in both paediatric emergency and paediatric general practice was the quickest and simplest way to transition to paediatric cardiology. I have a few exams here and there, then I'll start operating on the little ones.

"Still keen on surgery?"

"Not really, but I'm great at it, and I have invested time into it. I'm at a crossroads, and I'm taking what I think is an easier route. Less stress in paeds, and hopefully the egos are not so overinflated," I said resignedly.

"I'm here for you, Braithwaite, whatever you need." Izzy took my hand again and held it in hers. Some people have a sizable quantity of friends, but I had Izzy, who was quality. "Still, you didn't tell me about the talent at the children's hospital, or do they all wear multicoloured bow ties?" She laughed again.

My mind raced to the obscenely handsome parent, the man I had met only hours earlier, who was more off-limits than my colleagues. I already imagined spending my time with him. Besides looking like a dream, he seemed fun, energetic and clever, with a sensitivity that bloomed only from a place of elevated emotional intelligence.

"You know me, always the hopeless romantic. For now, I'm just trying to navigate these rainy streets without getting lost."

"Good idea. Never mix work and romance. We've worked too damn hard to get here. The only thing I'm mixing these days are lattes and long shifts." The sobering remark crashed me back down to earth with a resounding thud. Still, I raised my third cocktail of the evening, shared a toast with Izzy and hoped she wouldn't notice my shift in mood.

The trapeze artist started her performance. I still enjoyed my time with Izzy, although ice cold water had been poured on my fantasy and served with a side of linguini. We parted ways at midnight and I ordered a car back to Queen Anne. I made sure to forget my workday, especially the man in the ER who would have certainly forgotten about me.

Late Friday afternoon, after a consultation with my last patient of the day, Melinda, the clinic manager and all round busybody, pushed a medical trolley into my consultation room and on it was a large bouquet of flowers.

"Looks like you have an admirer, Cara. I'll place them next to the window for you. Did you drive in today? It might be a struggle, but you must take these home. They are too beautiful to leave all alone over the weekend. You know, this arrangement means lust at first sight." She made a show of fanning herself.

"Is that a fact?" I asked, after I finally got a word in.

I stared in wonder at the unusually pretty arrangement of purple roses, lilacs, and pink baby's breath. I loved flowers. Grateful patients sent them often but they were never as elaborate as this bouquet. My last beautiful bouquet was from James Foxworthy, a man I was sure would be my forever, until he decided I wasn't good enough to be his. Like every good thing, he took time to get over. Now he was firmly confined to the trash can of history.

Melinda had barely left the room when I pounced on the card within the bouquet and read it hurriedly. A smile filled my face, and my heart skipped a beat. They were from Miles Masterson. It was three days since we met, and I had done a good job of getting him out of my mind, until the flowers brought him right back. This couldn't go any further than a bouquet of flowers. I also knew I couldn't be rude, so I dialled the number on the card.

As if he had been waiting for the call, he answered on the first ring.

"Miles, it's Doctor Braithwaite. How's Maxie?" I shook my head and rolled my eyes at my cringeworthy formal tone.

"Maxie is much better, as if the whole thing never happened." He was relaxed and even chuckled on the other end of the phone.

"I'm pleased to hear that. Thanks for the flowers. That was generous but unnecessary. I was only doing my job." I made sure to keep it as professional as possible, hoping that would be the end of it, but also wishing it wouldn't be.

"Doctor Braithwaite, I need to see you." His gravelly voice sent a tingle down my spine.

"I'm sorry, I only see kids. I can give you a list of good physicians who attend to adults." Again, I rolled my eyes, this time at my poor attempt at pretending to misunderstand him.

"I'll be at your practice to pick up the list in fifteen minutes, if you're still there?" His chuckle became a lot deeper.

"I was just getting ready to leave, but I'll be here for another fifteen," I said brightly, hoping to disguise the mixed feelings I had about seeing him again.

That hadn't gone as I had hoped it would; I only see kids. I huffed. *Note to self: Don't come up with lame excuses on the fly.*

It was going to be difficult to get out of whatever this situation was with him. Even though we had only just met and spoke a handful of words to each other, I was excited to see him. On the other hand, I was uneasy. What was the purpose of his visit?

My heart was pounding and my palms were sweaty. This time I wasn't wearing scrubs. I wore my royal blue sheath midi dress. I loved its sophistication, and the way it held my body made me feel sexy in an unsexy work environment. I especially loved the deep V-neck, which I always made sure to cover with my white coat during patient consultations. I doffed the white coat and hung it on a hook behind the door.

While lost in my thoughts, and what seemed like only five minutes later, Melinda announced Miles' arrival over the intercom. He couldn't have been far when we spoke.

We both faltered when I opened my door. I was taken by surprise at how good he looked. In three days, I had managed to forget that. He looked as stunned as I was.

"How are you, Doctor Braithwaite?" His breath caught while he gazed at me, unflinching. The tiny flutters from Tuesday returned to my lower belly.

"You're the one needing recommendations for general physicians. Are you well?" I tried not to smile. He didn't need a physician, he was the picture of health *and virility*.

As he walked further into my consultation room, the scent of something expensive filled the room. He, too, filled the small space, decorated in primary colours and dotted with stuffed birds, with his exuberance, the deep timbre of his voice and his tall, broad shouldered frame clad in a suit clearly made just for him. He looked out of place, but that was offset by his confident swagger. He hadn't spoken much, but it would be difficult to continue to pretend to be impervious to his charm.

"Not so much. I needed to see you again." He sounded sincere as he casually sauntered towards my desk and pulled out a chair, where a white stuffed Galapagos penguin took pride of place. *Galapagos penguins mate for life.* A fact , one of my young patients had rattled off when she sat in that very chair.

I quickly shook the thought from my head as he sat down and placed the penguin at the juncture of his legs where there was a promi-nent bulge. My mouth dried while my eyes darted from the penguin to his eyes, as I willed myself to maintain eye contact. The small room where I treated infants, teenagers and every little human in between would never be the same again.

"Just so there's no misunderstanding, in what capacity did you need to see me again?" I took a deep breath and steeled myself for his response.

"Doctor Braithwaite, you're not misunderstanding anything. I want to get to know you, personally. We could start with dinner," he declared, still watching me with rapt attention.

I could get used to being looked at like that.

"I'm going to stop you right there. Due to the nature of my work, and my professional responsibilities, that can't happen. I don't dine or socialise with patients."

A hint of regret leaked into his expression before he quickly recov-ered. "That's where you're mistaken. I'm not one of your patients –

and never will be," he added with confidence and a self-assured grin, seemingly emboldened by his assertions.

A smile threatened to show on my face. He was only half right. I could have been mistaken, but I was enjoying his presence and his company. This was a simple interaction but I didn't want it to end.

"You're my patient's father, I have a professional responsibility towards you too," I explained as his intense eyes met mine.

How long can I continue to resist his advances?

"You attended to Maxie only once, and I'll make sure you never have to be her doctor again. I know a bit about the law." That's why he was an intense negotiator, even for a dinner date.

"Sounds like I'm preaching to the choir." I didn't recognise my own breathy voice.

"Doctor Braithwaite, I usually get what I want, and I never give in." The hard set of his jaw showed a relentless determination, and I believed him.

"It's not you. Actually, it's me." Again, I cringed inwardly. It was dinner, and I was treating it like a marriage proposal.

"That sounds like the beginning of every bad breakup, but explain." This time he quirked a single eyebrow.

"I did notice you, and if it were any other situation, I would be jumping at the chance to umm ... have dinner with you, but I can't. Although I've never had issues with socialising with patients, I've been investigated, interviewed, interrogated and had my work inspected with a fine tooth comb. The process was soul destroying and one of the reasons I left everything for a new start here, so the stakes are too high for me. Even if it's just dinner." The last statement had become a mere whisper.

"The situation you mention, how did that work out for you?" The expression on his face became serious, and he wasn't able to hide his concern. *An empath, he must be a Pisces.*

"I was cleared of all wrongdoing and allowed to continue practising. I did for a while, but that situation became untenable, so I moved here eight weeks ago."

I had never had therapy; I preferred to rationalise it all in my own mind, but that sounded suspiciously like it. How could I be so candid and unguarded? With a stranger. All that was missing was the couch and an air purifier.

"That's a lot to go through, and I'm sorry it happened. All the more reason to put it behind you. If you let me, I can show you this city, and in the process, you might like me," he tried to reason with a smile, which I was sure always got him anything he wanted.

Even though I shouldn't, I already liked him.

"I don't think you understand. I can't see you, not outside of my work," I whispered.

I didn't owe him anything, nor did I know him, but I couldn't help the pang of sadness at not getting a chance to know him. I only knew how to hide from him from behind the very thin veil of my job, and that, too, was slowly coming apart at the seams, the longer he was in my presence.

"Could I be reading you wrong? But I'm not convinced you mean that. Tell me one more time that you and I can't see each other." His voice had gone down an octave and had become husky. It felt like a full body caress, even goosebumps appeared on my skin.

Note to self: Behave.

I hesitated, and he pounced on that momentary delay. He smiled, a full and genuine smile, almost boyish and endearing. His dimples were in full effect, the left one deeper than the right. How had I not noticed that knee weakening quirk until now? Just as I was about to speak, a dramatic bolt of lightning zapped across the sky outside my window, and the late afternoon slow pitter patter of rain became a downpour. Could that be a sign?

"Ummm ..."

"I have my answer, Doctor Braithwaite. No words are necessary." All I could do was swallow the lump in my throat. "Are you going far? You wouldn't want to get that dress wet." He let me catch his eyes openly run up and down my body.

"Thanks, but I'll wait until it stops." I didn't trust myself to follow any rules, not around him.

"I insist. My driver's downstairs, he can take you wherever you need to go."

Hmm, is he one of those pompous twits with a driver and a butler to wait on him hand and foot?

"I can't accept a lift from you, I don't know you or your driver." If his driver took me home, he would know where I live. Women can never be too careful in Seattle, or any other big city. I wouldn't let myself become a statistic.

"I want to rectify that. You can trust me, and I trust Clayton. He drives Maxie when I'm tied up and can't drive her myself." *He is one of those twits. Enter butler, stage left.*

"And how will you manage in this rain?" I was being stubborn, but I needed a lift home.

"I'm Seattle-born and bred, a little rain doesn't faze me. Besides, something tells me you don't want to be seen leaving here with me," he continued, while the heavy rain lashed at the window.

He stood up and came round my desk. He held out his hand, and I didn't think twice as I gave him mine. He held it and stroked my index finger lightly, leaving a trail of tingling nerve endings in its wake. It was excruciating, but I couldn't hide from how intoxicating it was. That was not the handshake I expected.

I took a deep breath as he walked away and reached the door in two long strides. He turned around and looked at me as I finally exhaled.

"I'll be in touch." His dimpled smile was all I could see. I couldn't let this man affect me as much as he already did.

Chapter Three

♥

Miles/Cara

Unsurprisingly, blue had become my new favourite colour, and her dress nearly buried me. Her scrubs didn't do her body justice. She put some work into keeping fit, yet she remained feminine and soft in all the places sinfully moulded by the blue dress. Today she left her hair loose, and its brown waves tumbled down her shoulders to her back. Her pink plump lips formed a smile, which I selfishly imagined was only for me. She caught me staring a few times. I couldn't help myself.

Everything about her overpowered me but somehow, I kept my wits about me. I could tell from our short interaction she didn't realise how beautiful she was. Perhaps she did, but that wouldn't matter to someone like her – intelligent, busy and purposeful. She was out of my league in every way. Could that be why she kept pushing me away? I didn't measure up to her standards, but what were they and would I ever find out?

I didn't need to wine and dine her and try to impress her with the superficial. If she was ever going to look my way, I needed her to see me. All of me. My flaws, my failures and my fissures. If she allowed herself to get over those, in time she would see who I really am.

I would split open any old wound of mine, just to let her peer inside it, not because she was a doctor, but because she was her. I missed being wanted and needed in a way I was sure only she would.

When I arrived at the car, Clayton held the door open for me. He didn't have to, but he always insisted on it. He was well-mannered, in a way men of his generation were.

"I won't be needing a ride from you this evening."

"Are you walking back to HQ? It's pouring buckets out here," he exclaimed in disbelief.

"I won't melt Clay, but take Doctor Braithwaite wherever she needs to go. She'll be out soon. She's hard to miss," I said with a grin.

I never tried to hide from Clay. I could let my guard down with him, I trusted him. I pulled the umbrella from its compartment in the door.

"I'm in no rush. I can take both of you in separate directions. Marianne is working late tonight," he reasoned. Clay tried his best to attend to me, more than he needed to. It started when my ex-wife left and became more apparent when I lost my father.

"That insufferable Michael. He'll drive me home. Make him pay for working Marie's fingers to the bone," I joked and started to walk hurriedly towards HQ.

As I walked away in the pouring rain, I tried to understand why Cara kept pushing me away. Would the brief consultation and very minor procedure she performed on her forehead count as being Maxie's doctor? Yet that was the very excuse she used to dissuade me from pursuing her.

Whatever happened and made her leave London had her terrified of a single misstep in her professional life, and she didn't want to break a single rule. Would I ever be able to convince her that I was worthy? She didn't tell me what happened to make her leave London, but I felt on top of the world when she became vulnerable with me, even as she pushed me away.

Although she oozed intelligence and refinement, she had a sweet naivety about her. All I wanted was to protect her, from everything. Even when whatever I wanted to happen between us was still in doubt, I was walking in the pouring rain so she wouldn't refuse a ride from me. *The last woman in my life had been a colossal mistake. Am I making another by pursuing her?*

♥

Cara

Losing my words had never been a problem, but something about being around Miles made me lose all sense of self. I wanted to get lost in him and with him. I was fascinated, but I couldn't put everything I worked hard for at risk for a stranger, even a seemingly perfect one like him.

Clayton drove me home in a terribly ostentatious silver Rolls Royce. I was drawn to the intellectual types, with a vast amount of knowledge and a raging god complex, and it always ended badly. Was Miles one of those guys? I hadn't given him much of a chance to find out but as soon as I saw it, his car offended my sensibilities. Even if its ride was smooth, tranquil, and if I allowed it, the backseat was soft enough and large enough to lull me into a dreamless sleep.

Enveloped by his lingering expensive seductive scent in the car, and the large bouquet next to me, I sat quietly for a while. It was hard to forget his commanding presence. It would be simple to be swept away in his charm and appeal. He could easily sweet-talk any woman into his bed, perhaps without talking at all, as his sexual magnetism spoke volumes.

With my eyes closed, I returned to our intense exchange in my consultation room. I wondered if caution could be thrown to the wind just once and allow him to be my one thrilling and decadent indulgence. Eventually I opened them and caught Clayton watching me in the rearview mirror. I had caught a hint of a familiar accent when we spoke.

"Clayton, I couldn't place your accent before. Are you from London?"

"It's Clay, and no one can. I lived in Finchley for years, but I was born in Swansea." It was then that I caught the disguised sing-song of his Welsh accent. *I did miss England sometimes.* He continued to look at me in the mirror.

"A Welsh man, and now you're here. When did you leave the old country?" My curiosity got the better of me.

Having met many Brits since moving to Seattle, all with fascinating backstories, I never tired of hearing them. They seemed to be drawn to the iconic Olympic mountains in Seattle's background, the breathtaking scenery on its doorstep and the perceived lower cost of living.

"Twenty eight years ago next month. I came on holiday, met my wife Marianne in Tacoma and I've never left," he smiled, his ruddy cheeks turning redder.

"Where's Marianne now?" The romantic in me was dying to hear their love story, and I leaned towards the front in anticipation.

"She works for Miles', umm, Mr Masterson's brother. In fact, she's worked for the family since Mr Masterson was nine. I've known him since he was a cheeky lad. May I ask where you're from?"

It was hard to imagine Miles as a boy. *Now he was all man.*

"We're talking, aren't we?" I laughed softly. I liked Clay. He was easy to trust, no wonder Miles trusted him with his sweet daughter. "I was born in Dorchester, but I lived and worked in London since I left school."

"Dorchester, in Dorset?"

"Not that popular one. Dorchester-on-Thames in Oxfordshire."

"Oxford, the city of dreaming spires. I went there once. There were some good pubs, but no decent chippies," he chuckled as his trustworthy eyes glanced in the rearview mirror.

"You've definitely been there." We both laughed, until he slowed down and pulled into the terrace where my townhouse was.

My pristine white door was blood red. Stunned into silence, I could only gape. Eventually a gasp left me and when Clay noticed my door, he was surprised too. The rain hadn't rinsed away much, as the portico sheltered the door from the rain.

"Doctor Braithwaite, if you could wait just a moment before you come out of the car, I'll check what's happening there." His demeanour changed and he became someone else. Someone to be called on in a crisis.

"It looks like paint. I'll come with you." The panic in my voice came through as I opened the door and grappled with my umbrella. As we stepped closer, I could smell the distinctive metallic odour of blood.

"Don't come any closer, we don't know what this is."

I knew what it was. It was blood. But there was so much of it. Wherever it had been drawn, a life had been taken.

"It's blood," I gasped, looking around, unsure of what I was searching for. My palms were sweaty, and the heavy thudding in my chest was making it difficult to breathe.

"Has this happened before?" The alarm in his voice roused me from my thoughts.

"No. This is horrible. This can't be human blood, can it?" I asked as my voice trailed off.

"This matter must be reported to the authorities. It could be an isolated problem or, god forbid, an ongoing one." His tone, full of authority and finality, was difficult to ignore.

"It seems trivial to involve the police. I'm sure they are inundated with real crimes, but you're right, I'll take it from here."

I expected him to leave, but he called the local police department, and two police officers arrived and took a detailed report. I realised then, Clay used to be with the police. As there was blood, a crime scene investigator came out and collected samples. The police suggested installing surveillance cameras and left.

"Doctor Braithwaite, where do you keep your garden hose?" He was still in crisis mode and very much in control.

"I...I don't have one," I stuttered, still shocked. Did urbanites in Seattle own garden hoses? It seemed redundant with all the rain.

"Show me your utility cupboard. You might want to change out of that dress, it will be ruined." His take-charge voice was difficult to ignore. I went upstairs and changed. By the time I returned to the front door, all that was left of the bloody scene was a light pink puddle of water.

"Thank you. That was so strange, but I'm glad you were here to help me." What would I have done if Clay hadn't been with me? "I wouldn't want to bother your boss with such a small issue." I hoped he wouldn't tell Miles Masterson about this. The man I got to know in my office seemed like the type who would move mountains to right this wrong, and I wasn't sure what it was.

"This is exactly what he would want to know. You're putting me between a rock and a hard place." His voice took an apologetic tone while he was hunched over the kitchen sink scrubbing his hands.

"I don't think there's any need to tell him now that it's sorted, do you?" I handed him a towel. He straightened up but hesitated. He seemed unsure, but I convinced him with a reassuring nod and the smile I reserved for kids terrified of going to the doctor.

"Not a problem, Doctor Braithwaite. Call me day or night if you need help with anything."

I programmed his number into my phone without a second thought.

After he left I packed an overnight bag and went to Dean and Charlie's. After that strange act of vandalism, I was afraid of being alone in my townhouse. The questions the police posed made me nervous: Was anyone threatening me? Did I have enemies to speak of? What else has been happening? Had I seen anyone suspicious lurking around my home or place of business? All from blood at the door? The questions terrified me, perhaps more than the blood itself. I wondered if any of this had anything to do with my neighbour's broken window the previous week.

Early the next day, Dean installed surveillance cameras, and while he was doing that I got an eerie feeling we were being watched. Who would be watching? Who cares what I'm doing? If I was really being watched, would Dean's surveillance cameras be all the protection I needed? I didn't tell Dean how rattled I was. He would have demanded I move back in with him.

After we returned to his house and ate a late breakfast of french toast and grilled sausage, my niece and nephew were excited about my unannounced visit.

"Aunt Cara, can we go and see the flying fish please?" Finn begged.

I didn't miss the twinkle in my brother's eye. Child-free weekends were rare for both him and Charlie. I wanted to go out, too, and I took every opportunity to explore Seattle. I was still a tourist in my new home.

"Of course, we can. You and Ava need to dress warm, then we'll go." The thought crossed my mind to stay home, just for the day, but the looks on the kids' faces swayed me.

After breakfast and a change of clothes, the three of us left for Pike Place Market. We strolled past the fishmongers and other stall holders, immersed ourselves in the market's thrumming energy while taking in the Saturday street performances.

"Aunt Cara, can we get those sticky cinnamon rolls? They are so yummy." Ava tugged my hand and pulled me towards the sweet pastry display. They already knew how to play me like a fiddle, taking turns to ask for stuff, knowing I would easily cave. Even though we had not long had breakfast, I decided to indulge them both.

As we made our way inside the bakery, I turned around. In the throng I fleetingly caught a pair of melancholy and moody grey eyes with a cold and piercing stare, gawking at me. Just as I saw the man behind the eyes, he disappeared into the crowded market. Who was he? Had I unwittingly put the children in danger by bringing them out so soon after what happened at my door? My excitement became tempered by a niggling anxiety, but I didn't let it get in the way of our fun. I wouldn't disappoint the kids by taking them back home.

Once inside the bakery, the fresh, just baked smell of breads, pies and sweet pastries seemed to get the children even more excited. We bought cinnamon rolls and made our way to the ferry – Bainbridge Island was soon on the horizon.

The rest of the afternoon was spent exploring lush parks, playing in sandy coves and skipping stones across the water. Although it was deserted, I felt safe on Bainbridge Island.

In the early evening, the three of us held hands, walked back to the ferry terminal and caught the five thirty five back to Seattle. We arrived home and were all worn out and ready for bed. Despite what had happened at my door, I was happy in Seattle. It was the best move I could have made.

Chapter Four

♥

Cara

While at work in the emergency room on Monday, Melinda excitedly phoned me from the clinic with news. Another bouquet of flowers had been delivered.

I had told myself I wouldn't call Miles. Sometime over the weekend, with time to mull over his visit to the practice and the ride in his car, I decided I wouldn't be drawn into what looked like a superficial world in which he lived. Even if it was just dinner, I wouldn't have it with him.

I didn't call to thank him for the flowers. I wouldn't encourage him.

Bouquets of flowers with a blank card were delivered each day. On Thursday I decided to put an end to it.

> *Thank you for the flowers you've been sending, but I've decided you and I can't be whatever you're trying to be. Please stop sending them. Cara*

After powering down my phone, I dived headfirst into work, seeing a revolving door of children and their parents. One or two were true emergencies. Most required only a Band-Aid and a gentle tone. The nurses referred to the parents of those as the hangnail moms, as no one wanted to label them as having a factitious disorder. Their sky could be falling, after all.

Parents of newborns were the majority, needing reassurance they were doing all the right things. Of all days, I missed the thrill of surgery, of correcting something which wasn't right. I was a natural investigator and problem-solver. Today had seemed like a waste of my talent. As I walked out of the children's hospital and powered my phone back up, I heard the chime as Miles's message came through.

> Miles Masterson: I'm sorry to hear that's what you've decided. I wish you well. I haven't sent any flowers, though I should have … Miles.

If he wasn't sending the flowers, who could it be? I didn't know anyone else who would. The few people I knew in Seattle were from work. They were preoccupied with work, and they worked hard to distance themselves from it when they didn't have to be there. Had I led someone to believe I was interested in them? Although, the frequency of sending the flowers was bordering on obsessive, and not from an admirer. If not Miles Masterson, then who?

Without Miles' pursuit of me to look forward to anymore, it had also turned out to be a bad day. Not after the message I sent him early in the morning. Why would I be undecided? I was usually confident in my decisions. Resolute and steadfast, but this time I was torn.

Although my mind and body were weary, I took the long way to get home and hoped to throw anyone off my trail. As soon as I arrived, it dawned on me how driving around had been a waste of time. Whoever the person was already knew where I lived after that blood incident.

After my windows were locked, and the front and back doors bolted, I took a much needed shower. It didn't take me long to fall asleep until my alarm woke me with a start the next morning.

It was a new day, and I wouldn't dwell on the what ifs. I dressed in a bottle green shirt dress and paired it with a black belted trench coat, which kept the light drizzle off me. After a hurried breakfast of homemade granola, natural yoghurt and mixed berries, I made my way into the practice.

Friday's bouquet came with a card written in red ink, which looked and smelled like blood.

It had two simple but ominous words:

You're Next.

Fear and dread crawled up and down my spine as my insides coiled and tightened with an unfamiliar bilious feeling. I was worried and afraid, and a wave of panic moved through me. I thought back to the flowers placed all over the practice. There were bouquets of carnations, lilies, gerberas, and orchids. It can't have been my imagination, but all of them could be funeral flowers.

"Melinda, can you come in here please?" I spoke hurriedly and somewhat hysterically through the intercom.

"Another arrangement? These flowers are beautiful. Are they all from Mister GQ who came in last week – without an appointment or even a child?" she asked with what sounded like disapproval, although mirth danced in her eyes. *How is she always chirpy?*

"I don't think so. I'm not sure who they're from. Who's been delivering them?" Flustered and nervous, my shirt dress had become drenched in sweat.

"College-aged girl, distracted. Easy to tell she hates her job. I think it's one of those delivery services," she said, morphing into a sleuth.

"Not the florist?" I asked nonchalantly, trying to hide the panic I felt.

"I doubt it. What's going on, Cara?" She looked mildly concerned. I couldn't tell Melinda everything. She was kind and solicitous but blessed with loose lips. I didn't want the entire practice to know about the threat within the card.

"Nothing, just had to know. Next time she brings them in, can you find out where she delivers from – which florist?"

"To be young and beautiful and fending off the suitors with a stick. Sure, I'll find out. Have you got any weekend plans?"

"I need to catch up with some studying. I have an exam," I said with a tight smile. I didn't need to study. I knew the content of the exam like the back of my hand.

"That's a shame. I've just heard all the bachelors in Seattle let out a collective sigh of disappointment." With a dramatic flourish she glided out of my consulting room. Any other day she would've been amusing, then my imagination was lacking.

It was all very strange, I didn't know anyone in Seattle. Why would anyone threaten me – in blood?

I finished work for the day, but I couldn't bring myself to go out and meet the other ER doctors for Friday night drinks. I even ignored a call from a number that I recognised as Miles'.

Again, my short journey home took me longer than usual. I drove around in my Mini, this time to think. After my arrival, I did a thorough walk through of my security – windows locked, doors double bolted, alarm set. I was relieved to be back in the warmth and sanctuary of my home where no one could come inside.

I ordered groceries to be delivered and decided to stay inside. I spent the weekend hidden in my townhouse and attempted to cook my sadness and fear away.

Cooking had always been my salvation and sanctuary from difficult cases, difficult colleagues, and even as I endured my first heartbreak when I was ten years old. My first foray was baking banana bread, one of my mother's favourites - I hadn't stopped cooking and baking since.

The cooler weather demanded that I make a simple slow cooker beef bourguignon, a winter dish my mother would make when she had to be at work. The simple act of cooking it brought me comfort. Before we left for school in the morning, she would place all the delicious ingredients in a slow cooker, and by the time we returned home after school, beautiful smells would waft towards the front door as we walked in.

She always assured my father it was safe for us kids, as the copious amount of red wine she added to it reduced. I didn't want to waste the rest of the bottle of burgundy and made a red wine and blackberry sauce to pour over a duck breast I seared.

Those dishes, and the sweet breads I baked, kept me occupied for hours. I didn't eat much of the food; I wrapped it and put most away. I would take it to work for the doctors and nurses in the emergency room on Monday.

When Sunday evening came, and I had spent the weekend feeling sorry for myself, I answered my ringing phone without looking at it.

"Doctor Braithwaite, I hope you don't mind me calling. I thought I would check in and make sure everything's fine after that issue at your door," a welcome voice said gently.

"Clay, what a pleasant surprise. Thank you for checking in." I breathed deeply and hoped he wouldn't hear my sigh of relief. The relief of knowing I wasn't entirely alone.

"Is everything good? Have you had any more trouble?" His sincerity, care and concern came through over the phone.

I couldn't talk about it and chose to pretend everything was fine.

"All is well, Clay."

"Good to hear that. Remember to call if you need to."

"I will. Thanks for checking up on me." I hoped he heard the smile in my voice. His kindness was refreshing. I wondered if he had told Miles anything. A small part of me hoped he had.

Another week came around. Although I was spending all my time at home, and only venturing out for work, I was weary. How could my life in my new city have gone horribly wrong already?

The saving grace was that the blood poured all over my door was deemed to be bovine by the crime scene investigators. *Who would draw blood from a cow? A vet, a farmer, maybe a butcher.* Did I know any butchers, vets or farmers? Here, or even in England?

I had become obsessed with checking the surveillance camera feed on my phone. I returned home one night after work and found a dead fox on my doorstep.

Daily, after that, there were varieties of dead rodents awaiting my arrival at home. It was difficult to make out who was leaving these, as they seemed to know how to avoid the cameras and were always fully covered in black garb.

I couldn't keep living this way.

I went into work early and did what I should have done when help was offered to me. Even though I had lied to him before, I called the one man who cared but was far removed from me to panic. I told him all the things I should have when he reached out the first time.

Surprisingly, I opened up and told him all my fears and how in a few short weeks I had been reduced to a shell of my former self. All the while, he listened intently without hysteria or theatre. He told me what needed to be done and the tension lifted. I felt as if I had finally taken my first real breath in weeks.

Chapter Five

Miles

Clay never came to see me on the 45th floor. I had known him for most of my life. His wife, Marianne, had been our housekeeper when we were kids. When he retired from the police force seven years ago, still sharp and needing to keep busy, he started to drive Marianne insane. To help her, I took him on and kept him occupied driving my family when we needed him to. As soon as he arrived, Alistair let him in.

"Clay, what brings you by?" I was happy to see him and the unexpected visit piqued my curiosity.

He cleared his throat and pushed back a few wayward wisps of hair, which he never could tame. It was his tell when he was nervous.

"Miles, this is a little delicate, but I thought I should bring it to your attention. Doctor Braithwaite asked for my help to retain a private investigator." I stood without thinking and strode towards him.

"Why would she ask you to help her with that? How are you in contact with her?" I was surprised, puzzled and intrigued. She had grown to trust Clay after all.

"Things have been bizarre in her life, and she didn't know who else to turn to. She didn't want to worry her family. You see, we're both from the old country and have a shared background, a kinship, so to speak."

His eyes darted around my office, glanced out of the wall of windows towards the mountains, then became transfixed on my great grandfather's two-foot Japanese maple bonsai. One he acquired and personally trained when he took over the company from his father. It had become mine when I lost my father. Tending to it kept me focused and tethered to my reality.

"A kinship. She's half your age. There are hundreds of young British women in this city. Do you have a kinship with all of them?" I thundered, then composed myself when I realised I still didn't know why she needed a private investigator.

"I don't, but if Marie and I had been blessed with children, a daughter perhaps, I imagine she would be Doctor Braithwaite's age, and if we were lucky, just as lovely as she is. I don't know why I haven't seen her again with you, but in nearly three decades I haven't seen you act the way you did that rainy day." The weight of his words spoke to how I had never felt about a woman I had only just met the way I felt for Cara. Not even the one I married and nearly lost my brother for.

That calmed me until he told me about the incident at her door and all the other strange goings on that had been happening to her.

"Why didn't you tell me that evening? The moment you saw blood at her doorstep? You were with her for hours and didn't think to tell me. How can I trust you with Maxie if you keep things like this from me?" I barked, unable to disguise my anger at the situation.

She doesn't have another suitor after all. I had turned green with envy when I wondered about the man she chose over me. I even tortured myself with thoughts of all the ways they were getting to know each other.

"Miles, I didn't mean to interfere, but Doctor Braithwaite asked me not to," he confessed as he tried to stand tall. I was taller. His stance wouldn't normally affect me, yet I felt small and insignificant, having been left in the dark by Clay, a man I'd grown to trust over the years.

"You work for me, not her. You'll do well to always remember that. Why are you telling me this now? You seem to have it under control." I fired back.

I wasn't angry at Clay and he didn't deserve the ire. He was trying to help Cara. Even though I hadn't been the man she called in her time of need, I was relieved she sought out Clay.

"I thought, as this is an ongoing matter, with an investigator involved you might want to know. She's also terrified and leaves her place only to go to work."

"Her friends?"

"She doesn't see them and has been avoiding her brother and his family to keep them out of harm's way. The threat to her life has her shaken." The air in my office became heavy as I tried to imagine what she was going through.

"Did you help her get an investigator?"

"I did. We were on the job together for years. He's a good man, meticulous too. And affordable so she was able to cover his fee," he added quietly.

"That's the investigator. The threat to her life? Did you put someone onto it? The police? Someone to protect her?" I sucked in a deep breath, while my focus veered to Cara. I wanted to be the one she turned to, not Clay.

"I did what I could to help her. I'm coming to you now. She's all alone and I'm worried about her."

"She chose to be alone," I said to myself as I looked out at the city. Seattle was home, and I'd always loved it. But I didn't need to own the news to know what a dangerous place it could be.

Sensing my hesitation, he pressed, "Can you do anything at all?"

While we were deeply immersed in our conversation, Alistair pushed his head around my office door and spoke timidly. He needed to come out of his shell.

"*Business Now Magazine* and the students are here for your interview. They're setting up in the conference room."

"Cancel. Now's not a good time." I was abrupt as I walked back to my chair and sat down.

I regretted my agreement to be profiled by the students studying at one of the local community colleges. That was my father's thing. He had loved to inspire the next generation and nurture talent. My brother was the face of the company, and I preferred to work behind the scenes away from public scrutiny. Until, in a moment of bumbling honesty, Alistair told me the same project profiling my father had turned his life around.

"Miles. Sir, with all due respect, the students have been looking forward to the interview for months. Their portfolios are based on this. It would be a blow to their final scores to cancel on them now." Alistair shook his head, with a stricken look on his face. That was how he had come to work for me, he had been one of those students when they did a piece on my father.

I sighed heavily. "You're right. I'll be there soon, let me finish up here. And Alistair," I called out to him before he left.

"Yes, sir?"

"Drop the sirs. It's stifling and overblown. Miles is fine."

I nodded at him and looked back at Clay.

"Leave it with me. The cheques you cash come from me. Don't ever keep something like this from me again." I didn't recognise my voice. I was worried about her, relieved she had Clay, angry I didn't have her.

I liked her, and it was unfortunate she had a stalker. I helped plenty of people, many of whom I didn't know. I didn't have to, but I had Alistair organise a security service to protect her from a distance. Their orders: to be discrete and not make themselves known, especially to her. I was a busy man, with a child to look after and a demanding job. I didn't have time to chase and woo her if she didn't want me, although she was constantly on my mind. I wouldn't be able to live with myself if I didn't help her, then some misfortune visited upon her.

Chapter Six

♥

Cara

"She lives," Izzy shrieked when I arrived at her office at St Mark's. "You don't answer phone calls or texts. I've been worried sick." She held me in a tight embrace. Affection was what I was missing. What I needed.

"I'm sorry. I brought lunch?"

I held up a bag with two serves of a healthy chicken salad, which she devoured the last time I made it for her. I had avoided her for weeks. I was ill with fright and needed my friend.

"Food's always a good start to a healthy grovel, let's take it out onto the courtyard. I've been here since six and I need some air. What's the scientific evidence behind starting work so early anyway? What's the purpose of that cruel and unusual punishment?" She chattered excitedly while she fetched some napkins and bottles of water she kept in a box in the corner of her office.

"Is it overlooked? The courtyard?" I didn't recognise the fear and worried edge to my voice. In a few short weeks, my zestful and happy self was reduced to a mouselike, timid girl. I didn't recognize myself.

"Of course it is. That's where you want to see and be seen. I need to show you off, get the boys winking," she added, waggling her perfect eyebrows. Where I looked and felt like hell, she was glowing, radiant and carefree. Without a stalker.

"I'd rather stay inside," I mumbled and looked around her small cramped office, which was no bigger than a postage stamp. She hadn't changed much since school, cluttered and messy surrounds but well put together with a genius level IQ.

"In here? What's come over you Braithwaite? In fact, you're as pale as anything. Have you been outside at all?" She narrowed her eyes and looked closely at me as worry lines marred her forehead.

"Yes, in here. I can't go outside. I don't feel ..." The dam broke. The tears I hadn't yet cried ran down my cheeks.

"Something's happened? You're worrying me now. You never cry. Ever." Her voice was stricken as she put an arm around my shoulder.

"I don't know what to do anymore," I spluttered between sobs and hiccups.

Izzy was dramatic, and in our friendship, I was the listener. This time the tables were turned and she became the ear I needed. "Sit and tell me everything."

I told her everything – the blood at my doorstep, the creepy flowers, the threatening notes. I stopped sobbing and angrily told her about the rotting smells of the dead vermin I came home to night after night.

"You have a stalker. How? Who?" She gasped, open-mouthed and horrified.

An involuntary shiver ran up my spine. "I'm stumped. I don't know."

"It's always the ex. All the true crime documentaries prove it over and over," she quipped in a matter-of-fact tone.

"It's not James. He's an ocean away with three children under three, the youngest one a twenty-seven-week preemie who's still poorly. He's opened a clinic on Harley Street and seems generally busy."

"Braithwaite, that's an unhealthy amount of info to have on an ex. I know a priest who can help you exorcise that demon." She widened her eyes dramatically and grimaced.

"Izzy, behave." I chuckled through my anguish. "I hired a PI. He looked into everyone. My pitiful number of exes, some unfriendlies I told him about. He even ran some background checks on some not so squeaky clean colleagues at the clinic and the children's hospital. He has kept me updated on the everything and nothing he has been able to find." I sighed.

"Okay, good you're taking this seriously. Where did you even get a PI? I hope he's not a numpty."

I smiled as I remembered how Clay had done everything he could to help me. "I was referred to him by one of the kindest men I've ever met. One of those who wants to take care of everyone."

"Does he want to take care of you?" she asked pointedly, eyebrows raised with arms folded across her chest.

"It's not like that with him. He's an older guy, retired police. He gave me a lift home once," I mused, while I thought back to his boss. A man who lived in my thoughts and gave me reprieve from the nightmare I was living.

"What was wrong with your car? You can't accept rides from strangers, not in Seattle. What's next if this PI can't find anything? You can't stay inside your house and not live your life. Avoiding me, avoiding the sun," she said softly jutting her chin towards the small window.

"All I want is to become invisible until it stops. Everything makes me jump, and I look at everyone and wonder if they are the person making my life hell."

"That's not practical. Let the PI do his work, and you go about living your life. Friday night, some of the doctors here are going out to the Purple Cafe, been there yet?"

"Pink Door, Purple Cafe, I'm sensing a theme here," I smiled weakly. "I knew you would get me out of my head. I should have told you sooner."

"Exactly. Now to the courtyard, to meet the talent before Friday."

Izzy was doing what Izzy did best, soldier on and make the best of a bad situation. I didn't have her gumption. I could only pretend until it was behind me. Socialising was the furthest thing from my mind.

My stalker had been inactive for three months, and it was a relief. He must have become bored and moved along, perhaps to another unsuspecting soul. The PI failed to crack the case and never found out who it was.

I eventually told Dean and Charlie everything, and they were disappointed I had kept it from them. As expected, Dean demanded I move in with them, but after a lot of reassurance on my part, he agreed I had enough security at my townhouse. I was settled into my new home and even hosted a dinner party for some colleagues I had become friendly with, yet I was still restless. And lonely.

In between seeing patients at the practice, Melinda walked in with a magazine in her hand. With a low and inward chuckle, I looked up knowing she wanted to know anything and share whatever she gleaned from anyone else at the clinic. That was the anatomy of her workday.

"Cara, what happened to Mister GQ and all his flowers?" she asked, a mischievous smile on her face.

"Not sure, Mel." I knew where he was, tucked away in the dark recesses of my mind, coming to the forefront every now and then.

"I found him. Right here, on an actual magazine cover. They are calling him the 'Reluctant Heartthrob of Publishing.'" She waggled her eyebrows and placed the magazine on my desk in mock reverence.

"That's a good picture," I croaked, with what I hoped was also a non-committal glance at the cover, and returned my attention to my computer screen.

"Earth to Cara. Are you serious? Look at him. He's something," she continued excitedly.

I am painfully aware.

"Leave the magazine there, I'll flick through it when I get some time. Still trying to get my head around the next patient's results before he gets here." I hoped I sounded as nonchalant as I tried to. All I wanted was Melinda to leave so I could immerse myself in the magazine.

"Alrighty then. Suki wants to see you in her office when you're free." She spun around towards the door and walked out, deflated without the gossip she had come for.

I didn't wait long. I pushed thoughts of the magazine out of mind and wondered why the principal paediatrician at the clinic wanted to see me. After what happened in London, being summoned to the boss's office spelt disaster. I removed my white coat and made my way to her office at the other end of the practice. With sweaty palms and palpitations, I knocked on the door, and she called out for me to enter.

"Cara, come in and take a seat." She was warm and friendly. I relaxed. No one had lost life or limb, not this time.

"Thanks. Suki, what's going on?" I must have looked nervous. She was quick with reassurance.

"Relax, everything's fine. There's nothing to worry about." I visibly exhaled and she chuckled. "The last job did a number on you, didn't it?"

"That's putting it mildly." I sat back in the orange chair opposite her and tried to relax. Like all the consult rooms in the clinic, hers was just as brightly coloured. The rooms all made the children forget where they were and lulled the parents into being just as comfortable too.

"We love you here, your patients love you, and you're doing wonderful work. We appreciate you. I am grateful you landed in my practice." She continued in the same vein of praise and I relaxed.

"Suki, that's kind of you to say." I was now at ease, and the little girl in me was pleased with the positive feedback.

"Thanks for taking over Grayson's patients in his absence. That must have been extra pressure on you. He's back on Monday and things will be back to normal."

"Excellent, although I didn't mind the bit of pressure. For some reason I work well under it." I groaned inwardly and realised I sounded like a bootlicker.

"I've noticed. That is why I believe you will thrive after your time at this practice and move on to practising paediatric surgery. Your attention to detail and high intellect will serve you and your patients very well."

"I love it here, but I am looking forward to surgery. I'm really great at it. I wonder if I'm allowed to say that about myself." We both laughed quietly.

Suki was nothing like any supervisor I had ever had. Whenever I spoke to her, she seemed to have a deeper understanding of my work life. I imagined it had to do with her being both a female doctor and a mother.

"Yes, you can. Sometimes we are our own worst critics. If you can see your strengths and acknowledge them, you're doing better than most. But enough of that. I called you in here to ask another favour. I have two tickets to a gala. A charity thing for one of the kids' charities. I attend every year with any one of the other paediatricians here, or by myself sometimes, as I have an old friend running things there. This year, I'm with my grandkids and I can't go. You can take a plus one if you like."

"Umm, sure. When is it?" I feigned interest. The last fortnight had knackered me, and I was looking forward to curling up on my couch in my flannel pyjamas with a good book, plenty of ice cream and a large glass of wine.

"That's the catch. It's tomorrow night. I've sprung this on you, and I'm sorry. Take the day off tomorrow, and I also hoped this would sweeten the deal," she said, as she pushed a healthy-looking envelope in my direction. Puzzled, I reached out for it.

"I don't understand." I shook my head when I saw what was inside.

"It's for you to get a dress. It's a glitzy event and I don't want you to be out of pocket."

"Thanks, but I can get my own dress." I pushed the envelope back towards her. I learned early that taking money from anyone without services rendered came not with strings but with rods of titanium attached.

"I didn't mean to offend you. It's a work-related expense, and I insist you take it." Her voice took a firmer tone. As I was about to continue my refusals, Melinda's voice came through Suki's intercom and announced my next patient's arrival.

"Thank you." I took the envelope with the money and the Gala tickets. As I walked back to my consulting room I wondered if Izzy would be free at such short notice.

After my patient and his mother left, I finally picked up *Business Now* and devoured all the information in the article. The first few questions of the interview, although fun and lighthearted, helped to set the tone to one of the most cerebral and stimulating interviews I had read in a while.

'What does a COO do exactly?'

'This one works a little different from most. He has the CEO's back, helps safeguard the founding fathers' legacy, while steering the company towards a highly profitable future.'

'Not an iconoclast then?'

[He laughs] 'That's subjective and open to interpretation. Although, if you study all successful institutions throughout history, they all seemed to have one of those in their midst.'

'You're one of the most successful COOs under forty, or in general. At age thirty-seven, and in the last fourteen years, you have single-handedly acquired thirty-three separate business entities. We understand you're still coming down from the high of your biggest accomplishment only three weeks ago, the acquisition of Publish Pro Media Group and their four thousand employees in North America, Eastern Asia and Western Europe. What is the secret to your success?'

'Sounds like someone's been up all night studying. Is it that many? It's not single-handed, it takes a great team who work well together and share common goals. But it's worth remembering

acquisitions are not the litmus test for business success. There are a lot of other factors to take into consideration.'

It went on and on until Miles answered personal questions expertly but evasively, and they still read as authentic and honest as the rest of his interview.

'How does your significant other cope with all the work you put in? Does she play much of a role in what you do?'

'The little lady in my life is very understanding. When I work from my home office, which I do most days during school breaks, she tries not to disturb for the first hour at least, then makes up for any ensuing interruptions with bribes. You know, the usual kind – glasses of water, pieces of fruit and carrot sticks'.

'Okay, final question. Most of the guys wanted me to ask - Any fitness tips? You look like someone who would have plenty.'

'Can you print that last part in bold letters, so my brother doesn't miss it.' [He laughs again] 'Consistency and protein.'

I studied the five-page article intently, only stopping short of annotating it. Were these all Miles' words?

He was guarded and didn't give away anything about his love life. Instead he spoke with passion about the vision and the values of the company and his father's legacy. His father who lost his life in a drowning accident as he tried to rescue his granddaughter, a child Miles lost. *How does he make it through the day without an aura of sadness around him?*

That made me wonder about my own father's legacy. Had I been too much of a coward by not staying the course and becoming a cardiothoracic surgeon like him? Instead of the coward's way out, of choosing self-preservation? I'm certain my father would still be proud. I had steered slightly off course but I would still be just like him.

Miles was thirty-seven years old, but never had an interview from a person so young given way to so much introspection like this one had. The interview made me want to know him even more. It was impressive and polished, produced by journalism, business and photography students from disadvantaged backgrounds. Was this some type of publicity stunt or had I been too quick to judge him harshly?

The photographs accompanying the article were a bonus. They showed a relaxed but professional side to Miles, one who was still as devastatingly handsome as the last time I saw him sitting across from me. The rest of my day was spent in a daze, wondering if I was a perpetual bad judge of character, or if I had done a sensible thing by keeping my distance.

I woke up early the next morning, and even though Izzy couldn't attend the gala, she came shopping for a dress with me.

"I know you want to keep it cheap and cheerful, but for this gala, you need to dazzle. That's why your boss went out of her way to give you five grand. I think it might not be enough. Shoes, accessories, makeup – it all adds up." She was flustered as we walked into the dizzying flagship Nordstrom in downtown Seattle.

"I know about looking the part. I love a pretty dress like the next girl, but spending a vulgar amount of money on a dress to wear on just one occasion for only a few hours doesn't sit well with me."

"Yes, Ms Logical, you're right, but let's for once, not overthink things, loosen up a little and buy you something you deserve, even if you're wearing it for a few hours. I'm pleased the creeper is gone and you're finally letting your hair down." At this point she was on fast-forward as she took pictures of dresses we deemed worthy for me to try on.

Within fifteen minutes I had five gowns hanging on a rack outside my changing cubicle. When I stepped out wearing dress number four – the red one – and her eyes widened, I knew it was the one, as I loved it the minute I tried it on and admired it in the mirror.

"That dress suits you perfectly. It's so sexy and so classy. If you wear your hair like so, you'll look like a real life Jessica Rabbit," she said as she moved all my hair to the left side.

"This is the one. Thanks for coming with me and convincing me to buy something so pretty." She helped me out of the red dress, which made me feel like a naughty mermaid with its small fishtail train.

"How are you going to get out of it? You're going to have to bring someone back home to rip it off you." Although she was encouraging and urging a night of brazenness and depravity, her tone was surprisingly prim and proper.

"This is a work thing, I need to be on my best behaviour. Come to think of it, I'm always on my best behaviour," I sighed heavily as I thought about my dismal dating life.

"Which is a shame if you ask me. No one will be taking notes, and this dress is made for seduction. It clings to every curve of your body like it's painted on. Use it wisely and seduce someone, anyone, and dust off the old cobwebs. It's been three years. I'm not saying wear your heart on your sleeve. But put yourself out there, at least."

"I've been to kindergarten, Izzy, I can count. And leave my cobwebs alone, they help trap flies." We both giggled while she helped me out of the dress. "This is exciting, I had no idea I would enjoy playing dress up. Are you sure you can't come to the gala with me?"

"I wish I could, but I can't get away from work today. In fact I really need to go now. Spin class on Sunday, no excuses." She kissed me on the cheek and I headed toward the counter to pay for the extravagant dress.

Izzy went to work while I went to my long overdue hair appointment. I didn't let my hair down, instead I wore it up. What better way to show off the boldest feature of the dress – its plunging neckline, than to let it speak for itself without something as pedestrian as hair in the way.

After an afternoon of primping and heightened anticipation, I walked out of my townhouse. At first, I hadn't recognised myself in the dress, and the simple square diamond pendant, a birthday gift, gave the outfit a delicate edge. The stole I wore over the dress, a steal from the sale rack at Marks and Spencer, finished off the outfit. My first night out in months, and I looked sensational.

When I arrived at the Lotte, all my expectations were surpassed. It was a glamorous event, and everyone was well-dressed. I silently thanked Izzy and Suki. The flashing lights were blinding. I tried not to stare when I recognised some famous faces. After I checked my stole at the coat check I walked into the ballroom in awe.

The well decorated ballroom was the most beautiful room I had seen in a long time. It had bold four foot crystal chandeliers dotted along the ceiling, elegant drapery and a large dance floor where the well-heeled guests were already dancing the night away. I had been to some events like this one, but none on such a grand scale. Even though the event was to benefit children, there was nothing childlike about it. The ballroom's lights were set to dim, giving the place a moody and sultry feel. As I continued to look around, taking in the atmosphere and not quite believing how I was spending my Friday night, I looked up, and my eyes met with a pair of familiar, intense brown ones.

Chapter Seven

♥

Miles

My mother liked to host parties, second only to running her children's foundation. Since my father's death, she spent even more time raising money to help sick children through the foundation. Although she had hosted the same event over the last twenty years, this one was different.

Last year she had been upset, her emotions still too raw. She missed my father too much to host the gala, and it was cancelled. Those who expected a party understood, as it had only been a year since we lost him.

This year, my mother was back and felt better. The gala was bigger and filled with more influential people than I had ever seen in one room, and from early numbers the donations pledged were more than expected, having surpassed forty million dollars. I was pleased it was a success, but all I wanted was to be back on Mercer with Maxie.

I hadn't spent much time with her all week, and tonight she was with her nanny. We were reading *The Chronicles of Narnia*, and I was missing the wonder on her face as we turned each page. In my twenties, I had enjoyed a party as much as the next guy. Now all I wanted was a quiet night in, to be swept away in a fantastical book with my daughter.

As I turned around from the hundredth person to greet me as the heartthrob of publishing, I looked straight ahead and recognised a woman I resigned myself to never seeing again.

How was she here? I couldn't help the grin on my face as I made my way to her, only to be stopped by my brother.

"What's the rush? Are you leaving already?" He needed someone to help him work the room, and I had threatened to leave too many times.

"I see someone I need to speak to." I grew impatient, hoping none of the leering men would approach her. *Hell, I am one of those leering men.*

"You didn't want to speak to anyone before, who do you need to speak to now?" he quizzed, clearly making fun of me. He had seen me see her and the delay tactic was straight out of his playbook of mischief.

I stooped to his juvenile level. "Stop or I'm telling Mom." Then I strode past him while he chuckled behind me.

When I got to her side, I was lost for words. I leaned in closer to kiss her on the cheek and caught a whiff of her perfume. I remembered how it had filled her consult room four months ago, the last time I had seen her.

"Cara, how are you?"

"This is a surprise, what brings you here?" she asked with a disarming smile, the one which pulled me in the first time I saw her.

I couldn't help the broad smile as I looked at her, not believing my eyes. "You won't believe this, but my mother made me come here."

The blue dress had buried me, but the red one made me come alive. Her breasts defied gravity, and I had to make a concerted effort to keep my eyes on hers.

"I've heard that line from some of my teenage patients. I think I get the picture." She laughed, and I laughed with her until I saw my brother advancing towards us. He lived for moments like these, devolving to the age of twelve.

"Miles, are you busy? There are some people here I need you to speak to." The amusement dancing in his eyes took me back to our childhood.

"Big brother, this is Cara Braithwaite. Cara, this is Michael. He wants us to go outside and play. Always," I added drily.

"You've probably heard this before, but the resemblance is uncanny. It's good to meet you, Michael."

He regarded her with a momentary seriousness, a searching look in his eyes. I recognised the look – watchful, vigilant and protective. He needn't have worried, I didn't need protection from Cara.

"Pleasure's all mine. How do you know Miles? I ask because he never leaves the house. Right now, he's reading the *Chronicles of Narnia*, and he can't wait to get back to it." Charm came naturally to him, even when I was the object of his playful ridicule.

"Miles, is that true? You should've led with that. I'm stuck on *Prince Caspian*." She saw through Michael's ribbing. *She's perfect*.

"That's the fourth one, right? Come out onto the terrace so you can tell me more, but no spoilers. Michael, can I speak to those people later, or never?" It was my turn to be amused, and led Cara out onto the terrace.

As we stepped out onto the terrace, she shivered and goosebumps appeared on her chest and arms. I removed my jacket and draped it over her shoulders.

"Thank you, it's lovely out here. I never get enough of looking out at the lake." She wrapped the jacket tighter around herself and inhaled deeply, all the while staring in wonder at Lake Washington and the lights of Mercer and Bellevue beyond.

"How are you here? I'm glad you are, and that dress was made for you." She had a way of turning me into an inarticulate schoolboy.

"Thanks. The boss made me come here," she said casually. Looking me over, she threw my own words back at me with a smile on her face.

"Your boss needs an award. Were you being punished for something?" I joked, then she laughed softly.

"No, she must realise I need to get out more."

I loved seeing her like this. She was relaxed, not hiding behind her professional veneer. Could I try one more time for her to give me a chance?

"I still think about you. Maybe too much," I said, exhaling, while I continued to look out at the view. I was afraid of looking into her eyes and facing a second rejection, head on.

She wasn't cowardly, and she turned to look at me. "I'm not sure what I'm supposed to do with that."

"Will you give yourself a chance to figure it out? I can promise you discretion. I understand why it's important to you." This time, I turned and faced her.

I couldn't believe I had the attention of the belle of the ball.

"Why me? I'm sure you have your pick of women. You may have had plenty in the last four months. Who's to know?" A small smile showed on her perfect features, coupled with a shoulder shrug.

"I like that you think I'm more fun than I am. In reality I work two jobs and have little time for debauchery, so I haven't been doing what you might be imagining." She giggled and gave me a sidelong glance. I started to wonder what she had been imagining and smiled to myself.

"I know all about working two jobs, although your second one, if it's what I suspect, is most rewarding."

"It is, and I consider it job number one. I wouldn't change anything there. It's the biggest part of who I am. I think it's something you would understand, and why I can't seem to forget you, no matter how hard I try."

"How can I? I don't have children and I've never been a parent," she said with a faraway look in her eyes, which was clear to see even in the low light of the terrace.

"You may not have any, but you're surrounded by them every day. Though it's your job, it takes a special kind of person to do what you do, and the everyday you is the person I'm hoping you would let me get to know."

"Sounds like you want to have dinner with me because I have a great bedside manner," she quipped with a chuckle.

Even though it was only the two of us on the terrace, I leaned in closer, dipped lower and whispered in her ear, "Your job is not the reason I want to be next to you."

When she giggled, I realised my breath had tickled inside her ear, and I couldn't help my own smile. I wondered where else she was sensitive. "Okay, dinner. Somewhere quiet, without the cameras."

I exhaled, relieved she had finally agreed, also because she had stopped quizzing me. I wouldn't have been able to bite my tongue and not tell her all the other ways I needed to get to know her.

I tried to hide my excitement with humour. "Wow, she said yes."

"You're getting carried away. Like you told me once, it's just dinner." She gave me her enchanting smile. That was all I had wanted for months.

"This isn't my everyday life. Dinner will be quiet, just you and me." A small shiver went through her and I guessed that we may have stayed out on the terrace for too long. "Let's get back inside, before my brother starts to sulk. Can I take you home when you're ready to leave?"

"Sure. You two are close. That's sweet." She handed back my jacket, which as I put back on, I was sure held a heady mix of her delicate feminine scent and my cologne.

"Sweet? No, we are two very manly men." I caught her looking me over again. I'd had many admiring glances and some eyebrow raising propositions all evening. All tawdry compared to when Cara Braithwiate looked at me and appreciated what she saw.

"Yes, you are," she whispered under her breath, but I caught every word.

As we walked back inside, I realised how late it had become. The dance floor was still full, but the music had slowed. Would I be pushing it if I asked her for a dance?

"Do you feel like dancing?" I was glad the lights were set to dim and hoped she wouldn't see the desperation on my face, although I suspected my voice gave it away. I needed to hold her close and feel her body next to mine.

"I like this song," she agreed, and I didn't give her much time to change her mind as I wrapped my arm around her slender waist and pulled her, a little too hard against me.

I held her close and breathed her in. I didn't dwell on how the curves of her body were plastered against me or how her warm breath felt against my neck. She finally gave me a chance, and for the first time in a long time, I wasn't dancing alone.

While we danced and I felt her body against mine, I listened to the lyrics, which seemed to have been written for the two of us. They were about a man and a woman who were both alone, with an undeniable attraction to each other. Why not take a chance and get together? Perfectly cheesy, but perfect for our first dance. When the song ended, she took a step back from me and reached out for a drink from a passing server.

"Best dance of my life. I'll mingle some more, but whenever you want to go, send me a message, and we'll leave." I spoke softly, but loud enough to be heard over the din. She was flushed and looked dazed, maybe from the drink in her hand. She nodded, and as I made to leave her side, she placed her hand on my forearm.

"I don't have your number," she confessed, looking mildly embarrassed.

"You deleted me, didn't you?" I teased in a mock serious tone. I took my phone out and sent her a message.

> *Keep it, for as long as possible this time. Miles*
> *X*

She pulled out her phone from her purse and read my message with a smile. "Yes, I guess I did. This time I won't."

Chapter Eight

Cara

Of all the places to be tonight, I walked into the gala hosted by Miles' mother, and he was there too. His flirting was subtle yet so obvious. I didn't remember the last time a man had made me feel wanted, sexy and interesting. Feeling his hands around me was a sensation I wouldn't soon forget. Only hard, consistent work would yield a body as solid as his, and the closer we danced, the closer I wanted us to get. The song came to an end too soon, and I hadn't wanted him to let go. The dance had hardly been discreet and I clung to him as if we were one, but the lights were low. I told Izzy I would be on my best behaviour – one slow dance wouldn't make me a liar.

I hadn't wanted to come to the gala, but I did. Was it fate that brought me here? To run into a man I hadn't been able to stop thinking about, even as another made my life miserable? He promised me discretion, he understood what was at stake, but how could I readily trust him? Could it be his sincere brown eyes, his gentle manner with me, or was it that article?

I mingled a while longer, nibbled canapes and sipped champagne. I felt eyes on me all night, but I didn't dare look. Worried my eyes would betray how giddy I was, and whose eyes they would catch watching me. For a while I lived in fear of being watched, but Miles could watch me as much as he wanted to. I loved knowing his eyes were on me. I longed to be alone with him again, to hear his voice, and to watch him watch me.

After another hour I decided I had put in enough time to justify the expensive dress.

I sent him a message.

> I'm ready to leave, Cara x.

> Miles: Meet me out front, I'm in the silver car you've been in before.

I remembered the car, it was the one that made me discount the idea of spending time with him. I had packed him away in a box marked rich, arrogant and pretentious. I wasn't sure he belonged there anymore.

After leaving the coat check, I walked towards the car. Clay stepped out of the driver's side and opened the back door for me.

"Clay, it's lovely to see you again. Is Marianne well?"

"You too, Doctor Braithwaite. Marianne is very well, thank you."

"How long have you been here?" I asked, feeling a sudden flash of happiness after I stepped into the car and sat next to Miles. Despite the long night, his dark hair was still in its place. I longed to run my hands through it, to have it out of control and perhaps even have him lose control.

"Not long. I knew after talking to Mrs Barrett you would be ready to leave," he said with a chuckle. He must know her well.

"She's a charmer, but a little exhausting."

"A little? She's the foundation's biggest donor and will let anyone who will listen know how generous she is."

"Funny. She told me this year's number, and my jaw nearly hit the floor."

"She wasn't lying. You've created a monster, she'll expect you to swoon again next year when she tries to blow your mind with a predictably higher number."

"Sounds like future Cara's problem. Who's to say I'll be here next year?" I felt comfortable in his presence, I even let my guard down and giggled.

"I would love it if you were here next year." The melodic timbre of his voice had become a caress, dropping an octave when he moved closer to me.

"Were you following me all night?" *I can't help myself. I might just want him to follow me everywhere.*

I got comfortable and found my thigh pressed against one made from steel. In the dim light of the Rolls Royce, his eyes and his smile were all I could see, all I needed to see. The rest of him I felt; his strength, the power he projected, and just the right amount of softness to make me feel safe.

"Not following, but I was aware of where you were in case you needed to leave." I glanced at him, and my eyes landed on his lips. The pillow-soft lips, which even in the near darkness of the car I couldn't tear my eyes from.

"I had a great time. Your mother knows how to throw a party."

"She would be happy to hear that. She loves a good party, always has. I'll let her know you approve."

I couldn't help the ghost of a smile which appeared on my lips. For the first time in weeks, I didn't feel alone. I wanted to lean into him and just for a second have his arms around me again. Would that be too much, too soon? I must have been tired. It was my first night off work in a fortnight.

The drive to Queen Anne was a short one, and Clay drove through the last of the Friday night traffic with practised ease. We were outside my townhouse within minutes.

"Would you like to come inside?" I hoped he would. I didn't want the evening to end.

"I would love to." His movement was fluid and graceful, as if he had been expecting me to ask. He exited the car and held his hand out to help me and the dress out of the car.

As we walked towards the front door, I mentally congratulated myself for having the foresight to hire a biweekly cleaner. It was an embarrassing luxury, as well as a stretch financially, but it was a sacrifice I had to make, as I didn't have enough time in the day after the hospital shifts and consultations at the clinic.

Entering the small foyer in my townhouse, he followed closely behind me, his scent filling the space. He shut the door behind him, then leaned casually against the doorway. The reluctant heartthrob was in my home, and the photographs in *Business Now* didn't do him justice.

"Would you like a drink?" I swallowed thickly as my eyes darted again to his, down his torso, which deliciously filled his jacket, and I felt a wave of heat wash over me.

"Yes, please." He stepped towards me and watched me closely while I found the exact bottle I had in mind. It was an easy search, as I didn't keep many bottles of wine.

I poured two glasses from a Bordeaux that Izzy had given me. A housewarming gift, and I was saving it for a special occasion.

Nothing could be more special than this. I handed him the wine and my fingers grazed his. I felt my pulse quicken and my heart's rhythm went haywire.

"I hope this will do, I don't know what you like to drink." I was breathless, wishing I'd stocked up on everything.

"I don't drink much, not anymore, but this is perfect." His brown eyes remained on mine as he brought the glass to his lips. The lips which I wondered about again – would they be soft against mine, or would they be rough and plundering? I couldn't keep letting my thoughts wander.

I only knew enough about wine to help when I got lost in cooking, but when I brought the wine to my lips, I caught its scent, then savoured it. It evoked a sense of the man before me. I appreciated the traits the wine shared with him; rich, complex and bold.

"This place is great, I didn't realise there were new residences here." He took in my townhouse, which was decorated with my mismatched, but comfortable, furniture shipped from London. Some of the pieces were antiques, albeit unassuming ones that I collected on my rare days off from work.

I was a décor enthusiast, but I'd never made my mind up about the type of décor and furnishings I liked. All I knew was if it was beautiful and made me feel good, I loved it. Although it was a modest townhouse by what I imagined were his standards, it was perfect for me, with its large master bedroom and Dean's bespoke contemporary kitchen. It even had a guest bedroom big enough for when Ava and Finn came to stay.

"My brother put me onto them. Follow me, I'll show you the best part." I led him upstairs to the rooftop deck.

"Your brother?"

"He lives up the hill, an easy five minutes, with his wife and kids."

"That's convenient. This is a hidden gem. I see why you love it," he said after I had slid open the terrace door and we were standing outside, taking in my view.

It wasn't as vast and expansive as the view from the Lotte, but it was mine. The peaks of Mount Rainier to the south, Puget Sound to the west, Downtown Seattle northward and the wonders that were the Cascades and Lake Washington to the East.

"I love it. It's the perfect spot to unwind after a hard day's work."

"Do you feel safe here?" he asked, sounding concerned.

Note to self: Clay cannot keep a secret. But he is loyal and trustworthy.

"Clay told you, didn't he?"

"He did. Was he able to help you?"

"Yes, his man did all he could, and I can finally breathe again. Enough of my view, you need to tell me everything about you." I gazed into his eyes, hoping to diffuse the tension that seemed to have taken over his body when he asked about my safety.

"Everything? We might need all night," he chuckled softly as he pulled off his bow tie and undid the top two shirt buttons, exposing the gym-honed division between his pectorals.

I lost my train of thought.

"Do we have all night?" I didn't know this man, but already I wanted to spend all night talking to him and learning about him. *Could he be worth the trouble?*

"Not tonight. I left Maxie with her nanny, and she'll be waiting up for me." He sounded apologetic as he moved closer and surrounded me with his vigour and energy.

"She'll wait up?" I squeaked, aware of the flood of warmth that cascaded and pooled within my core.

"Yes, to make sure I come home," he explained with a small smile.

"Do you not go home sometimes?" My voice came out in a whisper.

"I always do, but it's at times like this one when I would rather stay out until morning." His throaty voice, and his closeness continued to set me alight. The throbbing in my core caused me to lose concentration at his confession.

"We have time. It's late and you should go home to her."

"When will I see you again?" He came closer, yet didn't lay a finger on me. I longed to have his arms around me again.

"Work keeps me busy, but I'm free this weekend, if you can squeeze me in." I drew a shaky breath.

"It's not about fitting you in somewhere in my schedule. I want to give you the time you deserve." Was he honest or just silver-tongued? Either way his words melted me.

"I don't want to take away from your time with Maxie and the *Chronicles of Narnia*."

I suspected he was reading that with Maxie, and I briefly wondered what memories I would have shared with my father, had he lived longer.

"Yes, keen to move on with that series. The goal is to finish it before she leaves home for college," he added with a light chuckle. "Will tomorrow work for dinner?"

"I think I can fit you in somewhere."

He smiled his dimpled smile. "Thanks for the wine." Boldly, he slipped one hand around my waist, the other behind my neck, brought my lips closer to his and gave me an almost chaste kiss, one which held a lot of promise. I could just about taste the wine on his lips, and I realised Miles and the Bordeaux were a perfect pairing.

I looked up into his brown gaze, hoping he would kiss me again. The way I imagined his lips could. "See you tomorrow." He reluctantly let me go, and my body was bereft without his touch.

We left the rooftop and walked downstairs, where he continued to his waiting car. I stood in my doorway and watched as he glanced back at me, then waved gently.

It wasn't lost on me that his daughter was his main concern, as she should be. From that magazine article, he had a high-level job, and I couldn't help but wonder what I wanted from him, or if he had time to give it to me. I went to sleep that night pondering if he was the charming prince I had read about in fairy tales. Although, I learned at the age of ten that fairy tales would always belong in between the pages of books.

Chapter Nine

♥

Cara

I had been restless all day, and couldn't focus on much. Miles told me to wear something casual and comfortable for our dinner date. I'd always found casual to be subjective; one woman's casual might be the next one's couture. By five o'clock I was dressed in a nearly sensible olive sweater dress. It kept me warm in the Seattle chill, but its length was laughable as it hit mid-thigh. The black skyscraper over-the-knee boots completed the look, and I hoped I didn't look like the vamp I felt. When I heard the doorbell, I expected to see Clay, but this time it was Miles.

"Hi." I looked him over, appreciating how he was night and day in a pair of distressed denim and an expensive looking cashmere sweater.

He slowly devoured me from my eyes right down to my feet. "You're perfect."

"Thanks, you don't look half bad yourself." His muscle bound torso filled out his soft taupe sweater. He looked younger, casual and relaxed, different from how he looked the night before, stifled by the formal attire.

He led me outside to a white Range Rover with blacked out windows. "We're driving for a while, to get out of the city," he offered, and I felt his warm hand linger on my waist as he helped me into the car.

He shut the car door and I settled into my seat. Although the interior of the car was warm, I had goosebumps from nowhere as a combination of his sandalwood and vetiver scent coupled with the soft aniline leather enveloped me. I even felt a flutter in my centre.

He walked around the car and placed my coat in the back. Our eyes locked as he got into the driver's seat.

"Everything okay?" he asked, his voice deep and husky. The flutter turned into a rabble of butterflies.

"Yes," I whispered, hoping he wouldn't notice how only the slightest touch from him could make me forget my own name. I needed to calm my racing heart and quell my inconvenient need.

He drove us away from the city lights, out of the dense metropolis of Seattle. I reluctantly tore my gaze away from his angular jaw before my palm would decide to pick itself up and run up and down the day-old growth he didn't have last night. His was an enthusiastic and infectious persona, a Seattle local who gave a history lesson about each place we drove past. Each time I looked at his stacked arms straining against the soft cashmere and the smile on his full lips, all I wanted to do was kiss the dimples on either side of his face. We arrived at what looked like a Georgian era stately home.

"I thought this would remind you of home. They call it 'The Manor.' It's mostly a wedding venue but also hosts other fancy parties." He continued to be the best tour guide.

A wedding venue on a first date.

Note to self: Don't be pathetic and read into that.

I stepped out of the car and looked around. "I love this place, it's grand." Its exterior reminded me of Somerset House, a gallery in London I visited often to unwind after work.

"Good, it's private too. Let's go inside." He took my hand and I let him.

We held hands and threaded our fingers. I didn't think it was possible to be aware of three pulses in my body at the same time – the one beating wildly against my chest wall, the one booming in my ears and the one achingly and deliberately thrumming between my thighs.

We were greeted at the entrance by the maître d' who led us to a dining space fitted with four small tables with classic crisp white tablecloths. Heavy red and gold drapery covered the windows. One visible stained glass, floor to ceiling cathedral window gave the dining room an air of high drama and a nod to a romantic mediaeval past, while small pieces of art common to the neoclassical Georgian era adorned the space. The dining room alone was a history lover's dream and we were the only patrons. I was taken aback at the grandeur and opulence and felt almost underdressed.

I realised he was wonderfully spontaneous if he arranged the dinner in such a small amount of time. "How did you find this place? It's fantastic."

"I'm pleased you like it. I wanted somewhere quiet and private." He smiled.

"Where's everyone else?" I pressed.

"It's only us tonight, the owners let us have it to ourselves." That provoked a jolt of surprise. He promised discretion and followed through. I liked him even more.

"It's perfect, but I think I should have worn a ball gown."

"You look flawless, no ball gowns needed. Besides, they are notoriously difficult to get out of." He looked at me with heat in his eyes, which warmed me up all over again.

"Have you had trouble getting out of one before?" I teased, and looked him over. Whenever I looked at him, he appeared more handsome than the time before.

"More times than most guys. Remind me to tell you about the time with the pink one," he smiled and looked at me in a way I was learning only he could.

In between fits of giggles, I tried to concentrate on the set menu and, as they were expecting only us, it didn't take long to order and be served. The wine, which the sommelier went to great lengths to explain was best paired with roast game, was long on the palate and easy to drink. He needn't have wasted his time on wine education, I wasn't a wine snob, and Miles stuck to sparkling water.

After the sommelier left, we fell into easy conversation while we ate one of my favourites, and a taste of home, venison with pancetta and fontina.

"Tell me about yourself. Where were you born?" he asked, after taking a sip of water in between mouthfuls of the venison.

"You're not ready for this one. I was born on the bathroom floor, in my parents' cottage, in a little village in Oxfordshire called Dorchester-on-Thames."

"Whoa, the bathroom floor?" he exclaimed in amazement.

"Yes, and my father delivered me. Is that uncouth, at dinner? In my line of work, talking about bodily functions, even socially, comes too easily," I laughed.

"No, it's fascinating. Please tell me more," he said and leaned forward.

Momentarily stunned by his good looks, I exhaled. "It was too late to get to the hospital, which was a bit of a drive. My father, a cardiac surgeon, rolled up his sleeves and took instructions from my mother on what he needed to do."

"Your mother kept her cool in that high stress situation?" He asked, still wide-eyed in awe, and took another sip from his glass.

"She was an obstetrician, so she knew what she was doing. As for dad, he knew a thing or two, but it had been a while since he dealt with anatomy south of the waist," I added wistfully.

"They sound like a couple with a healthy dose of common sense. Are they both still doctors?" he asked. The intrigue on his face made me miss my parents.

What would they have thought of Miles Masterson?

"No, umm. I lost them both in a car crash when I was ten," I answered weakly.

"I'm sorry. That must have been hard for you." The compassion I saw in his eyes told a thousand tales. He would understand, he lost his father too.

"I wasn't entirely alone, I had my brother. My aunt, Dad's younger sister, and her husband who were childless adopted me. Dean was already eighteen then. Still, they took both of us in, loved us and provided for us in a manner I wish for every orphan." I inhaled deeply as I recounted that.

I remembered fondly how my guardians kept me busy all the time. I realised when I was older that it was so I wouldn't be stuck in my own head. I was always with friends, made to read everything, volunteered at animal shelters and by the time I turned fifteen I had a Saturday job at the natural history museum where my love of science and the living world blossomed.

"So, you became a doctor, like mom and dad?" His powers of deduction led him to how I felt as an eighteen-year-old, desperate for a connection with my long-gone parents.

"Something like that. I wanted to feel close to them, and that was the only way I knew how. I begged my aunt and uncle to send me to the school my mother went to as a young girl, and after that I got into Oxford where they met."

"An Oxford boffin, how will I ever keep up?" He chuckled. His self-deprecating humour made him even more alluring.

"I remember reading somewhere, you were third in your class at some obscure law school in Cambridge." It was too late to be ashamed of myself for looking him up.

"Don't be fooled, it was a very small class." He laughed at his joke, which I suspected wasn't the first time he told it and that was most endearing. It was difficult not to laugh with him.

"Not to worry, I'll speak very slowly so you can follow along at your own pace."

"Why did you choose paediatrics, not obstetrics or cardiology?" he pressed as he tried to understand my logic.

"Now, that's another story. It's the dark cloud that hangs over my professional head. Last year, I was on my way to becoming a cardio-thoracic surgeon, until I made an error and lost the patient on the table. It became a big deal. The coroner had something to say about it, so did the medical council. I lost all confidence in myself and in my abilities as a surgeon and changed career paths." I gave him the abridged version. I didn't have the stomach to tell him about the day I went before the medical council.

I stood before the imposing panel of the General Medical Council. My heart pounding in my chest, the conference room felt suffused with an air of tension, every gaze on me scrutinising and judgemental. The silence hung heavy, broken only by the distant hum of the stark fluorescent lights. The GMC's spokesperson, Doctor Harold Major, leaned forward, his stern eyes locked onto mine.

"Doctor Braithwaite, you're here today to address the events in the operating room at King's College Hospital on October 12. Mr George Templeton lost his life. We need to understand how and why that happened. This panel has read through the documentation and all the reports, however, due to the sheer number of complaints we have received about this case from the deceased's family, the coroner and some observers present during surgery, we have convened this hearing in the interest of public safety. Do you understand?"

"I do." I was nearly in tears, public safety? Had I become a threat to my patients and the public?

"When you're ready, tell this panel what happened, to the best of your knowledge."

I didn't recognize my own voice as it quivered, while I recounted every step, every decision and every memory etched vividly in my mind. I explained how I had inadvertently nicked the circumflex artery, unleashing a torrent of crimson that had stained the sterile field and every other surface that surrounded the patient.

I couldn't help the tears that welled in my eyes as I recounted the desperate attempts to control the blood loss. I tried to make the panel understand how I fought with every ounce of my being to save George Templeton. As I looked around the room, at Sir Frost and Doctor Harrison absorbing my testimony, a deep sense of sorrow hung palpably in the air. It was my final chance to fight for my medical licence.

"I believe myself to be a brilliant surgeon, yet this tragedy occurred on my watch. It's a cruel reminder of the relentless nature of medicine, a field which demands perfection and doesn't allow for the inevitable human error. That is exactly what it was – an error. Please don't be too *harsh in your judgement ..." I was overcome with emotion and couldn't speak any more. The hearing was my worst nightmare as a doctor, second only to the event in question.*

Then came the moment of redemption. Doctor Harrison, the anaesthetist, spoke on my behalf, as did other surgeons who I had worked with over the years. Sir Frost surprisingly continued the chorus of support rising in my defence.

After a prolonged deliberation, the GMC returned, delivering their findings. Doctor Major spoke with kindness and an undercurrent of sternness. "Doctor Braithwaite, it is the consensus of this board that while a grave tragedy occurred, it was not due to any negligence on your part, rather a case of unforeseen human error."

A wave of relief washed over me as the tears streamed down my face. The compassion and wisdom of the members of the medical board had saved me from the edge of despair, but I vowed to myself that things needed to change.

"Is that the issue that made you leave and come here? You talked about that when I saw you at your clinic," he said with kindness in his eyes, not noticing I had briefly checked out of the conversation.

"One and the same," I said as tears glazed mine.

"I didn't mean to dredge things from the past. I'm sorry." Concern was painted on his handsome face.

"Don't be." Miles held my attention. I wanted to tell him everything. I wanted him to know me, in a way no other man had known me in a long time.

"What drew you to Seattle?" He smiled again, making me forget the heavy discussion we just had.

"My brother. I wanted to be where he was. We talked about it years ago when he encouraged me to organise some kind of US residency, a green card perhaps. By some stroke of luck, my residency status was finalised just as the case was wrapping up, and I took that as a sign and moved here."

Each time he smiled I couldn't tear myself from the dimples on his cheeks. After we finished dinner, we sat out in the courtyard and continued talking. It was cosy, with what I eventually realised was not a real fire but a gas one. There was no smoke, no soot and no sparks but that didn't take away from the traditional English-style ambience.

"Miles, if you don't mind my prying, how could your ex-wife ever let you go. Did you do something really wicked?"

He sighed deeply. "I didn't wrong her, but I wasn't blameless. The relationship may have been doomed from the start. The way we met was unconventional, and I believe the universe was punishing us, especially me." He was painfully candid as he tried to explain. Was he building up to the mother of all excuses? *I shouldn't have purposefully avoided reading about his past relationships.*

"How?"

"When we met, she was engaged to be married to my brother, but she pursued me relentlessly. I couldn't resist her, and we fell in love, we married, we had kids, but much later, she told me she was still in love with him." He closed his eyes briefly and took a deep breath. I couldn't be certain, but I saw contrition on his face.

"Ouch and ouch. I wouldn't have thought you had it in you to betray your brother like that."

My heart became heavy. I liked him, but I couldn't stand infidelity, whichever way it came wrapped. I had been at the receiving end of it and it had torn me apart, and this seemed much worse. Perhaps I wasn't such a bad judge of character after all. But who was I to judge? Unlike me, Miles hadn't ended someone's life.

"That betrayal is something I regret every day. I broke him in the worst way, and I despised myself for a long time. Sometimes I think I still do. For years I lost his trust and his friendship." He was pained as he owned up to that.

"How did he ever forgive you?"

I never bothered to forgive my ex. Instead, I got over him, with difficulty.

"Call it an act of God, or that of a madman. Did you ever hear about the Istanbul bombing two and a half years ago?"

"Yes, that story was everywhere for weeks. Admittedly, I remembered seeing your brother on the news when it happened, and then I recognised him at the gala. I just had never connected the two of you and it felt out of place to bring it up then. Is that what it took for him to forgive you?"

"It was a lot more complicated than that. His recovery was convoluted. I was overwhelmed with sadness, but I was happy too. My brother was back in my life, and needed me in a real and meaningful way."

"That must have been intense. It was good to see him vibrant and so full of life."

"He is full of life." He smiled, then half chuckled as if remembering a private joke.

"Before last year's events happened, sitting on my high horse, I would have told you how much you lacked integrity and even berated you for that infidelity. I would have excused myself from this dinner, indefinitely."

"And now?" he asked with keen interest.

"I'm wiser now. I've learned it's not fair to be judged on the worst decision we've ever made or the worst thing we've ever done."

"That's true, but our worst experiences, actions or inactions are the ones that always weigh heavily and shape us," he explained with sadness.

"Mmm, sounds like the only way to move past our worst actions is to forgive ourselves first," I mused.

I didn't realise we had been talking until after midnight when his phone rang. He glanced at it, ignored it, then changed his mind and answered it. He was irritated, and I could tell it was the end of our time together. While he was on his phone, I looked around the courtyard and realised it was deserted.

"Cara, there seems to be a problem at home, and I need to get back there," he said, agitated.

"Is Maxie okay?" What could be so urgent in the middle of the night?

"She's fine, but her mother is at my house and wants to see her."

"At midnight?" I asked, puzzled and disbelieving.

"I don't understand it either, but this needs my attention."

"Of course." I pretended to understand.

Dating Exit Strategies 101: The Crisis Phone Call. The evening had been going well, I couldn't have said something wrong, unless I did. *Did I?*

We silently made our way to the car. Within minutes Miles was pulling away from the beautiful manor and driving towards the city. We tried to make small talk, but the worry and apprehension on his face was difficult to ignore.

"Miles, does Maxie's mum do this often?" I asked with as much tact as possible.

"Maxie's mom signed away her parental rights. This seems to be something she has decided on the spur of the moment." He sighed dejectedly.

"She did? Who's with Maxie now?" I was horrified, as I tried to imagine why she wouldn't want to be mom to sweet Maxie.

"My mother, and she's very protective of all her grandkids, especially Maxie. But Vivian, my ex-wife, won't leave, and Mom is reluctant to get the authorities involved."

"I have met your mother, she's a force. I'm sorry about your father and your younger daughter."

"What do you know about that?" he asked softly.

"The little bit I read in *Business Now*."

He chuckled, and with a sad look on his face he said, "The infamous *Business Now* article. I didn't talk about them much but I miss them both everyday."

"I'm sorry. I can't imagine how to get over such a significant loss."

"You stay strong for those left behind, but it hurts every day." He spoke softly, with a wistful look on his face, which brought back the tears to my eyes.

"I'm sorry that happened, although after all you've been through, my words seem hollow."

"There's nothing hollow about them."

I looked outside and realised we had arrived at my townhouse. "Thank you for tonight."

"Cara, do you really feel safe here? When Clay told me about what was going on, I was worried about you, and I wanted to help in any way," he said, but why escape from our first date at the first chance, if he cared so much?

"Yes, that problem is not a problem anymore." My eyes met his as we both smiled.

"Good. Will I see you again?" he asked expectantly. He may really be needed at home after all.

"Definitely." I forgot the abrupt end to our date and was already looking forward to seeing him again.

"I can't wait."

"Me too."

"I'll go so you can get to Maxie." I hoped he would walk me to my door. I paused before I opened the car door; everything was different from when we had left hours earlier. This time, he was preoccupied with a distant look in his eyes, which I caught when the light briefly came on in the car.

Chapter Ten

Miles

Talking about losing my father and Laila had a way of sobering me up, and in a twisted way it made me count my blessings. I still had both Maxie and my mother, who could have gone too. But it would leave an impression on Cara, and I didn't want her pity. I needed her to see me as a man who could make her happy despite all I had been through.

Vivian's sudden reappearance riled me up and was messing up what I could tell was a good thing. I couldn't help reliving a midsummer evening I had packed away and hadn't unpacked in a while.

"Right, sweet little ladies, what shall we do now?"

"Nosh our dinner," giggled Maxie, who at five years old had a lexicon full of all the books she filled her days with.

"Yes, nosh our dinner," Laila squealed.

Maxie did all the talking, but Laila never passed up the chance to mimic her sister. Although there was a two-year age gap between them, they could've easily passed as twins. Laila talked like her, wanted to be like her sister and even wore her clothes, which Maxie always shared without much fuss.

While I was watching the girls, out of the corner of my eye I saw Vivian saunter into the kitchen towards the breakfast nook that looked out over the lake, where our dinner was ready. Fernando always got it right, and the girls loved him, Vivian, too, as she had never cooked a day in her life and had never bothered to learn, not even for the sake of the girls. I wasn't fazed, I loved Vivian for exactly who she was – sassy, sexy and underneath it all resided what I thought was a sensitive soul.

"Going somewhere, gorgeous?" I was puzzled. Her overnight bag was in her hand, and beyond her, at the foot of the stairs, my eyes caught two more pieces of luggage – large ones.

"I need some space," she said matter-of-fact, with a nervous glance at her short, clear nails.

She always kept them short, something she chose to do since Maxie was born, worried that if Maxie were to put any manner of objects in her tiny mouth, long nails would scratch the soft inside of it, I heard her say once. She took to motherhood like a duck to water.

"Here's space, Mommy," Maxie said, generously patting the spot next to her and sliding towards her sister at the banquette where they sat.

"Yes, Mommy, here's space," Laila parroted.

"Space from us?" I growled quietly as realisation set in.

"Space from you, Miles." I had never seen her that way. She looked cold, with a calculating glare in her eyes.

"Girls, time to play. We'll eat later. Viv, office, now." She had the good sense to follow me to the location of many lust-filled moments between us. Laila was conceived in that very office. It was private but close enough to the girls' playroom.

"I've interviewed nannies, you can choose one in the morning. The list is on the bathroom counter," she added coolly as she strutted inside and shut the door.

"Choose a nanny? In the morning? What's going on here?" My initial shock turned into a quiet rage.

She stared vacantly at me. *"I can't do it anymore. I can't keep lying to you, pretending everything is okay, when all I want is him."* Even as she broke my heart, she was still my gorgeous wife, the one who nearly cost me my family's love and favour.

"You've met someone else? Who is he? I thought you were focused on our family and your fashion line." I was in disbelief, angry and hurt.

I held my heavy head in my hands and slumped onto the couch.

Karma.

"It's always been him. I see him between you and I, in our every touch, every kiss and every glance. He's the one I'll never get over, the one I'll always miss no matter how hard I try not to. You two look so alike. I see him when I look at you sometimes." She had softened, and it dawned on me who she was talking about.

"You can't have been seeing him. He's met someone he's crazy about."

"No, we're not seeing each other. I haven't had any contact with him, other than during family stuff, and he makes sure to keep a respectful distance. Thoughts of him live in my heart and mind. I've never stopped loving him. I never will," she said quietly.

"You can't leave us for a fantasy, Viv. The girls and I are real, we're your life. You're my wife, my life, the woman I live for," I pleaded, and watched the warmth in her blue eyes leave once more. She'd already left our home, and I was no longer in her heart. From what she said, I never truly was.

"I can't live the lie anymore. Perhaps one day he and I will find our way back to each other, but while I wait for that day I'll be at my new house in Broadmoor."

"Your house? You bought a house? How long have you been contemplating this? On me, and on our children?"

"The first time I saw him with that flight attendant."

"Flight attendant?"

"The Kingman girl. It hit me – he's being wasted on her. She's a narcissist with her woe is me melodrama. We've all lost someone, the difference is we don't wear it like a badge of honour the way she does. As soon as he unwraps himself from her little finger, he'll come to his senses."

"And choose you? Viv, have you lost your mind?" I yelled. I couldn't contain my anger any longer.

"He'll realise we're made for each other," she sighed dreamily, ignoring my outburst.

"I don't recognise you. Was there even a time you loved me, at all? I can't believe I was deluded enough to choose you over him." I roared. The worst decision I ever made had come home to roost.

"I've borrowed one of my daddy's jets. I'll be away for a while. When I come back, we can talk about the kids, and the divorce. I've spoken to my lawyer. You did well for yourself with the prenup. I had hearts in my eyes when I signed it, but that's okay. I'll be just fine."

"A divorce. You thought just before dinner with our children was the best time to do this?"

"When should I have told you? At bathtime, or story time? There was never the right time," she said, as crocodile tears glazed her eyes. I was the one who was hurt, not her.

"Go. You've broken my heart. Tell the girls before you leave."

"No, you tell the girls. The jet's waiting. The saddest thing about this is you haven't even tried to fight for me, to beg me to stay, to prove to me that I chose the right brother."

"Who's the narcissist now? There's nothing to fight for, Viv. I don't like who I see, not anymore."

"*I'm the mother of your children,*" she cried out, tears falling down her face.

"*The children you won't kiss goodbye. They are my greatest gift, and I've got you to thank for that, but I'll never fight to be second string. I put you on a pedestal, and I should've belonged on yours.*" I was dying inside. My heart broke as my world crumbled but I spoke with a calmness I barely felt.

She picked up her overnight bag and walked out of the front door, then sent Clay in for the rest of her bags.

As I fought for the composure I needed to return to my girls, it dawned on me. I had suspected Vivian's disenchantment. I sensed the feelings she still held onto for my brother, the way her breath hitched when he walked into the room, the way she looked at him a little too long and the feral hunger she had whenever we made love after we had been around him. I was in denial for years. I was the architect of my own marriage's demise on the basis of the foundation of deception it was built on.

I had, with great success, gotten over that heartbreaking night when she ended our world and tore our family apart.

When I walked inside, she stood up from the bench in the foyer and rushed towards me.

"Where have you been? It's late." She had never asked me that question throughout our marriage. I never gave her a reason to. It was laughable, that tonight of all nights was when she chose to.

"You lost the right to ask me that question a long time ago. What do you want?" I was brusque and irritated. Cara was on my mind. I should have kissed her before she left my car and even taken the time to walk her to her front door. Without warning she burst into tears, and I couldn't help the groan of exasperation.

"I made the biggest mistake. I never should have left you and the girls like I did, and signing away my parental rights like that, I wasn't in my right mind."

"You're just realising that now? On a random Saturday night, two plus years later? Again, what do you want?" I asked calmly.

"I want you, and I want our family back," she said, adding a quiet sob, perhaps for effect.

"You want your parental rights reinstated?" My expression remained bland. Years of a high-pressure career, losing my daughter and a divorce fraught with her endless mind games transformed me into a humourless pillar of stone when confronted with another one of her antics.

"I want more than that, I want us to be a family again." She stared up at me with her doe eyes. I vaguely remembered a time I would have fallen for them.

"You want your family back? You have no idea what family is," I barked, fighting hard for composure.

"Don't be absurd, she's my daughter too, and I'm her mother." Her tone was tinged with bitterness.

"Mother? You checked out when Maxie needed you, when she didn't know what to do with her emotions. When she woke up night after night with piercing screams, when she didn't have the courage to get into a bath or a pool, terrified she would drown too. For a long time she was adrift and all she needed was you."

"She had you, Michael and Chris. I'm sure the flight attendant was here too, swanning around like she owned the place. If it wasn't for her, Laila would still be here, but she had to have her dream wedding, in the middle of nowhere." She was still fixated on Michael.

"Viv, will you stop and listen to yourself?" The even tone I fought hard for was on its way out the door, replaced by frustration.

"I want to be there for her now. For you too, Miles. You can't have forgotten how good it was between us?" she whispered.

I wasn't surprised. She ignored every struggle Maxie went through after she had watched her grandfather and sister drown. How could she parent Maxie, when Maxie was still invisible to her?

"You made your choice years ago. I'm sure there's a judge somewhere in this state willing to consider your parental rights, but you and I are over, and we have been for a long time. You can't have forgotten that." I fought hard to keep my voice even.

"I would do anything to show you how much I need you, and how much you and Maxie mean to me," she pleaded.

"I've moved on, and I can't be with you, ever." I shook my head, still angry that my time with Cara was cut short for her performance.

"You've got a beautiful home. I can't believe I've never been here. Can I visit and see Maxie?" she asked softly. If it were a different time, under different circumstances, I would have been eating out of her hand.

"Have your lawyer send through what you're proposing, and my lawyer and I will take a look at it."

"Don't blow this out of proportion, we don't need lawyers. You and I can hash this out alone, over dinner and anything else you want. You can come over to mine." I wasn't interested. Ever.

"Oh, but we do need them. Don't come here unannounced again. My house, and I don't want you upsetting Maxie." I took her elbow and walked her towards the front door.

"Think about what I've said and call me." She turned around and placed her hand on my chest.

"Lawyers, Vivian." I pointedly removed her hand from me and shut the door.

I went upstairs to Maxie's room where she was asleep. The light in the guestroom was still on and the door ajar. I knocked and my mother opened it wider and led me inside.

"Is everything okay, son?" My mother's concerned tone disturbed me. Like she had been with Michael, Viv and me, she was now caught in the middle again.

"She's gone. But she will be back, she wants to see Maxie." I sighed.

"She wants to be alone with her?" My mother couldn't hide her dread and apprehension.

"Perhaps. I'll get into it with my lawyer tomorrow. Get some sleep, Mom, it's late." I tried to smile, to reassure her that all was well in my world.

"Did you have fun tonight?" A wide smile appeared on her face. Since my divorce, I had been on a handful of forgettable dates, and my mother had never been privy to any of them. Tonight had been the first time she had caught wind of one.

"Too old for that question." I chuckled, and she laughed with me. "Good night, Mom."

"I'm the one who's old. See you in the morning."

I walked away from the guest room and as soon as I shut the door to my suite, I took a breath, then called Cara, who answered on the first ring.

"Hi." I was already missing her voice. I couldn't get the little dress she wore out of mind. Every time she moved in her chair, it would ride up and show her creamy thighs, which I wanted to run my hands over.

"Cara, were you asleep?"

"Not yet."

"I'm sorry about how the evening ended. That's not what I had in mind."

"How did you intend for it to end?" she asked softly. I wondered if she realised that her voice was her most honed tool of seduction, and she was already using it on me. She didn't know it, but talking to her was the calm I needed.

"You would be in my arms, as close to me as possible."

"It could still end that way," she said quietly.

"I want that, too, but I need to be here."

"Did you sort out the wife issue?" she asked after a few deep breaths.

"I don't have a wife, and not quite. That issue looks like it might take a while." I couldn't help the loud sigh.

"Oh. Why?" She started to sound distant.

"She wants to be a family again and wants her parental rights reinstated." She remained silent for a while.

"How do you feel about all that?" I couldn't read her. Not yet. Being on a phone call made it worse, but she sounded wounded.

"I'm open to parental rights, every child needs their mother, but I can't ever be with her. I've moved on and there's too much bad blood."

"She doesn't seem to think so. If she came over in the middle of the night. She might actually have a chance if you're able to drop whatever you were doing to be by her side."

Ouch, I deserved the dig. She sounded deflated, and I was starting to see where her mind was heading.

"I still want to explore things with you and me. Vivian and I are over."

"Got it. It's late and I'm going to sleep." She erected a ten-foot high wall between us. Shut me out. Was this the end already? Before we had even started. I hoped she was just tired, it was late at night, or early in the morning, depending on perspective.

"Not like this, talk to me please."

"Good night, Miles." She hung up.

I settled in for the night and lay in bed with images of her iridescent green eyes in my head.

Early in the morning, while Mom and Maxie were still asleep, I jogged to Michael's house. He had always lived close to me. Even when I sold my marital home, I made sure to stay close to him, to my parents. And a bonus, close to the water.

It was late October and already the air was sharp with the promise of a cold winter. The nip in the air helped to clear my head, but Cara's face came into my mind, followed by an image of her toned thighs and ample breasts. Not even the fresh crisp smell of the early morning could take away from Cara's scent that lingered in my nostrils. I hadn't been interested in a woman since Vivian ripped me to shreds. I hadn't imagined I would meet another woman I wanted to know. I arrived at his house, and he was already awake, swimming – a habit he could never shake.

"Miles, this is early, even for you. Can't sleep?" He came out of the pool and started to dry himself.

"Busy night, that's why. Sofia and the twins asleep?"

"For now. Is Maxie all right?" Concern was written all over his face. He was Maxie's cool uncle, and her favourite person in the world. He was just as smitten with her.

"She is. It's Vivian. She came to the house at midnight while I was out and demanded to see Maxie. Mom wouldn't let her, and when I got home, she told me she wants to be a family again."

"Did you kick her out?" He knew firsthand how manipulative Vivian could be.

"I was a gentleman, but yes, something like that. She wants her parental rights reinstated."

"She can do that through her lawyer, not come to your house at midnight." he said, protective. Besides my mother, my brother was the other constant in Maxie's life.

"That's exactly what I said."

"Now why were you not at home at midnight, Miles? That's way past your bedtime," he added with a chuckle.

"I was out."

"You were? Who with?"

"Cara Braithwaite." His face broke into a wide grin, and he couldn't hide his glee.

"I knew you liked her. The display on the dancefloor at Mom's gala nearly caused an inferno."

"It was just a dance, I didn't realise." I felt the heat too, but I didn't think it was obvious. We needed to work on being discreet.

"Red hot chemistry is hard to disguise. Ten seconds into it, I got security to move the press along. They were starting to ready their cameras. How was the date?"

"It's complicated." I sighed.

"Already?" He laughed.

"We met when she was Maxie's doctor, four months ago when Maxie hit her head on that field trip to the city."

"In the emergency room? Is that what your life has come to know? You have no shame." He chuckled, clearly enjoying himself.

"She only agreed to see me when you met her at the gala. She's worried about dating the patients' parents."

"Yeah, that's unethical. Is it not? Law school?" he quizzed, with a smirk.

"It's sexual misconduct."

"If Friday night was a precursor to things to come, it really is complicated. " He was thoughtful for a moment.

"I want to see her again, then again after that. You get the picture."

"Vividly," he said and shook his head. "But slow down, Romeo," he chortled. "Aren't you worried about getting her into trouble with her employer or whoever?"

"Yes, the state's medical board. We'll be discreet."

He laughed again. "How does the reluctant heartthrob of publishing date discreetly? Trips to Mars? You're plastering yourself all over magazine covers. Have you seen the underwear addressed to you that our mailroom staff keep having to take out to the incinerator?"

"I leave the perversions to you, big brother." I chuckled. "Besides I'll keep a low profile, it's the least I can do." I tried to convince myself more than him.

"If you say so, but be careful. For her sake," he said with a serious look on his face. We both knew how relentless the media could be if there was even a slight whiff of misconduct.

"Can you drive me home? I can't jog back, my thighs are on fire."

"Anything for the old and decrepit." This time he didn't hold back the laughter.

Chapter Eleven

Cara

I was disappointed at how our date ended prematurely. I didn't know what would have happened between us, but I wanted to find out. Sleep didn't come easy for me as I lay in bed and imagined how Miles' arms would feel around me, on me, and every way I would let him have me. After the reluctant Seattle sun rose, I gave up trying to sleep, and went to the gym a short walk away.

As I walked briskly, down the tree-lined avenue, I felt a presence. One I thought had disappeared from my life.

My skin prickled in awareness, and a cold sweat ran down my back. The gait of whoever was following me seemed light, lithe and calculated, almost feminine. Could it be a woman, or a slight male? I needed to turn around and look, to be sure my imagination wasn't playing tricks on me.

I slowly turned my head to look over my right shoulder and caught my brother's scent. He had worn it since he was eighteen, one of his coming-of-age gifts from our parents. Anyone who had ever set foot in a department store could easily buy it. Was I losing my mind? Maybe I was being paranoid, but given the events from a few months ago, that was highly unlikely.

My step faltered, and he must have noticed. From the corner of my eye I saw a quick and nimble movement. He could have ducked behind a parked car, as I didn't see anyone after I stopped walking and turned around. The city was not the friendliest place, but a young mother pushing a stroller kept walking in my direction from behind me. She would have seen him.

"Hi," I said brightly, without feeling it. "Did you see someone around, a man perhaps? He must have been right in front of you?

"No, I haven't seen anyone, only you, but I barely notice anything these days. I haven't slept in weeks, this one keeps me awake." She smiled indulgently at the baby in her stroller.

"I bet she does," I answered drily. All the small talk I possessed died on the tip of my tongue, while the sweat continued to soak my clothes. He was back and bolder, and had followed me in broad daylight. I thought the whole episode was behind me.

My brisk walk became a trot. I needed the safe haven of the gym. I finally arrived and while in my spin class, Izzy eventually made an appearance.

"I'm sorry I left you waiting," she apologised and got onto the bike I saved next to me.

"I wasn't waiting," I answered breathlessly as I pushed myself harder and faster on the spin bike. Frustrated, terrified and angry. We finished the rest of the class, and as we jumped off our bikes and were catching our breaths, she spoke up.

"How was your date with your mystery man?"

"It was good while it lasted. His ex-wife interrupted in her own special way." Although the date ended abruptly, thinking about him made me feel calmer, almost at peace, after the disturbing events of the morning.

"Ex-wife drama, do you have time for that?" She scoffed and rolled her eyes as she zipped up her sweater.

"I fancy this guy, and I want to see where this goes." I owned up to how I felt about my patient's parent. A man who was off-limits, but a man who had me twisted in knots even the most seasoned fisherman would have a hard time untangling.

"You work fast, cobwebs. How can you already? You met him on Friday night."

"I may have missed out the part where I actually met him four months ago," I said giddily.

She squealed with delight. "You've been holding out on me, you need to tell me more. Name? Age? Diagnosis?"

"I will, but first, do you want to sign up for a kickboxing or MMA class? I've always wanted to try one of those."

"I'll just hold you back, love, I'm not as agile as you are." She smiled ruefully.

I nudged her in the side as we walked towards the back of the gym where the combat classes were held. "Think of all the fun we would have." As we walked past the glass-enclosed rooms towards the group classes, Izzy stared wide-eyed at the built instructors.

"I think I will sign up with you. Do you think we can sign up for that Krav Maga? The instructor looks like he could teach me a thing or two." Her eyes opened even wider, and a huge grin filled her face.

"I don't know much about it. Is it good for self-defence?" I flipped through the brochure, and while we were speaking, Izzy's treasured instructor strode towards us.

Despite his large size and build, he seemed friendly. "Can I help you ladies?" he asked in a cheerful tone.

"Yes, please, my friend and I are interested in Krav Maga. We're not sure if it's a good fit for us." Izzy took charge and I let out a soft chuckle.

"I highly recommend this class, it's practical self-defence that can be applied in real-world situations."

"What will we learn and how long will it take for us to become effective?" I feigned confidence, but inside I was rattled by the re-emergence of my stalker. Izzy saw through me and a quick glance at her showed her face falling.

"It's all individualised. Everyone learns at their own pace, but it's a comprehensive class, so you'll learn techniques drawn from karate, boxing, wrestling and judo. You'll also learn how to defend yourselves in various situations and even against multiple attackers," he explained patiently.

"Will you be our instructor?" Izzy smiled sweetly after recovering from my unspoken bombshell, which she had gleaned. I shook my head slightly and fought to keep a straight face.

"Yes, and I take every class seriously. I expect all my students to do the same." He spoke with the practised ease of a professional, used to fending off advances of overzealous women.

"We're very serious students, right, Izzy? Where do we sign up?" Already, I was pleased with my decision. It was the control I needed.

We both signed up for the class in silence, and I felt Izzy's gaze on me. She put her arm around me and I sighed, silently thanking the universe for the quality friend given to me.

As we were walking out of the gym, Izzy turned to me. "Cara, talk to me. I thought this was over."

She knew me well, and I looked at her with teary eyes. "He's back and I'm terrified," I whispered, looking around us.

"When? We're reporting this now," she said as she clutched my arm and walked us hurriedly to her car.

"I think he followed me on my way here. What is there to report? I didn't see him, the only other person on the street didn't either," I said, dejected.

"You didn't think your oldest friend in the world would want to know what you've been dealing with?" Her eyes were sad and understanding.

"He's been absent, Izzy, for three months. I thought I felt his presence again today," I continued as she drove the short distance to my townhouse.

"You say this has been going on for four months?" Worry etched on her face while she concentrated on the road.

"Yes."

"That's when you met your mystery man. Could it be him?" She was thoughtful, and I became worried.

That was strange, when Miles came into my life, so too did this man. Could they be connected? "It can't be. He doesn't have time for that. He might even be busier than you and me combined."

"Who could it be? Any ideas?" she asked, panic-stricken.

"I've asked myself those questions a million times, and each time I draw a blank. I haven't been here long enough to have anyone obsess over me like this." I confessed, shaking my head.

"That PI you hired was a numpty. We need to take Krav Maga seriously," she said, resolutely.

"Yes, we do, so no flirting with blondie-what's-his-name." I laughed, trying to lighten the moment.

"His name's Colby, and that will be a hardship." She held the wheel with one hand and fanned herself with the other. We arrived at my townhouse and when she stopped the car, I looked around. The terrace was deserted, its usual peace. I let out a sigh of relief and smiled at her.

"I'll see you during the week."

"You will, and call me or text every night before you go to bed. Triple lock doors and all your windows."

"I will." I shut the car door and walked towards my front door.

Just as I entered, Miles called, and his phone call turned my day around. He asked to visit me at home, and I was quick to agree. I didn't remember ever being excited about seeing anyone the way I was excited to see him.

I'd never paid too much attention to what I wore. I spent most of my life in scrubs, and when I wasn't in them, I always stuck to casual, elegant options. This time, although I was shaken by what happened in the morning, my playful side was raring to show herself and I couldn't deny her the chance.

Miles and I didn't know each other well. And this had to be a good start. I found my shortest shorts and a tank top, laid them out on the bed and excitedly got into the shower.

As I was getting dressed, the doorbell chimed. I opened the door and found him on the other side with a bouquet of mixed pink and purple pompon dahlias. I instinctively looked over his shoulder past him.

"Expecting someone else?" he asked with a smile, while he tried and failed to keep his eyes trained on mine.

"Only you. Come in, these are pretty. They look like a picture, I love them." I took the dahlias from him and placed them in a vase I kept underneath the kitchen sink. While I arranged them, I felt his eyes on me.

Note to self: Perfect outfit.

"Something about them reminded me of you." The earnestness on his face replaced the blatant desire from before and was difficult to ignore.

"Really, like what?" I couldn't help my amused tone. How would he explain it without sounding rehearsed?

"When I saw these, I thought they were charming, elegant and delicately feminine."

I smiled. He was the charming one. "You have a way with words, how do you not have a trail of swooning women behind you?"

"Take a look outside your door. They are all there, in the recovery position."

"A little medical humour, I like that," I giggled. My bad day was turning around.

"I'm sorry about last night, that wasn't a good ending," he started to speak as he moved closer to me, his eyes roving all over my body again. I still couldn't believe I hadn't worn a bra, with a see-through tank, in October. *When did I become this woman?*

"It wasn't your fault." I looked up at him, and the butterflies in my stomach took flight.

"You have nothing to worry about with my ex-wife." He seemed sincere, or could it be each defined muscle moulded by that long-sleeved T-shirt making me lose my mind?

"Look, you and I only went out and had dinner. She's the mother of your child. Nothing trumps that." I didn't want to believe that, I wanted to be important to him. Important enough for him to drop everything, like he dropped me for her.

"It doesn't work that way. She'll always be Maxie's mother, but she's not with me," he said, walking slowly towards me.

"Right." My breath caught, each step he took bringing us closer.

"Last night ended too soon, and I was thinking about that." He was a hair's breadth away as his arms bracketed me against the kitchen island.

"What have you been thinking about?" I asked, my breath hitching, the action heaving my chest towards him.

My belly flip flopped as he pulled me into his arms and ardently crushed his lips against mine. It was happening, our first real kiss, stolen from us last night. I slid my hands underneath his T-shirt where I felt the hard planes of his body. I felt his skin too. If I could, I would've burrowed deep inside it and lived within it for as long as I could. His skin would be safer than mine. My body moulded into his, and he held me close while our tongues vied for control, without inhibition. His deep moan had a direct line to my centre, where I started to liquefy.

He tasted like I imagined, heaven with a side of mint. I was cocooned in the safety of his arms and my world was right again. Eventually we stopped kissing, but I wanted the kiss to last forever. I opened my eyes and found him watching me.

"You have the softest lips."

"I do?" I asked breathlessly.

"You do, and I can't get over how beautiful you are."

"Miles."

"Mmm?" He looked at me, his lips poised to kiss me again.

"You can stay longer, so you can kiss me some more. All day if you want to," I said softly. *When did I become painfully shy, and yet so bold?*

"Just kiss you all day? I don't think I could hold back. I'm already obsessed. Do they know you're leaving work with squares of gauze and sewing them into tank tops? Then greeting a consumed man at the front door wearing nothing else but hospital property? What am I to do?" he whispered, then softly rubbed his thumbs over my puckered nipples.

"Please don't tell them." My voice had mellowed, and I lost all ability to form any coherent thoughts.

"Don't worry, I can keep a secret," he said as he effortlessly picked me up and sat me on the counter, the movement of his hands pushing my tank higher and baring my midriff.

"Stay, and I can share more of my secrets, and you can tell me some of yours." Was I begging? I didn't recognise my own voice.

"I want to, but I can't. Are you free next Saturday?" He let his eyes slowly fall from my eyes to my lips, linger on my barely covered breasts, then down the rest of my body.

"I could be, why?" I tried to hide the excitement in my voice.

"I promised to show you around. I want to take you somewhere."

"Somewhere?"

"Have you been to Mount Si yet?"

"You want to take me into the woods?" I was shocked. Why into the woods? We would be alone. Would I be safe with him?

"Deep into the woods, Cara," he said suggestively.

"Ahh ..." I was letting my fears seep through every aspect of my life.

"Is that okay? You look terrified. It's a hike. I got this all wrong, we can do something else." He looked at me intently as he took a step back from between my legs, where the warmth of his body left. I already missed it.

"It's good, great actually. I would love to go hiking. It will be cold though."

"It will be, but it's still a good day out. Make sure to dress warm, and wear sturdy hiking boots, something waterproof. It is Washington after all."

"You have no idea how excited I am. That will be the highlight of my week." I made sure not to shriek. I hadn't had much luck getting Izzy or any of my new friends from work to go on a hike. They were always too tired after twelve hour days spent on our feet.

"Good, I'll pick you up at five," he said, then came back closer to me where I trapped him between my thighs.

"In the morning?" I gasped. He took hiking seriously. *What did I agree to?*

"Yes, in the morning. Is that okay?" he asked, pushing a tendril of hair out of my face.

"It is. I'm used to early mornings." Not on my days off, I preferred to sleep in until mid-morning.

"Good. I should leave, but I was relieved you let me come and see you today. After last night I thought I had blown my chance with you."

"Thanks for coming. I think you might be the best kisser in the whole city."

His voice held mock disapproval. "Have you kissed all the boys in this city?"

"I don't need to after kissing you, no one else could ever compare."

He kissed me again before he left. I could taste him for hours after he was gone. Even his expensive and seductive scent lingered in my townhouse.

Chapter Twelve

♥

Miles

The week was long, and all I looked forward to was the hike with Cara. The look of terror on her face at going into the woods worried me. I would have to find out what it was about. I finally had a chance to show her what I loved, and I hoped she wasn't as delicate as she looked. At five o'clock, I rang her doorbell, which she answered within seconds.

"Perfect, you're on time. Let's go." She grabbed a well-worn rucksack and walked ahead of me to the SUV. We buckled up and were on our way.

"You seemed unsure about a five a.m. start, I'm surprised you're ready and so ... sprightly." I sipped the now lukewarm coffee I had in the cupholder and offered her the other cup.

"I didn't want us to be late, and I've been looking forward to this hike since you asked me," she said, gingerly sipping her coffee. She needn't have worried. It had cooled down since I poured it at home, after long minutes spent agonising about how she took her coffee.

"You have?" I asked with a measure of disbelief. "When I asked, I got the impression you were afraid of going into the woods." I hoped to hear why the woods would frighten her.

"I'm not afraid of the woods. I was out of sorts last Sunday. Wait, you weren't testing me, were you? Do you really want us to go hiking?"

Out of sorts? It must have been about how our date ended on Saturday night. I wouldn't press it, she was happy now.

"Definitely, I want to. I love hiking, and I figured it would be fun if by some chance you liked it too."

"I do, but I never have time. I don't know the trails here well, and hiking is best with a hiking partner."

"Anytime you feel like taking one, let me know."

"Don't say that yet, you might not be able to keep up with me." She gave a teasing smile. Even in the low light of the car it was a distraction.

"I love a challenge, and how is the coffee?"

"A drop of cream and no sugar is just how I like it, thank you," she said, still smiling. I had forgotten how it was to have someone pleased with only a simple pleasure like just the right coffee.

After the thirty-minute drive out of the city we arrived at the Mount Si trailhead in North Bend. The parking lot was deserted, and that was a treat on the popular trail. We parked the car, grabbed water bottles, some trail snacks and set out. I offered to carry it all in my backpack, as I needed Cara to enjoy the hike without the extra pounds on her back. She had a grin on her face, one I never thought possible. Already, it was the best date I had ever been on.

"I can't believe the woods are this thick so early into the hike," she observed with undisguised wonder as she walked ahead of me.

Despite the time of year, the foliage remained dense, and the trees formed a deep canopy over the trail. Besides some occasional muddy pools, the trail was in good condition and the terrain was easy for us both.

"That's why I love this trail. You can lose yourself to it really quickly as soon as you're out of the city."

"How long is it?" she asked, her eyes lingering on my lips.

I had wanted to kiss her since she met me at her door, but she bounded out of it in excitement, and another opportunity hadn't presented itself yet. I was hardly a prolific lover, but I had been with enough women to realise Cara was different. Every now and then she reduced me to a nervous boy trying to impress his first crush.

"Only four miles, but it gets steep and has a sharp elevation. Anytime you want a break, we can take one." We walked another mile while she cooed at the chipmunks that darted blindly back and forth across the trail. Although it was still near dark, I could see she was already starting to struggle. She was determined but needed to rest. "I'll call that first break."

"Sure, I'm dying for a breather. I'm not as fit as I thought," she said, breathless from the exertion. My thoughts wandered, imagining her breathless from other pursuits. She opened a bottle of water and took a small sip, then handed it to me. "I'm curious, why did we take an early hike?"

"This trail is very popular and gets busy later in the day. I wanted you to see it for yourself, but since you asked, the sunrise from the top is the best you'll ever see."

"A sunrise. If I didn't know any better, I would think you're trying to impress me." This time she ran her soft hand across my cheek and down my jaw. It took all the willpower I had to stop myself from pulling her against me.

"I hope it's working," I said, taking her hand and holding it in mine.

"We'll see. How much longer to the summit?" she asked in a breathy voice and looked at our entwined fingers.

"At this pace, another thirty-five minutes, but it's not a race, we can take our time."

"I'll just peel off some of these layers and I'll be ready to go," she said, letting go of my hand.

She removed her jacket and handed it to me, filling up our small corner of Washington with her scent. Next, she removed a hooded sweater and was left with a white thermal T-shirt. She probably wore a utilitarian bra underneath, but I had never enjoyed looking at a thermal T-shirt the way I did then. It was moulded to her body like a second skin. I wondered if they were all this figure-hugging. The bulky winter clothes had been hiding the body that I had made a poor attempt to forget all week.

"Miles?" I missed what she said and found her smiling. "Caught you staring didn't I?" Her melodic laugh filled my ears.

"I'm sorry I got caught, but not sorry I was staring. You're stunning, and I can't stop looking at you."

"Don't sell yourself short, you're pretty too," she teased. "I'll take the jacket back please." She put her jacket back on and I put her sweater in my backpack, then we continued on our way.

She was more energised after the break, and in thirty minutes, just as the sun was coming up over Mount Rainier, we reached the summit.

"I see what you mean. This was worth the four-mile trek."

I handed her a bottle of water and felt the peace this exact place always gave me. The sunrise didn't disappoint. The early morning fog, which shrouded the summit, started to clear and the orange glow illuminated the vegetation all around us. I took in a deep breath and filled my lungs with the fresh mountain air. I closed my eyes and, just for a while, allowed my mind a visit back to the Seychelles.

"Miles, Miles, you need to wake up." I felt a firm hand on my shoulder and knew only Michael would be the one waking me up.

"We're in paradise, and you have a new bride, wake her up instead." I groaned, keeping my eyes closed, and felt the thudding headache that comes only after a great party. I played the role of best man very well. I even toasted myself over and over and the effects of the previous night's party were making themselves known.

"Miles, I need you." His voice cracked.

Waking me up in tears was light years from who he was. Without much thought, I bolted upright. The world spun faster as I kept my eyes tightly shut, protecting them from the glaring Seychelles sun spilling through the sheer curtains in my suite.

"What is it?"

"Dad's gone." He whispered.

"Has something come up at HQ? It's your wedding. But the old man's never been good at switching off." I would have chuckled, were it not for the tears threatening to fall from Michael's eyes, which I noticed when I braved the sunlight and opened my own eyes.

"Our father is gone. He's dead." This time, he spoke louder.

I became sober as the gravity of Michael's words hit me.

"No, he's not, he was dancing with Mom just before I fell asleep."

Could I have watched my parents have their last dance only a few hours ago?

"Get dressed, we need to get to the hospital now." He changed his tone. He was still broken but had become forceful.

My father was gone.

In a daze, I started to get dressed, but not fast enough for Michael. The remnants of the alcohol in my system made my body slow and sluggish.

My father was gone.

"Sit, I'll tie your shoes while you dress your upper half." In another minute we left my suite, and Michael jogged to a waiting chopper. I couldn't understand the rush.

My father was already gone.

I rushed too. It wasn't the time to try and be logical.

"Where is he? I need to see him," I cried out, while Michael hustled me inside the chopper. I had barely sat down when the chopper lifted and was flying low over the azure waters of the Indian Ocean.

"In good time, Miles," he said. This time he avoided my eyes, while his swam with tears. I had woken up to the worst day of my life.

"Where's Mom? She shouldn't be alone," I shouted for him to hear me above the noise.

"She's at the hospital," he said with a finality that didn't leave room for any more questions. He couldn't shut down. I needed him, my mother needed him, the business needed him to step up.

The chopper ride was less than five minutes long, but my stomach churned and all I wanted was to get off it. As soon as we arrived and entered the hospital, which was marginally larger than my house's great room, I followed my mother's voice. I could hear her, wailing, and with the little French I spoke, I understood she was begging someone to keep trying. Someone answered with compassion how they had already tried everything they could. She must be in shock, my father was beyond help.

When I rounded the corner, my world ended. Everything faded away except Laila lying on the gurney. She wasn't moving. She had her mother's medium skin tone, but the colour was drained from her lifeless body. Michael wouldn't have had the words to encapsulate this, so he let me see for myself.

"What's going on? What happened here? Who did this?" I bellowed as my legs gave way. For the second time that day, my brother helped me to my feet.

"Miles, no one did anything to her. We went out in one of the boats and she fell into the water. Your father went in after her, but they both got caught in a rip current. I only just managed to pull her out, but she was already so weak." My mother's voice was pained, but she was trying to be strong, strong for me. I noticed then she was soaking wet, her teeth chattered and she was shivering. She needed a towel, better yet, my father.

"Michael, help me give her CPR. You know how to. Please help me, help my baby girl," I cried out to him as I held Laila against my chest. He walked towards me. Sadness, pity, resignation and grief all resided on his face. He hadn't shut down on the chopper, he had run out of the right words to say.

"She's gone too, Miles. I'm sorry. I didn't know how to tell you." I held her close and didn't want to let her go. As the minutes ticked by while my mother's silent sobs filled the tiny hospital, I realised Maxie was nowhere to be seen. I gently placed Laila back on the gurney.

"Where's Maxie?" I cried out. I needed to know, but I didn't want to. I couldn't have lost her too.

"She's back on the other island with Sofia. She's safe and well." Michael was gentle with me and let me cry on his shoulder, all the while he held my mother's hand in his. He had already stepped up.

"Are you okay? You seem to have drifted somewhere." I heard the concern in Cara's voice and saw a worried look on her face.

"Yes, more than okay. I came here often in the first months after I lost my father and Laila. This will sound unreal, but I felt their presence in the wind and the rustling tree branches as I walked past them. The predawn calm always allowed my heart and mind to still and appreciate life as it had become."

"It's not unreal, it's what helped you heal. You must still miss them both terribly," she said with compassion on her face and a small smile on her lips. I wished she had been in my life when I lost them. Her smile, her voice and her understanding could have made things somewhat bearable.

"There's not a day that goes by that I don't think about Laila, my father too, but it's become easier. My father was not just my father. He was my mentor and my friend, too. The only friend I had for a while after what happened between my brother and me." I stared into her vivid green eyes, which looked more vibrant and intense at the break of dawn.

"Thanks for bringing me somewhere special to you." This time she took my hand in hers.

"There's a spot a little deeper where we could have breakfast before we descend. Would you like that?"

"You've thought of everything! Now I'm impressed. Something about the mountain air always makes me hungry."

"Good. The descent will be much easier. I hope I didn't push you to overdo your first hike in a while."

I led her towards a picnic table with two picnic benches. The morning dew still covered them, but we were both too tired to care. She chose to sit on the bench next to me. I enjoyed the closeness while I removed the mix of sweet and savoury pastries from their brown bags.

"You didn't. This is exactly what I needed. I would never have imagined you did this type of thing." She removed her jacket and placed it next to her on the other side of the bench and closed the small space between us. *She wants to be close to me too.* She let her hair down, and I was surrounded by a scent I needed to drown in.

"This type of thing?" I asked, in a daze, while my eyes glanced past her lips and dipped down to her breasts.

"You know, ordinary, regular guy stuff," she explained animatedly, with a chuckle, and tore one of the sweet pastries with her fingers.

"I don't know what regular guys do, I'm not one of them," I joked and bit into a ham and cheese pastry.

"I thought you would have waited for date number six before 'the cocky' was in full effect." She used air quotes as she laughed.

"I wouldn't want to mislead you. The cocky is part of the package. My chef made these pastries just for this hike so don't be fooled, the date wasn't as cheap as it looks." I chuckled and watched her blush.

"You're twisting my words, I'm not whining. This is perfect." She smiled sweetly as a small piece of pastry didn't quite make it into her mouth and hung precariously on her lower lip.

Distracted by her heart-shaped lips, I asked, "Is it something you might want to do again?"

"Are you asking me on another date before this one is over? You must've enjoyed yourself." She was stalling, and the thought crossed my mind that she may not have enjoyed herself as much as I hoped.

"Can I help you with something you have stuck to your lip?"

"Is it a bug?" She stilled, closed her eyes, and a look of terror flushed across her face. I didn't wait for permission. I moved closer to her and licked it off her lip. Before I could stop myself, I took her lower lip between mine and gently sucked on it. She slipped her tongue inside my mouth and moaned softly, while I took control of the kiss.

"No, it's not a bug," I whispered, after she had let me taste her for a few long minutes.

"What was it then?" she asked breathlessly, looking at me expectantly.

"Something edible, something I want to taste again." I crushed my lips against hers one more time, until a group of hikers arrived at the summit.

"Was it delicious?" She giggled and sipped some water.

"More than you would ever know. Although I didn't get an answer to my question."

"Which one? I got a little distracted," she teased, with a smile.

"Would you like to do this again next weekend? All weekend?" Right then, I realised she was the first woman I had ever almost begged to spend time with. *She was extraordinary.*

"I want to, but can you leave Maxie all weekend?" If my mind wasn't made up about how much I wanted to get to know her, to have her in my life and to have all of her, that question confirmed it.

"I like how you're considerate and Maxie's on your mind, but I want to get to know you, and I want to take you somewhere you haven't been to yet."

"Next weekend's tricky, I'm on call. Can we try the one after that?" She seemed apologetic, but I was impressed. I would never have expected her to drop everything for me. Everything she said, even that which should have disappointed me, impressed me more and more. She was refreshingly honest and principled.

"I don't know if I can wait that long to see you again, but it will have to do. Even a quick lunch? Midweek?" I was reduced to pleading again.

"I would love to. The weekend after next is all yours." As soon as she agreed, I kissed her again, other hikers be damned.

Chapter Thirteen

♥

Cara

I enjoyed the hike, but one thing was for certain, I needed to work on my fitness. After hiking a mere mile, my lungs were on fire but for Miles it was effortless. He had the stamina of an athlete. How would he find time to stay fit between his job, looking after Maxie and whatever other social appearances were demanded of him?

I had never been on a hike with a man I was attracted to. Everything he did, even the mundane, made me want to get to know him more. He was generous, funny and sexy without trying. Somewhere along the way he may have been told he was cocky, but it was his confidence misunderstood, and that was the best part of him.

When he drove me back home after our hike, shortly before lunch time, all I wanted was for him to come inside so we could help each other shower off the sweat we worked up on the way down from the summit. It was clear we were two adults who wanted to get to know each other, the way only two adults can. He may have wanted to come in, but I didn't have it in me to hear him let me down gently again. It was Saturday, and I imagined this was a day for him and his daughter, and he had already spent half of it with me.

Studying for my paediatrics certification, as well as putting in the hours required for it at both the clinic and the emergency room, was catching up with me and I was tired. I attended two invigorating Krav Maga classes weekly and they also pushed my limits physically. It was only Wednesday night. I needed the week to be over and to see Miles again. We hadn't seen each other since the morning at Mount Si and he was all I could think about. The choreography of trying to sync our busy schedules was tricky and talking on the phone and texting wasn't enough anymore.

I arrived home, and as I walked closer to my front door it was clear it had been kicked off its hinges. I realised the stranger in my life had escalated. Tears filled my eyes as I imagined what horrors were to be found inside my home, my sanctuary, my safe place. I wouldn't go inside alone, he could be lying in wait.

I dashed across the terrace and banged loudly on my middle-aged neighbour's door while I looked around me. She opened her door and hurriedly let me inside her townhouse as soon as she peered outside and caught sight of mine.

"Come inside, Cara. What's going on? Has someone broken in? Could it be the same person who broke my window?" She gasped, her right hand on her heart, worry written all over her face.

"Yes, it's a break-in. I've called the police. Any chance I could wait for them here?" I stuttered as I walked inside.

All I wanted after a long, exhausting day was to get home and relax. And talk to Miles, as our late-night phone calls had become the highlight of my day. Could I call him now? I didn't want to seem needy and clingy. Whatever was happening between us was still new.

"Of course. Look at you, shaking like a leaf, you can't even get your words out. You must be losing your mind. Sit. I'll bring you some water, maybe a Xanax. God knows I need one."

She put her arm around my shoulder and ushered me further inside her townhouse, which, besides the bold maximalist multi-colored decor, was a mirror image of mine. I didn't know her well; she kept to herself like my other neighbours. We only spoke briefly when I moved in, and she, too, lived alone.

She didn't take long to return to her unique living room where, for a moment, a busy and bright green pine-forest-themed wallpaper made me forget why I was there. "Here, take this," she said, handing me a glass of water and a Xanax.

"Thanks, I'll skip the Xanax. The police will want to talk to me, and it will knock me out." It wasn't the time to educate her about the perils of sharing prescription drugs. Even if I wanted to, I could barely speak.

"Can I call someone for you? The young man with the two children, your brother, was it?" For someone who didn't know me much, I realised she was observant. How could she not have noticed someone breaking in? Could she have seen someone lurking? How does something like this happen in Queen Anne? It was supposed to be a safe neighbourhood.

"Yes, my brother. I'll call him. You haven't seen anyone around my place in the last few weeks have you?" I asked, hopeful she could tell me something and inadvertently give me a clue about who this could be. Even though we didn't talk much, she was giving off nosey neighbour vibes, and this one time I adored the trait.

"Only your brother, the children. Your friend, the bold and bubbly girl, knocked on my door accidentally the first time she visited you. I did see a car I didn't recognise. Something European, a Bentley perhaps. It looked expensive. That's all I can think of." She sighed. She had taken note of my visitors, but not the one who posed a threat. He had even managed to evade the nosey neighbour.

The police didn't take long to arrive, and when I saw their lights, I thanked my neighbour, left her townhouse and met them outside my door. When I eventually entered my house behind them, I stood still and scanned my living room, stunned beyond belief.

Everything was strewn everywhere. An axe or a machete had been taken to my furniture. Everything was destroyed, and as I walked further there was a strong smell of urine in the centre of my bedroom where all my clothes were piled, save for the ones in the laundry basket in my bathroom. The sight was horrifying and unbelievable. A baby-faced officer looked at me and spoke, but I didn't hear a word.

"I beg your pardon?" I asked, in a trancelike state.

"Does it look like anything has been taken, Miss Braithwaite?" he asked louder.

"It's difficult to be sure. The place has been turned into a tip."

"I know, I'm sorry. Sometimes it's obvious when you walk in. Do you have any valuables in the house? Money, jewellery, documents?" He stared at me a little too long, until he remembered he was taking notes. Was I now suspicious of everyone?

"My mother's jewellery. Its value is mostly sentimental."

"Okay, can you check it's still here? While you're at it can you pack a bag? Is there somewhere you can stay tonight?"

I packed a bag, called Dean and asked him to bring a front door with him. I poked fun at him for having some doors propped against the wall in his garage. The police took photos and fingerprints, but that was in vain. It had all been done before. I was shattered. Everything I had ever bought in my working life was reduced to rubbish, ready to be taken away by the Friday morning rubbish collection.

When Dean arrived, I broke down and cried. He asked if I checked the cameras, but there was no feed on my phone. He went outside to check on the cameras he installed, and he found those destroyed too. My townhouse wasn't safe; I couldn't live there any longer.

I arrived at his house and showered the day away. The stalker had won, and I was terrified. I wondered if I had ever been safe in my own home.

While in the guestroom, the front doorbell chimed, but I didn't take much notice of it until Charlie knocked on my door and came in.

"Cara, a friend is here to see you," she announced excitedly, eyes bright and face flushed.

I was confused. "Izzy? She is?" I hadn't called her, though she would've wanted me to. My safety, the state of my house and the expense I faced was all that was on my mind.

"Definitely not Izzy. He said his name's Miles." I couldn't help the weak smile that formed on my lips. How did he know where Dean and Charlie lived? I had never been specific.

"Oh, Miles. Sure," I said, pretending to shrug the visit off, although inside I was turning somersaults. If Charlie realised how excited I was she would prematurely make him a part of the family.

"What does that mean – oh, Miles, sure?" she asked, mimicking my accent.

"We're establishing, cultivating or whatever," I said with a sigh, while I tried to come up with the right word to describe what was going on between Miles and me.

"Establishing? Hmm, that's a new one. Well, by the looks of things, he's dying to get established and desperate to get cultivated. Knocking on your brother's door with good manners, handshakes and that swoony eye contact. He even brought two bouquets of flowers – one for you and one for the lady of the house. I nearly died. Looks familiar though. Is he an actor or something?" Her rapid fire monologue finally died down and she grinned.

"Or something. I'm glad you've been provided some midweek entertainment," I said with a chuckle and quick shake of my head.

"Hurry downstairs before either of you change your minds and de-establish. I had no idea they built them like that in Seattle." She rubbed her hands together and giggled like a schoolgirl. Miles made me want to giggle too.

"I'll be down in a minute." I pulled on a comfortable sweater over my leggings. That was very different from the last outfit I had worn for him, and one of the few items that hadn't been caught in the madman's fit of rage.

I arrived downstairs and wasn't surprised to find that Dean and Miles had become acquainted. Dean was always welcoming, and Miles, I was starting to realise, was affable and friendly in social situations. When I entered the room, Miles stood up and walked towards me. He held me close, and his familiar scent was the comfort I didn't know I needed.

"Are you okay? Clay told me what happened at your house."

Clay, my surrogate protector. I was surprised he would've learned about this so quickly, relieved I didn't have to relive it all by telling Miles. "He did?"

"Yes, his old colleagues told him." The baby-faced one seemed to have been too engrossed with me to have been focused on anything else.

"Thanks for coming." I stayed close to him. His presence comforted me and all I wanted was for him to hold me close and never let go.

"How are you? You should've called me. I want to be the one you call when you need someone," he said gently, with a worried look, after Dean slipped out of the room.

"You're right, I should've called. The thought crossed my mind." I didn't miss the small smile on his worried face. "I'm shocked about everything."

"I'm sorry this happened." He brought my body back closer to his, held my face and kissed me softly on my head. *He read me perfectly. That was all I needed.*

"It's not your fault. This is something that has been happening for a while," I confessed into his compassionate eyes.

"It might be my fault." He sounded apologetic as we both sat down and he held my hand.

I was surprised and afraid. I let go of his hand and shuffled away from him. Izzy asked if this was a possibility. "How?"

"When you asked Clay for help, the first time, he told me about it. I know about the PI you hired, but Clay was worried that wasn't enough. So we had a security team watch you for months, until the morning after the manor, when you told me this person was no longer a problem. I dismissed the security service when I thought you were safe."

"Miles, I had no idea." I smiled as tears filled my eyes. *Why would he do that for me?*

"You weren't supposed to know. In that respect, they did a great job."

"Why would you do that for me? We weren't anything then."

He moved closer to me and spoke in a hushed tone. "Are we something now?" He cocked his head to the side and smiled a sweet smile.

I smiled at him. "I'm still vetting you."

"What will it take to turn this into something?" He took my hand in his, like we had been doing it for years, and kissed the tips of my fingers.

"I can't tell you that. We can find out together." I smiled coyly.

"Can I at least kiss you? I've missed you." He didn't know it, but I missed him too. I answered him with a kiss, one I didn't want to end until his lips reluctantly left mine.

"Are we still on for the weekend? After everything that's happened, you need to get away. If you're feeling up to it."

"I want to, but I need to sort out my house and my life. Short of setting a fire, he destroyed everything I have. I don't think I'll be returning there, I'm terrified of what could happen."

"I'm sorry. Will you let me help you?" He kept my hand in his large one.

"You don't have to do that. Dean's onto it." I let my eyes wander his face, and understanding lit his eyes.

"And he will sort it out. All I want to do is help him help you. A few things: I'll put the security service back onto you, get some people on this to find out who's done it and get a service to help with clean up and some new furniture. That way you can be done by Friday."

"Did you just come up with that plan off the top of your head?" I stalled while I tried to figure out how much of his generosity I was ready to keep accepting.

"Maybe I did," he said with a devastating smile.

"I don't need you to buy me anything, but I'll take all the help I can get."

"I want to help in any way I can," he said as he brought his lips closer to mine.

Charlie chose that moment to walk in, but did her best to execute a blank expression. The twinkle in her eye and the redness in her cheeks gave away what she had seen. She smiled and spoke directly to Miles.

"Would you like to stay for dinner? We've got plenty." *Step one: Bring him into the fold.*

"No, thank you. Not today, but next time I will, if you'll have me," he said with a smile as he stood up and picked up his grey peacoat. He only just arrived but was already leaving.

I peered at my watch and realised it was just after dinner time with Maxie. He missed that to check on me. The least he could do was make it back to her in time for her bedtime. I wanted him to stay, but even without his explanations, I understood why he had to go. I blinked back the surprising tears that filled my eyes.

"Sure, it was good to meet you, Miles," Charlie said as I walked him out to the front door.

Chapter Fourteen

Miles

On Friday afternoon, I sent Clay to the clinic for Cara, and we met at Boeing Field Airport a little outside the city. I arrived just as she stepped out of the car.

"This is a surprise," she said, while I took advantage of the empty hangar and held her curvy body close to mine, inhaling her scent. My body jerked to attention, but I let her go before she noticed.

"A pleasant one I hope?" I tore myself away from her. She wore a dress that hugged her tighter than I just had.

"It's all very James Bond, isn't it? The DBX you've parked over there, the plane behind me," she said with a teasing smile. "Where are we going? It's not fair you kept me in suspense, giving me only wardrobe clues." Her hand lingered on my chest. It had been two days since I had seen her, and they had been very long days. All I had been able to do was talk to her on the phone when I longed to have her with me and take away all her worries and burdens.

"Almost right, it's a DB12. And we're not going far. It's only a two-hour flight to California."

"Oh. I didn't bring my bikini," she said as her face fell.

"You won't need it. We're going to the mountains this time. Do you have sensible shoes?" I asked as I took in her six-inch heels.

"Always. They're not hiking boots, but they'll do." She had lost a lot of her clothes from the intrusion at her house, and I planned on replacing them for her. I didn't know how I would since she was fiercely opposed to overt acts of generosity.

We boarded the G700, and a soft gasp left her. I always forgot how the plane looked when seen for the first time. I was impressed too when I first saw it, a gift from the company board six months prior after intense negotiations and winning a high-value acquisition. I made sure to only use it when necessary. The last time I was on it with Maxie she asked me to explain carbon emissions, and that was a tricky conversation to have without sounding like a hypocrite.

"We don't have to leave this hangar. I could happily spend all weekend here," she said, smiling.

"If that's what you really want, that can be arranged too. Where would you like to sit?"

"Right here will do." She chose a pair of seats that allowed the passengers to take in the whole plane, including the cockpit, which she could tour if she wished, and a small kitchenette, where all manner of snacks and drinks were available. On the other side was a powder room and the stateroom, which was ideal for sleep during transatlantic flights.

I sent a message to the pilot telling him we were ready for take-off and within minutes, we were in the air.

"I've missed you. I can't stand how I couldn't see you since Wednesday happened." I leaned into her space. She was finally close, and she was all mine, all weekend. I had anticipated today, but never imagined it would feel this way.

"I'm excited too," she said and ran her hand against my jaw. That touch was what I longed for since I left her nearly in tears at her brother's doorstep. I had wanted to stay longer, but I was torn between her and Maxie. Whichever decision I made was hard to live with. Maxie was thriving, though in some ways still fragile. I tried to never break my promises to her, and I had promised to be home before her bed time.

"I'm sorry you had to leave your townhouse. I know you loved it. I have a downtown penthouse you can live in. It's safe, and close to everything." I couldn't stop myself as I brought her lips closer to mine, and gave her a slow lingering kiss.

"That's generous, but I've found something new," she said, letting go of my lips and biting into her lower one. I was still learning her tells, and I didn't understand that one yet. I fought hard not to show my disappointment. The penthouse was the perfect place for her. She would be comfortable and safe. It was even close to HQ, making it convenient for us to see each other as often as we could.

"Is it safe?" I pressed. How could I protect her if she wouldn't let me in the best way I knew?

"I believe so. It's in a gated golf community with security at the entrance." That wouldn't be enough to prevent another break-in.

"Do you like it?"

"It feels like deep suburbia, and not how I imagined living in Seattle, but I feel safe there. Over the weekend it will get some repairs and a lick of paint."

"I'm sorry you've compromised on the location you loved, but safety is important until this is all behind you." I sighed. She would have been safer in the penthouse, but I wouldn't push her.

"Yes, Daddy." She laughed softly.

"Do you think you could say that again, later?"

"You might be a little too presumptuous," she said, bringing her lips back to mine. I loved her flirty tone, and it was all for me.

"You have no idea about all the things I may have been presuming, all day and all night," I whispered against her lips.

She gasped as her eyes widened. "Day and night? You're not as busy as I imagined you to be." She chuckled and crossed one leg over the other. Her dress rode up her thigh and she let one heel fall off her foot. How would I make it through the flight without dragging her to the stateroom?

"One more serious thing. Do you know this man?" I showed her a picture of the man who may have been stalking her.

"That sullen face looks familiar. I may have seen him at my gym, or was it Pike Place while I was out with my niece and nephew?" She blew out a heavy breath as a look of recognition seemed to cross her face. "Who is he?"

"The investigator suspects that might be the man who has been following you, but he hasn't been able to identify him yet."

"I can't believe this is happening. It's every woman's worst night-mare." She appeared deep in thought as she shook her head, and her eyes watered.

"I didn't mean to upset you." Who was this man? Would just a guy from the gym stalk and obsess over a woman like he was doing? Did she know him, but didn't want to let on? I was obsessed with her too, but I would never make her life hell. Could she have rebuffed his advances?

"You haven't upset me, you're trying to help me. The stalking situation is what's upsetting, and possibly ruining my first trip to California," she said, smiling through her tears.

"Trust me, I'll do anything to help find this man, and the trip isn't ruined. We don't have to talk about this, not anymore." At that point, the flight attendant brought some sparkling water and left it quietly.

"Thank you, Miles." she said as she kissed my cheek and gave me a sweet, seductive look. "I need the loo, which way is it?" she asked, sliding her heel back on. I caught a glimpse of her creamy calf. *I am definitely obsessed.*

"The *restroom* is straight ahead, and it's the third door on your right," I corrected her and laughed. She laughed softly with me, stood up and walked towards the bathroom, her hips swaying from side to side, and I was in awe of how perfect she was. I twisted the cap off the bottle of water and took a sip. The moment the bubbles hit my tongue, and I savoured the tingle, I imagined how she would taste.

As she walked back, my eyes travelled up her legs, past her hips and became transfixed on her breasts. Just as she was walking past me to take her seat, the plane jerked and the gods of turbulence delivered her straight onto my lap. She tried to get up and our eyes met.

A heavy breath left my lungs. "You don't have to go anywhere." I couldn't stop myself as I wrapped my arms around her, feeling every curve and contour of her body against mine. I grew underneath her, and again when she moved against me as she tried to get up.

"The pilot didn't warn us the turbulence would be this strong," she said as she shivered in awareness, while her green gaze stared hungrily at my lips.

"That part wasn't turbulence, it's all me." I breathed her in while I softly ground her against me. She let out a quiet moan. I needed to stop. We were twenty minutes away from landing. I wouldn't rush her; I wanted to have her, the way she deserved to be taken, slowly and thoroughly.

She stood up and returned to her seat, flushed and breathing heavily. I chuckled at her obvious arousal, then forwarded her a message from my doctor, received after our descent from Mount Si. I didn't want her to worry and think about any other woman who had come before her. She picked up her phone and looked at it, then her gaze returned to my lips.

"Well done, you passed your test with flying colours, Heartthrob," she said as her breath hitched. *I love hearing her call me that.* "Although I didn't take one of those. " I heard a hint of an apology.

"When did you last take one?" I leaned in closer, pinching the sapphire on her neck between my fingertips.

"Three years ago, after a breakup," she whispered, biting her lip. I saw it then – she bit her bottom lip when she was nervous. It wasn't an easy conversation, for anyone.

"Why is that?" I asked. Then I nipped at her bottom lip, hoping to set it free and get her to relax. *I have a history too.*

"That's the last time I was with someone," she said breathlessly. I felt a pang of jealousy and dread. *Three whole years, what could she still be holding on to? Unless ...*

"Is your heart done with him?" I asked, while mine thudded wildly in my chest. I didn't want to be caught in another perverse love triangle.

"Definitely," she murmured.

"Why haven't you been with anyone since him?" This time I coaxed her mouth open, and she took control. She softly sucked my tongue and deepened the kiss. *She has to be the most sensual woman walking Earth's surface.* She slowly let go of my tongue and licked my lower lip. That small action had me at attention again.

"I was too busy for a real relationship, and I have a hard time with one night stands. I need a connection. Friends with benefits sounds too complicated in my simple mind." She ran a finger against my straining erection. *A woman after my own heart.*

"You're hardly simple. It's biology, Doctor Braithwaite." We continued to kiss softly, and in between kisses I said, "Some view it as a release, others a more intimate act." My legs widened as my body shifted involuntarily towards her.

"I can't believe I've owned up to that. You must think I'm about to ask for your hand in marriage." Even as she chuckled, she kept her fingers against me. I hoped she would never stop.

"If you're asking, I've always had my eye on one of those DeBeers engagement rings. Classic cut and not too showy, my friends might get jealous." I smiled and took her hand off me and held it in mine. We were close to landing, and I was losing control. The rhythmic drumbeat in my chest was a testament to how nervous I was. Had I ever been anyone's first before? Technically I wasn't hers, but whatever was going to happen tonight felt just as important.

Right then, the pilot announced we were five minutes out from descent. We fastened our seatbelts as I tried to calm my body.

Our destination was a short drive from the airfield where we landed. A car waited to drive to the spa and wellness resort, deep in the mountains. After sharing what we had on the jet, she was lighter. She chatted excitedly about where we were going. When we arrived, she wasn't disappointed.

It was a tranquil green paradise in a lush and natural forest setting. An exclusive spa, with eight small but luxurious villas perfectly suited for couples, it was the perfect place to help her forget her hellish week.

"Miles, this is heavenly. I love it. How do you always find the best places? Have you been here before?" She chattered after we had been led to our villa through a canopy of overhanging banyan trees. Despite the expansive walls of windows, it was private like I had hoped it would be.

"No, it's my first time too. I'm not disappointed. The best part's the look on your face." I leaned into her kiss. How did I ever live without knowing her? *Could I be falling too fast and too hard?*

Chapter Fifteen

♥

Cara

Miles had taken me to another beautiful and discreet place. I started to wonder if I was overthinking the doctor-patient relationship and didn't need to duck and dive. I put that to the back of my mind as we entered our suite. It was dreamy, inviting and decorated in all shades of green like the views outside.

Note to self: I'm never leaving.

"When you're ready, we could go and have dinner," he said, after we had looked around the single bedroom luxe suite. We were both amazed at the lush green mountain views out of the window and for miles beyond.

"I can be ready in ten minutes."

I walked into the bathroom with my overnight bag. I wasn't sure what came over me on the plane, but the desire I saw in Miles' eyes made me bolder than I had ever been. He was smooth, sharing his test results before things became too heated. I hadn't dated in a long time. I even forgot the "I'll show you mine if you show me yours" unspoken rule.

Just as I finished getting changed into a short, frilly black playsuit, and was letting my hair down, I felt him behind me. I looked up and found him leaning against the jade-green backlit onyx wall. His reflection in the mirror was a picture of intensity. His heavy-lidded gaze didn't leave any doubts in my mind about what he wanted. My core throbbed and tightened while I shook my hair and pretended not to notice the raw masculinity which had taken up residence in the bathroom. Freshening up had become an act, and I turned around and faced him.

"Need the loo? I'll be out in a minute." My voice shook, while my body rippled.

"I couldn't help myself. I had to see you." His eyes roved all over my body as he moved closer to me.

"See me?" I could barely hear myself think over the loud thud in my ears, but I continued to playact the ignorance. I understood what he meant. I felt it too.

"I've tried to be a gentleman, but I can't wait anymore. I. Want. You."

"And dinner?" My cheeks heated as those two words failed to convince either of us that we needed to eat.

"You know we aren't leaving this suite for dinner. I've wanted you since we arrived at the hangar. Tell me you didn't feel it too. That you don't feel it now."

The sexual tension thickened as we looked at each other. He was easily the sexiest man I had ever met. He wanted me, but I wanted him more.

"I think ..." He didn't let me finish. He easily picked me up and placed me on the marble counter. Standing between my parted thighs, his body heat continued to set me alight.

"Say no right now if all you want is to eat," he whispered, his voice heavy with desire, as he tasted my lips. He unzipped the side zip of my jumpsuit, hidden beneath the elaborate seams. *How did he find the zipper so easily?*

"I can't say no," I whispered hoarsely.

"Why can't you?"

"Because I want you too. I've wanted you for a long time. I didn't want to be wrong," I said, panting into his handsome face while he unclasped the black lacy bra I chose with this moment in mind.

"Does anything about this feel wrong?" He exhaled, gazing at me, at my body, as he finally had the upper half of my jumpsuit off me.

He held fistfuls of both breasts in the possessive palms of his hands and was hungrily sucking, biting and nipping at my now braless breasts. I was starved, so was he. I lifted my buttocks off the bathroom counter and he pulled the rest of the jumpsuit off me, together with the little scrap of knickers I wore.

"It doesn't," I moaned. Then I finally had the sense to get his clothes off.

He wore a sky blue dress shirt and navy slacks, which had come from somewhere where thread count and quality mattered. I fumbled with his shirt until he was shirtless, then an involuntary whimper left me. The solid planes of his body were as hard as I imagined every night in my bed while the hollow space between my legs, which I had wanted only him to fill, desperately quivered.

The warmth of arousal making its frenzied way all around my body was something I'd only ever read about in medical books. I had never felt this way before, not with any lover I had ever had.

"I've thought about you, about this, for months since I first met you, and nothing I imagined comes close to the real thing." He kissed my lips savagely, with fervour and hunger matched by my own, while his hands continued to explore my body. That was the connection I had waited for my whole life.

"And what have you imagined?" I urged, arching my body towards his.

"You've been the subject of my fantasies for too long. I get to lick and taste every bit of you. Touch you in all these places I've wanted to touch. You and me, all night, with nothing between us. You would bend to my every will, and I would give you all I have, in every way you'd let me."

"I want that too. All of it." I groaned as my thighs parted even further and his gaze dropped to my weeping centre.

"When did this happen?" he asked in amazement as he brushed two fingers lightly against my core. I moaned as he pushed them inside.

"Since you came to the clinic, but more recently on the plane," I confessed. My grip tightened on the counter while my head fell against the mirror behind me as his digits teased and prodded.

That seemed to galvanise him. His brown eyes snapped and his pupils dilated. With my legs wrapped around his waist, he hauled me from the bathroom counter and walked us into the bedroom. All the while he kissed me hungrily, tasting and biting, finally giving in to his baser instincts, then sat me down on the bed.

I watched as he pulled the rest of his clothes off. He was even more impressive without them. Once his slacks came off, the cords of muscle in his powerful legs were on display. Evidently he never skipped leg day. His desire was undoubted as it throbbed in time to his heartbeat. The power emanating from his body made me whimper in anticipation, as I dropped both my knees to the bed in open invitation.

He prowled towards me with an unmistakable hunger, and once he was close enough he returned his fingers to my core. He moved closer to my centre and took a deep breath, then looked up at me. "You smell delicious. I need to taste you."

His focus shifted from my face to my breasts, then to my thighs. He gazed at me like he was a starving man, and I was his meal. My heart thundered in my ears as he turned me around and helped me position on all fours, my centre arched and my head against the pillow. "It's all yours," I moaned into the pillow.

"I want all of you," he rasped, then pulled me backwards towards him. I felt his lips and his tongue, moving with intense ferocity, without rhyme or reason. He devoured me from top to bottom then around, and sucked on me mercilessly. I whimpered his name while I writhed against his face, until I lost all control.

"I can't wait," I panted deliriously, pushing back towards his pelvis, still mindless with need.

He didn't make me wait. He moved his body closer and sunk in slowly, an inch at a time. He was gentle, far removed from the animalistic growls that came from deep within him. After a while he was seated deeply. His size took my body by surprise, and I convulsed against him. I must've been teetering on the edge for too long. He paused until my composure returned, then started to thrust against me.

"You are something special. Everything about you and your body is a wonder." He shuddered and fought to stay in control of his movements. I was spent from the surprise orgasm, barely able to hold myself upright, when he briefly left my body to lay me on my back, then returned to fill me up again.

I took in a sharp breath knowing it would take a while to get used to taking him all. Still, I needed to feel him closer and wrapped my legs tightly around his waist. That drove him wild, as he plunged every inch over and over into my heat. Panting and with a keening cry, my body shuddered. He, too, was close, and just as he was about to retreat from me, I held his body closer, my core squeezing him tight.

"I want it all," I begged. I needed the warmth, the intimacy, the safety and the comfort. I needed this to take me away from everything that made me feel unsafe. He pulsed continuously inside me with a thunderous roar.

We both lay on the bed, drenched in each other's need, and fought to bring our breaths back to normal. He looked at me, like he never had before.

"I don't know what to say."

"I loved that too. I think I'm ruined." In between kisses, I wrapped myself around him. Without much effort, he rolled me onto him, where he was surprisingly coming back to attention.

"No. I'm ruined," he grunted, then slipped inside me again. We were both restrained this time, while I moved against him to another soul-shattering release. The sweetness didn't diminish the pleasure and we clung to each other, breathless and spent.

"This wasn't the plan. I wanted us to have dinner tonight and look around the place."

"I liked the change of plans. Everything took me by surprise."

"Everything?"

"I'm not spelling it out. Your ego will get bigger than it already is."

"Right, it's my ego that's big, is it?" He chuckled, bringing me closer to him, where I caught our musky scent brought on by our coupling. I breathed it in, and I couldn't help myself as I sucked the base of his neck. *Will I ever get enough of him?*

When I started to feel an exquisite heaviness settling into my muscles and my eyelids started to droop, I looked at him and said, "I'm going to need a quick shower."

"I'll come and keep you company."

"You mean, you'll come and attack me again," I giggled. I wanted his company in the shower, perhaps everywhere else too.

"That's highly likely," he said with a satisfied grin that sent tingles straight to the nerves within my core.

I left the bed and entered the bathroom, where he was quick to follow me.

"I'm sorry about before ... I should've asked, are you on something?" He pulled my back against his chest and our eyes locked in the mirror. Then he began to trail hungry kisses down my neck.

I moaned softly, finding it difficult to concentrate. "What do you mean?"

"The pill or something like it." He moved my hair out of his way, sucking, biting and tasting my neck while he gently kneaded each breast.

"I know a doctor, you don't have to worry." Fatherhood must be the last thing he ever wanted to do again, after all he'd been through.

I moved gently out of his arms, tied up my hair and walked towards the luxurious shower. I lost count of the showerheads, but five of them seemed to turn on at once. He followed me inside, where he stood behind me and put his arms back around me. *I haven't felt this safe in weeks.*

"I'm glad I found you. Now do you think you have vetted me enough? You even said I was full of surprises."

"Easy, tiger. You are full of surprises, and today you've shown me the biggest and the best one yet." I laughed softly, turned around and lathered his chest and arms with a floral scented body wash I wished I could take home with me.

"I'm flattered that you're impressed, but someone like you won't base your decision on that. I don't let just anyone close to me. I want to let all of you in," he purred, as one of the two rainfall showerheads drenched his hair and tiny rivulets of water ran down his handsome face.

"I need the rest of the weekend to continue my vetting process. I could be a simpleton and base my decision on that one thing," I teased.

"Then I'll continue to enjoy being vetted."

"Do you have something in mind?" I goaded him.

To my delight he decided to play. "Turn around, I'll show you. For the purposes of due diligence, there's a review you need to conduct."

"Is it scientific? I love conducting reviews," I laughed.

"I want you to closely examine the growth potential and tell me if what I bring to the table is sound and to your satisfaction." Our moans echoed in the shower enclosure as he pushed himself gently inside me.

"You don't play fair," I exhaled softly, then pushed back against him with my palms against the glass enclosure. He took me gently, his slippery hands wrapped around my body. He rocked back and forth against me slowly and deliberately until I felt his warmth, hotter than the shower, explode inside me.

Eventually, we left the shower and towelled off in the green bathroom. We didn't get dressed. It was after ten thirty, and the restaurant was shut.

"I never meant to starve you." He murmured, his breath tickling my ear while I reclined between his strong thighs, lying against his solid chest. His defined arms wrapped around me and he weighed my heavy breasts in his palms, teasing. Nibbling and nipping at my earlobe. It was an assault to the senses, and I never wanted it to end.

"My hunger was sated, but if you're talking about food, there's a room service menu on the console as you walk into the suite," I whispered, while we basked in the dimly illuminated living room.

"I need to feed you. In the morning, we're getting out of this suite and going on a hike." Even as we were planning a meal and a hike, I felt him grow against my back.

"I want that. I've always been one of those Brits who thought California was all about the beach. Thanks for bringing me here."

I turned around, straddled his waist and kissed him. We built a rhythm as my thighs hugged his hips, causing unimaginable pressure in my core. His velvety smooth rod of iron sent me on a wave that I rode over and over, until his warmth cascaded inside me and I finally floated back down.

We both ordered a club sandwich and I tried the chocolate ice cream, while I assumed he inwardly fretted about his ten percent body fat. He was right, we were both starving. We eventually fell asleep just as dawn was breaking, both tired and spent from a night of love-making that was both frenzied and sensual.

Chapter Sixteen

♥

Miles

I couldn't remember the last time I slept soundly. Being a single dad would do that to a man. When I woke up to Cara's soft snores, I couldn't believe she was with me. Her sleeping allowed me to watch her in repose and take in her features – the slight flaring of her nose, the small moans she made in her sleep, and when she moved the mint green sheet shifted and left her body bared to me. The body which had driven me wild all night.

She was sensitive and responsive, her body shivered with every kiss and every touch. She turned me into an animal as I brought her out of her three-year, self-imposed celibacy. Cara in private was a contradiction to the Cara she showed to the rest of the world. When I met her while she was working, I would never have imagined that she would be so uninhibited, passionate and unguarded.

My phone's vibration caught my attention and, in turn, woke her up. As I made to get out of bed to answer it, she moaned in her sleep.

"The great escape?" she joked sleepily.

"Good morning, I didn't want to wake you. I need to speak to Maxie, unless you don't mind me calling her right here," I said, then tasted her kiss-ravaged lips.

"You can talk to her here. She must be missing you." She opened her eyes sleepily.

"Don't think so, my brother has a pair of one-year-old twins, and Maxie is obsessed with them, and they are with her." I dialled Maxie's number. She had a phone that she used only to call me and her uncle.

"Hi, Daddy, I got a haircut and some ballet slippers." Her excited voice was loud and clear through the phone. "Can we do a video so I can show you?"

"I can't do a video now, beautiful, but I'll see your hair soon. I didn't know you needed ballet slippers."

"I did. I danced and danced like Clara and one got a hole in it. They are so pretty. They have lilac ribbons to match my tutu. Aunt Sofia said it was okay to get them."

"Did you remember to say thank you?"

"Yes. When will you come back home?"

"I'll be back tomorrow. I miss you, sweetheart."

"Me too. I love you."

When I hung up, I felt Cara's eyes on me and turned to look at her. I caught her wide smile, and for the second time in my life, she took my breath away.

"That was a comprehensive update. Who's Clara?"

"She's from *The Nutcracker*. Maxie started ballet classes and she's moved past aspiring to be the tooth fairy to a prima ballerina when she grows up."

"Okay, it's official, I feel terrible. You should be with her instead." She wrapped the sheet tighter around her naked body.

"I'm where I need to be. She's with family and having fun. She's got new ballet slippers and a haircut, that's more fun than she would have had with me," I explained, while I wondered why Cara would hide from me.

"As long as she's happy. Now, you promised me a hike?" She avoided eye contact and didn't sound as excited as I had become used to.

"We may have overslept and the weather forecast this morning isn't on our side. Although we can still see the mountains from the air. I'll make a call."

"While you do that, I'll freshen up and get dressed." She stood up with the sheet still wrapped tightly around her. She was different, almost guarded.

I pulled on a pair of shorts from my forgotten overnight bag and went out onto the terrace to give her some space. Something wasn't right.

After a while, I returned inside to find her dressed in simple jeans and another gauzy tank top. This time she had her luscious breasts encased in a bra that could hardly contain them. It was hard to focus when she looked like that, but I still needed to know what was eating her.

"A little shy today?" I tucked some flyaway hair behind her ear.

"I'm not shy. Things are different with the sun up." She seemed thoughtful, with a distant look in her eyes.

"Nothing's different. I'm still being vetted, you're still irresistible with that perfect body. We can go out and finally eat something warm, then take a chopper over the mountains. What's different for you?"

"I can't help feel like last night was some kind of transaction."

I couldn't keep the edge out of my voice. "A transaction? Did I do something that made you feel uncomfortable?" What could I have done? She loved everything last night.

"No, but you paid for a security service for me when you didn't have to. It felt like I was returning a favour," she said, still beautiful, yet forlorn, staring at the mountains.

"I didn't see that coming." Predatory: Is that how she saw me? "I thought you wanted me, like I wanted you."

"I did want you, I still do. It's this dynamic between us. You have everything, and I don't have much."

"That doesn't have anything to do with what's happening here." I was surprised, almost defensive. What did she mean?

"Not for you, but I feel a certain way about it."

"Have you not dated a wealthy man before?" I didn't need an answer to that question, but I had to understand the one-eighty.

"I may have, but you already know there's only one you." She sighed unhappily, but inwardly I smiled at the compliment which may not have been meant as one.

"In your mind, I want you for your body and nothing else. And I'm paying for it?" I closed my eyes in disbelief and did a quick mental walkthrough of last night's events.

"Something like that," she answered softly.

I breathed deeply. How would I fix this? "Your reasoning is off. I have a lot, but I'm just a man who's trying to get to know a woman. I don't want you to feel that way, ever."

"I've offended you, haven't I?" she said with her eyes closed and a quick shake of her head. The confident, bold and sexy woman from last night was replaced by a weak-kneed version I hardly recognised.

"I'm more worried about how you feel. We can pump the brakes. We don't have to do anything you feel is transactional."

"This is strange even for me. I've never felt like this before, afterwards, you know."

"Would you like to leave? I can take you back home if that's what you want." I offered half-heartedly. I wasn't ready to leave California yet.

"No. This is all me. Last night took me by surprise. I'd never felt so free with anyone like I did with you." She seemed torn, confused, and I was doubtful any of it had anything to do with my actions.

"Why would that get you down?" I asked, bending at the knees, bringing us to the same height.

"Because I fear last night can't be replicated. You're a busy guy, with a busy life, and the night we shared could be a fluke," she said with a wry smile.

"Where would you get the idea?" I wanted to wrap my arms around her, but I didn't want to upset the delicate balance we had for now.

"I may have memorised your article in *Business Now*."

The article had some reach, more than I imagined it would. I still heard about it every day from my peers, the competition, people I didn't know and from college and high school kids who said they wanted to be like Miles Masterson when they were older. A lot of boys and men. I hadn't imagined it touched Cara deeply.

"I was only trying to impress you with that article. Did it work?"

"It was eye-opening and the reason I would think you're busy."

"I am, but I have learned to balance all aspects of my life. I've been doing that since I joined the family business fifteen years ago and I like to think I do it well."

"You need to tell me how you learned that fine balance, over that hot meal you promised."

"Sure, give me ten and I'll be ready," I said as I made my way into the bathroom for my legendary four-minute shower. I still didn't understand why Cara felt the way she did. I may have all the money in the world, but in my mind's eye she had everything else.

While at the restaurant, an electrical storm started, coupled with a heavy downpour and unimaginable winds. Our chopper ride over the California mountains wasn't meant to be, and an hour later Cara was at the spa, while I stayed in our suite and caught up with work.

When she returned two hours later, I tried to give her space, but her time at the spa seemed to have worked to help relieve her of the tension from before. She went into the bathroom and came out wearing only a thigh length silk robe, which reminded me of a kimono. She sat next to me on the bed and shut my laptop with a dramatic snap. She was relaxed and playful.

"I want to show you what I've been doing all afternoon." Her breathy voice reminded me of the night before.

"Show me," I said, looking at her. She was glowing and smelled delicious. I would be buying all the potions in the spa before leaving. "You smell good."

"It's the flower bath. Have you not had one before?" she asked, bringing her torso closer to my nose and letting her robe fall off her shoulders, which she left exposed. I was onto her game, and I would play.

"No. No flower baths for me," I said, chuckling.

She wiggled her slender fingers in my face and showed me her short French tip manicure, then lay down with her head towards the foot of the bed, lifted both her feet and wiggled her toes at me. That had the effect of spreading the robe open. As the robe fell down the sides of her body, it was hard to ignore that she was completely bare and waxed to within an inch of her life.

"You seem to have lost your panties, Doctor Braithwaite." I worked hard to remain steadfast, but all the blood in my body rushed down to my groin.

"You, on the other hand, seem to have developed a really huge problem. You might need a specialist." She smiled a victorious smile and rested her foot gently against me. I pulled it closer and ground against it, eliciting a giggle from her.

Within a short time, I missed her body. But I would let her take charge. She had to show me what she wanted. I released her foot and watched, enthralled, as she threw her robe off and her naked body crawled up mine.

"You have too many clothes on," she pouted, with a needy moan.

I already loved when she needed me. My will power slowly ebbed, as the intoxicating mix of smells from the flower bath, her massage and her feminine scent assaulted me and caused me to be harder than I had been since we arrived in California.

"What will you do about that?" My voice was strained.

Her mouth came closer to mine, and she deliberately licked my lips while she worked my shirt off me.

"You'll just have to wait and see," she murmured, pulling my shorts off too. She slid down my body, and when she came face to face with my hard length, I was done for.

She slowly teased and licked my tip for what felt like hours while I fought hard to stay in control. Just when I thought I would explode, she took all of me in her mouth, and when I hit the back of her throat, I saw stars. That was all I could take. I slid out of her mouth and hauled her up the bed to my lips.

While our insistent tongues fought for control, she slipped me inside her right to the hilt. She languidly rode me until she couldn't keep upright, her soft moans music to my ears. I heaved her onto her

                    SANDY J MCNEILL

back and parted her thighs, until I noticed how swollen and sensitive she was.

"Did I hurt you last night?" Could that be why she was upset in the morning? How could I have been so careless? I slowly shifted away from her.

"No, it's not you, it's the wax. It makes me a little sore, but so deliciously sensitive." Like an acrobat, she wrapped her leg around my waist and pulled me back towards her.

"I'm going to have to kiss it better," I said and thrust gently.

"Later. Now, let me feel you. I want you," she moaned, gripping me tighter.

"I didn't catch that. What did you say?" I teased.

"I want you, Miles. Please," she begged and canted her hips towards me, pulling me deeper inside her.

Her pleas unleashed a madman, and I had her all afternoon and well into the evening.

The obliging spa staff delivered baskets full of fragrant petals and she soaked in another flower bath.

After the bath to soothe her aching muscles, I parted her softly, licked and sucked. Tasted and nibbled without letting her float into oblivion. I held her orgasm at ransom until she begged for mercy. She moaned as she quivered in my mouth, then released a gush that surprised me as much as it did her.

"That's sexy, I need to see it again."

"I can't take it anymore, you're killing me," she panted, desperate for a break from the delicious torture.

We spent the rest of the night in each other's arms, loving each other's bodies, learning each other's nuances and listening to each other's words. She was who I had been waiting for.

Sometime overnight, the storm let up, and in the morning after the fog cleared we eventually went out into the chopper and flew over the mountains. As we rose high into the clouds, I realised Cara also rose above her insecurities. Her excitement was evident as we flew over the Sierra Nevada mountains, and she was in awe.

"I thought California was all about the coast," she gushed. "This is magic."

"Next time, will we see the coast?" I needed to know if there would be a next time.

"Yes, we will," she said, and her eyes rested on mine.

Much to my dismay, the weekend was over quickly, but not before I spent our two-hour flight licking her sweet centre better and committing her heady scent, her quivering thighs and her moans to memory. After our arrival back to the city, I drove her to her townhouse where we packed the few things which she had salvaged from the destruction and chaos into her car. She drove to her new home and I drove home to Maxie.

Chapter Seventeen

Miles

I was in a daze when I arrived home. Cara was everything I expected and more. We were in sync. She was ambitious, but she knew how to relax and live in the moment. She didn't mind that I had Maxie, and in a short time she knew what drove me wild.

When I entered the house, I was met with the delivery from Vivian's lawyers. Skimming through the documents, I realised the extent of Vivian's seriousness about renegotiating her parental rights. That included a clause that the three of us would spend one evening a week together. It seemed like a veiled ploy, but I knew legally it would hold water and I would be obliged to follow through. I would still run it past my lawyer.

I went to Michael's to pick up Maxie, and when we arrived home, Vivian was waiting for us. The greeting was cordial. I didn't want to cause a scene around Maxie. Viv was her usual vivacious and bubbly self, but Maxie was polite, distant from her mother and reserved. It tore me apart. After Maxie was settled in, Vivian and I went into the kitchen.

"You can't drop by whenever you wish."

"I had to see my family," she said with what looked like a sickly sweet smile.

"Why is your family important to you all of a sudden?"

"My family has always been important to me. I had a momentary lapse in judgement, and I need you to see that."

"Momentary lapse?" I uttered in surprise, but kept my voice low."Your lapse was two years long and destructive. Viv, you seem to have a very short memory. But mine is long and I'll remind you. You left because you fell out of love with me. You signed away your rights to parent Maxie because you were too grief stricken over Laila to get yourself out of bed and look after her."

"Miles, it was more than that. I was heartsick. Michael—"

"Maxie burnt down your kitchen because it was three in the afternoon without breakfast, and she was making it herself. She couldn't wake you because you swallowed half your medicine cupboard, while you were supposed to be looking after her, then locked your bedroom door on her. It was all too indefensible, and you decided giving up your parental rights was an easier way to face the music than to face a criminal court. And that was the one time disaster occurred, what about the rest of the times you left her to fend for herself?"

"You've just brought up the lowest point in my life to spite me. It was only four Ambien, I needed to sleep. Michael nearly died and that was the biggest thing in my world."

"Michael was alive. You lost your daughter, then abandoned her sister. How do you propose she learns to trust you? That I learn to trust you with her?"

I wasn't getting through to her. I never had, not after the fire. She had what she thought were valid excuses for everything that went wrong that day. Her father tried to help her see sense but that, too, had been an exercise in futility.

"I've never had a mother, and I didn't know how my decision would affect her."

"Another excuse. You're more astute than you're letting on. You were a great mother, until you weren't." I felt my anger rise. I had never got over Viv's neglect of Maxie.

"I'm here now to make up for that. I would love to have dinner with you and Maxie." It sounded like a plea, and I was drained at the cyclical tone of our conversation.

After ordering in, the three of us sat in the kitchen and ate together. Maxie came out of her shell and insisted on taking pictures with us both. Vivian took some too. After our heated exchange, we both calmed down for Maxie's sake and the evening wasn't too unbearable.

She eventually left after reading to Maxie and helping her to bed. That was the most time she had spent with her in the last two years, but I couldn't help wonder what the current mind game was leading to.

Before I fell asleep, I sent Cara a message. I missed her already.

> *I enjoyed our weekend. I can't wait to see you again. I can still taste you on my lips. x*

> *Cara: Missing you too.*

I arrived at work the next morning, another busy Monday, and I didn't come up for air until three o'clock that afternoon. Alistair knew better than to insert himself into my personal life, but this time he sent me a link to an online news article, which I clicked on.

Vivian's true colours, again, punched me in the stomach. My Sunday evening was laid bare for the world to see, including the toppings on our pizza. The photos, out of context, told a multitude of lies. Thankfully, Maxie's face had been blurred out. Vivian and I were visible, smiling and seemingly happy. I sighed and scoffed, and I realised she would never change.

I wondered if Cara read gossip magazines, and if she would see this. I thought back to her bookshelf at her townhouse – her reading material had more substance. She loved conducting scientific reviews, after all. I smiled to myself as I thought about the woman I was falling for. I couldn't wait to see her again soon. I closed the story and went back to work.

Chapter Eighteen

♥

Cara

The weekend with Miles was everything I had hoped it would be. I didn't understand what came over me after our first night together, but I must have sounded naive and immature. By mid-morning on Monday, I returned to work after spending time settling into my new home.

In between seeing patients, I caught up with online news. As a bit of fun, I set up alerts to receive news about Miles and his work.

My heart sank when I saw the piece about Miles and his ex-wife. There were photographs of the two of them with Maxie. I stared at it in disbelief for what felt like hours as I re-read the short article accompanying it.

> *Single no more!: Worldwide Media heir and aptly named "reluctant heartthrob" pictured above with his ex Vivian and their daughter, enjoying a pizza dinner amid ongoing rumours of a reconciliation. "They are made for each other. This has been a long time coming," several mutual friends of the pair report after the couple jointly released the intimate family snaps.*

How could I have become that person? The one who comes in the way of family. My first instinct of having felt used after our first night together was right. Why hadn't I trusted that instinct like we had been taught at Krav Maga?

I looked closely at the pictures. Miles wore the forest green shirt he wore on our way back from the spa, the one he said would always remind him of my eyes and our time in California. That confirmed the photo was recent, and they were together last night. *How could I have been such a fool? Again.*

I decided to throw myself into work. I called the emergency room coordinator and put my name forward for all shifts – evenings, night shifts, even the weekends. Not only could I lose myself in work for hours and avoid life, but I would also be safe from my stalker. It was a win-win. The heartthrob had his fun, and all I had to do was move on.

Miles: When can I see you again? It's been three days since I last held you.

I've been swamped at work and working round-the-clock shifts. Can I get back to you?

Miles: When you take a meal break, can we meet then?

If I do, you'll be the first to know.

> *Miles: Huh? I've been calling you. Can you call me back?*

> *Sorry I can't. I'm working crazy hours and fin- ishing work at crazy times.*

> *Miles: It's finally Friday, let's meet some- where. What time are you free?*

> *I'm needed at work all weekend. Sometime during the week, I MIGHT be free.*

> *Miles: MIGHT in caps? Is that a Briticism?*

> *Miles: Let's talk. It's Wednesday, Your security say you hop from one job to the next. You don't go home. That can't be healthy.*

> *Miles: Can you call me back? Please …*

I ignored his last messages. Miles and I had been going back and forth for a fortnight. He would call, I wouldn't answer. I didn't let on that I knew he was getting back together with his wife. I didn't want to confront the situation. I was exhausted, burning the candle at both ends. But I felt alive and in control, until at one o'clock on Saturday morning, Ivie, the emergency room coordinator, gave me the two-finger summons from across the nurses' station. It had been a long day, first at the clinic then the emergency room.

Rolling her eyes and shaking her head she said, "Your American brother is here."

"Dean? He is? Okay. I'll take ten, and I'll be back." Shocked and panicked, my mind started reeling to why Dean would come to find me at work at nearly one in the morning. Had the stalker gone to their house? Was it the kids? I should never have taken the kids out to Pike Place the very next day after the blood was poured at my door. He must have seen them there. I was horrified and broke into a cold sweat.

She put her hand on my arm to calm me. "Honey, I've met Dean, remember. He has that upper crust accent you both have. This guy isn't fooling anyone. He's upper crust, too, but homegrown. Although he was cute trying to be incognito with a hoodie and baseball cap. I told him to wait in there for you." She cackled, too loudly for one o'clock and definitely for the emergency room, while motioning with her head to the break room.

As I started to walk away, I stopped in my tracks and turned back to Ivie, "Did you check his ID? Ask for a name? Anything, before you confirmed I was here?"

"No, he looked like a friendly. We let each others' walk-ins back there all the time. What's wrong?" she asked, unnerved.

"Ivie, the hospital has protocol for this. I have a complex situation I'm dealing with in my personal life and, of all places, I imagined I didn't need to explain myself here because of our protocols."

"What do you mean? Is someone harassing you?" The seriousness of the situation became clear to her straight away. She talked about the horrors she saw in different emergency rooms with victims of harassment. One of the reasons she worked in a children's emergency room instead.

"Yes, Ivie. Someone is. I don't mean to snap, but I'm tired and walking on eggshells," I confessed. Unlike Melinda from the clinic, Ivie was a vault.

"Sorry, honey, you're right I should've been more diligent. This one had a trustworthy face, dark hair beneath his baseball cap, piercing brown eyes, good looking in an unforgettable way. He looked like that cologne model from the billboard across the street. I'll call security, they'll be here in seconds." As we continued to speak, I realised who it was, and a familiar thud returned to my chest.

"Don't call security Ivie. I have an idea who it is. Back in ten." How could I let this happen? After ignoring him and his messages, he would come and find me at work.

"Take more than ten. You might need it." She winked, fanning herself. "Then we'll talk and see what else we can do here at work about your situation, okay?" She tried to reassure me, but my mind was already in the break room.

As soon as I walked into the small, cosy space and was enveloped by his familiar scent, it stirred a cascade of all the emotion I tried to escape for nearly two weeks. All my senses recognised his distinct, commanding and sexy scent, which ignited a flame low in my stomach. My mind and body returned to our green suite in California where I let him have everything I kept guarded for years. Everything, which I realised hadn't meant a single thing to him.

He waited at the bulletin board while he browsed the notices posted there – an apartment to rent, a litter of beagle puppies that needed homes, somebody with extra fruit to share from their kitchen garden. He was in my workspace, and again he managed to invade it. Effort-lessly.

"Hey there. Brother," I murmured with a restrained smile.

He removed the baseball cap and his hair seemed longer. My knees became weaker. How could I have fallen so fast? All I needed now was to get over our lost weekend in California, and over him. *How do I get over someone I only just met?*

He turned to look at me and exhaled. "You have no idea how much I've missed you." His long strides ate up the small distance between us and he tried to pull me towards him.

"No, don't. I'm at work, and I'm grubby. These scrubs have been in battle for the last eight hours." I gently pushed him off me.

I hadn't allowed myself to miss the safety of his arms, still livid at how I started to fall for the same type that broke my heart three years ago.

"I don't care," he whispered as he held me and tried to kiss me. I took a step back.

"That's not a good idea," I whispered back.

"I know you're at work, and I shouldn't be here, but I needed to see you. You're not picking up your phone. You really should work on that work-life balance." He smiled that smile, the one I was working hard to forget since I last saw it, thirteen days ago.

"Did you sneak out of your house? Does your wife know you're here? I know you're working hard on the reconciliation, with jointly released photographs and all that." The bitch residing inside me reared her ugly head, and I didn't try to put her away. His brown gaze fell on me, and he slumped into the shabby fire engine red couch.

"Right. Okay." He was thrown, but only for a second. "I suspected you had seen that. I'm sorry."

"You're sorry I'm familiar with the internet, or you're sorry I'm a fool?" I perched on the seat opposite him, glanced at my watch and like muscle memory, waited to hear the excuses.

"Cara, you need to listen to me. I've been honest and transparent with you from the first time we met. I don't have a wife. Vivian and I are over. We won't be reconciling in this life, or any other."

"You say that, but I saw the photos of you, Maxie and her. The least you could have done was tell me about it before I read about it, with the rest of the Miles Masterson fanatics," I returned, then exhaled the breath I may have held for a fortnight.

"Fanatics, really? Anytime you see or read anything about me on the internet, talk to me first."

"What, so you can worm your way out of things and lie, lie and lie again? No, you should have talked to me, laid it all out for me, so I didn't get caught in another web of lies." Why was I upset? *Because I want him to be all mine.* I could hear my voice becoming louder, and I became more distressed, but I wasn't going to back down. I wouldn't allow myself to be his plaything.

"I've never lied to you about anything." He turned down the volume and sounded sincere, and the pleading look in his eyes was enough to break me.

"You may not have lied, but you've omitted things, and the three of you looked happy in your pizza pics. I won't stand in the way of that. I must go now, I have work to do."

"Cara, wait. I loved our time in California, and I really want to —" While he was speaking, Ivie walked in.

"Cara, honey. Can I talk to you for a minute? This won't take long." She appeared apologetic.

Note to self: The workplace is not the right place for a lovers' spat. Especially one I should never have been with in the first place.

I moved closer to her, although in the small space, it wouldn't matter. Miles would still hear our conversation. "Sure, what's up?" I tried to smile.

"Like a halfwit, I double-booked you and Noah. As specialists, I can't have both of you here at the same time, it's too expensive for the hospital, and Doctor Stevens will tan my hide." She was flustered, and I decided to give her an easy out.

"It's okay, I'll go home. Let Noah deal with the gastro outbreak," I replied with a half-hearted mischievous chuckle.

"Thanks for understanding. Would I be pushing it if I cancelled tonight's shift as well? Same issue."

I mock sighed. "Ivie, at this rate I'll be begging for scraps on the streets of Seattle but go ahead, take away my livelihood."

"Thanks, I owe you." With her single eyebrow raise, only reserved for use when talking down to her insubordinate employees, she looked at Miles, but spoke to me. "Say hi to Dean for me, will you?" She turned and walked out, leaving Miles looking at me sheepishly.

"I hope I didn't get you into trouble. I didn't think this through. I needed to see you."

"Even if they knew you, I don't think anyone recognised you. They are all very busy," I replied curtly, trying to reassure myself more than him.

"Dealing with the gastro outbreak? How bad can that get to need the hospital?" he asked with his eyes narrowed.

"Really bad. The younger ones can get quite ill with it," I replied seriously while I fleetingly forgot about his lies of omission.

"Sounds terrible. I don't think Noah will cope. Can I take you home before he realises it?" He tried humour, but I wouldn't fall for it.

Striding past him, I mumbled, "My car's parked here, and I still need to hand over patient care to Noah."

"Can I follow you home?" I heard him speak to the empty break room.

When I finished with Noah, I retrieved my bag from my locker and met the burly security guard at the exit, and he walked me to my car quietly.

I drove away from the hospital to my golf course bungalow and, just as I arrived at the entry, I noticed Miles' Aston Martin driving behind me in my rearview mirror. There had been no security team on my tail.

Miles must have dismissed them at the hospital. How presumptuous of him. Did he think he would be spending the night? Even though I didn't want to, I felt a rush of excitement. I stopped and spoke to security, letting them know he was my guest.

I arrived at my new lease, the smallest and sweetest house in the subdivision. It was the greenkeeper's residence until his family started to get bigger. A lick of paint and a two-day minor refurbishment, courtesy of Dean's subcontractors, freshened it up. It was small, at only eleven hundred square feet, but it was perfectly formed and perfect for me, with views of the green. Best of all, it had a backyard, something I never had in any of my homes as an adult.

Although the leaves had the red, brown and yellow hues of autumn and were falling off the trees and leaving them bare, I still loved the signs of life in my backyard. The scurrying squirrels, the starlings, the sparrows, and the occasional woodpecker all made me smile in the mornings. And now in the dark of night, I could just about hear the last of the crickets chirping. Miles' car eventually turned the corner, and he stopped in my driveway.

"They are thorough with their checks here. They took a copy of my ID and looked me up in some database. It's a safe spot," he said while he unfolded his tall frame from the small car.

"I do feel safe here," I mumbled, still unsure about him following me home.

"Do hospital security walk everyone to their car or is it because you're special?" he asked, trying to lighten the moment.

"Only if one asks them to. You followed me home, am I safe from you?" I snapped.

"Of course, you are. Can we talk?" he added soberly.

I unlocked the front door and the sweet, fresh smell of cardamom, orange and vanilla welcomed me back. I loved everything about my house. After stepping over the threshold, I turned around to look at Miles.

"I'm not avoiding you, but I need to shower the hospital off me first. I won't be long," I said and walked towards my bedroom.

I stripped out of my scrubs and put them in a black bag filled with others to return to the hospital, then finally stepped inside the shower and scrubbed off my seventeen-hour workday. Ivie double-booking Noah and me had been a blessing. I didn't realise it before, but I needed the weekend off, and the heartthrob was now in my living room making himself at home. I didn't want to fall back into his arms, but the treacherous throb in my core was hard to ignore.

Chapter Nineteen

♥

Miles

Cara was a paradox, a level-headed scientist who used logic and reasoning, but also a hopeless romantic who wanted to be swept off her feet. Her new house was an extension of her personality. Sweet, feminine and tidy. She even had a jar with *Italian Lemons* scrawled in chalk in her powder room. I wondered why, until I opened it and realised they were miniature decorative soaps, which filled the bathroom with a fresh citrus scent once I popped the top. I had never met a woman like her – accomplished, serious and passionate. Yet playful and funny, in the same breath. Would she still want me?

As I was looking through her vast collection of medical books arranged neatly on a wide bookshelf, she walked back into the room and brought in with her a fresh, just-showered scent. She had removed all traces of Doctor Braithwaite, and all that was left was Cara. *How will I make her mine?* She wore a zip-up sweater and another pair of micro shorts. Already I couldn't think straight as all the blood in my body seemed to rush down south.

"I'm happy I'm here with you," I said, stepping closer. She still wouldn't let me hold her the way I wanted to. "It's been too long."

She ignored that statement. "Who's Maxie with while you're out at all hours?" She was determined and on a mission.

"She's in San Francisco, at the ballet, with my mother. Nothing's changed, Cara. Those photos were exactly that, just photos."

With her brow furrowed, she sighed "The stuff in the article seemed so … I don't know, normal and real. Stuff anyone would do with their family on a Sunday evening."

"Because it was. Everything was real except the family dynamic. Vivian fed whoever wrote that piece everything. We ate together, she spent the evening at my house, she put Maxie to bed, then left." I made sure to explain it all as it had been. I needed her to understand.

"It was difficult to see and I didn't understand how you and I could share everything we shared in California and before, only to find out you had been reconciling for weeks."

"California was special to me too. I'm not a cold bastard. I would have thought the time we've spent together was enough for you to know just that little bit about me." I walked closer to her, but she was still closed off with her defences up.

"It seems she still has your heart, or some type of hold on you, or you on her. She might not be over you or something." She was intuitive, but wrong. I'd been over Vivian since she walked out and left.

"We're never reconciling. I don't like to speak ill of her, she's Maxie's mom, but she's a little unhinged, and a touch manipulative. I should have known when she came to my house, she would seize the opportunity and weave her own intricate tale of a happily ever after."

"Why did she visit?" Her piercing green eyes looked into mine while she waited for an excuse, perhaps a lie? I wouldn't lie to her.

"To talk about her parental rights, to see Maxie and to try and get back together with me, which will never happen. Is this why you've been avoiding me? Telling me you don't take meal breaks?"

"That's exactly the reason why. If you look at the situation from my lens, it's simple enough to understand. That report made a mockery of everything you and I had been doing together."

"I see that, but all you had to do was talk to me." This time she let me put my arm around her waist and bring her closer to me.

"So, it is true then," she murmured, giving my lips a lingering look and resting both her arms around my neck.

I sat her on her kitchen island. "What is true?" I asked, unzipping her sweater and finally kissing her. As our kiss deepened, she moaned into me and let her sweater fall off her shoulders. She wore nothing else underneath, and I breathed in sharply when I was met with nothing but warm, soft skin.

"That you shouldn't believe everything you see on the internet. That conversation isn't over. I still have many unanswered questions, and you're distracting me." She moaned louder as I dropped my lips from hers and onto her already hardened nipples.

"And I will answer every last question you have. Don't let her come between us. Now, which way to bed? I need to taste you. I've been dying to have you back on my tongue." She wrapped her legs around me and softly ground against me. Then I picked her up and followed the vanilla scent that led to her bedroom. The sweater was lost on our way from the kitchen, and her short shorts easily slid down her thighs. Her soft body was warm and pliant underneath mine.

"It might feel better for both of us if you lost the jeans," she panted, nipping gently at my lower lip. I got back up with her, and she stood on the edge of the bed and kissed me while I fought a losing battle with my zipper. She gently moved my fingers out of the way and easily pulled it down. She fell to her knees and took me between her lips. *Surgical precision.*

While she painfully teased and ran her tongue torturously around my tip, the rest of my clothes came off in a blur. I moved her off me and lay on the bed. She was now just as frenzied as I was. She still tasted my tip, only this time she turned herself around so I could taste her too. As I probed and prodded her warm depths with my fingers and my tongue, I felt myself start to lose control.

Breathlessly I begged, "Stop, not this way. I need you." She stopped and slid down my body, leaving a trail of her arousal on me. Without warning, she drove right down onto me and her warmth hugged me tight, from root to tip. Her moans of pleasure ricocheted against the bedroom walls, while I fought hard not to spill.

"I forgot how you fill me full," she gasped while she ground against me.

After I composed myself, I sat upright and held her back against my chest. I reached around and my fingers found her plump bundle of nerves. I couldn't help myself as I feverishly rubbed against her. Before long, her moans grew louder and her movements became more frantic as she came apart in my arms.

She fell back onto my chest, her body limp and languid, and fought to catch her breath. I laid her down while I breathed her in, and got lost in her sweet scent. I brought both her legs up to my shoulders and thrust into her again and again while I held onto both her soft cheeks. As she quivered against me for the second time, I lost all control and poured all I had, deep inside her. Still, I didn't want to sever our connection as I caught my breath, while I marvelled at her body in the soft light cast by the bedside lamps.

Eventually, I lay down next to her and brought her body closer to mine. "You don't have to forget." I whispered into her neck and shoulder as her body moulded perfectly into mine and she took my hand in hers.

"I missed all of you," she said with a sigh. Post orgasmic honesty. I wanted to understand more of what had been playing on my mind since she said it.

"I need you to be honest with me. Are you going to be begging for scraps on the streets of Seattle, hmm?"

She sighed before she turned around to look at me. "If this thing between us is going to work—"

"Thing?" I interrupted. "Are we La Cosa Nostra?"

"You know what I mean," she said, giggling. In turn, I lost myself in everything she was, and my fact-finding mission was discarded.

"Does this mean I've been vetted completely and thoroughly, and I cut the mustard?" I dared to ask, tracing a finger against her cheek. Her eyes shone in the dim light. *She just might want to be with me.*

"You're on a trial period," she whispered and took my finger between hers.

"Sounds like dicey relationship probation. What will make me fail?" I murmured.

Slowly, she licked it. "You're almost perfect but trying to rescue me from my abject poverty and keeping me in the dark about Vivian," she said as she slipped it in her mouth, sucking hard on it. Her green gaze was on me, daring me to argue.

"I promise to do better on both counts," I quickly agreed. "Although I only have one request. The thing you were just doing to my finger—"

It was her turn to interrupt. "I'm not taking any requests tonight. You're going to have to lie there and see exactly what you've signed up for. Now, to find my whip and ball gag," she joked.

"Can you rethink taking 'this thing' of ours public? I want you to meet my family and get to know Maxie."

"I've met most of your family, remember?"

"Not in this capacity, you haven't, I need both you and my family to know you're not my dirty little secret. And I need you to know that too."

"Perhaps *you* are my dirty little secret," she said, distracting me with her body, which she rubbed against mine.

The next morning, after an epic wake-up call of Cara's tongue on me, we reluctantly left the bed. As she walked me to the door, I realised this was my chance to take her home, prove to her I want to let her in in every way

"Come home with me to Mercer, for the weekend. We'll have the house to ourselves. We can cook, go out for dinner or order in. Whatever you want. I'll even show you my bedroom," I coaxed, right before I brought her lips to mine, which were swollen and tender after our night together. We hadn't been able to let go of each other until daylight broke through her heavily lined curtains that were perfect for daytime sleep.

"I'm only coming for the bedroom tour. Let me grab some things and a change of clothes," she gushed excitedly. I should have invited her sooner.

"You won't need clothes."

We got into my car and pulled away from the golf course. Cara was a breath of fresh air. It was still a wonder to be around someone who wanted to know me just for me, and nothing else.

"Have you been on Mercer before?" I asked as we approached the end of the bridge connecting the city and Mercer Island.

"In the months I've been living here, I haven't yet ventured over this bridge. Although it's close enough."

"That's reasonable, there's so much more to see in Seattle. As soon as I travel a mere seven miles and cross the bridge, I find peace here."

"Okay, Robinson Crusoe, sell me your little island," she mocked playfully.

"Right, I was born and raised on this island, left it when I went to school. When I came back, I lived downtown for a while. It was a great place but realised it wasn't for me. I needed the space to breathe, to run, to hike, and I wanted the lake within touching distance."

"You like the water?"

"I love the water. I played in it as a child, it was my escape in my short-lived but awkward teens, and now as an adult. If I can't get to the mountains, I spend my time on the lake."

"You're full of surprises, although I can't imagine you were ever an awkward teenager."

"Believe me, I was, and what's so surprising about me?" I laughed, as I remembered like a reel the embarrassing highlights from my awkward phase.

"You. I misjudged you badly when I first met you. I thought you were ... I can't even bring myself to say it."

"You thought I was an over-indulged, vapid, trust-fund playboy who spent his time charming lady doctors up and down the Pacific Northwest?"

"Not in so many words, but yes. I couldn't have been more wrong." She seemed pensive as she owned up to that, and I decided to rescue her from her thoughts.

"Maybe you're not wrong, it's too soon to tell." I pulled in at the gate. Unassuming and understated, just the way I liked it. "This is home." The reason for this location was in the back, where I had two hundred feet of private lake frontage. My own slice of heaven.

"What's the code to get in?"

"You want the gate code? Soon you'll want a drawer and a toothbrush too. It's 341687," I said slowly, to make sure she would remember it. I wanted her to use it. Often.

"I won't be burgling you any time soon, I've already forgotten it," she said and giggled. She couldn't have forgotten it. She trained her mind to remember all manner of weird and wonderful things. "I can't wait to see how a real life heartthrob lives," she joked as the garage door shut behind us.

"I usually come through the garage door, but the front door is to the left. You can use that next time you come over." I hoped this would be the start of sharing more of her time with me.

"The tradesman entrance suits me perfectly," she quipped as she looked around the garage. "You're not a patriot? Six cars and not a single American one in this garage."

"We've already established I've got a soft spot for a sexy Brit, and my mother's people have roots in Italy and Germany, so that makes me more patriotic than you might think. You like American muscle?"

"Not as a collective. Maybe just the one." She grabbed my forearm and smiled coyly.

"I'm going to need to hear you keep repeating that for the rest of the weekend." I pulled her into me. It had already been too long since I held her close, tasted her lips and felt her soft body melt into mine. I already needed her close, always. Breathlessly we pulled apart.

"Where are your manners? Invite me in."

"I got distracted. Your eyes are a different shade of green today, got lost in them for a while."

"I like it when I lose you to them," she said softly, only marginally louder than the beat of my heart in my chest. She was finally mine. I couldn't shout it from the rooftops, but it remained true.

I led her downstairs to the basement, my favourite part of the house. "Once Maxie's in bed, asleep, this is where I usually am."

"The basement? What have you got down there?" she whispered, conspiratorially, then broke into a small laugh. As we walked down, and the first glass enclosed space came within our line of sight, she gasped. "This is where the American muscle is made. I would be obsessed with my body too if my basement was decked out like this one. It's a gym junkie's toy store."

"When you put it like that, it takes away from all my hard work. It's not the machines that do the work." My pretence at a wounded tone remained unconvincing.

"How long have you lived here?" she asked as we moved away from the machines, past the sauna and towards the pool while she took it all in. She gave a backward glance to the reformer. I would give anything to have her on it while I did my own work.

"About two years. I found this huge parcel of land with a half-built house, a very grateful but bankrupt owner and water views for miles. I had an architect and designers who were able to bring my vision to life. It was the perfect escape, in both the literal and figurative."

"How so?"

"When I came across it, I had been a single dad for five weeks, and my brother was hanging on to life by a thread. I wanted somewhere new but still close to my family to raise my girls, and everything about this house, even some of the sourcing trips I went on with my designers, helped me forget reality, even if it was just for a little while. It gave me something to look forward to."

"When you do retail therapy, you do it big. The house is new, but it has a soul."

"You call it retail therapy, I like to imagine it as a labour of love."

"Hmm, they aren't putting you to good use at work – acquisitions and such. You need to be in the love letter and flowery language department." She laughed and I loved the sound.

"That would be the propaganda squad known as marketing. Come upstairs, there's more to see."

Cara wasn't disappointed by the main floor and continued to be amazed. "The décor is a mix of everything I love – modern organic, transitional, California casual, and the styles are married well."

"Thanks, sounds like you're the one not being put to good use with EKGs, blood tests and such." She laughed softly and looked up.

"That chandelier is gorgeous, where's it from?"

"A furniture fair in Gothenburg. Maxie and Laila picked it because of two butterflies etched in each arm. That's the maker's signature," I added wistfully, remembering the day vividly. Both my daughters had been together. Excited, vibrant and noisy. A furniture fair hadn't been an appropriate outing.

She smiled and looked at it intently. "I would give it pride of place too, it means everything." She hugged me from the back, and that, too, was everything.

"Next Friday's Laila's birthday," I announced out of the blue. It had been weighing on my mind. Maxie had remembered too, and wanted cake. She had drawn one, heart-shaped and yellow, for Fernando to recreate an exact but edible replica.

"It is?" she asked softly, compassion still pouring into the protector hug. "How will you celebrate?" She kept her head resting against my back, where I suspected she could hear the sound of my heartache.

"Mount Si first thing, then dinner and cake with Maxie and her cousins. My mother and brother may have invited themselves over too."

"Sounds like you'll have your hands full in the evening. Want company on Mount Si?" she offered.

"I would love that. No work on Friday?" Her compassion overwhelmed me, and I was relieved we were not looking at each other. She would have noticed how affected I was.

"Even doctors call in sick sometimes, and it sounds like you could do with a hiking partner."

I was knocked off balance and even my heart became lighter. She understood me. I could only answer hoarsely, "Pick you up at five."

We continued the tour, despite the heaviness of our exchange, I was on cloud nine. Could she be the half of me that was missing? When we walked into the kitchen, her eyes darted everywhere, then settled on one spot.

"An eight-foot La Cornue range, with your name engraved into it. What have you cooked on it?" she asked with a twinkle in her eye, as if she already knew the pitiful answer.

I couldn't help the chuckle and decided to be honest. "Some breakfasts, cheesy eggs mostly, and I've warmed some milk for hot chocolate a few times."

"That's bordering on blasphemy," she said and sighed dramatically. "I'll make us something later."

"Do you cook because you like it or you have to?"

"That's how I unwind. It seems my mother was the same, but she did one better and kept a collection of her favourite recipes. I've been practising those for years, over and ..." Her words trailed away when she looked outside the huge floor-to-ceiling window towards the lake. I followed her eyes to see what caught her attention and her eyes led me to the dock at the bottom of the backyard.

"How about this for an idea? I'll help you make us something to eat, and we'll take it onto the yacht, and we can eat out there? You get to see the lake from a different vantage."

"The yacht's yours too?" She swallowed audibly. "Of course it is. This is your house, so is the dock, stands to reason the yacht is too."

"It is, you'll love it. It's compact, perfect for use on a lake."

"I would love to eat out on the lake," she said, lost in the views across the water towards the mountains. I got lost in the view too, it was always the perfect end to any day.

"Later, we've got time. I promised you a bedroom tour."

Chapter Twenty

Cara

The more time I spent with Miles, the more I realised I misjudged him, over and over. My preconceptions had become my worst enemy.

After arranging to meet, the end of my work day couldn't come soon enough. All I wanted was to see him again. To hear his voice, to hear about his day and to have him hold me. I never felt so wanted, so needed and so safe as I did when I was with him. I called a car to take me to the address he sent, and it pulled up to a hotel entrance.

"Hmm, I think we might be lost," I mused when the driver stopped.

"This is the address you gave me. I never get lost around here, this is my turf." His turf? The driver was barely out of his teens. "This is the nicest hotel downtown, you're not lost." He looked at me appreciatively, which disturbed me. I was skittish. It was difficult to know who was genuinely flirting and who was making my life a living hell, or if they were the same.

A valet dressed in a sharp uniform opened the car door, and held it open while I stepped out. I walked towards the entrance where a smart hostess greeted me with a smile.

"Hi, I'm looking for this address. Is this the right place?" I showed her the address on my phone.

"That's the South Penthouse. This way, please."

She led me to the desk, where she looked something up, while I looked around the vast and expansive foyer. The ceilings looked to be three storeys high with an art installation – a clustered group of large gold, beige and cream flower-like linen structures which represented an anatomically correct action of respirations. The rest of the foyer was a marble nerd's dream with rich tones of brown furnishings and glossy chandeliers intermixed with a cream and gold marble, which had to be seen to be believed.

"Right, I've got it. Are you ..."

"Doctor Braithwaite, Cara Braithwaite."

"Yes, I have your key here, and that elevator will take you straight up to the penthouse." *My place? This is a hotel.*

True to the hostess' word, I was on the forty-ninth floor and walked straight into another polished and elegant foyer, smaller this time but just as showstopping. I smelled and felt Miles' presence before I saw him. The light flutters in my core intensified the further I walked into the penthouse. In two strides he was next to me, picked me up and held me close.

That was all I had looked forward to all day. Carefully he placed me back onto the floor, took my face in both his hands and kissed me with everything he had. He tasted familiar and we both lingered, reuniting, reconnecting and remembering. It had only been three days since we were on Mercer together, but it felt like a lifetime.

"This is a great place you have here. Never had I pictured a home in a hotel," I said and let our lips part.

"Imagine being twenty-four years old and finding a condo close to work, with five restaurants downstairs, a gym and a view. I thought I was a king for a while." He kept his arm around my waist as he walked us to a bay of windows where the prominent Olympic mountains were the backdrop.

"You could afford this at twenty-four?" I gasped as I looked around and briefly remembered my living situation when I had graduated and worked in London. I could only chuckle at the worlds-apart comparison.

"One of the wisest investments I've ever made. I haven't used it in years, but it would be foolish to sell it now. The hotel maintains it and it's booked up throughout the year." He was great at acquisitions, even unexpected real estate ones.

"This is the place you left for your island, and the place you offered me. You skimped on a lot of details. It's gorgeous." We looked out at the Olympic mountains, and he tugged my back against his chest. I couldn't help resting my head against him, while he placed open-mouthed kisses on the side of my neck. I was content and felt safe.

"No, you're gorgeous. It's still yours if you want it." I couldn't stop myself as I turned around and kissed him again. More ravenously than before.

"Thank you, but no. I've fallen in love with the golf course. How are we here, on a school night? You should feel really naughty, Miles Masterson."

"Let's sit. I'll explain. I hope you don't mind but I've ordered for us, food will be here in twenty. "

"After making life and death decisions all day, I don't mind when you take one decision off my plate, and I'm starving." We sat down on a comfortable cream couch, where he swiftly removed my heels and rested my feet in his lap.

"Your work is demanding, and busy, I had an inkling you would want to eat. How was it today?"

"This case will stay with me for a while. A four-year-old boy was brought in, starved and emaciated, with tissue paper dry skin from dehydration. I don't understand how a parent can do that."

"Will he be okay?"

"Still touch and go, but I think he will be."

"After the hospital, and he's better, how can I help him? I want to." I hadn't expected him to offer help, although I should have known he would. I was slowly coming to the realisation Miles would do anything he could to help anyone or a cause close to his heart. He seemed to have a soft spot for kids.

"You're kind and generous, nearly perfect. I'll get you his social worker's details."

"You're great, you know that? Ever thought about having kids?"

"Hmm, I did consider it once, a long time ago, when I thought the relationship was right and I was ready."

"What made you backtrack?" The conversation should have been awkward, but Miles made it seem like every word I spoke was the most important one he had ever heard.

"He decided he would rather make one – a child – with someone else, someone who was more available and not preoccupied with her work." I expected to feel a pang of something, jealousy, loss, heartache, as I recounted that. I didn't, not while Miles' hand was running up and down my leg, under the guise of a foot massage.

"This happened while you and him were together?" He tried to hide his shock, it never worked. He wore his feelings on his face. How did he make it in acquisitions? A poker face would be a better asset.

"Yes, and what made it even crazier was the three of us worked together." His hand stilled on my leg as the affected glance on his face morphed into an understanding look.

"That must have been brutal. I'm sorry I put you in a situation where you thought it was happening again. With the photos, online." He had apologised on Mercer. He didn't need to apologise for James' actions. "Did you work closely with her?

"Yes. She was an exercise physiologist and I referred patients to her all the time, face to face, or perhaps belly to belly – her round one next to my non-existent one." I chuckled. "I laugh now but for a while I thought I was jealous. Little did I realise how hurt and broken I was."

"I suppose evidence of his infidelity would stare you in the face every time you walked into work."

"The pain of that experience turned me off from dating for a while, until you, Heartthrob," I said, moving closer to him, swapping my foot with my body on his. He wrapped his hands around me, as I sunk into him.

"I can't believe you took a chance on me after that. It had to be this handsome face." He chuckled softly, but I saw through that throwaway comment too.

"You wanted to tell me something. What is it?" I wondered if he needed me, like I was starting to need him.

"This shouldn't affect you and me, but it's important you know. I wouldn't want you to find out any other way."

"Tell me, what is it?" I asked hurriedly, worried about what it could be.

"Maxie's mom wants back in her life. She wants visitation, and moving forward it may lead to shared custody. We met this afternoon with both our lawyers."

She gave up her rights in the first place, was it fair to ping-pong into Maxie's life like she would be doing?

"What changed? Why did she sign away her parental rights in the first place?"

"That was the legal advice, and perhaps the best thing she could have done – for herself at the time."

"In what reality is abandoning your child the choice which makes sense?" I couldn't hide my outrage as Miles chuckled softly and held me tighter.

"She was charged with child neglect and endangerment. Both charges were dropped after she gave up her rights." *How could that happen, in the world which Miles and Maxie lived?*

"Child neglect? Oh, Maxie," I whispered. My mind raced to the sweet girl I met, the one who I had fallen for through Miles' eyes.

"A few weeks after we laid Laila to rest, Maxie was spending time at her mother's house. Vivian locked her bedroom door so Maxie wouldn't disturb her while she was asleep. Her excuse was she looked too much like Laila and seeing her at night caused too much anguish."

"This is too surreal."

"That's not even half of it. Mid-afternoon the next day, Vivian still hadn't woken up. Maxie was hungry, lonely, sad and generally neglected. She decided to make herself breakfast or lunch, whatever a starving child eats at three in the afternoon. That's when she accidentally set fire to her mother's kitchen."

"What?" I couldn't believe it. It was my turn to wear my feelings on my face. Did mothers really do this to their children? Of course they did, I saw varied iterations of it at work. This was different. It was Maxie and her very polished mother, who I had spent too much time looking up on the internet. With her designer clothes, flawless makeup and well-heeled friends.

"After talking to Maxie some more, I found out this had been going on every time she was at her mother's house." He let out a deep sigh.

"I have to ask. Is she safe to look after Maxie? Do you trust her?"

"When this goes before a judge, we will be requesting supervised visits, with my mother."

"Not with you?"

"No, I won't be giving her any ideas about her and I." As we were speaking, a buzzing sound made me jump. My heart leapt and I was terrified.

"Cara, it's okay, it's room service with our meal." Again, something simple had unnerved me.

"I don't recognize myself sometimes. I've become a bag of nerves."

"Don't be, you're safe with me. And when I'm not there, someone's watching you. I've made sure of it." I was reassured as he unwound his body from mine and started to walk towards the door.

Chapter Twenty-One

Cara

Heartthrob: You worked right through Christmas and New Year. You need a holiday.

You read my mind. St Valentine would love you.

Heartthrob: Can you get away next Monday? For a week? I have an idea.

I might be able to. Let me finesse it with Suki and Ivie. Where are we going?

Heartthrob: One clue, you will thoroughly defrost.

Perfect! Somewhere warm? In the southern hemisphere?

Heartthrob: Yes and yes.

Mmm…

I was always able to find familiarity and grounding when I was working. I easily passed my second certification exam. Between Miles' time with Maxie, his work and mine, we tried to see each other as often as we could. Even though our thing was official, and we were four months strong, he agreed to put some distance between the first time we met and our coming out as a couple. I still hadn't met his family the way he wanted me to. I finally owned up to Izzy about how we really met. She pretended to disapprove but moved on from her shock by renaming me the ER Vixen.

It was finally Thursday evening and Monday couldn't come soon enough. I finished work at the emergency room and attended my six p.m. Krav Maga class, which had become a thrice-weekly fixture in my week, and I enjoyed it. It gave me a measure of control over my life. Although it was physically and mentally intense, I was pleased with my progress. I felt fitter and stronger and as a bonus I was more toned than I had ever been.

I walked out of the gym, tired but upbeat, ready to walk the six minutes it took to get home. Thanks to Dean's clever home automation, my lights and heat would already be on by the time I arrived. Out of the corner of my eye, I spied the security car from Miles' security team, which had also become the norm.

They would watch me walk out of the gym past the car, get out of their car, then follow me home at some distance, watch me get inside my house, confer with golf course security, then in the morning they would follow me to work. That was repeated day after day.

Today was different. They must be new, or could they be trying to change up their sequence? *They have to stay dynamic after all*. This pair didn't leave the car, instead they drove, I assumed, to the gated entrance. That was all right too. I would arrive home before they did.

We were well into the new year, and wintery Seattle remained bitterly cold, but after the class I was warm and energised, unfazed by the weather. I loved the peace and tranquillity of the golf course in the evening, and I took this route like I had become used to since leaving my townhouse in Queen Anne.

As I was rounding a secluded bend, I came face to face with one I had seen before.

My world, without warning, ceased to spin on its axis and I was doused in fright and fear.

His commanding stature continued to advance towards me and I instinctively let out a piercing scream. I turned around and ran back towards the gym, and with each stride, the gravel crunched beneath my feet. As he got closer to me, his thumping footsteps and grunting breaths behind me became louder and more ominous, and I didn't get far.

He caught up to me and we both tumbled to the ground. He stunned me with a single solid blow to my face, and as if a faucet had been turned, blood poured out of my nose. *Where is security when I need them most?*

Jet black terror gripped me. "What do you want from me?" I cried, while the pain in my face took my breath away.

He dragged me from the grass verges and, under the cover of near darkness, hauled me, shoved me and pushed me towards the greenkeeper's shed. Clumsily, I stumbled along as we made our way to what I was sure was my death. I felt useless, artless and hopeless. All the misogynist non-verbal and verbal tirades ever directed towards me played in my head at the same time. *Is this what it means to be the fairer sex?*

"Wrong question, Doc," he snapped. I grasped then that this man knew me in a professional capacity.

Besides seeing him at my old gym and at Pike Place, I'd never seen him before. As we reached the shed, I grabbed hold of the cold, heavy rusty metal door and hoped he wouldn't shove me inside. I also hoped the action would be dilatory and give security a fighting chance to find me.

"Please, don't take me in there, please," I whimpered as my eyes frantically darted everywhere. There was no point in screaming for help. The golf course was deserted on the cold and lonely night.

He hustled me into the shed and I stumbled onto the floor. While I was down there, in the shed's semi-darkness, I scanned the floor feverishly for anything to defend myself with. All I saw was a thin channel along the wall where, if I was lucky, something could have fallen and become trapped inside.

Meanwhile, his sturdy running shoes rammed into my torso over and over. My insides convulsed with pain and rage. He was furious, but I didn't know why.

In that vulnerable position, all the work I put into Krav Maga was of no use. I was immobilised by both the fear and the pain he was inflicting. He was just past six feet tall, I was five eight, but he had taken me down with ease.

"Stop, please, what is this about?" I sobbed and wheezed through the worst pain I had ever known.

He paused briefly and looked me straight in the eye, "My father," he snarled. His asperity was more obvious with dialogue.

Note to self: Keep the questions to a minimum.

"Your father?" Silence reigned for a minute. Blood trickled down my nose while I discreetly studied him and searched his features for anything to help me recognise him.

The question worsened his anger. He knelt on the ground, sat astride my chest and pummelled me with his fists. After a while I couldn't see from my right eye, and that must have been when I passed out.

I came to, with a start when a bucket of ice cold water was poured on me. I wondered how long I had been out for. It could have been hours or mere minutes. Painful shivers racked my numb body. The shed was dimly lit by an overhead light, but from my one functional eye, I could tell it had become pitch black outside, accompanied by an eerie silence.

Disoriented and too shattered to move my head or even speak, I could barely see my assailant in the low light. *Do security know I never made it home? The lights on in my house could be misleading.* In my light gym clothes and the freezing conditions, my body convulsed uncontrollably as my teeth chattered. My whole body hurt, but I needed to stay awake. He knelt next to me and spoke in a deceptively soft tone.

"Doc, if you and I had met in another life, you would have been just my type." He ran his tongue over his brilliant white teeth. He was well-groomed and somewhere beneath the American twang was buried a cockney accent. Who did I know from East London?

From nowhere, he ripped open the zipper of my sweater, grabbed and squeezed both my breasts. I didn't recognise the squeal I let out, but I avoided talking. He was furious, and I didn't want to set him off again.

"That tiny waist and those sweet tits could have been perfect, but after that vile act they let you get away with, everything about you revolts me. I still had to check if these were real, and I'm pleasantly surprised." Long seconds became agonising minutes as he continued to grope my breasts, while I took shuddering breaths from the cold, the fear and the repulsion.

In my haze, the pieces of the puzzle finally came together, and I realised this man was George Templeton's son.

Disbelief, amazement and devastation at realising he followed me all the way to Seattle to exact his revenge made my soul conciliate with the thought that death would soon follow. I hoped it would be swift.

I let out a deep breath, and as my teeth chattered, and against my better judgement, I asked, "How are you here?"

"Don't flatter yourself, I didn't follow you here. You're the one who came to my city. You keep a very low profile, Doc, but your old friends at King's, not so much. That was quite the farewell party you had. When I found out you were coming here, it was providence, and I had to do this for my father," he sneered.

"What's your name?" I whispered.

"Easy. It's George. As you lay there dying, remember you took George the elder's life, then junior took yours."

I was surprisingly calm. I felt anything but. "I'm sorry about your father, we tried everything to save him."

His response was a garbled cry. He was too far gone, and I wasn't reaching him. "After you murdered my father, with those pretty man-icured fingers, the coroner called it ... what was it, again? Death by medical misadventure. What does that mean? Did my dad go on a quest into your operating room and, as if by magic, he just died?" he murmured quietly. He had become contemplative, but it was clear he was cold and calculating. In a silent rage.

I tried to sit up, but my battered body sagged. George helped me and propped me up against a golf buggy. His assistance was deceptive and only served to assert his dominance.

"What are you going to do to me?" I wheezed.

"A lot more than that impotent pretty boy can. I know he didn't seal the deal, not in this house anyway."

"I don't understand. What house?" I tried to think as the throbbing in my head robbed me of all coherence.

"Did you think I wouldn't find you? 'Goddess of Seattle Children's.' Did you know they call you that behind your back? Your colleagues, the parents. The ones who don't love your work are all lusting after you, and you pretend not to see it. I've been watching you closely, Doc. Even your hapless security. Where are they now? I knew they could be outsmarted, all it took was patience."

"When? How? You don't have to do this. Please."

"They don't know the Goddess is nothing but a murderer. After today they will know you gutted my father like an animal and let him bleed to death. What were you even doing as he lay bleeding? Touching up your makeup!" He bellowed with a booming roar.

I didn't think it was possible to be more frightened than I already was, but the reverberation in the shed from his anger was enough to remind me how my life was close to ending.

"And now they've let you loose, looking after little kids." He lost control again and garden implements made a clanging noise as he kicked them in frustration. *Someone must have heard that.*

"We did everything we could for your father. I promise you," I cried feebly.

He came closer and sat next to me. He may have started out clean, but his clothes were muddy, bloody and sweaty. The cologne he wore had become stale and the pungent odour filled my nostrils.

"That's neither here nor there," he scoffed.

He took out his phone and scrolled through what I realised were hundreds of videos from inside my old townhouse, sniggering and sneering when he was entertained.

I took a long, hard look at him. He couldn't have been more than thirty years old. On a good day he would have been difficult to escape from, but in my current condition, it would be impossible.

"You didn't know I put cameras in there did you? You thought four perimeter cameras could catch me. I had twelve inside, even in here," he sneered.

He showed me a feed from my bathroom. Despite the broken bones, and my right eye swollen shut, the invasion of my privacy devastated me.

"Before I kill you, we are going to take all these clothes off, so I can get a clear view of what's underneath." The menace in his voice caused me to gag.

"George, please. No, you don't have to do this." I heard myself whimpering.

"You took my father from me, from my mother and from my kids. I'm going to take whatever I want from you. Then I will take you from everyone in your world."

"That won't bring him back. I'll be dead. But you'll spend your life in prison. You've got kids, what about them?" I tried breathlessly to reason with him, using the little energy I had left.

"Nothing will bring him back. No one will ever give my mother flowers. He brought flowers to my mother every Friday after he got his paycheck, small as it was. He loved her, and you turned her into a textbook lonely old hag." That explained his neurosis with flowers.

It was getting difficult to breathe and even harder to speak. My body hurt and I could feel my strength ebbing. The tears rolled down my cheeks, and I couldn't stop them from flowing. I wanted to hold on but I had nothing left to hold on to. I silently recited a prayer, one I last said at school to the archangels, fierce warriors and protectors, to fight my battle which I had already lost. Instead, all I saw were the four horsemen coming for me. The one on his pale horse galloped faster and faster, and its hooves got louder and louder.

"We're done talking, Doc," he said with a menacing finality.

He found a scythe and cut my gym clothes to shreds. He didn't try to be careful. As he ripped through my clothes, he also ripped through my skin. I sobbed silently and resigned myself to a horrendous death in the greenkeeper's shed at a golf course. Thoughts of my family ran through my mind. Dean, Charlie and the children, how would they ever live through this? If I had lived, would my thing with Miles have stood a chance?

After I was naked, he hit me with a rake over and over, and kicked me again and again. He took out all his anger on me, grunting and moaning as he used all the strength he could muster.

In the frenzy, I heard a cluttering sound. When I turned my eyes to it, I saw his phone fall into the thin channel against the wall. It didn't register to him, as he concentrated on his grim task of breaking me. He had put a lot of thought into it, and he must have fantasised about hurting me for a long time.

He had his chance and didn't waste it. I was at his mercy.

He straightened up and I mistakenly thought it was all over, until he unzipped his pants, and a wave of nausea came over me. As he pulled my legs apart to continue his gruesome assault, I used all the power left in me and kicked him off me. He staggered backwards, landing on the stone floor. I didn't recognise it, but I let out a bloodcurdling scream that shattered the silence. That was all in vain, as the golf course would be deserted.

When he returned to me, he was angrier than before and kicked me repeatedly before he knelt and forced himself inside me. He let out a hiss. The hiss of misplaced pleasure and a power trip signalling my pain, my loss and the theft of my dignity. I turned my head away and vomited all over the floor in revulsion. Before he started to push against me, the shed door crashed open.

I made out two figures. *Is that St Michael and St Gabriel, the archangels finally arrived? They took their time.* The next instant, George was off me and flung against the wall. For the second time that night, I succumbed to the mercy of unconsciousness.

Chapter Twenty-Two

Miles

Cara and I would be leaving for our trip on Monday. On Friday, by six o'clock, I arrived at HQ to go over an important new acquisition with Michael, when Alistair came in and spoke quietly.

"Miles, there's a Ms Charlene here to see you."

"Can it wait? I'm busy, and it's too early to start seeing anyone, you should know better," I chided impatiently. Alistair was still nervous but had become a quick study. His problem was separating the wheat from the chaff when it came to unannounced visitors at the office.

"I don't think it can. She's in tears and she's told me it's a family issue. I also have Defense Shield Security on the line."

"Alistair, I'm only one man. Probe what these people want, prioritise then deliver. We've gone over this before. You're my assistant and gatekeeper."

"Yes, Miles. Okay. I'm sorry."

"Who's family? Hers? Let her in," I called out to Alistair as he scurried out. It was rare in my work to have someone see me with a family issue. This one I decided to hear about, at six in the morning.

"Why haven't you fired him yet?" Michael asked, bemused.

"Unlike my previous assistant, he doesn't have a crush on the boss and he never will. He has a lot of potential and will grow into the role."

"All very good points, but send him down to research and development. They need new thinkers, and get someone more effective to be your assistant."

"No, sir. I'll hire and fire my own personnel. Sir." I chuckled and sipped my coffee, waiting for Michael's clever comeback. This time he didn't have one.

"Who's Charlene anyway? I thought you and Cara were in a ... thing," he said with a smirk.

"We are, she's the next Mrs Masterson. She just doesn't know it yet." I wasn't able to hide my grin. It was the first time I owned up to anyone, even to myself, about how I felt about us.

"Once she catches wind of that she'll be swimming the Atlantic, straight into the arms of an Englishman who speaks her language and knows how to fire ineffective help," he returned, amused but clearly happy with my confession.

The surprise visitor walked in and when I looked up, my heart sank as a feeling of impending doom washed over me.

"Charlie. It's you. What's happened to her?"

Loud sobs filled my office, and fresh tears rained down her already tear-stained face. She couldn't speak and seemed to be having trouble breathing. Michael was soon beside her and helped her into a chair.

"Miles, she's having a panic attack. Hand me that brown bag. Charlie? Is that your name? I'm Michael, Miles' brother. Look at me. Good, you need to take deep breaths like I'm doing." He took slow, measured breaths and encouraged her to sync her breaths with his.

While Michael helped Charlie, I called Cara, but she wasn't answering her phone. It took some minutes to calm Charlie down while I paced my office helplessly.

"Charlie, can you tell Miles why you're here?" Frown lines etched his face as he crouched next to her chair.

In between sobs and hiccups, she started to talk. "Miles, he attacked her, and she's not in a good way. I don't think she'll make it."

"What! Where is she?" Immeasurable guilt and anger constricted my chest as heat filled my body. In no time, I was a ball of fury and tension ready to explode.

"At St Mark's, with Dean and Izzy." Her sobs returned, louder this time.

I didn't wait around to hear any more. With the benefit of the express elevator from the 45th floor, I made it to the parking lot in seconds. The early morning rush was just beginning, but not a red light nor stop sign stood in my way. I broke road rule after road rule as I sped through the downtown streets.

Where was the security team? What had they been doing? They were getting paid a king's ransom. Where was I? I'm the man in her life. She seemed safe at her golf course home. I should have insisted she live at the penthouse or even with me on Mercer. She wouldn't have taken up much room. If she died, I would never forgive myself. As I was driving, Clay's call came through.

"Miles, I have some difficult news." He sounded like I felt, grave and sombre.

"I know, I'm on my way to St Mark's. Defense Shield dropped the ball, find out how."

"I'm on it."

When I arrived at the hospital, I was directed to the Step Down Unit. *Step down from what?* Did Cara ever talk to me about that? I never imagined I needed to learn hospital lingo. St Mark's was one of the newer hospitals in the city, modern and clean. But the minute I arrived on Cara's floor, a wave of nausea came over me. I needed to be stronger than I had been when I lost my father and Laila. This wasn't an unexpected rip current close to shore, it had been months in the making, yet I still failed her.

Would I ever make this right? I didn't want to believe this was the end for her, and for us. I had only just found her, I wanted to keep her for as long as she would have me.

I came off the elevator and came face to face with Dean, white as a ghost and trembling like a leaf. Him and others, who I later found out were detectives, milled around the corridor.

"Where is she?" I asked him hurriedly.

"In there with her doctors." He pointed weakly to a room with a closed door.

"What have they said?"

"Nothing good," he mumbled with his head down. I didn't want to wait. I needed to see her straight away. I knocked once and opened the door to her room.

"Sir, you can't be in here." A young doctor, who didn't look much older than twelve and looked too thin and too pale to be healing people, walked toward me.

"Excuse me," I retorted angrily as I pushed past him to Cara's bedside.

I was horrified at what I saw. Her face was unrecognisable. Black and blue, swollen and disfigured to a point where I had to do a double take to make sure it was her.

"Sir, you need to leave. This patient is not receiving visitors at the moment. I'm calling security otherwise." The juvenile-like doctor tried to deepen his voice, but I wasn't having any of it.

"Who do you think you are? I'm THE visitor, now let me have my moment with her. If anything, you should leave." I was livid. It wasn't the young doctor's fault, but he was getting in my way, and the state of Cara's face angered me. Why would he do this to her?

He returned mutely to where the gaggle of doctors continued to talk quietly among themselves.

That gave me a chance to take a good look at her. This was why she didn't answer my call last night. I would have called her back, but I fell asleep reading with Maxie. The crazed psychopath beat her half to death and left her beautiful face unrecognisable. Every part of her body that was visible to me was black, blue and purple. I wondered what she went through to look this way. Her sapphire necklace was even gone from her neck. While I stood there, I saw her lips move. She was conscious but weak and I knelt at her bedside, next to her head.

"Cara, can you hear me? It's Miles." I heard the crack in my voice. With some effort she turned her face to look at me. Although it was difficult to see her eyes, her face was wet with tears. She tried to open her eyes wider but squinted at the hospital lights. She tried to move, but winced. I imagined pain shot through her body.

"Stay still, there's no need to move. I'm here now. I should've been with you," I whispered. In my periphery, a doctor who had just entered the room came closer to her bed.

From nowhere, she yelled how I imagined an army sergeant would, "Everyone out. What are you all doing in here, standing around as if you don't have anywhere else to be?" Another British doctor in a Seattle hospital.

The other doctors looked over and stopped talking in their hushed tones. She started again, "If you have no business in this room, get the hell out. This patient is not a circus animal, for heaven's sake." Her voice cracked. She was taking Cara's condition personally.

One of them dared to say, "Her brother gave consent for us to be here."

"Have you seen the state her brother's in?" she shrieked. "He would give consent for her to blast off into space if he thought that would help her. Consider it withdrawn. It can't have been informed consent. None of you are coming near this patient again, and if you do, it will be my personal mission to have you all expelled."

They quickly filed out, save for one doctor who sidled next to the screaming one. Before they started speaking to each other, she looked at me.

"Good morning, what's your business here, sir?" she asked as her voice broke and her eyes filled with tears. Her strength was a façade, she appeared deeply distressed.

"I'm here for Cara, she's my ..."

She sighed and smiled weakly. A U-turn from her heated performance. "You're the secret heartthrob, aren't you?"

"Please, call me Miles." I extended my hand out to her. She ignored it and gave me a warm hug instead. She knew who I was.

"I'm Isobel Wallace. Izzy. Cara's friend." She walked around to the other side of the bed and knelt next to Cara. Her name sounded familiar, Cara may have mentioned her. "Braithwaite, you were right. He is dishy, but you never talk about me, do you? I'll forgive you this time," she murmured softly as a lone tear trickled down her face. Cara was important to this woman.

The other doctor who had been in the room came closer to me and introduced herself.

"I'm Doctor Penrose. I need to examine Cara," she said softly.

"I'm not leaving, Doctor Penrose."

"I'm sorry, who are you?"

"I'm Miles Masterson, Cara's my girlfriend." I had promised to keep our relationship under wraps, but I didn't care, not now. I would scream about us if I had to.

"All right, Mr Masterson. I'm sorry to do this. I'm a gynaecologist and I need to perform an intimate exam. Everyone else has left the room, it will be just me and Izzy. We'll be respectful, and it won't take long."

Without needing further explanation, I understood. Everything. My head fell and tears filled my eyes. Cara squeezed my hand, and the tears which had stopped streaming down her face started again.

I whispered in her ear, "I'll be right outside. Izzy and Doctor Penrose will be with you, but as soon as they are finished, I'll be back. Okay." She tried to speak, but she could barely whisper. Instead, she nodded her head. Reluctantly, I tore my eyes from her face. "Doctor Penrose, when you're finished here, please dim the lights. They are too bright for her." As I spoke, my voice broke, and I fought hard to hold back my tears.

"I will. I'll try to do this quickly so you can come back and be with her."

When I left her room, my body sagged against the wall and the tears fell down my face freely.

After trying to compose myself as much as possible, I walked into a magnolia-coloured waiting room, where I found Charlie, Dean and

Michael. Michael was quick to get up. It had been a while since I cried on his shoulder, and he let me until he spoke up.

"I'll take Miles to the cafeteria. He'll be back." As we walked out of the waiting room and down a quiet corridor, we found an empty room and went inside. After the door clicked shut, Michael sat me down.

"She's not doing well, he broke her like a ragdoll." My voice cracked as my tears escaped again.

"I'm sorry. Has she said anything to you?" he asked gently.

"Yes and no, she's too upset and so weak. I don't know if I'll ever get her back."

"Do you know what happened?" The dread in his tone broke through the momentary silence between us.

"Physical and sexual assault, and months of emotional torture. We both thought this was over."

Concern streaked through his expression. He was an expert at being strong for me. "I'm sorry. Charlie and Dean filled me in on some of what's been going on. Why did you never tell me? How could we let this happen to her?" He was quietly outraged.

"I thought a security detail was all she needed. It seemed she was in good hands."

"Is this Defense Shield? They've provided security for us since I can remember. After today, they are done in this city. I'll handle them. What can I do for you?" It was laughable how Michael was plotting his version of vengeance, while I slowly died.

"Send Zane to represent her. He needs to do everything to keep this matter sealed. Look after Maxie, just for a while. Cara needs me. When you can, I need a change of clothes and a toothbrush. I'm not leaving her." I needed to stop the tears. For the second time in my life, I didn't know how.

"Say no more, consider it all done. Go back in there, looks like her doctor's out. I'll be on the phone if you need anything."

I nodded and returned to Cara's room. As soon as I entered, I heard a soft sob. I couldn't help myself, tears filled my eyes too. I sat down next to her, took her small hand in mine, looked into her eyes and forced a smile.

"Cara, I'm sorry. I wish I could have been there." She nodded her head gently. I suspected I saw her smile too, but her face was too disfigured to be sure. I got closer to her and kissed her lips. She flinched, and the worst of what may have happened to her ran through my mind. "Can you talk to me?" I asked gently.

Again, she nodded her head and mouthed the word phone. I took my phone from my pocket and tried to hand it to her. She shook her head.

"Do you want your phone?"

Again, she shook her head. I tried to understand what she was trying to tell me. She had been through the worst ordeal of her life, and the first thing she wanted to talk about was a phone. I suspected it had something to do with his phone.

"Does he have something on his phone?" She nodded over and over with as much vigour as she could muster in her weak state, while the tears streamed down her face.

"Did he record what he did to you on his phone?" She shook her head and tried to speak. I leaned my ear right to her lips and heard her speak softly for the first time. Her coppery breath broke me all over again. *Every breath she took was laced with her own blood.*

"He had cameras recording me in my Queen Anne house." In disbelief, I moved my head from her lips, looked into her eyes and saw her pain. It seemed worse than the physical pain. She beckoned me to bring my ear back to her lips. "His phone fell down a small channel against the wall in the shed on the golf course," she whispered.

I had to focus, and I understood what she needed, but how would I deliver? The place was a crime scene and would be crawling with investigators.

"Can you give me an hour? I'll be back." She nodded and squeezed my hand weakly. I fought hard to keep my tears at bay. I wouldn't let her see me cry.

The breadth of what he did shook me. If that phone fell into the wrong hands, whatever was on it, would be entertainment for the whole world as long as the internet existed. As I was leaving her room, Charlie and Dean were coming in. They wanted to talk, they needed comfort, words I didn't have, and I had the business of the phone to attend to. I excused myself and called Clay.

"I need to see you now," I said brusquely.

"I'm at St Marks."

"Good, meet me in the cafeteria."

As soon as I arrived, I asked him what he knew, and he explained what happened with what I suspected were broad brushstrokes. He went on to explain that the attacker was in police custody.

"Did you find out about Defense Shield and their negligence?"

"I did. Their CEO is on his way to HQ, to see you."

"He'll be dealing with Michael. What happened to them?"

"They saw her leave the gym. Instead of following her on foot, they drove to her residence, found her lights on and assumed she was already in the house. At three o'clock, when they noticed every single light in her house was still on, they caught on to the fact she might not be inside her house. That's when they traced her route and found her."

"Found her?"

"Yes, and him. They detained him while they called the emergency services."

"In what state did they find her?" *How am I a glutton for this kind of punishment?* He took a huge breath, pushed the wisps of hair on his head down and stared at the box of condiments in the centre of the table. He was about to lie, and I didn't have the time.

"Forget it. I need you to do something for me, and if you can't do it, I will be asking someone else." Silent fury made me tremble. I wanted to kill, the fierce beat in my chest egging me on. I had never been one to fight, I never needed to. Everything in life was seemingly handed to me, but this time I wanted to hunt and take out a man with my bare hands.

He looked uneasy, I had never spoken to him like that before. "Do you remember that kinship you have with Cara?"

"Miles, what are you asking me?"

I explained all I knew of what Cara told me about his phone, and what was on it. I understood about tampering with evidence, and the repercussions if it were to ever come to light. The need to protect Cara's privacy outweighed the police's investigations. I wasn't conflicted with my decision. But I was asking Clay to commit a crime. Marianne would never forgive me if it went sideways.

"Clay, while you're there, see if you can find a necklace with a blue stone, a sapphire. It's important to her." I showed him a photo of Cara and I where the necklace was prominent.

"And Templeton?" he asked, with a vacant look. One I had never seen on his face before.

"He doesn't exist to me," I lied. I wanted him dead.

I'd always kept my hands clean, but both Clay and I knew Templeton could cease to be if I made the smallest insinuation. I couldn't and I wouldn't. No matter his crimes, and what he snatched from her and from me. I wouldn't be able to live with myself, and if Cara found out, I would lose her. She was in the business of preserving life. I could never take one, not in her name.

"I'll do everything I can," he said sombrely, then left.

I needed to find out the extent of Cara's injuries. I didn't know Izzy well, but she was the person to talk to without going through the annoyance of a lack of next of kin privilege. I had her paged. Within five minutes I made my way to meet her in her office.

"Sorry, I didn't think I would be entertaining polite company in this wretched shoe box. Bet you didn't know these were the working conditions of the hoi polloi," she muttered while she cleared medical files from a chair for me to sit down. I could see how she and Cara would be friends. She was witty and knew how to laugh at herself, but after today I didn't think I would ever laugh again.

"Thanks for seeing me. What do you know about Cara's condition? I need to know everything you know."

"This won't be easy to hear. She arrived in the emergency room after physical assault by the son of an ex-patient of hers. One she treated in London."

"In London? Do you mean the one she operated on, and it didn't go well?" That was his fixation on Cara – his father's death.

"Yes, it seems so, but I'm more worried about our Cara."

"So am I. What are her injuries?"

"She has a ruptured spleen, fractured ribs, a perforated eardrum, a broken nose and facial fractures. There was a question about sexual assault, but Doctor Penrose wasn't able to determine that, and Cara isn't talking much to answer questions."

"Is she in much pain?" I stumbled. I fought with the idea of sexual assault, with how Cara would have felt, how she would have fought and how I should have protected her. I grappled with how she got the broken bones. The brutality she faced while I slept soundly in the comfort of my home on Mercer. My personal trainer had been a professional boxer, and from him I knew how debilitating broken bones could be.

"Her team has made sure she's not. Miles, what you saw earlier, the medical students in her room, finding a subject for their theses – that won't happen again. I'll make sure of it. Dean is understandably not himself, and he won't sign anything else unless he talks to me first."

"Thank you, I appreciate that. Cara would, too, she's a private person."

"That she is. She kept you a semi-secret from me," she said with a sad smile on her face, which nearly broke me. I couldn't break, not again.

"Do her team of doctors know what they are doing? Are they competent? I've been around Cara long enough to know, not all doctors are created equal."

She chuckled softly. "Perfect, she's taught you well. She has the best team in the Pacific Northwest, but there's one thing I want for her, and I'm not sure if I should ask you."

"You can ask me anything. Cara has easily become my everything, and I would do anything for her." I leaned forward, eager to hear what I could do to help Cara.

She smiled a real smile. "Okay. I knew she liked you a lot, I didn't realise ... Anyway, the US has plenty of great doctors, Canada, too, but there's a plastic and reconstructive surgeon in Germany, who's also certified to practise here. She's in a league of her own and I want to get her here as soon as possible to fix Cara's face. We're talking hours, we can't wait too long with facial fractures." She lost all composure as the tears started to stream down her face.

I got up and, in her shoe box office, knelt on the floor next to her and covered her hand with mine. "You're a good friend, and Cara is lucky to have you. All we need to do now is be strong for her. Organise everything, send me the bill. If the surgeon's need to get here is as urgent as you say, charter her a plane or I'll send her mine. Whatever it takes. Perhaps we could get Cara's aunt and uncle on the same plane. I'll talk to Dean."

"Thank you, I'll make sure she's looked after well. She's my oldest and dearest friend," she said, smiling through her tears.

Chapter Twenty-Three

Cara

When I woke up in hospital, I couldn't calm my racing heart as I tried to understand what happened to me and how I got there. For the first few seconds before I remembered everything, I was blissfully unaware. Until it all came crashing back to me.

I remembered the terror I felt at the realisation that my time on earth could be coming to an end at George's hands. The brutality of the attack. His cruelty. I never imagined I would ever see daylight again. Drifting in and out of sleep was both a blessing and a curse.

I woke up again, disoriented. The small whiteboard in front of me showed it was day three of my hospital stay. Just as the nurse walked out, my aunt and uncle walked in.

Unbelievable. I had last seen them at Heathrow Airport, when they wished me well and I told them I was excited and looking forward to a fresh start in Seattle. I saw the longing in my aunt's eyes. She had wanted me to stay. She had the same look as she walked closer to my bedside.

"Hello, love, how are you?" she whispered as tears rolled down her face. Even though a top one percent specialist took my broken face and put it together again, I still couldn't bring myself to look in the mirror. The same face she was looking at. *No wonder her tears were unstoppable.*

"Hi, Aunt Delia, Uncle Charlie." I looked over her shoulder at my uncle, who wouldn't look at me. I could hardly open my mouth, but they had flown from England to see me. I had to give them something.

"Your uncle is too upset. I am, too, love. We should have begged you to stay. This would never have happened in London," she sobbed quietly.

"Cordelia, don't. Please. Many women have been hurt under the Met's watch. This could have happened anywhere." My uncle walked closer to my bed and took my hand in his. "I've missed you, Cara, we both have. Our Sunday afternoons haven't been the same since you left. I've been reduced to eating your Aunt Delia's roast," he said and chuckled. That made Aunt Delia smile too.

Aunt Delia's roast had always been difficult for Uncle Charlie, for anyone. Her undercooked potatoes, overdone meat and store-bought yorkshire pudding were never his favourite. That moment of nostalgia brought a small smile to my face as I returned to a simpler time, when I could never have imagined where I was now.

"Aunt Delia, lamb is easier and you can't go wrong with sweet potato." My voice came out in a hoarse whisper. "I missed you, too, Uncle Charlie. How did you get here so quickly?" Before he could answer, there was a soft knock at the door and Miles walked in.

The last seventy-two hours had done away with self-consciousness. He had already seen me at my worst, but Miles still looked and smiled at me like the most beautiful woman in the world. Aunt Delia stopped crying and took out her compact, dabbed some powder on her cheeks and gave Miles a smile. If my face didn't hurt so much I would've giggled. She'd always been a shameless flirt, much to Uncle Charlie's chagrin.

"The lovely Miles made it happen. I was glad to meet him but not under these circumstances." She was overcome with tears again. Her new favourite person held her while Uncle Charlie sat with me and after a while started to talk softly over her sobs.

"Aunt Delia joined a wine club. They don't take long to empty those bottles." He chuckled as he made a drinking gesture.

"A wine club?" I asked in disbelief, unable to open my mouth but still surprised.

My uncle would talk about anything to distract me from pain. He had done that when he and Aunt Delia had taken me in, and every other time I had needed comfort.

Aunt Delia stopped sobbing and came to her own defence. "It's not a wine club, Charles, it's a book club. The wine is to chase down the books, some are hard to swallow don't you know?"

The three of them laughed, yet none of them had a laugh I recognised. They were all in hell, theirs a little different from mine. I tried to laugh too. Although Miles sat in a chair further away from me than usual, he kept glancing at me. I read worry, relief and the occasional flash of anger on his face.

While we sat together, they updated me on their latest exploits. From nowhere, something came over me and I was back in the shed. I focused on breathing through the intrusive thoughts and the sudden pain I felt in my ribs.

As if we were in sync, Miles looked over towards me. Anguish must have been written on my face, as he quickly and quietly made my aunt and uncle file out of my room. I held onto a scream I didn't want to let escape.

"Cara. Look at me," he whispered. I opened my eyes and met his concerned ones. The heavy sigh which left me caused him to also exhale.

"You're safe, it's over." He nodded reassuringly. I knew that, but how did I get back to the golf course?

"Will it ever be really over? I see it when I close my eyes, and now with them open," I wailed. Aunt Delia's histrionics had rubbed off on me.

"It's already over, I promise."

"You don't know that, what if he comes to finish me off?" I stuttered. My nerves and my left jaw, which I could hardly move, made it difficult to get words out clearly.

"He won't. He's locked up, and his bail amount is eye-watering." I had security and he still managed to outwit them. "I'll do everything I can to make sure he stays locked up."

My heart was broken. My face hurt, so did my ribs. I couldn't talk anymore. Miles sat on the bed next to me, his solid chest a comfort as long nights of sadness, quiet anguish and apathy erupted through loud wails, soft sobs and violently painful ribs. Through it all Miles didn't waver.

It was day ten. Breathing still hurt, and I was bruised all over. The pain meds and thoughts about what I went through had me in a perpetual state of queasiness.

I still hadn't looked in the mirror, insightful Izzy taped a pillowcase over it. I got the feeling I looked like the bride of Frankenstein. I was given a host of antibiotics to treat all manner of infections. My gynaecologist's exam was inconclusive, but George had raped me. That didn't need a doctor's diagnosis.

As I had been unconscious at some point, the assumption by the police was sexual assault had taken place during that time. I didn't correct them. I wasn't ready to talk about that with anyone. Talking about it made it real, and I didn't want to go back to that shed. Not yet. Maybe not ever.

My aunt and uncle returned to London after a week. I had loved seeing them, but it had been a difficult trip.

Dean and Charlie took turns visiting. I welcomed and dreaded their visits. Their appearances without the children reminded me of how bruised I was. Dean was angry and blamed himself for my ever being in Seattle in the first place. Charlie kept me company and looked at decor magazines with me, but I could only concentrate for minutes at a time.

Izzy was still my friend, but she had also become my nurse, my doctor, my voice, an all-round mother hen as she constantly hovered over me.

Miles was my other constant. For the first five days I was in hospital, he didn't leave my room and slept in the chair next to me. Every time I woke up and opened my eyes, he was awake with a comforting smile and sips of water.

He brought me different chef-prepared soups every day and during the moments he wasn't with me, he sent heartfelt messages. When he was with me, he made me feel beautiful, though I didn't look it. The thought of his touch, replacing the vile one left on me, was what I held onto. I imagined his reverent touch on me. His lustful gaze, his lips and his powerful body, which knew how to love me. I fell in love with him in my hospital bed. I couldn't tell him then. I suspected it was my vulnerability that made me feel that way.

He arrived with a soft cheesy pasta, which he insisted on feeding me, even though both my hands worked perfectly.

"I think my taste buds are getting back to normal. This is delicious." I still wasn't able to open my mouth fully, but the meal slid down my throat easily.

"I'll be sure to let Fernando know. Have your doctors talked to you about going home?"

"Not yet, but I'm going stir-crazy in here. There's a small complication, but I want to leave in the next two days."

"What's the complication?" His worried look broke me. I shouldn't have said anything. His inquiring mind would want to understand.

"I've got aspiration pneumonia." And to confirm that diagnosis, I was racked by a coughing fit which made my broken ribs scream.

"I didn't realise there were different types. What's special about this one?" He asked, handing me tissue from the box next to me. I discreetly looked at what I had just coughed up and sweet Miles averted his eyes, to give me that moment. *Thankfully no more blood.*

Note to self: Keep it simple and spare Miles from too much detail.

"I have this one because of something I inhaled," I added quietly. I hoped he would take the hint and drop the subject.

"Do you know what you inhaled? Would it still be in your lungs? How do the doctors get it out?"

"My own vomit," I said quickly. Hoping, somehow, he wouldn't hear me.

"What? How?" He was pained, with a searching look on his face.

"It's hard to explain. I just want to go home. I've already been on antibiotics through the IV and another two days of them is all I need," I whispered.

"I want you to come and live with me, so I can take care of you." That took me by surprise, and I was bewildered. *Why was I terrified?*

"Are you asking me to move in with you? You told me I was safe." I felt a tightness in my chest as my heart thudded wildly. The hospital room became smaller, while Miles became bigger.

"You are safe from him. He won't be seeing the light of day. Not in this life," he said with conviction. No one knows that for certain, how can he be sure? "The prosecutor can talk to you and answer questions you have." I didn't need to talk to more people and answer more questions. The questions after this ordeal were half the reason I was exhausted.

"No need, I understand what you've already told me," I conceded weakly.

"But I want you to move in with me," he said, softly, as if he was afraid to break me. *I am already broken.*

"Can we have this conversation when I'm better?" My breathing had become uneven and my words choppy.

"I thought the natural progression of our thing would be you and I moving in together." His tone was encouraging.

"It is, but not in the next two days. Please understand." From nowhere tears filled my eyes, and I was petrified. That should have brought me comfort, instead it filled me with dread. I had been to Mercer plenty of times when Maxie was out. I loved it. This was different. I felt different.

"I didn't mean to upset you. I'm sorry," he whispered, with a worried smile.

I shook my head and smiled at him, a small smile, which didn't hurt my face. "I'm not upset, I don't know if I'm even thinking straight."

"Why wouldn't you be? What's on your mind?"

"It's not just you and me. You have Maxie. How would we explain the way I look to her?"

"She would understand that a bad man did this," he said, trying to convince me.

"She's been through a lot and doesn't need more examples of how terrible the world can be. I want to be at my best when she and I have our second debut." I hoped he believed me. I wanted to believe me too.

"And this is all about Maxie?" he asked softly, looking at the tears swimming in my eyes.

I willed them not to fall, but they let me down, one teardrop at a time. As he had become used to, Miles held me close and let me cry on his chest. His clean scent was a comfort. It took away the scent from the greenkeeper's shed, which overpowered me when I least expected it to.

The tears rolled down my face freely as I wondered if I would ever get over what happened. If every little thing would continue to set me off. If I had been reduced to a bag of nerves. If all Miles was good for would be an eternal shoulder to cry on. After what felt like hours, he created some space between us and looked at me with a smile, one which would ordinarily melt me.

"There's no need to be overwhelmed. I won't pressure you, but I'm insisting on sending you Fernando so he can cook for you, and someone to help you around the house." He was being generous, and I wouldn't continue to turn down every kind offer he made.

"I would love that. I don't think I could tie my own shoes, even if I wanted to."

"Moving to Mercer with us is an open invitation. You are welcome there whenever you want. Maxie and I would tie your shoes all day if you wanted us to. Although velcro is also an option."

"Don't make me laugh, it's too painful." He tried to make light of my meltdown and gave me a wide berth, but he expected us to talk. Would I ever be ready? I wanted to heal my body before I could think about healing my mind. "Do you remember what we talked about when you first came to see me after this happened?"

"That's been handled. Don't want you to worry about that, and no other copies exist anywhere else." We held hands and talked about everything except the most important thing.

Miles looked at me as if he knew what was going through my mind. "Babe." He had never called me that before, and my heart skipped a beat.

"Yes. Babe?" My interest piqued.

"I love you and I want you to feel better soon, in every way. I want us to talk, but you are reluctant to talk to me, and that's okay. But you need to talk to someone."

"You love me?" I was still reeling from his declaration of love.

"I do, with all that I am," he said with sincerity.

"Even after everything that's happened to me?" The thumping returned to my chest again.

"That has no bearing on my feelings for you. I fell in love with you over the Sierra Nevada mountains, and nothing can take away from that."

"What did I do in that chopper, so I can do it again? Perhaps you can keep falling every day, over and over." I put on the charm but didn't feel an ounce of it. Instead, my heart was heavy, and my soul was weary.

"You were just you. That's all you ever need to be." I decided not to make light of what he said by parroting a declaration to him. I was certain I loved him too. I moved my lips closer to him and kissed him softly. Although my face hurt, I gave him another small smile.

"My sister-in-law gave me a recommendation for a therapist. She's discreet and can visit at home. Will you call her? To help you and to help us?"

"I will."

Note to self: I won't. I don't feel like talking, especially to a stranger.

He handed me a card and I recognised the name. She was highly regarded and respected in her field. I wouldn't argue with Miles, already my honesty had nearly taken me back inside that shed.

Chapter
Twenty-Four

Miles

I was hopelessly in love with Cara, and I wanted to shout it from the rooftops. I had been in love before, but not like this. She was hesitant to talk about her ordeal with me. She had shut down and shut me out, pretending to be upbeat. I wasn't fooled. Dean and Charlie told me the same. She wouldn't live with them either and preferred to be in her own house.

Her doctors warned that healing would take time, but I was impatient to have her back. I hadn't expected her to tell me that she loved me too, although I suspected she did. Alistair made the arrangements for an in-home nurse and a housekeeper, and Fernando continued to prepare meals for her.

The arrangement in place for Vivian's visitations was grating. She tried to get attention from me in any way she could. I refused to play her game and to be involved when she spent time with Maxie. Instead, my mother was present during the visits. Vivian would call me after every visit, pleading to see me at the next one. I told her each time I was unavailable to her indefinitely. Eventually, she stopped calling, but I suspected she was regrouping.

Two days after I told Cara I was in love with her, she left the hospital to go home. When I arrived at her house, Dean was leaving after helping her to get settled in. The bruising to her face and arms had become lighter, and the swelling improved. I tried to kiss her again when I arrived. Again, she recoiled, and I decided to broach the subject.

"Cara, why won't you let me kiss you?"

"I don't know," she barely whispered.

"Do you want to talk about it?"

"I do but I don't think I can, not to you." Only a few short weeks ago we were able to talk to each other about everything. I was angry at the stranger who came between us and stole from us.

"Do you trust me?"

"I do."

"What's on your mind?" She was silent for a while, fighting to come up with the right words to say.

"I'm terrified about how you see me now." Her shame and sadness were clear to see. What she didn't realise was she was still the woman who was out of my league.

"My perception is that you're healing, you're still a little sore, you're a little sad but the woman I have a thing with, and who I'm crazy about, is right here with me."

The tears which she held back came thick and fast. She cried all the tears she could cry while I held her. She cried until she fell asleep, and I carried her to bed. I got undressed and slid into the bed with her, but I couldn't fall asleep. Nothing I tried could give her comfort. I wasn't enough for her, not then. She needed more. *Should I call the therapist now?*

Sometime in the middle of the night, she was sobbing again, this time in her sleep. She let me hold her. By the time I woke up in the morning, she was gone from the bed and where she lay was cold. *She must have been up for hours.* I made a call to the therapist, then went in search of her and found her in the kitchen.

"Good morning." I moved closer to her and kissed her. This time she didn't flinch. Much. I felt some of the tension from my sleepless night start to leave me.

"Imagine my surprise when I saw the heartthrob in my bed this morning," she said and smiled sweetly.

Relief. *I missed her.* She was still guarded, but pretended it was a usual morning.

I chose to humour her. "Was he everything you imagined he would be?

"And so much more. Thank you for staying with me," she murmured. I needed to, so I kissed her again, and it was still a chaste kiss. "Did you get any sleep?"

"A little," I admitted. I hadn't slept much as I listened to her sob in her sleep.

"Where did you tell Maxie you were? She must be missing you for breakfast."

"I told her I would be with you." All I wanted was to hold her, like I would whenever we were lucky enough to wake up together.

"Does she know about us?" she asked, surprised.

"Not all the specifics, but she knows I've met someone special."

"You're special to me too, Miles," she said as she wrapped her arms around *her* body, the one I needed closer to me.

"Last night was difficult for me, Cara. I felt helpless. I guess it was difficult for you too." I tried to ease us into the difficult conversation.

"Being there for me helped, and you made my first night home bearable. It would have been a million times worse if you weren't with me."

"Good to know, but you need more than I can give you. I made the decision for you, and I've called the therapist. She'll be here at twelve." For the first time ever, I was forceful, and I had gone over her head. It needed to be done, and I was the one to do it.

She gasped. "I don't know if I'm ready to talk about anything and everything," she stuttered, the tears in her eyes threatening to fall.

She was broken, and her anguish nearly broke me too. Michael was right, how could I have let this happen?

"Talk about what you can. Please. It's still a few more hours yet, if you really don't want to talk to her, I can call her back and cancel," I begged, tucking my knees so my eyes could look into hers.

She took a step back from me, sighed, and then surprised me. "Only on one condition." I loved it when she was like this. It wouldn't last but I would take it when she gave it to me.

"What's that?"

"Can you make your specialty, those soft cheesy scrambled eggs? I don't think I could chew granola or fruit." For the first time since last night, I finally felt useful.

"Sit down, I'll take care of it."

"Do you have to be at work soon?" She sat at her small kitchen island, with a pained expression on her face. She didn't realise as she was pushing me away, she was also pulling me back at the same time.

"Only for a few hours after lunch, then I'll get Maxie from school. She has a ballet recital in the evening. She's Sugar Plum."

For a moment, she appeared and sounded brighter. "She is? I hope she isn't nervous." I placed the breakfast ingredients on the counter and looked at her. She seemed to be the nervous one.

"Not really. If she does well and wants to do another recital, can you come with me and watch her?" I coaxed, trying to gauge what she was thinking and hoping to get her out of her head.

"Maybe when I don't look like I do now," she whispered. "Wouldn't want to give the poor girls and their parents a fright." She looked through me as if I had become invisible.

The playful Cara appeared briefly and just as quickly, she was gone. In her place was the broken version. The one who left me feeling inadequate and racked with guilt. I rounded the counter and sat down next to her.

"You're beautiful and you will heal with time. The fancy German said so." I made a feeble attempt at humour, which she seemed to appreciate. Although tears filled her eyes, she broke into a smile.

"Okay. Let's shut down the pity party and have those eggs," she said and smiled. I wasn't fooled, but I stood up and returned to making breakfast.

Chapter Twenty-Five

Cara

Miles surpassed all the expectations I had of him. Not only had he found George's phone, which had all the recordings taken by George inside my old townhouse, but he also spent all night with me and had even held me. Like him, I had been awake most of the night too.

After breakfast, he ran a bath and poured a bath mousse which I recognised from the spa in California. The scent brought me comfort and a small smile to my face. Miles looked at me and smiled too. *The Pisces I fell for when I least expected to.*

I hadn't considered the bathroom logistics until he started to help me.

"I can undo the buttons." I felt a fresh impulse to push him away.

He wouldn't have any of it and continued to undo them. "I've undone them many times before, why not now?" Like he had been while I was in hospital, he remained persistent and patient while I stood before him, weathered and weary. My body and soul battered and broken.

"It's not the same," I whispered. I barely heard myself. I wondered if I had spoken loud enough for him to hear me.

"We're still the same. You're still mine and I'm yours." He spoke in muted tones while he gently pulled the pyjama top off me. I didn't look at myself, I was afraid to. I imagined my body was an eerie kaleidoscope of colours. Instead I focused on Miles' unflinching gaze. As my tear-filled eyes ran down the length of his face, I didn't miss the tick in his strong jaw and the determined look, and behind his eyes I imagined I read a silent promise.

"Thank you," I whispered while he helped me into the bath. He studied my body and my face carefully, as he had been given instructions to look out for the signs of infection. I'd heard that doctors become the worst patients. I didn't want to be like that so I let him look. My body screamed its reluctance for any intimacy of any sort, and his help was kept strictly to the business of taking a bath.

His phone rang and I nodded for him to answer it. We both needed a break from the intensity of a simple bath.

Alone in the bathroom, the warm water soothed my battered body. The comforting scent calmed my mind and helped me realise talking to a professional might be the tonic I needed for my broken spirit. I made my peace with the therapist's impending visit.

Miles returned some minutes later and helped me get dressed. My wardrobe had been scant since Templeton had turned it into his personal urinal, but while I was in hospital Miles snuck a brand new wardrobe into my house. All the things I would have never bought and never could afford organised as they would be in a chic boutique, on shelving and in cupboards Dean had installed. Had it been any other time, I would have excitedly spent hours trying everything on.

The doorbell chimed, announcing the arrival of the emotional cavalry. Miles smiled reassuringly, kissed my cheek and let Andrea in as he left for work.

When she came inside, I slowly led her into the living room, where she sat on the bluff France and Son swivel chair, which Charlie insisted was perfect for the French country cottage décor I was attempting in suburban Seattle. Charlie believed we got the look right, whereas I just loved my home. I sat on the couch and tried to get comfortable. It still hurt to breathe, and after the bath and getting ready, I felt tired.

"I'm Andrea. I'm glad you've agreed to see me."

"Thank you for coming out here." I wondered if I sounded resilient and resolute, but I didn't dwell on that too long. Honesty was what was called for.

"It's good to get out of the office sometimes," she said. She was cordial and set the stage for me. I still wasn't sure if I could share much with her.

"I was very nervous about this session. I still am. I've never met a psychiatrist who's also a life coach. One is science, and the other is art," I confessed with a shoulder shrug.

"Interesting observation, I never thought about it that way before. I love the clinical aspect of psychiatry, but after I had been doing it for some years, I got the feeling I wasn't realising the full potential of how I could help my patients. At certain stages in their treatment I needed to palm them off to someone else, and now here I am."

"Mmm," I said, as my mind started to drift away.

"You don't agree?" she asked after what felt like long minutes of silence between us.

"I'm sorry, I don't mean to be rude. I think I zoned out for a minute there." I stifled a yawn. I didn't want to come across as bored and uninterested. In reality, all I wanted to do was to stay in the moment.

"Is this something that's happening often, zoning out, losing your concentration?"

"Sometimes, when the conversation develops any type of technical or medical jargon. I feel like I want to switch off from medicine. Forever."

For the first time since her arrival she wrote something down, and I felt like her patient. Had both Templetons succeeded in advancing the loss of my sanity and sense of self? I thought about both men and the impact they'd had on my life, and my shoulders sagged. She smiled a gentle smile.

"Okay, we'll keep this jargon-free. Now, do you think you can tell me what's on your mind?"

"I don't know where to start from," I said hesitantly. I needed to shift my mindset. This wasn't about the Templetons, it was about me.

"How about I ask you a question?"

"Sure."

"Why am I here in your home today?" *Psychiatry rotation day 1: Ask open-ended questions.*

Again, I let out a heavy sigh. "Two weeks ago, I was dragged to the depths of hell, by Lucifer himself." I swallowed the beginnings of a sob. I promised myself I wouldn't cry, not until I said all I had to say.

"It won't be easy, Cara, and talking about it could make you feel worse before you feel better, but I would like you to tell me more about that."

Recounting the details of what happened was hard, but in between sobs I was able to push through and tell her.

She gave me a safe space where I felt no judgement or ill will. We spent an hour and a half talking. She taught me relaxation techniques and guided imagery to help me cope. She warned me it would take time and practice.

I was able to laugh and cry. In that hour and a half, she helped me realise I was the victim, not a villain, and I hadn't deserved to be attacked. She was kind, and not once did I zone out.

"This has been productive," she said cheerily. A far cry from the content of our session. "Well done. Before I go, I'll leave you with some homework. I want you to think about what you meant by switching off from medicine forever. I want us to dig deeper into that, not tomorrow or the day after, but sometime."

"Sure, I will. Can you come back here again? Do you think?" I asked hesitantly.

"I can see you tomorrow at three, if that suits you?" I should never have worried about meeting her. Miles was right, I had needed to do this.

When she left, I was spent and took a nap, only waking up when Izzy limped into my foyer with more food to add to the prepared meals in the fridge.

I sat up on the couch and watched as she walked closer. "What happened to you?" I exclaimed, trying not to open my mouth too wide.

She chuckled and winced as she made herself comfortable next to me. "Torn ACL," she said flippantly.

"That's a first, how do *you* have a sports injury? You don't do sports." I snorted and laughed.

She laughed with me until the tears rolled down her cheeks. "I'll have you know, I'm doing Krav Maga, and for the last couple of weeks I *do* it so much, I take it home and *do* it all night, and well into the next day."

My eyes widened as I finally understood. "Blonde Colby? How did you break him? With the serious 'I'm a professional' seriousness he has going on." She giggled at my poor impersonation of our Krav Maga instructor from the gym in Queen Anne.

"That's where you come in, Braithwaite. I didn't mean to, but I was upset about everything, and after his class he asked why I was off. I told him over copious amounts of alcohol, and one thing led to another."

I smiled and meant it. "The big guy took advantage of your vulnerability. Not very original, is it?"

"Being taken advantage of is underrated." We both giggled.

"Still doesn't quite explain the torn ACL, but at this stage it feels safer if you don't explain in technicolour."

"A good rogering was in order. You'll see what I mean when you're feeling up to it," she said softly with a small smile.

I let out a half-hearted chuckle. "Rogering? You say all the cutest things, but I'm finding myself a tad revolting, and something tells me Miles might be too."

"You should know better than that. There's nothing revolting about you," she reassured me.

"My head tells me you're right, but it's how I feel," I said quietly, as everything stopped and I momentarily returned to the greenkeeper's shed.

"I'm sorry you feel that way, it will pass. Try not to push him away."

"I'm not pushing him away, I can't have him too close right now. I imagine Miles can smell him on me. I can still smell him on me."

She shuffled closer and sniffed. Smiling indulgently, she said, "Actually, you smell like a rose garden. Takes me all the way to Grasse on that trip we took in the sixth form. What's that scent you're wearing? I love it."

"Apparently it has two hundred and fifty roses in one bottle. It's by Kurkdjian," I said, trying to roll my eyes. I wasn't sure it was possible with the state my face was in.

"Braithwaite, did you just roll your eyes? Allow me to write that down, for posterity," she chuckled. I was already smiling, she always had a way of taking me out of my head. "How did this Kurk person juice two hundred and fifty roses? Like your new wardrobe, it sounds like an expensive undertaking. Did the heartthrob get it for you?"

"He did. I wouldn't spend so much on such a small thing."

"Oh dear, someone sounds like they are still offended by wealth. I blame the toffs at school." She shook her head, moved some hair out of my face, and studied its state.

"I don't know, it's ..." I trailed off.

"Miles would never say this, and I bet he would kill me if he knew I told you. But did you know - that most offensive wealth bought you a most priceless gift?" She sighed as tears filled her eyes.

My own tears ran down my face as it occurred to me. I had a great health insurance plan, but it wasn't good enough to fly the eminent plastic surgeon Karoline Neumann to work on me. "I'm a brat, perhaps an ungrateful one," I whispered.

Mother hen returned. "Of course not, but here's some unsolicited advice: Don't let your imaginary relationship with wealth get in the way of your actual relationship with the most authentic man you'll ever meet."

"How are you so wise?"

She tapped her temple. "I studied under the best dons, don't you know? Well, here's this for a wise idea. When you're feeling up to it, and my knee isn't the size of a granny smith, we're having a spa day."

"Izzy. What do you know? Is this your way of telling me I need a thorough grooming?"

She laughed. "Between you and me, I'm the one in need of one." She was working hard to make me smile, and it was working.

"You're my favourite person to laugh and cry with. Thanks for coming to see me. We'll have that spa day soon. Before you go, can you unhook my bra?"

"Braithwaite, you're really pushing the boundaries of this friendship. I'll unhook you. Then I need to feed you, and tonight it's you and me. I'll be in Finn and Ava's room. My starfish might hurt you if I'm in your bed."

"You're staying the night? I love a sleepover. And Colby?" I'd always craved my own space, but I was grateful she was spending the night. I couldn't bear to be alone with my thoughts.

"He loves a sleepover, too, but not tonight. I need to give the knee the right kind of elevation," she said and giggled.

After dinner and helping me to get settled in my bed, she went to sleep in Finn and Ava's bedroom.

When I woke up sometime in the middle of the night, Izzy was in my bed with her arms around me. We both didn't sleep, as the nightmares had been unrelenting. My screams woke us both. I still wouldn't take the Valium or the Xanax, not even the gentle Melatonin. I begrudgingly agreed to chamomile tea so I wouldn't seem so petulant.

It had been six weeks of hopping on and off a roller coaster of emotions. In the first week of our meeting, Andrea visited me daily and we both worked hard. After my first week of therapy, we saw each other twice weekly. The previous week I visited her practice, driven by Clay, who kept our conversation light.

I could see the pity in his eyes, and I suspected he read the police report. I never asked Miles for the specifics about George's phone, but my guess would be Clay was the one he sent for it. I wanted to thank him for that. One day I would find the right words.

I had the spa date with Izzy, and I looked like my old self. The bruising and discolouration completely disappeared. My ribs were still sore when I took a deep breath or stretched, but my face and nose in their perfection were the canvas to Doctor Neumann's Mona Lisa. Dean joked that the new nose was an upgrade. He put my fragility aside and started to treat me like his little sister again.

Miles never wavered. He spent many nights with me, and those seemed to be the most difficult times. He never tried to make love to me, and that was a relief. Although my body felt normal and healed, I couldn't bring myself to think about being close with Miles in that way. I couldn't understand why he would still want me.

Chapter Twenty-Six

♥

Miles

Cara's physical recovery was quicker than I expected. She looked like her old self again. Yet, she was still not Cara. She was withdrawn and had trouble sleeping, plagued by constant nightmares. She wouldn't take sedatives, not even for one night of relief. She worried about becoming dependent on them. I spent many nights in her bed, but she was reluctant to spend nights in mine. I needed to take her somewhere, even just for a weekend, to get her mind off things and for a change of scene. On a late Friday afternoon, I arrived at her house with the jet fuelled and ready.

"Hi, beautiful."

"You're too sweet to me, and you want something don't you?" She smiled a big smile.

Could she really be back? I walked closer to her.

"Yes, there's something I want." I pulled her closer to me. She didn't flinch, but she was still delicate, and walking the tightrope of her emotions was a fine balancing act. My heart hammered in my chest as the air was squeezed from my lungs. I couldn't tell her how much I longed for her, longed to have her back in all the ways I still couldn't.

"What would that be?" She brought both her arms around my neck.

Progress – today was a good day.

"To take you to the coast just for the weekend, you'll love it." It didn't take long before her arms dropped to her sides and her demeanour changed. Her voice trembled, as did her body. This had the makings of a panic attack. I had become familiar with those.

"What do you want from me? I can't give you what you want. What will it take for you to understand that?" She was on the brink of tears. My plan quickly turned on its head.

I kept my voice even. "It's just a trip to get away for a little while. You've been cooped up in here for too long and I want to take you away. It's what you love."

"I know what your trips are all about. I thought you would give me time, but instead you're thinking with your small head." She walked away and slammed the bathroom door in my face.

I stood helpless on the other side as I listened to her sob and whimper. How could the most confident and fun-loving woman I had ever met be reduced to being afraid of going away with me?

"Cara, open the door. Let's talk."

"I can't, the pressure from you is too much. The last time we went on a trip, we didn't leave the suite. We didn't sleep either. I can't give you what you want. Don't you see that!" She wailed. I had no choice but to talk through the door.

"Listen. I have no motives, except to take you somewhere different and spend some time with you outside of this house. I only want to make you happy, show you some places I think you would like, that's all."

"I don't believe you." Her sobs became louder on the other side of the bathroom door.

"Okay, we won't go anywhere. Open the door, and we'll cook something together. You can show me another one of your mother's favourites – please?" I begged, while I sent a message to my pilot, cancelling the trip which would never be.

Silence.

"If you prefer, we can watch a movie – something with the old British guy you like so much?"

Silence.

I sat outside her door for an hour, and she didn't move. I considered taking the door off its hinges, but that was her shield. From me. Begrudgingly, I accepted that.

I had done everything I was supposed to. I was patient, attentive and understanding. She was right, I longed to make love to her and have her melt in my arms, but I could wait until she was ready. The trip wasn't about that. It was also for me. I was drained from the demands of having to be strong for her when I was broken too.

After a while, I heard a rustling behind the door.

Relief.

Until she called out to me softly. "Miles, are you still there?"

"I am. Are you ready to come out?"

"Yes, but only if you leave. I want to be alone tonight."

I would never give up on her, but tonight I had given it everything I could.

When I got home last night, it was still early, and the nanny was pleased when she finally got a rare night off. Maxie took advantage of my presence and excitedly filled me in on *Prince Caspian,* which she was reading with Michael and his family, the nanny and even Vivian during their visits. I wondered how much I could keep pouring into Cara, while being neglectful of everything and everyone else in my life.

As Maxie gave me a thorough and detailed account of the rightful heir of Narnia, and how he took his duties and his birthright with the utmost seriousness, my own dereliction of duties occurred to me. I was only one man, and it was finally time to bring my two most important worlds together.

After an early morning swim in the basement with Maxie, my mother arrived to spend the court-stipulated family time with Vivian and Maxie. Vivian would arrive at nine o'clock and they would be together until lunchtime, giving me three hours at HQ to catch up with work. Although it was a Saturday, it was necessary. Michael had been carrying my workload for too long.

Today would be the day Maxie, Cara and I spend together for the first time, the way I wanted us to. Cara wouldn't turn me away if I took Maxie with me to see her. It might even do Cara some good to get out of her own head.

Chapter
Twenty-Seven

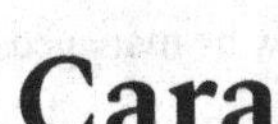

Cara

Although the breakdown last night had been a jolt, I was able to sleep better than I had since the attack. When I woke up, I had more clarity than I had in weeks. My body was healed, I was alive and I needed my control back. I needed to focus on my friends and family who helped rescue my mind and my body. First I needed to see Miles, to apologise for last night. He planned a sweet surprise, and I hadn't seen it for what it was.

On the occasions I had been to Miles' home, we drove together, or Clay did. Today, I would drive my Mini and make my own way. Being a Saturday, Maxie would also be at home. That is what Miles had been asking from me for a while, for us to come out of the shadows to everyone important to him. I was ready, and I felt strong enough.

After a self-indulgent and luxurious bath, I wore pink. Today was the day for it. The weather was slowly changing and it was a beautiful spring day. The dress was perfect, with a sweetheart neckline, sitting an inch or two above the knees. Both father and daughter would be impressed. As I made my way over the bridge towards Mercer, I was excited and considered calling Miles. I decided against it, as that would've spoiled the surprise.

I arrived at the house I had come to love. Large, loved and well curated. with the restrained electric gates, which, despite never using it myself, I remembered the gate code – a six-digit hybrid of Miles' and Maxie's birthdays. When the gate opened, a light thud started in my chest, until I stopped in the circular driveway that led to the welcoming walnut front door.

It always left me awed how he managed to create an inviting, warm and almost cosy home from a house so large and imposing from the outside. I had been here only a handful of times when we both needed each other and needed to know each other in the only way a man and a woman need to sometimes. *Will we ever know each other that way again?*

When I got to the door, the fingerprint entry with its flashing red light silently mocked me. I had to ring the doorbell. I didn't need to wait long before Maxie's grandmother appeared.

"Cara, this is a lovely surprise," she gushed, giving me a warm embrace. "Does Miles know you're coming?" I heard a sudden edge to her tone, which I couldn't place. Could I have overstepped some boundary?

"Just a Saturday morning surprise," I said, staying close to her. She was, as I remembered, warm, elegant and looked too young to be a grandmother of three.

"You look beautiful. I'm happy to see you looking well. If I didn't know better, I would have thought you were a figment of Miles' imagination," she said, tears filling her eyes. "Come in, although it's best you wait for him in his office." *Why?* Miles said I was welcome at his home anytime, could I have misunderstood? Although Chris was welcoming, she was uneasy.

I walked in and started towards his office when I heard a shrill voice. "Doctor Cara, you're at my house," Maxie screamed as she ran into the foyer and wrapped her arms around my waist. Her welcome brought tears to my eyes and a burst of warmth in my chest.

"Yes, I'm here. How are you?" I couldn't temper my own excitement, as hers was infectious. I was just as happy to see her and noticed how much she had grown in the ten months since I first met her.

"My head got better, look," she said, moving her dark hair out of the way.

"Good and there's no scar. What are you doing?"

"My mommy and I are decorating cupcakes. Do you want one?" she asked excitedly.

That was why Chris was trying to quickly usher me into Miles' office. Saturday morning, one of Maxies's twice weekly visitation days with her mother.

"That sounds yummy. Can you save one for me, and I can have it later?" I heard the unmistakable slow tap of approaching stilettos on the warm oak floors.

I looked away from Maxie and came face to face with the most striking woman I had ever seen.

In her heels she was easily six feet tall, her olive skin was flawless, and her short, cropped hairstyle showcased a long neck which gave her an air of elegance. Although it was her large, expressive, vivid blue eyes boring into me that were most remarkable against her light brown skin. The daughter of a beauty queen from Caracas who survived only a few hours after childbirth, and American royalty. "The Lost Tycoon of Washington," I had read. She had been a sometimes model and fashion designer but mostly socialite, until she stole the hearts of two of Washington's most eligible bachelors.

"Who's this?" she asked, in a tone deceptively cheerful, and looked between me and Maxie, who still had an arm around me.

"This is Doctor Cara, she glued my head when I fell, and she's very pretty," she said with a childlike and innocent sparkle.

"Yes, the prettiest. Hi, Doctor Cara. I'm Vivian Masterson. Maxie's mother. You're Maxie's doctor? Is she still sick?" She held out her dainty hand, which I shook.

"Far from it, she's perfectly healthy." I smiled and was as polite as can be. It was their time together, and I didn't want to cause too much upset.

"Yet you're here with all your prettiness on a house call, wearing Alexander McQueen. Straight off the runway." She narrowed her eyes, and her cocked head made her neck look even longer at that angle. Nothing could have ever prepared me for her sass.

"I'll get out of your way and wait in Miles' office," I said with what I hoped was an unaffected tone.

"Join us for cupcakes. We've got plenty to share, don't we Maxie?" She sounded sincere, but the looks she threw my way were hard to miss.

"Viv, if you take Maxie back into the kitchen, I'll see to Cara," Chris offered with charm, perfectly diffusing the rising tension. Highly skilled in diplomacy, she must have found herself in many awkward situations, as she didn't miss a beat.

"It was good to meet you, Doctor Cara," Vivian said, giving me the once-over, one more time.

"You, too, umm ..."

"Mrs Masterson, to you," she retorted.

"Right, Mrs Masterson," I muttered as I made my way to Miles' main floor office.

That wasn't how I imagined today would go. Miles and I kept our relationship low profile and inconspicuous. It wouldn't take the former Mrs Masterson long to read between the lines and realise Miles and I were together. She already may have, given the frosty reception. Knowing what little I did about her, I wondered if she would use it against Miles in their custody saga? Would she ever use it against me?

While I was at home, feeling sorry for myself with a broken face and a broken body, she had been otherworldly and every man's fantasy. She had called herself Mrs Masterson – could she and Miles have rekindled their flame? It was a possibility, I hadn't been a real girlfriend for a while and Miles was passionate and tireless. It wouldn't be the first time I lost a man I was in love with to another woman.

I hadn't been waiting long with my thoughts when I heard Miles arrive home. Within a few minutes he walked through the office door and shut it softly behind him.

"This is a surprise," he said with a wide grin.

"It was a good idea, until I realised I intruded on Maxie's visit with her mother. I'm sorry, I should have called first," I apologised and met him at the door.

"Don't apologise, I'm happy you're here." He let his eyes openly rove up and down my body. He held me close, and I breathed him in properly, for the first time in a long time. I missed him, and I missed us.

"You look ravishing, I still can't believe you're mine, and on my little island," he whispered.

"I'm sorry about last night, I don't know what came over me. I don't think I've ever thrown a tantrum like that before."

"Long forgotten. You seem different today, much happier, brighter.
"

"It's a new day, but we've got time to talk. Mrs Masterson might need you in there." I offered a small smile.

"No need to call my mother that, her name's Chris, or Mom, if you prefer," he said, beaming.

"The other Mrs Masterson, at least that's how she wants *me* to address her. Still a little proprietary. Are you and her on the same page, or even reading the same book? Or am I the confused one?" I groaned inwardly. I sounded hopelessly needy, my confidence had suffered a real blow.

He held my chin in his hand and whispered softly, "You're not confused about anything. You're the woman in my life, the one who races through my thoughts night and day." Just as his lips touched mine, Maxie burst into his office.

"Do you want a cupcake?" she asked excitedly.

"Yes, we'll have one. Will you say goodbye to your mommy?" He reluctantly let me go.

"I already have. Daddy, is your pulse broken?" His arms fell to his side as he regarded Maxie.

"My pulse? Do you mean my heart?"

"I mean your pulse. Mommy told her friend on her phone Doctor Cara came to feel your pulse." He kept calm, despite the angry look that momentarily flashed across his face.

"Beautiful, what did we say about eavesdropping on adult conversations?"

"But Daddy, they are such fun," she quipped, until she saw the stern look on his face. "You said not to."

"I need to tell you something, Maxie. Sit next to me." He patted the plush couch. He looked at me and smiled, and I looked at him expectantly.

"Tell me, are you sick?"

"I'm not sick. Doctor Cara is my girlfriend, and she's here to see you and me." He smiled his irresistible dimpled smile. Miles and I had defined our relationship, and we were both aware of what we were to each other, but hearing him take ownership of us, even to an eight-year-old, made my insides turn somersaults.

"She is? Can I show her my room? Do you want to see my room, Doctor Cara?" she asked with wide eyes, then held her hand out to me.

"I do," I said with a chuckle, both surprised and humoured at her non-reaction to her father's announcement and being more interested in giving me a tour of her room.

As the three of us walked out of Miles' office, we came face to face with Chris, who was preparing to leave. She smiled brightly as she donned her coat, then looked at me, her voice taking a motherly tone.

"I'm so sorry. About everything. How are you feeling?"

"Much better, thank you." I willed the tears filling my eyes not to fall. When did the tears stop? I wasn't crying, but they had a mind of their own.

"I'm happy you've come today. I've wanted to come and see you for a long time, but Miles has been like a guard dog." Not only had Miles inherited her eyes, he also had her compassion.

"I haven't been in a good place for visitors, but it's getting easier now."

"That's wonderful, and if you're feeling up to it, come to mine for lunch, although I don't cook as well as you do. I loved the tortellini from last week."

"You had that? I always make too much. I'm pleased you enjoyed it. I'll be in touch about lunch," I said with my eyes still glazed with tears. Her kindness was overwhelming.

"Sure, baby steps," she said softly, looking up at Maxie who left the adults talking and was at the other end of the foyer.

"Okay, kids, I'm off to see the twins. Anyone else coming with me?" She spoke louder, looking over at Maxie.

"Thanks, Mom, not today. Maxie will spend the rest of the day with us." *We are an us.* I shouldn't have had doubts when 'Mrs Masterson' showed her teeth.

"Great plan. It was good to see you again, Cara. Miles, walk the old lady to her car." She smiled as her eyes lit up.

"Grandma, you're not old, you don't even have a stick." Maxie came closer and kissed her grandmother. As soon as Miles and Chris walked out of the front door, Maxie smiled at me.

"Come, Doctor Cara, my room's upstairs." She took my hand in her small one and led me upstairs. "That's my daddy's room, and that used to be my little sister's room, and that's the twins' room when they stay over, and that can be your room when you stay over. There are more rooms in the basement," she said without stopping to take a breath. When I first met her as a patient, I thought she was delightful, now I was smitten.

I made a show of enjoying the tour. I didn't want to let on that I'd seen the house before nor did I have the heart to correct her about my own room when I stayed over. I left that awkward conversation to Miles.

She led me into her room, which had been redecorated with pink and purple calm tones since I last saw it. She now had a low white desk too, and I smiled when I remembered Miles telling me her current obsession was homework.

"I love the colours in your room, they are beautiful," I gushed.

"I picked all the colours. And grandma got that lilac light from Chihuly where they do the glassblowing. Do you know it?"

"I think I've heard about it, but I haven't been there before."

"It's such fun. I like it. What's your favourite colour?"

"I love all shades of blue." I automatically reached for my pendant until I remembered it was lost forever, the one thing which made me feel closest to my mother

While Maxie showed me around, she asked a lot of questions.

"Have you fixed someone's head like you did mine? And saved their life? Is it fun saving lives?"

"Yes, I have fixed some heads, some sore throats, too, and saved some lives." I couldn't help chuckling, Maxie was a delight. "What have you been doing since I last saw you?"

"I've won two medals at swimming, and I was Sugar Plum at ballet."

"You have kept yourself very busy. When do you get time to play?"

"I play every day with my friends, but I don't have a puppy, not anymore." She hung her head dramatically.

"Why? What happened to your puppy?"

"He ran away when we moved here from my old house. My daddy looked everywhere and my uncle put up signs with a reward, but he never came back."

"He didn't? I'm sorry."

Note to self: Ask Miles if Maxie would like a new puppy, I've always wanted one too.

She showed me her favourite books, her swimming medals and photos she had of everyone important to her. She had plenty of friends and seemed well-adjusted. She spent a lot of time with her uncle and his family, and she was taken with her aunt. We spent a good part of an hour together, and I realised not once during that time did I think about what happened to me. Before we left her room, she took me by surprise.

"Doctor Cara, do you love my daddy?"

I smiled at her and gave her a truthful answer. "Yes, I do, with all my heart."

"That means I love you too," she said, then threw her arms around my neck.

Her sweet declaration brought tears to my eyes for the second time that day. We left her room hand in hand and found Miles in the living room with a big smile on his face.

"Does anyone feel like going to the aquarium?"

"Yes, Daddy, me."

"Okay, get some shoes on. Something sensible, then we'll go."

Once we were left alone, he pulled me closer to him.

"I'm sorry about Vivian. Thank you for keeping it civil and shielding Maxie from a front door showdown."

"No need to thank me. It was their quality time, and I didn't want to detract from it. Maxie wasn't too bothered when you told her about you and me." I smiled and leaned into him. I closed my eyes, and for a moment allowed myself to be truly with him. Like I hadn't allowed myself to be for weeks.

"Don't let her fool you, she's a thinker. As we speak, she's consolidating all she's learned today. Then tomorrow, and perhaps the rest of the month, there will be an inquisition."

"Okay, it's a good thing you give great interviews and have all the answers," I said.

"The complex ones, I'll defer to you. Is the aquarium okay? I'm sorry, I should have asked you first."

"It will be fine, I'm sure," I reassured him. It would be my first excursion since the night at the golf course, and a first with Maxie and Miles. Before yesterday, I would have been self-conscious in public, but now I finally felt comfortable in my own skin.

"I love you with all my heart, too, and thank you for being kind to my Maxie," he said as he picked up a cube of decorative marble from the coffee table. I was puzzled, until he said, "This is a monitor."

"Like a baby monitor? I would never have guessed. It blends into the décor." I loved Miles' home from the first time I stepped inside it. "Although we need to talk about eavesdropping on girls' conversations," I said and giggled.

"But they are such fun," he said with a laugh. "I'm surprised Maxie found out how you feel about me before I did," he added softly, gazing at me.

"You're right. I should have told you first. I'll just follow her upstairs and take it all back, shall I?" I smiled, pushing myself up from the soft couch.

"No, stay. I can't believe you're this close to me. I've missed you," he whispered, turning into me and kissing, nipping and sucking the junction of my neck and shoulder just the way I liked him to, his new stubble tickling me and sending signals to my core. I saw then how much I had missed the little things. His touch, his mouth on my body, his tongue laving all over me, him inside me, fast or slow until I felt his warmth inside me. I especially missed how he sounded when he reached his peak. I turned my body towards his.

"I'm in love with you, and if I could shout it to the world I would. I never imagined I would fall as deeply as I've fallen for you." He didn't let me finish as he took my bottom lip between his teeth. I pulled him closer where I wanted him, and we fed into our needy and hungry kisses for long minutes. I moaned against his lips, then felt him still and break our kiss.

"Are those the most sensible shoes you could find?" He turned to Maxie, who had been standing over us.

Reluctantly, we let go of each other, as Miles held out his hand, inviting Maxie to join us on the couch.

"That was a big kiss, Daddy. A really big one."

"It was, I love Doctor Cara. Let's make a deal."

"With money?" she squealed.

"No, no money, Maxie." He chuckled, looking at her with what I was sure was all the love he possessed. "If you see me give her a big kiss, you don't watch like you were doing just now."

She sighed before she expertly changed the subject. "My shoes look just like Doctor Cara's." Miles groaned.

"I suppose they do, but how will I carry both of you when you start to complain that your feet hurt?"

"You're strong enough, those biceps aren't for decoration," I said, in a fit of giggles. Maxie and I held hands and walked behind Miles towards the car.

The trip to the aquarium was the most fun I'd had in a long time. Heels were not sensible shoes, and Maxie and I decided we wouldn't wear them out to the aquarium again. As we sat and enjoyed an early dinner at The Capital Grille, I realised I needed to get out of my head and start living again.

Chapter Twenty-Eight

♥

Miles

Cara and I enjoyed the day we spent with Maxie, but I needed to get her alone. She needed to talk, but she couldn't, not with Maxie's eager ears clinging to every word. I could sense this every time we held hands and she would squeeze mine a little tighter, in the tender looks she gave me when she thought I was distracted with Maxie, and every now and then when she bit her lip with a thoughtful look on her face. That would all have been lost on anyone else but I was in tune with her, more than she knew.

After our day at the aquarium, Maxie begrudgingly stayed on Mercer with the nanny, while I followed Cara home. When we arrived, she went to her bedroom and changed clothes. I wanted to follow her, but I still wasn't sure what barriers there were between us when we were alone. She came back dressed in workout gear, and it reminded me how her soft curves were still off limits to me.

"Can we go out? I want to take you somewhere," she said with a haunted look in her eyes. This had to be serious. "We could walk, but driving is quicker."

When we left, she directed me to drive towards a gym, the one she had come from when she was attacked. She held my hand as I drove, and she seemed comforted. She had a serene look on her face, but I wasn't fooled. Her inner turmoil was wrapped up in her tense shoulders, her tapping right foot and the way she kept biting her lower lip. When we stopped in the deserted parking lot, she was hyperaware and kept looking around.

"Cara, you're safe," I whispered, and she gave me a forced smile and a quick nod and beckoned me out of the car.

"This is the route which I would walk after the gym. It's very pretty at dusk, and the golf course makes it perfect."

"I wish I had been with you. It would never have happened."

"Tonight's not about that, don't be harsh on yourself." Our roles were reversed, and she was reassuring *me*.

I held her trembling hand and we walked along the track in silence. As we came closer to a bend she stopped and looked at me. The tears shone in her eyes as she spoke hoarsely.

"How much do you want to hear about that night? It's burned into my memory, and when I sleep, it's all I see. That night was awful. My logical mind kept telling me to do something to help myself, but I was weak, and beaten. All I did was call on angels and saints, mythical beings, anything to rescue me from that shed. I tried to escape into my imagination just to preserve a small part of me."

I looked at her and saw something – a true stoic.

"I want to hear everything you want to tell me." I wasn't sure how much of it I could bear. I hoped she couldn't hear the rapid thud in my chest, as I felt each beat of my heart, and each felt like it would be my last. Is that how she must have felt then, when she was under attack? I felt the slight tremble in her hand and the moisture that had begun to coat her palm. I had the moisture too. Beads of sweat formed on the back of my neck, but I wouldn't let her know I was as destroyed as she was.

"When I came round this bend, I saw him, and he saw me. His gaze was brutal, like he was out for blood. He chased me as I tried to run back towards the gym." Her voice quivered.

"Did you recognise him then?" I stayed strong and tried not to crack. My heart was breaking, just as it had the first time I had seen her in her hospital bed that morning at St Mark's.

"I did, but only as someone I had seen at the gym in Queen Anne, and that one time I told you about, at Pike Place. I ran hard, but he caught up to me and he punched me, right here in the midface. I heard a crack. Blood poured out of my nose, as if a faucet had been turned on. From my ENT rotation, I figured it was a nasal septal fracture. At that time, I thought it was the worst pain I had ever known. Little did I realise, it was a sneak preview of what he had in store for me." She raised her eyebrows and quickly shook her head. I pulled her closer into my arms and held her.

"Please, let me finish. If you keep being so kind, I won't be able to without crying," she said into my chest, while I tried to keep my eyes from hers. I didn't want her to see the tears in my eyes. I hadn't let her see them, now wasn't my time to break.

"I can't help it, I can't believe what you suffered all by yourself that night. I should have been with you." My voice cracked again as I swallowed the large lump in my throat.

"Shhh, this isn't about that. If you keep talking, the grand tour will be cancelled," she continued, her tears wetting my shirt.

We walked in the general direction which he pushed her along. She showed me the shed where he dragged her into and continued his vicious assault. She even explained his motivations. By then, I couldn't help myself as I felt the tears on my face. I wouldn't have imagined hearing what happened to Cara in her own words would rip me apart.

In her bravery, she wanted to go inside the shed, but we couldn't, as it was bolted and had a security lock system to rival any I had ever seen.

"Miles, after he beat me and had me helpless on the cold stone floor, he raped me. I'm ... I'm sorry." Her silent tears became loud heart-rending sobs as her body sagged into mine. She clung to me for long minutes until she eventually stopped.

I should have taken Clay up on his silent offer to end him.

But would that end Cara's suffering?

Would it make her feel whole again?

"None of that was your fault." I held her face in both my hands and hoped the anger and frustration I felt wasn't written on mine.

"You have no idea how guilty and filthy I feel. I'm yours, but I don't know how we'll ever get back to being us."

"You're not filthy, you're mine. I'm yours." I didn't try to hide my tears from her anymore.

"But he just didn't do it to me, he did it to us. Look at us, we don't even touch any more. I'm a nervous wreck, and you're patiently waiting for me to get a grip. I don't know how to make our thing right," she whispered, pointing between the two of us.

"This is a huge step. You trusted me and let me in."

"Do you now understand why I'm not good enough for you anymore?" Her confidence was crushed. Knowing that crushed me too.

"You're mistaken. I'm in love with you, and you're everything I want. You can't let him take away from what we have."

"Are you real? I don't know how you can be understanding. In there, he took something from me, and I don't think I could ever get it back. I'm not the woman I once was. I don't feel like her, and when I look in the mirror, sometimes I don't recognise the reflection staring back at me," she said, the tears rolling down her cheeks unbidden.

"You are still the woman I fell in love with." I wiped her tears with my fingers, wishing I could wipe away everything else too.

"It can't have been easy on you. I was wrapped up in my own feelings, I never once considered how you might have felt about everything. Now I realise when I was attacked, you were too."

"I didn't take care of you like I should have done. I'm angry at myself all the time. Seeing you hurt and hurting, and knowing I could have done better makes me feel less than a man."

"You didn't do this. You did all you could have done. There was no way any of us could have known any of it would happen. Don't blame yourself."

"It's not easy not to," I confessed.

I wouldn't tell her Andrea gave me guidance too. When I felt inadequate and helpless. That was not her cross to bear.

"You said you wanted to take me somewhere?"

"Yes, anywhere."

"Can you take me home, please?"

"Of course."

"I mean to the source, Miles. I need to go to England, just for a while. We can take Maxie with us," she pleaded.

"I'll rearrange some things, then we can go on Tuesday. But we can't take Maxie this time. She's in the middle of school. I try not to disrupt her routine as much as possible."

"I didn't think. You can't leave her alone either," she said and sighed.

"She won't be alone. She'll be with her grandmother, and that's okay."

"Thank you, we'll keep it short, a week or even less." She tried to reason with me, she needn't have. I would fly her to the ends of the earth if it meant I would see a real smile on her face.

"A week's fine. I want to be there with you."

We held hands and walked the rest of the way in silence. When we entered her house, I pulled her closer, our lips colliding in a searing kiss. Even though we were home, alone, all I could do was kiss her. All I wanted was to kiss her. I still had her, and we would make our way back to each other.

"I almost forgot you were the best kisser in the whole city."

"Not good enough. I might need you to keep reminding me for a while."

We kissed over and over. I needed to erase any other touch that had been on her. In twenty four hours she had made greater strides than she had over the last few weeks.

Chapter Twenty-Nine

Cara

The two days before we had to leave came and went quickly. I saw Andrea again. I was fully healed, save for the emotional wounds, and my shattered self-confidence. I went out for a walk along the golf course and faced my demons head-on. Talking to Miles, retracing my steps and telling him what was taken from me that night felt like a huge weight lifted from my shoulders.

It turned into a crisp evening and only a few remaining golfers were brave enough to be on the course. It was hardly golfing weather but I walked around the course. I felt free and unencumbered. In the corner of my eye, I caught two men following me briskly, their suits and ties made their efforts hilarious. I longed to have had them there on the night I needed them.

All the while my work situation played on my mind on a constant loop. Changing specialties to paediatrics was what I needed to do, and it was the right thing at the moment of making the decision. I enjoyed treating children, but inside I knew practising medicine was not my calling anymore.

I wondered if George Templeton, both junior and senior, may be the reason I was second-guessing my career choice. Or could there be other changes going on within my psyche? Andrea and I touched on it during our last session, but I wished for my parents, as I imagined it would be the kind of dilemma I would discuss with them if they were still here.

Early the next morning, Miles arrived at my door, ready for our trip to London. As he loaded my bag into the car, I noticed how different he looked. I had seen him before, but today felt like I was seeing him for the first time.

His dark hair was shorter and newly trimmed, the clean shave gave his jaw more definition. Thick curly eyelashes framed his eyes and I wondered if his thick and tidy eyebrows were professionally groomed. I always thought he was handsome, but today he was on a different plane. He looked darker too. Had he been out to the mountains? On the water? To think? For comfort? I wanted to be the one to comfort him.

"You got a haircut, you look very handsome."

"I couldn't have the Brits thinking we are uncivilised across the pond."

"Noone would ever doubt how civilised you are, Miles. Was Maxie okay this morning?"

"She's never cried whenever I go away, but today she did. She wanted to come too and have afternoon tea at the 'Ritzy.'"

"The Ritzy huh? I wish she could have come too, I really do."

"There will be a next time." Hope bloomed within me. Miles was looking ahead to the future, our future.

We arrived at Boeing Field, where the jet was ready. This time there were two pilots, who introduced themselves in the hangar.

"Where are we landing?" It hadn't occurred to me to tell Miles where in England I wanted to go.

"Luton Airport, Doctor Braithwaite. It's the most convenient to travel on to Oxfordshire," the older pilot said.

Tears filled my eyes when I realised Miles was taking me home, where I was born. The place I was with my parents for the last time.

"Thank you, that's perfect." I hurried up the airstair, hoping Miles hadn't caught on to my change in mood. I was wrong, I didn't hide it well.

Once we were inside the plane he asked, "Did I mess something up?" The concern in his voice and on his face caused the tears to fall freely. We stood in the middle of the plane, and he held me close while I sobbed quietly.

"You didn't mess anything up, it's exactly what I wanted. Just surprised, happy and sad all bundled up in one inexplicable ball of feelings. And now I'm holding up the plane."

"You're not holding up anything. The plane leaves when we are ready," he said reassuringly, holding my face in both his hands.

"Thank you, home is exactly where I wanted to go, and you made that happen. You're very sweet to me."

"Not sweet – manly man, remember?" he said with a smile. "Let's get ready for take-off."

"Sure." I led him to the exact spot we sat when we flew to California. He sent a message to the pilot. Before long the plane was taxiing down the runway. He held my hand as we took off and when it was safe, we both removed our seatbelts.

"I'm tired. I think I'll take a nap." I looked at him, and even in the spacious plane, his long legs filled up the space.

"Use the stateroom, you'll be more comfortable." He smiled, kept my hand in his and walked us to the back of the plane.

"How will I ever fly British Airways again? I still can't get over a queen-size bed on a plane," I said after he slid the door open.

"You don't ever have to." He looked at me soberly while I removed my shoes, put my hair up and lay down.

I didn't remember falling asleep, but I woke up four hours later refreshed. It may have been the circadian lighting specific to the plane, which I later found out mimicked daytime across time zones, or the low cabin altitude. Whatever the case, I felt great.

I freshened up in the luxe master suite. I hadn't been in many six- or even five-star hotel bathrooms, but I imagined that is how they would look, with calacatta marble and well-thought-out fixtures and fittings. The last flight I had taken on this plane lasted two hours, not long enough to notice the opulence and comfort all around me. This one gave me time to take it all in.

I left the stateroom and ambled towards the seats, where I found Miles, brow furrowed with his focused face reserved for work and his gym. A pen between his lips, fingers clicking on his keyboard. As soon as he heard me approach, he looked up.

"Sorry, I didn't mean to distract you."

"Perhaps, you're the very distraction I need," he said and smiled. He stood up, pulled me closer to him and sat us both down on his seat, where I felt him grow underneath me. I felt an ache deep within. Even if my head wasn't sure, my body knew what it needed from him. He gazed at me, and I realised I lived for the moments his brown eyes fixed on me. "Did you sleep well?"

"I did."

"No nightmares?"

"Not a single one." It registered how well I had slept and how for the last three nights I hadn't had any nightmares.

"Good, happy to hear that. Hungry?"

"Did you cook while I slept?" I teased. He had a modest number in his repertoire of simple meals, and meal prep was never featured at the top of his to-do list.

"That's all I did while you slept. I can offer a sizzling steak with a creamy crab oscar topping, or a healthy creamy-spinach-stuffed salmon in garlic butter." He smiled.

"Talk dirty to me, chef, everything sounds delicious. What's for dessert? I'll leave room for some." I kissed him, hoping I was finally ready to let him have me the way I hadn't been ready for in a while. The oxygen left the cabin as he abruptly brought my body closer to his and kissed me back hungrily, all-consuming and possessive. We were both breathless, fifty-one thousand feet above the Atlantic, as we reluctantly severed our connection.

"If it's dessert you want, we have a caramel flan, with its sweet yet bitter taste, which will leave a tingle in your mouth, and a portion so small it will have you crying out for more." The hard set of his jaw caused a flutter of desire to race through me. That wasn't the first time, but I was still afraid when we made love, it would never be the same again.

"Yes, hungry now. For everything, the caramel flan too." I couldn't resist running my hands through his naturally glossy dark hair.

"I'm hungry too," he murmured, kissing me softly this time, while he sat me astride him. I boldly rubbed my throbbing core against him and hoped to ease the ache.

"I've missed you," I whispered, looking down past his lips and to his chest where his casual shirt was moulded against his defined shoulders. *How have I gone for so long without his body?*

I continued to grind against his thickness, and that caused my skirt to bunch around my waist. He held my cheeks in both his hands and moved me harder against him. Our soft kisses had become desperate, and he groaned into me. His eyes sought permission from mine before he brought his fingers to my needy centre, all the while kissing me.

He made gentle contact with my swollen nub and, in slow deliberate circles, rubbed me the way I loved. The way I craved. The way he knew how to. I moaned as I sought more friction from him. Underneath me, he grew larger while I became hotter. As soon as he let a finger breach my centre, I closed my eyes and gently pushed his hand away.

"The flight attendant," I sighed and dropped my head against his shoulder. I couldn't look at him. I didn't want to see the hurt on his face as he took in a lie. An excuse concocted in the heat of the moment to stop us from taking what we both needed from each other.

I loved him even more when he sat me up and gazed into my eyes, understanding written all over his face, and said, "She does have a habit of appearing when you least expect her to." He righted my panties and pulled down my skirt.

"Yes, perhaps we can have that steak." Subdued, with a small smile, I moved to the seat opposite him and looked out at the wispy clouds in the distance.

"Good, I'll serve it to you now. By proxy, of course," he joked.

After the heated moment, banter didn't come naturally for me as I wondered how much longer it would take for me to relax and do what previously came naturally to us.

Chapter Thirty

♥

Miles

Cara had needed a change of scene, we both did. Even before we landed at Luton Airport, she was happy. She was free and, apart from the moment when I thought she was ready for us to get closer and I touched her, sending her into her own thoughts for a short time, she seemed much like the usual Cara. Was she happier because she was at home, or was it the distance from what happened to her? All I knew was I couldn't live without her. Wherever she needed to be to be happy, I would make it work and be wherever that was.

I trusted Alistair to find somewhere suitable for us to stay in Oxfordshire, close to Dorchester-on-Thames, and the best he was able to do at short notice was a place in Great Milton ten miles away. As I drove and we neared the chocolate box cottage, Cara cooed, and I groaned inwardly. I wondered if I would be able to stand up tall in the place. Some things about England always seemed bite-sized to me – the narrow country lanes, the crowded pubs and now the cottage.

"This is perfect. How did you find this place?" she gushed. My imagination went into overdrive to find the charm.

"Alistair organised it for us," I said, still doubtful about its dimensions in relation to mine.

When we walked inside, I was relieved. Although it was a classic seventeenth-century cottage, it was refurbished sympathetically with surprisingly tall ceilings and the typical English cottage beams. Everything else was in the elegant white style of a boutique hotel and it had a surprise inglenook fireplace in its centre to keep it warm. Alistair had got it right.

"He's good, tell him thank you from me." Cara knew about Alistair's shortcomings. He didn't know it, but that one statement swayed me towards him.

After we settled in and I spoke to Maxie, I found Cara in the backyard, staring out at a field.

"Look, Miles, this cottage even looks out over a meadow, and there are daffodils and forget-me-nots everywhere!" The excitement in her voice reassured me the trip was what she needed to get out of her mind

"A meadow?" I chuckled.

"Okay. A pasture, a paddock, a mead. What would you call it?

"A field, but you speak English and I speak American." I chuckled, putting an end to the debate before it started.

"You've finally owned up to that true fact," she said with a laugh.

"Let's go somewhere. Are you feeling up to it?"

"Yes, I can't believe it's still only lunchtime. Are we driving?"

"We could take a train, if you prefer. It's a quick trip."

"No, Heartthrob, let's not. I saw the looks you gave the cottage when we arrived. This is light years out of your comfort zone," she said and chuckled.

"Are you calling me spoiled?"

"No, the quaint English countryside charm isn't to everyone's taste. Although I love watching you drive on the right side, and by that I mean the correct side of the road."

"You're having too much fun, at my expense. Are you sure my brother didn't put you up to this?"

We had a spacious SUV to drive in Oxfordshire. It made driving around seem safer. I punched our destination into the GPS and pulled carefully out of the driveway. Even though the trip was only ten miles long, I had a death grip on the steering wheel as we drove to Dorchester on the narrow country lane.

We arrived, and when I stopped the car, Cara's eyes opened wide in recognition.

"Miles, this is the street I grew up on. How did you know? Was it Dean? I can't believe I'm back here. It's been forever." As her words tumbled out of her mouth, her eyes filled with tears.

"Happy tears?"

"Definitely happy tears," she said and launched herself over the console and kissed me.

"Okay, let's go inside. Someone's expecting you."

"What? Who?" she asked expectantly. Her curiosity and interest took over.

We stepped out of the car, where she took my hand and walked towards an olive front door with a large number eighteen on it. It rested on a charming stone cottage, Cara's childhood idyll. By the time I rang the doorbell, her tears had become unstoppable and they spilled down her face. An energetic woman in her sixties greeted us at the door.

"Hi. Rosie?"

"Miles, and you must be Cara. Come in. I'll just put the kettle on. You all right love?" she asked, smiling at Cara.

"I'm sorry, I am. Just surprised, and happy." She inelegantly rubbed the tears off her cheeks and I fell in love again.

"He's clever, your Miles, arranging all this. How did you find us? When I talked to him on the phone, he was difficult to resist. I had to see him for myself." She gave Cara a gentle pat on her arm.

"This is all a surprise to me, Rosie. How long have you lived here?" Cara asked as Rosie led us into her kitchen, where we sat down around her bite-sized kitchen table.

"Since you moved out, love. I'm sorry. The neighbours told us about you and your parents, that must have been hard on you and your brother."

"Thank you, that's very kind."

"Well. Imagine my surprise when five years ago we were digging up the garden, the weeping willow in the back developed root rot you see. We dug something up, and I knew it belonged to you."

"What did you dig up?" Cara asked. Her tears stopped, and she was intrigued.

"I'll get it for you. Help yourself to a cuppa and some biscuits while I fetch it." Cara was nervous and made to get up to follow Rosie. I stopped her in her tracks.

"Cara, pour yourself a cuppa, add a dash of milk and nibble on one of these jammy dodgers." I tried my best English accent.

"How can you eat a biscuit, Miles? This is huge," she stage-whispered.

"How can I not? Rosie thinks I'm irresistible, the least I can do is eat one of her biscuits, and this is a real-life English tea set," I joked, trying to help Cara become at ease while I sipped some tea.

Rosie wasn't gone long before she returned. "Here it is, dear." She brought in an oblong wooden box. Written on it in a faded child's handwriting was an instruction: "Do not open until 2015."

"Do you know what that is?" I was intrigued too. Tea and biscuits were forgotten. Rosie didn't mention the box when we spoke. That must be why she insisted on a visit.

"I don't remember it, but I would guess it's a time capsule, and it's nine years overdue to be opened. Thank you, Rosie, for holding onto this. I don't know what's inside, but I already know it will make me very happy."

"That's all right, love. Everyone loves a bit of buried treasure. Do you two have children?"

"Not together. Not yet," Cara said hurriedly. She became flustered and quickly glanced at me.

What does that mean? She doesn't have children yet, or WE don't have children yet? What does she want? Was it too soon to think about that? Having siblings as a child kept me on my toes, and I had a lifelong friend. I would want the same for Maxie despite the heartache with Laila.

"You'll see, once you get around to it. You will understand why I could never throw this out."

"Thank you, Rosie, for your hospitality, and for the time capsule."

"It's my pleasure. Would you like to look around before you go?"

"If it's not too much trouble, we would love to." It was an emotional journey for Cara, but she looked like she wanted to be there and take it all in. To immerse herself into what once was. She was stronger than she knew.

"Show yourselves, I'll be in the garden. It's lovely out there today."

Slowly, Cara and I walked around Rosie's cottage. The house Cara was born and lived in as a child. Where her childhood was cut short, and where her dreams stalled. The home she lost when she lost her parents, and perhaps where she lost her identity. The identity which she fought for, all her life. The identity which Templeton tried and failed to snatch from her. As I looked around the cottage, and at Cara taking it all in, I got to know her in a way I never had. She was the woman who rescued me from my bitterness and loneliness and made me believe in love again. Would I be able to rescue her, from her despair?

"Miles, I loved coming here, but it's not my home anymore. Can you say farewell to Rosie? I'll wait in the car." Tears brimmed in her eyes, but she didn't let them fall. I wanted to hold her in my arms and show her how much I wanted to be there for her.

"Sure, I'll be right out." I handed her the keys and noticed a longing in her eyes.

I found Rosie and thanked her again for everything, then followed Cara to the car.

"Buckle up. Onwards and upwards to the White Hart," I said brightly.

"In three hours, you've caught the lingo and know the location of the local pub. You would be right at home here. All that's missing is a checked baker boy, a pipe and a brown wingback to relax in, on Sunday afternoons." She laughed.

I was glad she was laughing. The visit to Rosie's cottage was heavy, she could have been crying.

"I assimilate very well. Wait 'til you hear me order a pint of Guinness at the pub."

The White Hart, where Rosie directed me to, was very local to Cara's childhood home, and within minutes we pulled into the deserted parking lot.

"The pub is a religion in these parts, is it not?"

"You might be thrown by the time difference, Heartthrob, it's two o'clock in the afternoon, the punters are still at work." She took the time capsule from the backseat, and we walked into the White Hart.

Another old historic building brought into the twenty-first century by a contemporary renovation. From the entry we noticed an alfresco dining area, perfect for the springtime sunshine that shone from behind the clouds. We walked inside where a strong aroma of the day's special - Bangers and Mash hit us. Cara led us to the counter where we placed our order, then found a table outside.

"Miles, I can't believe the day we've had. How did you do all this? In such a small amount of time?" She took my hand, and held it tight. Physical touch was getting easier for her.

"You wanted to come home, and I made sure you did it right. I hope it was everything you hoped it would be."

"And more, it's been beautiful. Sad, but beautiful."

"Are you ready to open that now?" I gestured towards her time capsule on the chair next to her.

"I'm dying to open it." She let go of my hand, and I felt the loss of her warm one. She picked up the oblong box reverently, and her delicate fingers slid the latch, which seemed to catch onto something. "Oh, it's stuck."

"Let me see." She handed it over to me, where I reached the same conclusion. As we were trying to open it, the publican arrived with a pint of Guinness and a glass of white wine.

"Thanks, do you think we could borrow a screwdriver?"

"That's an odd request, but yes. We always keep one handy in case of situations like these."

His dry humour, another English quirk, was amusing, and he returned almost straight away with one. I unscrewed the rusty nails holding the box together, and the top came off easily. I returned the box to Cara, where she slowly picked up everything in there, one at a time.

"Do any of these look familiar?"

"Yes. These are my mother's recipes, I don't think I've tried these before, and this was her pinard. These are letters from our parents to Dean and I, and to each other. I remember when this was taken." She handed me a family portrait.

"I've got so many questions. What's a pinard, and what does it do?"

"It's an old fashioned way of listening to a foetal heartbeat. This side goes on the mother's belly, and this side on the doctor's ear. I think some old school midwives still use them," she explained animatedly.

"Fascinating, and do you remember when you sat for this portrait?"

"A week before we buried this box in the garden. Then the weekend after that, my parents died. It's all coming back to me now. Quite vividly actually."

"This must be difficult for you." I took her hand and held it.

"Not particularly, I'm remembering a painful experience, perhaps my worst one, but with the benefit of time and maturity. Surprisingly, I'm all right with it." Her gaze lingered on me, and she held my hand tighter.

"You should frame this. It's special. You've always been super cute."

"I was cute, wasn't I? I had no idea what was coming. No one did." She seemed to ponder, almost as if looking right through the portrait.

"It's a shame your aunt and uncle are travelling. When they visited you, I wasn't thinking straight, and not good company."

"They didn't notice. They loved you, and they enjoyed the ride on your plane. I don't think I've ever thanked you for everything you did for me, everything you still do. I don't think this was your idea of a girlfriend when you came hunting for one at the clinic."

With the sun out, in this light, her eyes were a deeper shade of green, a pool of emeralds that I wanted to drown in, and I could have easily stared into them all afternoon.

"I didn't come hunting for a girlfriend. I wanted dinner. You pressured me into a thing."

"Good, because I fell in love hard, like I've never been," she said, while she ran her hand across my jaw.

"I'm the luckiest guy in the world because I have you." I moved her body closer to mine. I needed her closer.

"I'm the lucky one," she said as she moved her lips towards mine and gave me a gentle kiss.

"I could easily lose my mind if you keep kissing me like that."

"I'm going to have to kiss you again. I'm in love with you, Miles Masterson. Everything you are and everything you do. You're the man of my dreams." She kissed me again, and this time she explored, tasted and probed. Her passionate kisses left me with a yearning for all of her. Reluctantly we stopped and pulled apart. The once deserted pub was starting to fill up.

"Would you like another glass of Reisling?"

"No, it's already getting to my head. Shall we order something light to go? I'm not sure what's at the cottage for later."

"Sure."

Chapter Thirty-One

♥

Cara

I couldn't believe everything that happened. Returning to Oxfordshire after many years surpassed all expectations I had of the trip. Thanks to Miles, who took me back home only to discover a priceless relic from my past, I found myself seized by an aching nostalgia.

I didn't know the contents of the letter from my parents, but I hoped to find answers. Some guidance, a light for the darkness I found myself in. They were gone, but my parents loved me for a while, and if nature allowed, they would have loved me for eternity.

We arrived at the cottage and put away our salad, for if ever we got round to eating it. We took a shower together, and held each other close. His body throbbed, yet he kept it together. My skin prickled in awareness, my core slick and hot for him. Still he didn't push for what he needed, what we both needed. He brushed his soft lips against mine as I lightly felt his taut abdominal muscles beneath my fingers. *Will I ever remember how to touch him again?*

"I want you, Cara," he eventually said, with a longing gaze. "I've missed you."

I wanted to remember how it was to be made to feel, to be held close to his skin, wrapped tight in his arms, his torso covered with the unmistakable sheen that appeared only when we loved each other right, and hard. I needed him to plunder and pillage my body, in the way he had mastered. I needed him to erase my memory of all invasion, the unwanted intrusion. But I was still afraid.

"I'm terrified. Things might be different for me, but especially for you," I whispered.

"You know that can't be possible," he said gently as tiny rivulets of water ran down his face.

"The water's getting cold. Country cottages, right," I said cheerily and severed the tiny thread of connection that could have led us back to each other. He still smiled at me, a gentle smile which reassured me he understood. *How long will he continue to be patient?*

"I need a cold shower. I'll be out soon."

He turned the hot water faucet off, his heated gaze running up and down my body. I walked out of the shower, my core tingling and aching. My mind and body's fulcrum was close to snapping. It was working overtime and I wasn't in control of it.

I left the bathroom, wore a pair of soft cotton pyjamas, and decided to read the letter from my parents from the time capsule. The fireplace made the cottage warm and cosy. I sat on the sofa in front of it and opened the envelope addressed to me. It was an eerie feeling, as I prepared myself to read words from beyond the grave.

Our Dearest Cara

If you're reading this, it means you've made it to the ripe old age of twenty one. Ready for the world and possibly chasing your dreams. We have always been proud of you, and we will always continue to be. You have always found ways to be true to yourself. A staunch believer in right and wrong, a lover of flowers, pastels and pretty things and devourer of all books. Remain fearless, always strong, always striving to be better. You have always loved hard, and we pray you will find someone who knows how to love just as hard.

The world is full of surprises, some pleasant, others not so. What we both agree is to always live in the present, and be grateful for whatever you have, however little it may be. Sometimes there's no need to chase the next shiny thing, the next best thing. Always remember the most important things are those which are right in front of you, and the easiest choices sometimes demand the hardest of considerations. It is wise to change your mind and to veer off course. Our path in this life, to success, whatever that may look like to you, is never linear.

We will always love you, we will always be proud, and we will always cheer you on, wherever we may be.

We love you, we love you, we love you.

Mummy and Daddy.

I didn't notice the tears dripping down my face until a teardrop appeared on the letter. I didn't want Miles to catch me crying. He had seen enough of my tears to last a lifetime. I carefully folded the letter and put it away. Then went into the bedroom, dimmed the lights, and lay down. Shortly afterwards he came to bed and held me close.

He whispered quietly while he nipped gently at my ear, "I don't want to hijack your trip, but how do you feel about driving down to London, in the morning?"

Even though I pushed him away in the bathroom, he still held me close. His bare chest against my back made me feel safe. *Always remember the most important things are those which are right in front of you.* I already knew, but for a while I had been trapped in a bubble of despair.

"I would love that. On one condition." I giggled as he kept his lips close to my neck. I felt his smile and the open-mouthed kisses he rained on me.

"What condition would that be, hmm?"

My flimsy pyjama top had ridden higher, and my midriff was bared to his touch. Despite his cold shower, his palms were hot on my body. My breath hitched as he caressed me softly. His was the only touch I ever wanted.

"I'm driving."

"Really?" he murmured.

While he continued to nibble and kiss my neck, he moved his palms higher, cupped my breasts and gently rolled my nipples. My breath caught. I wanted him, I needed him. I didn't want to keep pushing him away.

"Yes, really. I can't watch you white knuckle it for fifty miles," I said breathlessly. I turned around in the bed, and we were face to face.

"It's that obvious, huh?" He chuckled and softly caressed my cheek.

"I understand. The lanes are little, the car's enormous and you've been spoiled by Clay."

I didn't finish talking, as he caught my chin in his hand and brought my lips closer to his. Although the light was dim, I saw the flash of desire in his eyes. He groaned as he pulled my body flush against his, where for the second time, I felt the solid ridge of his arousal.

"You know the human body better than I do, but I know *your* body better than you do, and nothing's changed about how you make me feel. This is what you do to me every day."

He pulled my pelvis towards his, wrapped my leg around his waist and ground himself against my aching centre. I didn't recognise the moan that left me as I felt how much he wanted me. Just as quickly as he pulled me against him, he gently let go of my body and created space between us.

"You don't need to move so far away," I whispered breathlessly.

"Nothing's happening, not until you're ready. I didn't mean to put pressure on you in the bathroom or on the jet." He brought me back to him and kissed my forehead, serving to end the conversation. I breathed heavily, shuffled closer to him and fell asleep in his arms.

I woke up to an empty bed the next morning. Just as I finished getting dressed and packing away all we had at the cottage, Miles walked back in, flushed, sweaty, sexy. The muscle tank didn't disguise how seriously he took the time he spent with his personal trainer. It was money well spent. He kissed me as if it were the first time we had seen each other in weeks, then made his way to the fridge for some water.

"You're up early." I couldn't focus as my eyes shifted from his traps, down to his pecs and back up to his eyes. I avoided the bulge that begged to be freed from the confines of his shorts.

"I had to make use of that meadow you're crazy about. Those daffodils and the other little blue ones are something special. They are everywhere."

"Forget-me-nots, but I don't see any in your hands for me," I said, pouting.

"I don't know how to pick flowers while out on a run, but I'll fix that. I promise."

He trapped me against the fridge and kissed me again. Even after a night's sleep, he still wanted me. I was sure I wanted him too.

"Breakfast?" I asked breathlessly as I looked at him and felt a tightness in my chest, which in turn became butterflies in my belly, then moved lower becoming a familiar throb.

"I've had a shake. I'll clean up and we can leave. Have you had granola? When I spoke to Alistair, that was his main concern. He made sure there was some." He shook his head and chuckled.

"I did. Strawberries, too. See, great attention to detail. He's a keeper."

I drove us to London, and this time Miles was more relaxed as a passenger. As we approached the A40, he entered our destination into the GPS.

"Where's that taking us?"

"My parents' place, in Marylebone."

"Yes, you did tell me they had a place there. Marylebone is close to everything."

"It is. We stayed there often, but my mother can't bring herself to go back there, not without my father."

"I can see how that can be difficult. Are you okay with being here?"

"I'm not alone," he said as he put his warm hand on my thigh.

We arrived at the regency-style property, and I was speechless as I took in the magnificence of the exterior, with a small placard at the entry announcing its grade-two listed status. When Miles led me inside, I was awed at the grandeur. I hadn't expected dust and cobwebs, but I was dazed as I took in the classic monochromatic details of the house. Set over two storeys, the generous penthouse overlooked four hundred acres of Regency Park, which could be seen from every window, opening and crevice. How was it a possibility in the heart of London?

"I see why the cottage in Great Milton offended you. This is fit for a queen."

"Perfect. I'm glad you like it."

"Like it? I love it. Chris must miss this place. We must come back with her and Maxie so it's not so empty when she's here."

"She would love that." He had become subdued. I realised he hadn't been back here either since his father's passing.

"Right, let's put our things away. We need food," I chimed brightly.

He led me to the second floor where we found an equally beautiful, but surprisingly delicate, suite. Despite six thousand square feet of monochrome, the interior was unmatched.

"This was my childhood bedroom, and the other two on either side were my brothers'."

"Did you sneak plenty of girls in here, Heartthrob?"

"A gentleman never tells."

"Good answer." I had to kiss him. It felt too long since the morning kisses and they had left me wanting more.

Chapter Thirty-Two

♥

Miles

After Cara took in the Marylebone house, we left. We were both starving as I tucked into the burger that took me back to the times my father brought my brothers and me to the same steakhouse whenever we visited London. Only two of the Masterson men who sat in there were still alive, and it could've been just one if Michael hadn't made it out of Istanbul alive. That was a sobering thought, and I buried it. I was there with Cara, and she was finally happy again.

"This restaurant is the best." She brought the piping hot plate closer to her nose and inhaled. "I have a healthy appetite and even a zest for food and for life. I finally want to start living in the now again." The words I longed to hear from her for weeks.

As she was polishing off her dessert, which she always made sure to have, I couldn't stop watching her.

"You're staring, Miles, you should have ordered this mango thing. It's delicious. Have a bite of mine," she offered. I kept the desserts to a minimum, and she made sure to tease me incessantly, usually until I relented and we shared them.

"I'm not staring at the mango thing. I can't stop looking at the woman I'm in love with, and I still can't believe she's mine."

She became flushed as she looked at me with a smile, then said, "I need to buy some things for Ava, Finn and Maxie. The twins, too. Will you be okay by yourself for an hour?" That was perfect, I needed the time too.

"It will be a struggle, but I'll be fine. Take this with you in case you see something I might like." I slid a credit card towards her. That was the only way she would ever take money from me.

"What's the limit? I might buy one of these pretty houses." She stared longingly out of the large glass windows in the steakhouse. She surprised me and didn't fight taking the credit card from me.

"Go crazy, buy one if you like." I meant it. I wanted to give her the world, but most of all I wanted to give her all of me.

We parted ways at the restaurant, while she made her way towards Knightsbridge, I walked towards Bond Street. One of my purchases may have been bought on impulse, but the other had been playing on my mind for weeks. It didn't take me long to find what I needed and have it prepared and packaged.

One hour became three. I was pleased. She needed to forget everything. When she returned, I was surprised at the never-ending packages the black-cab driver kept bringing to the doorway. That was unlike Cara, but I loved it. As soon as she came in, I shut the door and pulled her further inside the foyer. As if we had been apart for months and not mere hours, I held her close, inhaling her delicious scent.

"Who knew she was a closet shopaholic? I might need to get another job."

"You just might." She had a gleam in her eye.

"Did you get everything you wanted?"

"I think so, although I need a minute," she said with an inviting smile as she left my arms and walked into the powder bath next to the front door.

Just as I finished moving her packages into the front living room, she came back out, all buttoned up. I was sure her coat was nearly off when she went into the bathroom.

"That's a new coat?"

"It is, but it's a little warm in here. I'll take it off."

She unbuttoned it and handed it to me. It took me a second to realise she wore nothing else but the sexiest lingerie I had ever seen, scraps of material which barely held her body together, and her usual sky high heels. My breath caught when I looked at her. She walked away from me slowly, towards the wide staircase, and looked coyly over her shoulder. My eyes were transfixed on her body and my legs wouldn't move.

"Coming, Heartthrob? I need your help upstairs to vanquish the spirits of girlfriends past," she called out. A mating call I had never heard, but I longed for the ritual which would follow.

Following mutely, having been reduced to a mere spectator in my own seduction, we entered my boyhood suite, where she sat me down on the plush white sofa. She sat astride me and put her hands around my neck. I was surrounded by her scent, her hair, her curves. It was a sensory overload.

"No wonder your shopping trip took you a while. You look good enough to eat." My voice had become hoarse.

"I think I reached that limit which your card doesn't have," she whispered, grinding against me softly, causing me to grow.

"Did you get this in every colour?" I still hadn't touched her, and my hands wanted to rest on her hips. I still wasn't sure how this was going to end.

"Maybe I did." She came closer to my lips, licked me slowly, sucked gently and moaned seductively. All the while she kept her eyes closed, while mine watched the unbelievable sight before me. She slid her tongue inside my mouth, and we tasted each other over and over, until we were both breathless.

Slowly she slid down my legs, onto the soft rug, and unbuckled my belt easily. When she pulled down the zipper, I lost my mind. Her wide eyes took me in as she swallowed thickly.

"That looks fierce," she whispered.

"I can't help it, I've missed you—"

She didn't let me finish as she took me in her mouth, slowly at first, letting herself remember how to take me. It was worth the wait. On her own terms. I held onto my self-control while she took her time. After I started to feel the tell-tale tingle at the base of my spine, I brought her up towards me and sat her back on my lap, where her warm arousal seeped out of her and onto my pants.

"I love it, but how do I get you out of this contraption?"

"It's a Saisha playsuit." She giggled, pushing her breasts towards me. She was back.

"What are these?" I ran my fingers on the clear stones that were dotted all over the playsuit.

"Crystals," she answered simply.

"I love Saisha and her crystals, can you wear her every day from now on?"

"I might be able to arrange that," she teased, then shrugged out of the thin scraps of material which barely held her ample breasts.

Saisha came off and her breasts tumbled free. While she unbuttoned my shirt I sat back and marvelled at how beautifully flushed she was, grinding hungrily against me.

"Pull these off, I want to feel your skin on me." She spoke with urgency, tugging at my pants.

I stood up, with her legs wrapped around my waist, and walked the few steps to the bed with her lips fixed on mine. She knelt on the bed, trailing my abs with her lips. The unintended benefit of all the core work was to have her worship them that way. Eventually the pants came all the way off while she sat back and took me in. When she had her fill she sat me down and crawled up my body. Her naked skin on mine. She ran her nose up my jaw and inhaled deeply. If anticipation could kill, I would have been buried.

Before I knew it, our lips slammed together again, and I was consumed. Consumed by her ardent kisses, her soft body on mine, demanding, taking and giving. Her moans and whimpers were unmistakably hers but had become foreign to me. I heard my own animalistic growl as I finally ran my hands up and down her body and touched her the way I couldn't for months.

"I want more," she panted. The lust took over and she lined her entrance above me, then sunk me into her slowly, inch by inch.

"So warm and soft. I've missed you." I didn't recognise my own voice as the pleasure took over all my senses.

As it was the first time, she gave herself time to become used to me, while I fought hard not to move and take what I wanted, giving her what she needed. I wanted it to last. Time stood still. I forgot where I was, who I was, when it was and nothing else mattered. I fought to keep my cool inside her.

"I don't know how I waited so long to have you fill me. I can feel you everywhere," she moaned.

She finally started to move rhythmically. How could she be so controlled? She needed the control, and I let her have it. I let her take it back. She rode me and ground onto me, filling herself up. After marvelling at her for a while, I finally brought her body flush against mine, and held her tight while I gave into my need. She was mine, and I would spend what I could of my life making up for what had been taken from her.

During it all, I heard the distinctive sound of my phone ring. All I cared about was the depths and the softness I was buried in.

As we moved faster and harder against each other, I felt her clenching walls against me, and her scorching arousal leaked out of her as she became undone.

As soon as she was composed, I flipped her over and her trembling legs wrapped around me. I drove into her, slowly at first. I wanted to be gentle, I wanted us to savour the moment, but my need was heightened, more than I had ever been. I gave her all of me over and over, until I couldn't hold back. With a roar, I erupted endlessly. She didn't let me go. She held me in a vice until she was composed enough to speak.

"You were right, Miles. Nothing about my body's changed. You and I still fit perfectly," she said softly, still trying to catch her breath.

"I never doubted we would, not for a second." She finally relaxed and let me go. I lay next to her, yet I didn't let go of her. I never would.

"I'm sorry it took so long for me, for us, to do this," she apologised as she circled my nipple with her delicate finger.

"That's not an apology I need from you ever. We're where we need to be." I kissed her fingers, then her swollen lips, relieved she had trusted me with everything, again. "Give me a second. Bathroom."

"Don't take too long. I don't want to miss you," she answered sleepily.

I wasn't gone long, but by the time I returned, she was snoring softly with a serene look on her face. I freshened her up and lay next to her, held her close and felt her soft curves mould into me. She was my heaven, and my sanctuary.

Chapter Thirty-Three

Cara

I woke up cocooned in Miles' arms, with a delicious exhaustion that had settled over my body and a throbbing in my core. The soft light cast by the wall sconces showed him stir in his sleep and move from his side onto his back. He threw his arm above his head. His breaths were measured and he was in a deep sleep. I couldn't wait for him to wake up and sat astride him, rocking gently, taking my pleasure from him. His body didn't take long to respond, and within minutes he was ready and had filled me up.

"Is it wrong that I've been objectified and I love it?" His voice was deep and husky from sleep, while a small smile played on his lips.

"Your body seemed to oblige and gave me what I craved." I moaned as he sat up against the luxurious ceiling-height headboard. He held my hips in his hands and moved me on him, in time to his own increased movements.

"That's because even on a subconscious level, I always want you."
He didn't hold back as he gave me what I had woken up for. He
groaned, then I felt his warmth coat me. "Is that what you needed?"
He pulled me closer and held me against his body, where our racing
hearts beat wildly.

"Exactly what I needed, you know my body well."

"I made it my mission to know you in every way that matters," he
said, his voice gravelly, with what seemed like a direct line to my centre.
He held me close, breathed me in, kissed me softly. I stayed in his arms
for a while, where I never wanted to leave, until I realised I needed to.

"Let's not make a mess." I got up and padded on the soft carpet to
the bathroom. I fumbled in the dark until I found the light switch. As
soon as the lights came on, my eyes caught the navy blue oblong box
from Harry Winston resting on the marble counter. *I wasn't the only
one who had been shopping.* I had the good sense to freshen up first and
just as I finished, he appeared in the bathroom.

"I love it," I squealed and threw my body against his, then wrapped
my arms around his neck and kissed him.

"Can I see it on you?"

"I haven't opened it yet," I said with a giggle.

"How would you know you love it if you haven't opened it yet?"
He used an indulgent tone, one I recall being used on Maxie. The
thought made me smile as I opened it to find a sapphire and diamond
forget-me-not pendant.

"It's beautiful," I sighed, while he picked it up and placed it on my
neck.

"You were offended I didn't pick forget-me-nots from your meadow. This one comes with a no-wilt guarantee. You miss the sapphire
necklace from your mother. That one is irreplaceable, but this one

seemed to check all the pendant boxes." He spoke softly while he kissed my neck.

"It does. It's thoughtful and meaningful, and deep," I whispered, swallowing the surprising lump in my throat. *I just fell in love with him again.*

"It's good to hear you say that. I'm happy I'm the one you chose to share your time and your world with."

"Okay, Mister Chosen One, there's something else I need to share with you. One I've been grappling with for weeks. Before I start, perhaps you could hand me that robe. I can't be in the nude when I talk about this one."

"I like the nude you, but this sounds serious," he said and handed me the plush soft robe that hung behind him.

When we both had the robes on, we filed out of the bathroom and sat in the dimly lit bedroom. It was only seven o'clock, but it was already dark outside.

"Okay, I've never said this out loud before, and I want to get it right the first time I do."

"It's only me, you can't go wrong." He smiled.

"Being a doctor has defined who I am for as long as I can remember. It's what I love, it's what I do, and I've mistakenly made it who I am."

"Right," he said, nodding in encouragement. I needed it to continue.

"After what happened at King's, my confidence took a knock. That's okay. I worked on that and got back to a good place professionally. But I've made up my mind. I can't return to clinical work, not anymore. The golf course was the last straw."

"It's out, you've said it. It didn't sound so bad." His smile made everything right.

"Good." I exhaled and lost the ton I had been carrying on my shoulders for weeks.

"If, as you say, being a doctor is who you are. If you stop clinical work, who do you think you'll become?" He tucked my hair behind my ear and tilted my chin upwards to look into his eyes.

"I will continue to be a licensed doctor, but I haven't completely figured out what my professional life would look like yet. All I know so far is where I don't want to be." *Our path to success is never linear.*

"That's a huge step, and an important decision to make. It must have been agonising to come to it."

"It was, and that final nudge came from beyond the grave. It was something I read in the letter from my parents which assured me I was making the right decision." He took my hand in his and placed delicate kisses on my fingers. The fingers I had decided would never wield a scalpel again.

"I would be an inattentive man if I didn't realise how much your financial independence matters to you, but have you made a plan in that respect?"

"I don't plan to be unemployed for long, but while I am, I will live off my savings. I don't need much." *My ever-dwindling savings.*

"If I weren't me, and I were yours, and I found myself in your position – between jobs and figuring things out – what would you do?" he asked gently.

"I would help you in any way I can. Miles, I see what you're doing. If I need anything I will tell you."

"Keep the card I gave you this afternoon. Your need to use it won't change how I see you. In our thing, we'll always be equals. Is that what you're worried about?"

"Maybe it is," I answered honestly. I'd never wanted my identity to be defined by who I was in a relationship with or who I eventually married, even if I took his name.

"You don't have to worry about that. The most important people in this thing, you and I, know we are equals."

Miles' phone rang again. As he made his way around the room to answer it, I realised it rang several times while we were preoccupied with each other. It may have been what woke me up from sleep. As soon as he answered it, his face fell. All I could hear were the questions he kept firing back.

"Is she at school this morning?" He was livid as he asked that all-important question.

It all seemed familiar, and while he was still on the phone I began to get our things together. I had seen a brand new luggage set in the hallway cupboard. That's where I would pack the shopping spoils, which were downstairs, as soon as he came off the phone. Once he hung up, I saw the pained look in his eyes.

"Vivian took Maxie from school, before my mother arrived there."

"Okay. Where is she now?"

"I'm not sure. They are both not at her house, Michael has checked."

"Where could they be, why would she take her?" As I was trying to understand, Miles had a thought.

"Perhaps at her father's."

"Where is that?"

"He has homes dotted all over."

"The country?"

"No, the world. I'm sorry, Cara, we need to cut this trip short. They could be anywhere."

"Of course, I can be ready in fifteen. Where exactly are we going?"

"I don't know yet. Can you get everything together? I'll call her and the pilots." He was angry, but in control. Again, Mrs Masterson had risen to the occasion and stolen more moments from Miles and me. Did she take Maxie because she wanted to be with her? Or was she seeking attention from Miles?

"Perhaps don't call Vivian. Call her father instead."

"Why?"

"She's expecting your call, and you would be playing right into her hand."

"Maybe her father has no clue where she is."

"I met her only for a few minutes, but it's clear she has a princess complex. All princesses are enabled by their parents first." Then their husbands.

Note to self: Don't kick a man when he's down.

"You're right. I may have spent too much time being reactive to her."

While I packed away all evidence of us from the Marylebone house, Miles was on the phone. I would have loved to enjoy more time in London with him. To catch up with old friends while I was here too. I wouldn't begrudge Miles. Vivian may have left for the one she let get away, but she clearly wanted to be back with Miles and would do anything for his attention.

Chapter Thirty-Four

Miles

The last time I saw and spoke to Cameron Carlisle was at Laila's funeral. I hadn't known which way was up, having lost both my father and daughter. Worldwide Media stock had plummeted, and Michael and I were working hard to maintain the confidence of our shareholders. Vivian and her father had been the least of my priorities. The only time I gave them any credence was in the last five minutes. Why had Cameron Carlisle abandoned his only granddaughter when Vivian did? And was he complicit in taking Maxie?

"Was Maxie's grandfather involved with Maxie and Laila before your divorce?" I heard Cara's soft voice while I was deep in thought.

"His style of grandparenting was different from my parents'. He lavished them with gifts and money, but not much attention. When he disappeared from Maxie's life, I don't think she noticed."

"She lost too many people at the same time. Perhaps it all became a blur in her five-year-old mind."

"I never thought I would ever have to make a call like this to Cameron."

"It might be easier than you think. You and he have some things in common. He, too, has a daughter he raised by himself. He would understand."

Cara had done a deep dive into Vivian. She didn't know it, but I did one, too, into her unfaithful ex when I was trying to figure out who her stalker was. Where I had become a jealous fool, she had gained some good insight.

"Not if his daughter has his ear. I'll call him anyway." I left the bedroom and went downstairs and called his number.

"Cameron, it's Miles Masterson."

"The son I never had. Today has just become a good day. How's your lovely mother?"

"Today's not a good day for her, Cameron."

"Tell me what you mean, what's happened to her?"

"I'm in London, and I left Maxie with her. Only when she went to collect Maxie from school, she wasn't there. So you can understand, she's beside herself with worry."

"You're telling me this because you know Maxie is with me?"

"I suspected she would be with you, but—"

"Son, I don't believe a mother can ever relinquish that title. A mother will always be that no matter the circumstances. Maxie is safe with family." *Safe? Maybe with you. Maxie is invisible to her mother.*

"I don't doubt she's safe, but this is a unique situation. I've worked hard to create a stable and uncomplicated environment for Maxie, one where she knows stability and routine. I keep surprises age-appropriate and to a minimum."

"I'm with you."

"Taking Maxie from school, away from her grandmother, and by extension away from me in this manner doesn't foster that stable environment. It's confusing to her, and it's not the plan for this week, which I went to great pains explaining to Maxie. As we speak, I still don't know where in the world she is."

"I'm sorry, I didn't realise she was taken without your knowledge. She's safe with me at the Brookville house."

"With you? Her mother?"

"Her mother's in the city." Why take Maxie if she wouldn't be with her?

"With all due respect, Cameron, she might be safe, but she hardly knows you. Not anymore."

"I'm her grandfather, you can't keep her away from me too."

"I'm not keeping her away. You disappeared from her life when Vivian did. There's a right and wrong way of doing this, and this is the wrong way."

"You haven't always been a martinet, have you?"

"If you were in my position, with an eight-year-old Vivian, you would've done the same. I'll be arriving at LaGuardia for her at seven o'clock your time. Make arrangements to be there with her when I arrive."

"Son, don't be harsh on an old boy. She's my family too." His voice shook, and for a second, I wanted to cave into his pleas. Maxie needed all her family and Cameron was the only grandfather she had left. But I wouldn't leave her there. If ever I was out of reach again, Vivian would repeat this, and that was not how I wanted Maxie to be raised.

"I'll make sure you see her as often as you want, you have my word. For now, prepare her for my arrival and have this time with her, as I'll be taking her back home to Seattle."

"She'll be ready," he said and sighed deeply.

"Thanks for understanding. May I speak to her?"

"Of course, I'll take the phone to her. Miles, I'm sorry, my daughter hasn't been herself in years." He sounded apologetic.

"It's not your fault."

"Here, Maxie, it's your father." I heard him say to Maxie.

"Daddy, I went on a plane just like you. Mommy came for me at school during recess, it was such fun, and grandad has millions of books in his library." Hearing Maxie's excited voice was all I needed to calm my racing heart. She was safe and looked after. She needed her grandfather after all.

"Millions?"

"Millions, Daddy. He said I can choose some to take home."

"Remember your manners, Maxie, and be good for your grandad. I'll see you soon."

"Did you have tea at the Ritzy?"

"I had tea, but not at the Ritzy. I'll tell you about it when I see you. Bye, beautiful."

"Bye, Daddy."

As soon as I hung up, I had the pilots ready the plane. It was already hangared at London City Airport, an easy drive from Marylebone. I returned upstairs where I found Cara with our bags spread out on the bed, packing.

"Have you found her?" she asked hesitantly, the worried look on her face reminding me she was still fragile.

"You were right. She's with her grandfather at his estate in New York, but her mother's in the city."

"Have you spoken to her? Is she okay?"

"I did, she's fine. We should leave for City Airport now."

"Is that where the plane is? Everything's ready. I just need to pack the packages downstairs in a suitcase. I'll do that while you get dressed, shall I?" As she made to walk past me out of the bedroom, I pulled her into my arms.

"I'm sorry," I whispered into her damp hair. She must have been in the shower while I was downstairs. "I promised you time here. This isn't what I imagined."

"It wasn't a waste." She wrapped her arms around my neck but I felt her disappointment.

"I promised you a week. We'll come back. You've made London very special to me. I could never be here without you." I breathed her in and promised myself Vivian would never interrupt our time again.

"It was special to me too. You planned everything perfectly." She put her soft lips against mine. I had to bring London to an end, else we would never leave.

When she made her way downstairs, I remembered the other package from Harry Winston and hoped she hadn't seen it while she was packing. I couldn't give it to her on this trip, it would have to wait. Would she take it? Was she ready to be with me always, like I was ready for her?

Within twenty minutes, we were both ready to leave. The luggage was in the SUV, and I walked towards the driver's seat, wondering how I would navigate the busy streets of central London.

"I'll drive, I know a quick way to City Airport," she said with a smile.

"You read my mind, it would take me hours." She took the keys and manoeuvred us from the on-street parking common in Marylebone, out onto the main city road. I took one last look behind us. Marylebone held some of my childhood memories too. Cara didn't realise it, but she had made it easier for me to be there.

"At this time of day, the secret is to avoid Kensington and Tower Bridge. Before you know it, we'll be at the Royal Docks. If there are no roadworks or road incidents, we should make it there in thirty minutes." I smiled as she easily took over and proved this was her neck of the woods.

"You're a local through and through."

"Look, that turn would take us to Great Ormond Street. That's where I did my paediatrics rotation."

"Was it a good one?"

"One of my favourites, second only to surgery. Kids are great to work with. They are surprisingly optimistic."

"When you worked here, where was home?"

"In Fulham, in the tiniest flat known to man. It can't have been much bigger than your closet, but it was what I could afford and where I wanted to be," she said and chuckled.

"I wished we could've stayed longer, I love to see London through your eyes. Does this route take us past Fulham?"

"No, that's the opposite direction," she corrected me patiently. She had needed this trip. We both had.

We continued on our way while Cara showed me her London. I may have been with her, but in the back of my mind I was worried about Maxie's state of mind. Her confusion at being taken from school from her grandmother, then taken to her grandfather who was nearly a stranger to her. We arrived at the airport and followed signs to the hangar, where we found the plane, climbed aboard and, within minutes, were cleared for take-off, flying towards LaGuardia Airport.

"You haven't had much to eat since lunch time, are you hungry?" Even though the plane comfortably sat eight, Cara sat in my lap, her body curled into mine. Her proximity brought me comfort.

"It's mealtime, but I'm worried about you. Maxie's fine, and you know it, but you're still uneasy. I can feel the tension in your body, and it shows on the frown lines on your face," she said, giving me a soft facial massage.

"I'm relaxed. You're here in my arms where you belong, but again I've failed to protect what's mine," I confessed.

"No one would've known this would be Vivian's next move. Is she still trying to get your attention and talking about being a family again?"

"She's not ringing a loud bell about it anymore, but she's dropped subtle hints to a few mutual friends. I avoid her, I spend all my time with you."

"You didn't tell me any of this. She knows about us. How can she still be talking about being with you?" She stopped the facial massage. Without opening my eyes, I felt her unease.

"We were preoccupied with more important things, Cara, I didn't think much of it."

"She's unpredictable. It's time to give this the attention it deserves."

"Before I do that, there's another matter that deserves my attention." I kissed her, because I wanted to, but mostly, I didn't want Vivian to take up more of our time together.

The plane touched down at LaGuardia at seven o'clock in the morning. True to his word, Cameron brought Maxie to meet us. As Maxie walked up the airstair onto the plane, Cameron and I talked on the noisy tarmac.

"Son, I'm sorry this happened. Can I see her again?"

"I don't have a problem arranging that. It's Vivian's deception I'm concerned with."

"Forgive her, she's heartbroken. She's been that way since we lost Laila, and she imagined that would have brought you two back together, but you never went knocking at her door. I think she might still be waiting for you."

"You're mistaken, Cameron. She's pining for someone else."

"I know a thing or two about Vivie. She's determined to have you back, and she will do whatever it takes." Conversations with both Carlisles seemed infinite and cyclical. Cameron pretended to be oblivious to Vivian's manipulative ways. He helped engineer the custody issue two years ago to keep his daughter's name clean and her out of jail. It was also beneficial to me and Maxie, we hadn't needed that kind of publicity.

"It was good to see you again, Cameron. I need to take Maxie home."

"I'll be in Seattle in two weeks. I'll give you a call to arrange something."

Chapter Thirty-Five

♥

Cara

My arrival back to Seattle felt like returning home. My life was finally full of promise, and I started looking ahead. *It was nine nights without a nightmare.*

Two days after we returned from London, Vivian arrived at Mercer after Miles returned from taking Maxie to school. I was upstairs in his bed, but his decorative marble child monitor was next to me. I trusted Miles, but my curiosity got the better of me as I listened to every word.

"I know you have rules and I shouldn't come here unannounced, but we needed to talk after what happened in New York."

"You disrupted my plans in the worst way possible with your selfish ways."

"Don't blame me, Miles, you chose to make this bigger than what it was. I'm not some perpetrator of irresponsible actions. The fact of the matter is, I'm a casualty of circumstances. You wanted to be off in London with your latest flavour instead of raising our child. I had to be an actual parent and take responsibility."

"You have no idea what you're talking about. That's your wounded pride clinging to some senseless justifications. You're not a victim of circumstance, you were the mastermind of those circumstances."

"I sacrificed everything for you, especially who I was. You wield your power and privilege like a weapon against me. The one time I had a chance to do something for my daughter, you took her away and embarrassed me. My father was livid, he thought I was the problem."

"You are the problem. Everything I do has Maxie's emotional well-being at the very core of it. What you did is not how to parent an eight-year-old. Co-parenting is not a game of tit for tat or one-up-manship. All you had to do was stick to the visitation schedule. I'll be speaking to my lawyer about the stunt you pulled."

"It's the doctor, isn't it? You looked her way and now she walks on water. She's only with you for that large bank account, your other large asset and the designer clothes. I saw through her last Saturday. She would need to work a whole month plus overtime to afford the dress she was wearing. I know a gold digging whore when I see one."

"You're projecting. Those are your motivations. I've been civil for Maxie's sake, calling Cara names has nothing to do with being Maxie's mom. Let's make this easier for both of us and continue to speak through our lawyers. There's the door."

"You can't kick me out, we're not finished."

"I am."

"Fine, lawyers it is."

Miles came upstairs and found the marble cube in my hand. He looked apologetic.

"That was intense, are you okay?" I asked before he had a chance to speak. I wouldn't let him apologise for Vivian's words. He was tense, and he took the monitor and placed it to the side.

"As long as I have you, I will always be okay." He sighed, then kissed me. He didn't let the visit get in the way of our time together. We left the bedroom and spent our time on the lake, until it was time for Maxie to come home from school.

On Saturday night, both Miles and Maxie had their first sleepover at my house together. For the first time, I imagined how life would be if Miles, Maxie and I were a family. I loved the feeling, but I didn't dwell on that fantasy for too long in case it remained that. Even though I had seen the ring from Harry Winston while I was packing in Marylebone, I hoped Miles would give me time before he asked. I was relearning to be comfortable in my own skin. I would need to learn to reconcile Cara Braithwaite with becoming Mrs Miles Masterson.

In the evening, I helped Maxie get ready for bed. She was excited to sleep in Finn and Ava's room and was looking forward to meeting them. As I was walking out of the bedroom, she called out to me.

"Can we read this book together? My grandpa gave it to me, and he said it was my mommy's favourite when she was my age." *Did she subconsciously long for her absent mother like I longed for mine?*

"He did? What is it about?" I walked back to the bed and sat down next to her.

"A prince who didn't want to be a prince anymore, and he switched places with a poor boy. Do you know the story?"

"I think I might know it, but I would love to read it with you."

As we took turns reading, I wasn't sure who I had fallen in love with more, Maxie or her father. When she finally fell asleep, I left her room and joined Miles in mine.

"You took a while." He met me at the bedroom door without a stitch on. In the dim light, all I saw was the outline of his body, the one whose ridges, planes and muscles I spent the last three days relearning and committing to memory. In his bed, in mine and on every surface of his yacht. He didn't give me time to marvel at him, instead he picked me up and carried me to the bed where we both tumbled. He fumbled with my high-low dress as he tried to get it off.

"I didn't know we were on a schedule," I teased and giggled, while I enjoyed his frenzy.

"What did you think? The neckline on this dress is a crime. Against me, perpetrated on purpose all day long, knowing I couldn't do anything about it with Maxie awake." He had me out of the dress and groaned when he finally held my breasts in his hands and kneaded them mercilessly. His lips left mine, and dropped to my nipples, where they didn't stay long. "I'm starving at a buffet and I don't know what to eat first," he whispered.

"Go lower," I moaned.

"Here?" he teased, licking my navel. He knew where I needed him to go.

"No, a lot lower, and start there." He didn't waste time. Within seconds he slid down my body and was between my thighs devouring me like his last meal.

Taking a breath, he spoke gently, a contradiction to the untamed beast he had become. "I can't get enough, I don't know how I lasted all day without having you."

♥

The Human Resources department at the children's hospital didn't work during the weekend, but they called me early on Sunday morning and asked me to come into the hospital on Monday morning. I assumed this was to cover their bases and have me answer some check-in questions, as I had been away for nearly two months. But when they told me I was coming in to discuss a patient complaint and needed to bring legal representation, I knew it had to be serious. Where and how would I get a legal representative at such short notice? The only lawyer I knew was drinking coffee in my kitchen, and he didn't practise law.

"There's been a complaint about me, at the hospital by a patient." I couldn't hide the shake in my voice. I shook and stuttered. I was nearly in tears as my thoughts returned to King's, both Georges and everything that happened since.

"You haven't been to work in nearly eight weeks, what's there to complain about?" Miles asked, puzzled, as he walked towards me.

"I don't know, but I need a legal rep for the meeting at nine tomorrow morning." I couldn't stop shaking, as everything I thought I had gotten over played in my mind.

"They can't spring this on you and expect you to jump to it. That's illegal. Postpone it until you're ready." Miles tried to hold me, but I gently shrugged him off me. I was terrified, and affection wouldn't help, not this time.

"They followed up with this email. It seems serious." I gave him my phone and he read the email with concern and alarm on his face.

"All the more reason to postpone, find out what this is about, prepare and plan your response."

"Just like a criminal?" I was worried. This took me straight back to the hearing with the GMC. This was how it started. What could I have done to be called back into work at short notice while away on leave?

"No, like any regular person would."

"I would rather get it over and done with, I can't have this hanging over my head. Not even for a few days. I can't believe I'm back here again."

"You don't know what this is. I'll call someone for you."

"Who is he? Is he any good?"

"Ryland Miller, I interned at his firm one summer, and we still bounce ideas off each other from time to time. He specialises in medical malpractice." He sighed, while I closed my eyes and tried to quiet my thoughts. I didn't have the strength for whatever this was.

"Call him, so I can prepare and plan my response, as you say." I exhaled in defeat.

"This time, it's different, Cara." He pulled me into his arms and held me while I simultaneously fought back the tears and wondered what error I made ... this time.

"How?" I whispered.

"This time, you're not alone. You've got me, and I've got you. Whatever this is, it's not insurmountable."

"I could've done with having you in my corner in London. I wouldn't have become the basket case I was."

"I'm here now." He held me tighter. Maybe I did need affection.

"Call your man while I make waffles for Maxie and I, and a slimy green protein shake coming right up for you." I chuckled and made space between us.

"I want waffles," Maxie said as she walked into the kitchen, still in her Trotters ballerina pyjamas. She and Ava had the same pair from our trip to London.

"Where did you come from? Come here and say good morning properly, Lady Maxie."

"Good morning properly," she said with a giggle as she heaved herself onto the stool at the tiny kitchen island, with its butcher board surface. "Daddy, I like Doctor Cara's house, can we have another sleepover soon?"

"I'm not sure she'll have us again if we're messy and don't clean up after ourselves. Did you make the bed, beautiful?"

"I didn't. Doctor Cara, if I make the bed, can I have another sleepover?"

"Let me see." I pretended to think, and that made Maxie laugh. "You would need to make the bed, help me make waffles and eat a bowl of brussels sprouts, then you can have as many sleepovers as you like."

"Eww, brussels sprouts. Only Daddy eats those."

"I think you might be right, Maxie." This time we all laughed.

That's what Miles meant. I wasn't alone with my thoughts, picking apart every case I ever worked at the children's hospital in the hopes of trying to understand who would make a formal complaint and why. Instead, I was with two people whose company I enjoyed, and who I had fallen in love with.

After breakfast, Ryland Miller arrived to see me at Miles' request. A middle-aged man with a mop of salt and pepper hair, his kind eyes made me trust him as soon as we met. He seemed to have walked off the golf course right into my kitchen, wearing a pair of brown chinos, a pink polo shirt and a Titleist hat in his hands. After the introductions, Miles and Maxie went outside and Ryland and I sat in my living room.

"Doctor Braithwaite, what can you tell me about the issue you'll be answering tomorrow?"

"See, this is where I'm stumped. They haven't been forthright with any information. All I have is the email you've read," I said apologetically.

"What concerns me is you're being called in to answer a patient complaint while you're away on illness leave."

"What are your concerns?"

"Patients complain all the time. In fact, when they do, the process drags out for a long time. That delay tactic is an open secret used by some hospitals. My concern is both the magnitude of your infraction and the level of influence the complainant may have."

"I see, now I'm really worried." I started shaking again. How could I make it through the meeting tomorrow in this state? Would Andrea have any tips?

"Does anything come to mind at all about any cases you handled, anything complex? Anything that went awry?" he encouraged, trying to jog my memory.

"No, nothing at all. It's all been straightforward." My voice came out in a hoarse whisper.

"In that case, we'll have to be surprised tomorrow. Is there anything else you think I should know?" The kindness in his eyes was replaced by a searching look.

"Yes, I wasn't planning on returning to clinical work. I wouldn't have returned to work at the hospital or at a paediatric clinic I also work at."

"Why? Have you got a job offer elsewhere? This case could jeopardise that offer. We need to proceed with caution."

"I don't have a job offer. I went through something difficult in my personal life and I decided clinical work wasn't for me anymore."

"Right. I'm sorry to hear that. I'm sure you'll find your feet when you decide on your next steps."

"Thank you, Ryland."

"There's not much we can do today. Let's meet tomorrow at the hospital cafeteria at eight forty five. Be punctual, let them see you're cooperative and taking this seriously. But don't speak to anyone without me, even if it's a colleague and you're exchanging pleasantries."

"Understood. Thank you for coming at such short notice."

I walked him out to his car. As soon as he drove away I joined Miles and Maxie in the backyard where they sat playing cards in the early spring warmth. Despite the dark cloud hanging over me, I made sure to enjoy my day with them.

Chapter Thirty-Six

♥

Cara

I didn't sleep much, and early the next morning I was up at four o'clock. I wandered my house aimlessly, straightened out books on the shelf, rearranged my clothes and kept my shaking hands busy. I didn't try to stomach breakfast, as the bile kept rising. I could taste its bitter taste in my mouth. I was worried, moreso about having caused injury to one of my patients again, and this time it was a child. This confirmed the decision I spoke out loud in London. I must avoid clinical work.

I decided to get dressed, as moping around at home sent my mind wandering to all places. I chose my red crepe couture dress. Although it was slightly short with a flouncy skirt, it had an air of seriousness and sophistication. I felt weak, and Valentino was the best and only armour I could find in my suburban closet. I paired it with a pair of black leather Anouk pumps and waited for Clay to arrive. Miles was right, I could never have driven myself. As the time to leave the house drew closer, my palms were sweaty and I trembled.

Clay arrived and we rode in silence to the hospital. When I arrived, I easily found Ryland in the near-empty cafeteria. We had ten minutes to spare before we needed to be in meeting room five, where the email had directed me to attend.

"Cara, can I get you a coffee or water?"

"I'm too nervous to drink anything." I grimaced.

"Try not to be. Follow my lead, and only speak when I tell you to. We need to check the temperature of the room before we say too much."

"No problem." My responses were clipped. My insides churned as I continued to swallow down the bile.

We left the cafeteria and arrived at the meeting room. Present was the director of HR, whose name I didn't try to learn, and Doctor Stevens, the director of emergency medicine and my immediate boss. He had hired me on the spot when we met.

To add to the gravity of the meeting, a transcriber was even in the room. The hospital's two lawyers were also present. Five of them for a preliminary meeting, and only one of me. Someone must have died. After the introductions, one of the hospital lawyers spoke first.

"We have received a serious complaint from the mother of one of your patients – Maxie Masterson. Do you remember her, Doctor Braithwaite? We've taken the liberty of printing out her patient record to help jog your memory."

My heart sank.

I glanced at Ryland, whose thoughtful expression had morphed into a small frown. He nodded slowly for me to speak.

"I don't need her notes, as I remember Maxie. Seven years old at the time, four centimetre split laceration to her forehead and a mild concussion. She and her grandmother spent a few hours in the emergency room with us." My voice shook while my stomach roiled. I already had my suspicions about where this was headed.

"Yes, that is correct. There is no question about the clinical care you provided, Doctor Braithwaite. That was excellent, as Doctor Stevens has advised all your work is," he said with a reptilian smile. It seemed he made up his mind about me when he received the allegation.

"Maxie's mother has reported to us through her illustrious legal team that you have and continue to deprive Maxie of a stable family life due to the nature of your ongoing relationship with her father." He cleared his throat and looked at me above the rim of his glasses. I held my head high, but shrunk in size as a cold sweat ran down my neck towards the centre of my chest.

"To name a few things, she alleges you have interrupted and inserted yourself into family activities, namely a baking session. You've flown to New York and taken the child from her maternal grandfather and a laundry list of other disturbing allegations. We have been led to believe the relationship is sexual in nature. I'm sure you are up to speed with the Medical Association's guidelines, as well as our hospital policies regarding matters of sexual misconduct. We have those guidelines printed out too." He finally took a breath after the unsettling monologue and pushed a brown file towards Ryland.

I knew this would happen.

"If I may speak to Doctor Braithwaite in private, please?" Ryland asked when he knew what the allegation was.

"Through that door is a room you're welcome to use," the HR director said with a look of exasperation.

As soon as we were alone, Ryland turned to look at me, took a deep breath and spoke quietly. He couldn't hide the apprehension on his face. *This is bad.*

"This is what I meant when I asked if there was anything else I needed to know. You said Maxie came in with her grandmother, does this mean you didn't meet Miles in this hospital for the first time on the occasion you attended to Maxie?"

"I met him then, and that was the first time," I said with a soft sigh. "He arrived after Maxie and her grandmother had been in the ER for about ninety minutes." The trembling, which stopped on my way here, returned. I fought hard to take deep breaths. *Why hadn't I followed my first instinct? But if I had, I would never have fallen deeply in love with the man I had been waiting for all my life.*

"That complicates things."

"I see. Whichever answer I give will be damning. Lying would be worse than owning up to the truth," I whispered.

As if a lightbulb had come on, Ryland's face lit up. "In that case, don't give an answer. What we're going to do here is the best and only way out of this predicament." He looked deep in thought as he prised open his briefcase and handed me pen and paper. "I don't see any other way out, and this is my best advice. You can call Miles if you like, he's the best strategist I know, but I'm sure he would tell you the same thing."

"I'm not making any phone calls now, Ryland. Miles trusted you to help me. What do you propose we do?"

After five minutes of conferring with Ryland and writing down what he told me to, we left the private room and returned to meeting room five, where Doctor Stevens gave me a look of sympathy as Ryland and I walked in.

The situation in London was beyond my control, but this one I let happen. I was embarrassed and felt like a silly schoolgirl with a crush on the most popular boy in school who didn't even know my name. I glanced back at Doctor Stevens while he momentarily closed his eyes.

"Thank you for giving Doctor Braithwaite and I this time, she would like to read something to you," Ryland said to the HR director. "Go ahead, Doctor Braithwaite."

"Dear sirs, please accept this letter as my formal resignation with immediate effect, and it's signed by myself, Doctor Cara Braithwaite, today, the twenty-ninth of April."

"Doctor Braithwaite, you're the most brilliant paediatrician on our staff. Your absence has been deeply felt by all your colleagues. I'm sure this is all a misunderstanding, right?" Doctor Stevens quickly interjected. I didn't make eye contact with him. He was always fair and kind to me, trusted my judgement and was always full of praise, and I let him down. Still, I couldn't talk about it to him, not now, not today. I must follow Ryland's instructions. In this room he was the only one in my corner.

"Hold on, everyone. Doctor Braithwaite, this still doesn't address the concerns raised by Mrs Masterson. We need to return to her legal team with answers," said the lawyer who looked like a viper.

"Doctor Braithwaite is no longer an employee here. If you have any further questions, direct them to my firm, and refrain from contacting her directly. Thank you for your time," Ryland said with finality, handing the lawyers his business card. "After you, Doctor Braithwaite," he said as he helped me pull out my chair. Everything was over before I had time to blink. I got up, glanced apologetically at Doctor Stevens and walked out.

The complaint would turn me into a cliche. Once it got out, I would lose the professional credibility I had done a good job of cultivating since my arrival in Seattle, and there was no one to blame but me.

"Ryland, what does all this mean?" I asked in a shaky breath as we hurriedly walked away from the meeting room. "What are the implications to my medical licence?"

"We've burnt bridges here, and you won't get a recommendation for starters."

"And the medical board?" I was dying inside. All I worked for, obliterated by one decision made in my Cinderella moment.

"Her legal team could advise Maxie's mother to take her complaint to the medical board if she's not satisfied with today's outcome."

"What have we achieved here today then?"

"You weren't let go. You resigned voluntarily. That will work in your favour in your job hunt. I've also bought you time to convince Maxie's mother not to take her complaint to the State Medical Board, but you need to act quickly, as her legal team would hear about this outcome as we speak."

"Thank you, Ryland." I wasn't sure why I was thanking him. The meeting was a disaster. I was unemployed and on a clear path to losing my licence to ever call myself a doctor in any capacity. I needed to tell Suki at the clinic before she caught wind of this any other way. That would be another embarrassing conversation. My only hope was she would let me resign with some dignity. We arrived at the hospital exit.

"Do you need a lift somewhere, Doctor Braithwaite?" Ryland was being kind, but I was too angry and sad, and I realised I didn't hear him the first time he asked.

"No, I have one." I gestured at the silver car waiting, which I had a love-hate relationship with. Currently, I hated it. When I got closer to the car, Clay got out and opened the door for me. As soon as I got inside, I broke down and cried.

"Cara, Ryland sent me a message. I'm sorry." I was startled by Miles' soft voice. My relief at him waiting in the car tempered, as he was the reason I was in this mess. His ex-wife's unresolved issues. But I was still at fault. I knew the rules and knowingly broke them.

"You're here?" I sobbed quietly, loving and loathing the man next to me in equal measure.

"I took Maxie to school, but I was worried about you," he said with sincerity.

"I don't know what to do. She's destroyed me and if I don't tuck my tail and go to her, she'll take everything I've ever worked for away. She has illustrious lawyers after all." I was hysterical.

"Cara, I'm so sorry, I never imagined this would happen. This is being handled as we speak." After the way he spoke to her when she came to Mercer last Friday, this was bound to happen. *She was a woman scorned.*

"Handle it all you like, but you and I are over. She can have you." I sobbed quietly.

"Cara, you can't mean that. You're the only one I want, the only one who'll ever have me."

"I must have been out of mind, thinking you and I could get away with this." I pulled out my phone from my bag and requested a car. There was one only three minutes away.

"Spend the day with me. You need some fresh mountain air. I promise you, clarity will make you feel better afterwards."

Clarity. Everything was crystal clear. I'd lost my job, the man I loved, the life I was building and my self worth.

"My ride's here. Don't call, don't text, don't visit. We're done," I said with a strength I didn't feel.

"Cara, we can't end like this. Listen, you and I are more than what's happening here. Look, you were leaving this job anyway. This isn't the way you wanted to do it, but it's still the same outcome." He tried to reason.

I no longer had a livelihood. I was insignificant and irrelevant. Who was I?

"Are you blind? You have more money than God, but after my savings run out, I'll never be able to afford a basic need, like the roof over my head. Clearly, you've never lost something you've spent half your life working for."

"I'll fix this. We're not done. We can't break things off at the first hurdle. I love you, and you love me. I see a future with you," he pleaded.

He never looked more handsome than he did then, and that had been my downfall. His looks, his charm, his mind, the way he treated me and made me feel. I had been his queen for a while, but the rightful one wanted him back.

"Fix this how? She wants her family back. The last time a patient's family member became fixated on me, I nearly lost my life. I love you, but I will not die for you. Vivian is on a mission and she's unpredictable."

"Listen, you're mistakenly angry and upset with me. I'll call Charlie or Izzy for you—"

"My ride's here. This is over. There's no need to call me, ever. Make it known to Vivian, she's played it very well and has won her family back. She can stay out of my life now, so should you." I walked away from Miles and had never felt unhappier and more alone than I did.

Chapter Thirty-Seven

Miles

I could have handled that better. Instead, I let Cara walk out of my car and out of my life. Vivian's actions had taken her from me. Even if Cara wasn't with me, I wouldn't be the reason she lost what mattered to her. While deep in thought, I heard the driver door shut. My furious eyes met Clay's concerned ones in the rearview mirror.

"Where to, Miles?"

"Broadmoor. Vivian's house." I looked through him, but didn't see him. I had lost Cara. Only a week ago I had been ready to beg her to be my wife.

"Do you want to take some time to cool down before you go there?"

"What do you know about anything, Clay? You have a kinship with Cara, not with me. You go where I tell you, when I tell you." I sighed in resignation.

"You're mad as hell and Doctor Braithwaite walked past me upset. Now you want me to drive to the former Mrs Masterson's. I'm only looking out for you." His eyes darted to my clenched fists then back to my face.

"Drive. Me. To. Broadmoor. Please." I looked out the window, signalling the end of our exchange. It may not have seemed like it, but all it took was the conversation with Clay to compose myself.

He drove quietly, and as soon as the car stopped outside the contemporary glass box Vivian lived in, I stepped out of it. As I walked towards the door, I wandered about living in glasshouses and throwing stones. It was fitting. Vivian was far from perfect, yet she had dragged Cara through the mud because she could.

Before I had a chance to ring the doorbell, Vivian opened the large glass pivot door with what looked like a mixture of hope and apprehension on her face.

As I stood in the doorway, the tension between us crackled.

"You're here because of the doctor? This has everything to do with her, doesn't it?" She nervously smoothed an imaginary wrinkle from her blouse, her eyes searching behind me for whom I imagined she dreaded to see but was eager to face.

"This has everything to do with you and what you've done," I spat, realising what she had done this time was the last straw to the vestiges of whatever parenting relationship remained between us. The veneer of civility I had worked hard to nurture between the two of us had been ripped to shreds.

"Miles, she was breaking the law and the rules she's supposed to follow. Taking advantage of you, worming her way into yours and Maxie's life," she said, her voice barely a whisper as she swallowed hard.

"Stop. Your benevolence is making my knees weak. It's my business who I let into mine and Maxie's life. What the hell were you thinking?" I couldn't help how my voice rose with each spoken word, as frustration continued to simmer within me. "You don't care who I bring into my life. You don't want me to move on with a woman I finally want to be with. A woman who loves me as much as I love her." She flinched. My raised voice took her by surprise, and it made me despise the man I was in that moment.

"I ... I need you and Maxie back. You and I have a real history. A shared past. We love each other, and our girls. You and her are nothing but a quick and torrid fumble," she stammered, her voice tinged with what sounded like desperation. "It's easy to see why you're losing your mind over her, she's a bombshell. But you need something real, with me."

"Something real?" I growled incredulously. "Do you have any idea how deluded you sound? You're Maxie's mom, that's it. Sabotaging my relationship reeks of the conniving manipulations of a selfish and lonely woman." I kept both my hands in my pocket, a pretence at being calm. I was heating up. I had lost Cara because of her.

"Can't you see? If it wasn't for that doctor, you, Maxie, and I would be a family. We would even be working on growing our family." This time she moved closer and tried to put her arms around my neck, which I shoved from me. I walked away and stood at the opposite end of her foyer.

"You'll be hearing from your legal team. Mine should have been in touch with them by now."

"About my visits with Maxie? Is this how you'll punish me?" she retorted.

"This isn't about visitation. It's about slander, harassment and lost earnings. Other things, too. I didn't have time to read the whole lawsuit. It seemed long and expensive. For you."

She gasped loudly. "Miles, this isn't you. It's her. It's all her. What has she done to you?"

As she continued to stand in the doorway and speak, I saw through her flimsy façade of fighting for her family, and I recognized it for what it was. She didn't want to be with me or with Maxie, nor did she want anyone else in my life. The idea of family was what she craved, and Cara was the first woman since our divorce who had threatened the ideal which she longed for. As the confrontation wore on, a tempest of emotions whirled within me. Hurt lanced through me and anger boiled inside but one thing remained true, Cara had seen through Vivian and warned me about how much she could tear apart any meaningful relationship I would ever have.

"She has nothing to do with this, and you've misjudged her. I wouldn't stop you from seeing Maxie. What I would do is pack up my whole life, and Maxie's, and move to the ends of this earth to be wherever Cara is. Make of that what you will, and do everything in your power to make sure I don't follow her with Maxie in tow."

I walked away from her to the car. Anything that threatened Vivian and her finances always made her sit up and pay attention. Using Maxie as a pawn and threatening to take her out of the country was low, but Vivian would know it was a possibility due to Worldwide Media's huge presence in Europe. I should have been satisfied, but I was empty. Only Cara could make me whole, and she had made it clear I was no longer welcome in her life. I rounded the car and went to the driver's side.

"Where to, Miles?"

"We're swapping seats, Clay. I'll drop you off wherever you need to go." I opened the door for Clay, and he glanced at me before walking over to the passenger door.

"Where do we search if we haven't heard from you?" The concern on his face reminded me I was more more than just a job to him. I needed to stop being abrupt with him.

"The mountains," I sighed. All I wanted was to bang on Cara's door and beg her to change her mind about us. But what did I have to show that Vivian wasn't her problem anymore? I needed time to think.

"Miles, that attire—" he continued as he got comfortable in the passenger seat.

"Will work. Where to, Clay?"

How much space and time did Cara need? I had given her plenty. Six weeks to be exact. Six weeks since she walked out of my car and out of my life. But not completely out of it. She had a new job right here in Seattle. Our indiscretion had never made it to the medical board, Ryland Miller assured me. She was within touching distance but I was growing impatient. Her new boss mentioned her employment in passing, so I wouldn't be caught unawares. But I wouldn't get any more information from this employer. She played her cards close to her chest and threw around words like confidential, privacy and trust. She begged me to stay away and not harass her new employee, not at her place of business. I had made a promise I was about to break.

The florist thought it odd that all I wanted were forget-me-nots in the largest arrangements they could come up with. She even tried to nudge me towards roses and lilies. The arrangements were delivered and all that was left was for me to follow the flowers and make my case. With the strangest feeling of déjà vu, I walked into a building I had been in many times before, but this time it was to see someone else.

"Good afternoon, Mr Masterson. Here to see Mrs Masterson? She's out." *I know. She's with Maxie.*

"Not this time, Nadia, I'm here for Doctor Braithwaite."

"Oh, okay. I'll just let her know you're here. Is she expecting you?"

"No, and no need to announce me. Just tell me where she is and I'll find her." She seemed to consider my request for a minute, then shrugged her shoulders.

"What's the worst that could happen? It's technically your building." I could have used the same rationale over the last six weeks, but the situation had been too delicate.

Nadia directed me to Cara's office, and when I arrived at her door I took a breath and prepared myself. Begging wasn't beneath me, my plan was to do anything to have her back. I knocked on her door, and the voice I longed to hear for weeks called out to me.

"Come in." I pushed the door open, and as I walked inside I was hit with pops of blue. The forget-me-nots, and Cara in that blue sheath dress, the one made to bury me. As I walked closer to her, I noticed she still wore her sapphire pendant from London. I might still have her heart after all. "Miles, what are you doing here?" She exhaled deeply.

I forgot everything I had planned to say as I took her in. Even in her office, surrounded by mountains of work, she was still the belle of the ball. The woman who lived in my thoughts, day and night.

"Your boss told me you worked here, right before she warned me against bothering you at work, but I couldn't stay away any longer." I walked slowly towards her, though she still wasn't giving much away. I was happy we were in the same room, and talking. "I gave you space, but I can't breathe without you," I confessed.

"But look at you, warm and well-perfused." She smiled as she stood up and walked towards her window to the six baskets of forget-me-nots. She had the view she loved of the lake. My father had bought this building for the woman he loved so she could fulfil her life's work. The words – full circle – came to mind. "I love the flowers. Picked them yourself from a meadow?" She laughed softly.

I gazed at her and remembered our time in Oxfordshire, our time in Marylebone. All the time we ever spent together, time which had never been enough. Time we wasted trying to be discreet. Time which was almost taken from us by a madman. We didn't need to hide anymore. There was nothing to lose except more time apart.

"I would give anything to go back there with you and pick every forget-me-not from that meadow."

She closed her eyes and took a deep breath. When she opened them, they were glazed with unshed tears.

"I'm sorry I didn't give us a chance, Miles. I shouldn't have given in so easily. I should have taken a leaf out of your book. You never gave up on me. I owed it to both of us to stay strong. I ran from you instead of running towards you." A lone tear ran down her cheek.

I didn't think as I walked closer to her and pulled her into my arms. My world was right again. We held each other close. I had missed her, her sweet scent, her curvy body, what she did to my body. Reluctantly, we pulled apart after some minutes.

"Let's have dinner. Figure things out together?"

"Not if she's still there. Between us," she said hesitantly.

"She's not, it's just you and me."

"I would love to have dinner with you. Somewhere loud, where nothing can ever be kept secret." She smiled the huge smile I had longed to see for weeks.

Fifteen Months Later

Epilogue

"Braithwaite, if I knew being laid off from a job looked like this, I would have been laid off a thousand times. You have not one but two assistants and a pretty lavender loo in your office?" Izzy gushed after she finished a tour of my newly redecorated office at the Worldwide Children's Foundation. I loved my office too – light, bright and feminine with an overabundance of complimentary pastels. It could be misleading as a place of easy workdays, as it was a showcase in charm and whimsy. Chris Masterson was the head of the foundation and she gave me carte blanche to redesign my office.

"Not too loud. I didn't get laid off. Remember, I resigned voluntarily." I shook my head, recalling that low point and how far I had come.

"Potato, potato. Whatever the case, the high priestess of hell did you a favour," she said with a scowl.

"Ancient history. Stick with me, you'll learn the art and science of letting bygones be bygones."

"What? You and Vivian are friends now? I've been away for only three months." We both giggled. I was glad Izzy was back.

"Far from it, but we're in a better place."

"Is she seeing Maxie?"

"That's an ongoing saga. After that breakdown she had when she found out about the baby, she has her one weekend a month, at her father's house. Underneath all that bravado was a broken woman who never got over losing her daughter. She's got a good therapist now."

"I don't know, Braithwaite, she put you through hell. It will take me a while to trust her around you. Keep her at arm's length, maybe a whole field," she said with a chuckle.

"Don't worry, she's far enough. How was London?" I pivoted. Izzy took a three-month break from work after she collapsed from exhaustion during her rounds.

"It was great to be back there. Thanks for letting me stay in Marylebone. I can't believe all I gave you two was dinnerware as your wedding gift, and Chris gave you a whole house."

"Don't beat yourself up, Izzy. We use the dinnerware for all our meals, so it gets more use than the house."

"That makes me feel a lot better." She smiled.

"Back to business, the second assistant is for whoever takes on the position you're interviewing for. I need help. The workload has become surprisingly heavy," I confessed. The workload might be increasing, but it was still easier than any other work I had ever done.

"It's because you're growing a honeymoon heartthrob in there. How are you more beautiful than usual while you do it?"

"Thanks, I might be beautiful, but I'm starving half the time, even now. My head hurts, but only when I'm awake and when I'm asleep. And before Miles is through the front door, I knock him to the ground."

"You're still gorgeous. I've heard the huge appetites are both normal, enjoy them while they last. Have you had the headaches checked out?"

"Yes, everything's as it should be. I guess it's one of those things I should expect."

"I'm sorry, love, it will all be worth it in four more short weeks," she said, giving a short, excited clap. As I paid closer attention to her, she seemed nervous, but she didn't need to be. We were just two girls who had done a good job of finally finding where we fit in.

"Let's get to the matter at hand. As you know, the foundation's Healthy Kids with Healthy Hearts campaign has taken off and it's gone from statewide to nationwide. In the last twelve months, the foundation has facilitated and partly financed northwards of three hundred minor and major heart surgeries for children in Washington State alone. Twenty nine hundred in the rest of the country."

"Right, I'm neither a cardiologist nor paediatrician. What would I be doing as an endocrinologist?"

"As is the case, there's a correlation between diabetes, drug and alcohol dependence, other metabolic diseases versus heart disease in children."

"Sounds like you're trying to court controversy, Braithwaite. Are you going public with this? How about congenital heart defects? Those parents would skin you alive for insinuating that their occasional glass of wine and a cigarette in their younger days made their children sick."

"This isn't anything new, it's all in the public domain. And no, we're not in the blame game, nor do we lord over people and their lifestyle choices. Just good old-fashioned health promotion. Heart disease takes lots of lives all over, we only want to get through to the kids before they form lifelong habits that are difficult to unlearn."

"Okay, I see. I think I love it already. When do I start, and will I get my own fetching office with a lav?" She beamed.

I was happy too. I would be working with my friend and a brilliant thinker.

"And then some. No shift work, no on-call hours. The pay isn't shabby either. Look at your phone, I've sent you the dollar figure you'll be offered." I gestured to her chiming phone on the table.

"Sold!" she exclaimed loudly. Her smile grew wider as she took in the number which appeared on her screen.

"You're my favourite doctor. The one who took care of me when I couldn't take care of myself. You need to be clear and certain about leaving clinical work behind. This is a different animal, but you'll love it."

"Clear as day. I've put in my time, and I want to finally own my weekends. I can't believe this is happening." She forgot where she was and squealed.

"Sorry to disturb you, Cara. The Senator is coming up the elevator now," my assistant whispered after a quick knock at my door.

"Sure, thanks, Nadia. Will you show him to the conference room when he arrives, and let Chris know he's here?" Nadia left just as quickly as she had arrived.

"A Senator has arrived? For you? Why?" Izzy's wide eyes and her hushed tone took me back to being thirteen years old. The thought alone made me smile and brought tears to my eyes.

"Come to this meeting with me. You'll have to meet with him regularly when I leave to have this little one. The work we do here has garnered a lot of attention and we're working with the state government. That's why we can now afford your expertise plus six more nurses."

"My godfathers. You have arrived. Aren't you nervous about this meeting?" She stared at me while shaking her head in awe.

"No, and you shouldn't be either. You've met the senator already." We both stood up and I felt a sharp pain in my back. One I never had before. Just as quickly as it came, it was gone. It would have to wait, this meeting was important. We walked towards the conference room.

"I have? I'm sure I would remember that." She looked thoughtful and shook her head.

"Yes, at my wedding. Richard ..."

"Elliston? Dicky? Oh. Braithwaite, I can't meet with him, ever," she whispered with a mortified look.

"Why not? You're both professionals." I giggled. The senator and Izzy had been playing a game of cat and mouse since they got close at our wedding nearly nine months ago.

"There you are. He's waiting in the conference room. Are you okay? You're favouring your left side." Chris looked worried. I saw her every day at work. We had become each other's sounding board ever since the day she called me.

"Cara, I've been trying to get a hold of you for days, how are you?" She spoke brightly, but my world was doom and gloom, as three weeks of unemployment, occasionally babysitting Finn and Ava and cooking away my feelings was taking its toll. My phone had been off for a week. I switched it on only to reply to Izzy, Dean and Charlie's messages. I erased everyone else from my consciousness, my friends from both jobs and Miles.

"I'm sorry, I don't recognise this number, who's speaking?"

"Of course, why would you? Sorry, darling, it's Chris Masterson." How pathetic, Miles had resorted to sending his mother to try and get us back together.

"Chris, hello. What's this about?" I needed to remain civil. None of this had anything to do with her.

"I got your number from Suki Henderson after talking to her about a position at my foundation, which needs just that certain kind of doctor." I sighed, exasperated. Even my old boss felt sorry for me.

"How do you know Suki?"

"If that's the most important question to you, I'll answer it. She's a friend. We were on the rowing team together at school and she speaks highly of you. Imagine my surprise when she told me the strangest story about how she lost her hardest working doctor over matters of the heart. What had me was how close to home the whole situation was. My son kept his heartache close to his chest and hadn't shared it with me, not until I asked." She spoke in a motherly tone, one I hoped wouldn't make me cry. I had lost my job, my livelihood and the man I was still hopelessly in love with.

"That would make me a pity hire. You don't have to do that for me." It was my turn to speak brightly, although I didn't feel an ounce it.

"Far from it, but if you know any other Oxford-educated doctors with vast international and local specialist experience, in both cardiology and paediatrics, who are hardworking, personable, knowledgeable, genuinely care for their patients and are out-of-the-box thinkers, I will definitely take their names from you and call them for this position. It's a very important one."

"You've got my resume there?" I laughed softly.

"I spoke to a knight who loves the sound of his own voice and he vouched for you, and Suki Henderson has always been thorough and highly intuitive. If you were good enough for her, I would gladly take a chance on you. Can we meet?"

"Just you and I, Chris?"

Just you and I, Cara, I would never interfere in your personal life. This is only about you and I. Well, and hundreds of children. I've got lofty goals."

I got up from my couch, took my first shower in three days, left the house and met with Chris.

"I'm fine, just some back twinges. The sky-high shoes don't help either. I'll go home straight after this meeting." I smiled reassuringly, and this seemed to put Chris at ease. I had worried about working with her when I took the job at the foundation. I needn't have, she was warm, kind and set clear expectations. She never let our personal relationship interfere with our work.

"Isobel, it's good to see you again. Is it premature to say welcome aboard?"

"Not at all, Mrs Masterson. The role sounds wonderful, and it would be hard to pass up the opportunity to work with Cara."

"Call me Chris. We're lucky to have her. Her work here has helped thousands of kids. Join us in this meeting, it will get you up to speed quickly."

"I'm home," I called out as I walked through the front door and kicked off my shoes at the threshold. Both my feet and back vying for the worst pain accolade. The twinges in my back had worsened over the last two hours. All I needed was the weekend to rest.

"You're home. Can I listen to the baby's heart before I go?" Maxie skipped towards the door with a stethoscope in her hands. At nine years old she had grown to be bold, fearless and determined.

"Is it today you're going to Grandpa's? I'll miss you so much." I pulled her into my arms and gave her a quick embrace.

"Doctor Cara, it's only for the weekend. I'll be back on Sunday," she reassured me, her bright eyes twinkling.

"Right, what did we say about calling me Doctor Cara? I'm not your doctor anymore, I'm your really wicked stepmother. You can call me just Cara."

In between giggles, she said, "You're not wicked, and my mommy said I can't call you Cara."

"She did, huh?"

"Yes, she said the baby will learn that and start calling you Cara, too, and you won't like it." Her matter-of-fact tone brought a smile to my face.

"Hmmm, your mommy is quite clever, isn't she? We'll think of something. Where's Daddy?"

"In his office looking at the squares and shapes that hurt his eyes on his computer, but we were playing cards before."

"I hope you let him win this time. Let me see him, then we'll go upstairs and you can listen to the baby's heart." She took my hand and walked towards Miles' office.

"You're not walking straight, Doctor Cara, do you need a doctor?"

"No, a good rest is all I need."

"Pivot tables?" I giggled after we had walked into Miles' office, where we found him staring out the window.

"What gave it away?"

"The glazed look in your eyes, and Lady Maxie told me." He stood up. I let go of Maxie's hand and walked into his arms.

"You smell so good, I missed you," he whispered into the crook of my neck, breathing me in.

"You saw her in the morning, Daddy," Maxie said and giggled, then walked out.

"Yes, you saw me in the morning, Daddy," I looked up at him and still couldn't quite believe he was mine. Would the fluttering butterflies ever go away?

"Are you two girls ganging up on me? I can't wait for him to get here, that way I'll finally have someone who can relate." He placed his hand over my belly, then gently rubbed it while he gazed at me. When he was sure Maxie left, he took my face in both his hands and our lips crushed into each other's. We both moaned as he found the side zipper of the shift dress I wore and slowly started to pull it down. It didn't take long for my centre to melt for him, but good sense won.

"Maxie is walking back any minute now, and we're expecting company soon," I whispered breathlessly. "Besides, you need to finish weeping over your spreadsheets. I thought you delegated those."

"I did. This is something else."

"The football team?" Miles was excited about having a son, and he thought the best way to celebrate was a British acquisition they could enjoy together. And it also gave us an excuse to travel to London more than we did.

"Soccer team."

"You need to get the lingo right. You can't be an owner and not know what you own."

"You call a restroom something else, but the output is still the same. How were your meetings? Did Izzy take the job? Did Dicky behave? He's partial to a beautiful woman. I don't trust him around you." He kissed me and pulled the zipper back up.

"Don't worry about Richard, he only has eyes for one woman. Izzy took the job and was in the meeting. Both she and Richard were flustered and wouldn't stop trying to look at each other when they thought the other wasn't looking, and he agreed to the extra funding."

"You've done great work." He caught my lower lip between his. "I never doubted you would make this job work for you."

Our lips crushed again and we explored each other, until I remembered Maxie was waiting upstairs. "Maxie and I will be upstairs, then I'm making us dinner."

"Fernando made some meals for the weekend, you don't want one of those?"

"They'll keep. Tonight, I want pan fried salmon," I called out as I walked out.

"Salmon is all you've wanted all week," he said, laughing. Salmon was all I'd wanted since we found out I was pregnant.

I walked upstairs to my bedroom, where I found Maxie in the sitting area, waiting for me. When I moved in, we redecorated. The burgundy, although sultry and sexy, had been too moody and masculine, but we found a happy medium with warm cream and tan tones.

"I'll get changed, then we can listen together, okay?" I walked into the store-sized closet and found a soft cotton maxi skirt and a loosely fitted tank. All I craved after a day at work was comfort.

"Can we use the stethoscope and your mommy's pinard?" Maxie asked.

"Well done, you got the names right." I sat next to her on the cream chaise and watched her put the earpieces in her ears, then place the bell against my belly, just as I had shown her. It took her a while to hear what she was listening for.

"I think I can hear something." She had her father's focused face and his resilience too.

"That's because you have very good ears. Now, try the pinard." She used it with a grin.

"I've heard the fast boom boom and whooshing. I think I want to be a doctor when I grow up, it's such fun." As she was talking, Miles came upstairs.

"Maxie, your mom's here for you. Where's your bag?"

"It's in my room, I'll get it. See you on Sunday baby brother." She kissed my belly, as she did every day before we left the house for school.

"I'll come downstairs with you," I said while I put the pinard away and wrapped the stethoscope to return to Maxie's room. I looked up and caught Miles watching me.

"You don't have to come down if you don't want to."

"It's fine. She apologised a few hundred times, and wrote those grovelling letters to the hospital begging for my job back. This is for Maxie. It's the little things she'll always remember." Like Izzy, it was hard for me to trust Vivian. She stopped trying to sink her claws into Miles and that was enough.

"I don't think I've told you how much I love you today."

"Is it the way I wrapped the stethoscope that did it for you?"

"Exactly."

We met Maxie at the top of the landing, and Miles helped her with her bag. Vivian was sitting on the foyer bench, still as beautiful as the first time I met her.

"Hi, Maxie, are you ready?"

"Hi, Mommy," she said, running into her mother's arms. "I'm excited, I miss riding La Jefa."

"I bet she misses you too. I don't know how you do it, Cara. You look effortlessly gorgeous," she said softly, turning to look at me. She was quick with compliments, but it was taking me a while to reconcile this Vivian with the one I first met.

"Thank you. Likewise."

"I've brought you something. Well, it's really for Maxie, but can you keep it for her and use it when you're ready?" she said and handed me a light blue bag, emblazoned with Tiffany and Co.

"What is it, Doctor Cara?" Maxie asked, intrigued.

"Let's find out together, shall we?" We sat down on the foyer bench. I opened the bag and inside was a picture frame, which had words engraved into the intricate silver.

"It says – me and my brother. Is this to put a picture of the baby and me, Mommy?" Maxie asked excitedly.

"I think you'll have plenty of pictures taken with your brother, and you can choose one and put it in here." She smiled a sad smile which didn't quite reach her eyes.

"Thank you, it's beautiful," Miles said, offering Vivian a small smile. I didn't want to read into the moment, but it was one shared by two parents who had loved and lost.

"This is perfect. I'll look after it for her."

"We'll be back on Sunday around seven, will that work for you?" Vivian looked between both Miles and I. Again she was saying and doing all the right things. Could she be setting up to have her access to Maxie increased? She had spent the last year working intensively with a grief counsellor.

"Yes, that's fine. See you on Sunday, beautiful," Miles said and gave Maxie a kiss.

"Have fun, Maxie," I said brightly as they walked out of the house, and I shut the door behind them.

"Let's figure out that salmon now." Miles said as we walked towards the kitchen, which I loved so much. It was still a treat cooking in it, even when I only made the cheese-flavoured microwave popcorn I recently acquired a taste for.

"I was thinking we could eat something Fernando's made. I'm starting to feel really tired."

"Long day?"

"I'm feeling it now, especially in my back and the tops of my thighs."

"I'll give you a massage after dinner, will that help?" Miles asked, coming up behind me and rubbing my lower back. I sagged into his body and, were it not for the rumble in my stomach, I would have stayed in that pose for the rest of the weekend.

"That would be perfect. I think I love you too." I turned to him and kissed him softly.

"Was it the promise of a massage that did it?"

"Maybe it was."

We found a baked salmon dish in the fridge. It may not have been pan fried, but Fernando always outdid himself. Of late he always made sure we had some to eat or cook on standby.

"Miles, I know you've been avoiding talking about it. But I know he was sentenced three days ago." We had both avoided talking about it, but I decided to bring it up.

"You have no business being upset, not now, when you're happy and preoccupied with important things in our life."

"He got exactly what he deserved. I'm happy I never had to face him again. He did me a favour by pleading guilty." I surprised myself. I could talk about my attacker without shaking or breaking out into a cold sweat. Andrea was a godsend, who had turned me into an advocate for talk therapy.

"Sixty-four years without parole is a record in this state for his crimes."

"Did you have anything to do with that?"

"I did what I do best. We did this to protect your peace of mind. I needed to be sure he would never breathe the same air you do."

"We?"

"Doctor Neumann, Doctor Stevens, Suki and I all wrote letters to the sentencing judge. So did some of your patients here and from London. Dean delivered them, as well as his own statement, which he presented directly to the judge."

"How did you do all that?" I gasped. How did I not know any of this?

"I had help, even from Frost. You're a lot of people's beloved doctor. A hundred and seven patients wrote all about it. Those who can't write made it clear with their crayons." He chuckled.

"Dean was in court, and this is all public record now?"

"Yes, he was. The only strings I pulled were to make sure there were no names entered into the public record. If it's something you ever want to talk about to anyone, our children perhaps, you get to do it on your own terms."

"All this was behind closed doors, and you kept it from me too? Maybe I wanted to have a say." I felt like a child among adults who were keeping a very important secret. I didn't speak with much conviction. I wasn't sure how much involvement I could have stomached or what I could've said.

"I took control of this one thing. I wanted to protect both you and the baby, like I failed to in the first place. I didn't know what the stress of it all would've done to you or our son. I would never take any control away from you again, but it had to be done this way."

"You left me in the dark, while you talked to everyone else around me, about me. You treated me like a child. On our first visit to London you promised me we were equals." The outburst was unlike me, but it needed to be said.

"We are equals. I was looking out for my wife. You would've done the same thing for me. In fact, I would expect you to help protect my sanity if you had a way to do it. I wasn't trying to infantilize you in any way." There was a stretch of silence between us while we both ate the baked salmon, and I calmed down and considered what he did.

Being involved in the court process may have brought me some closure, but at what cost? The weeks after it happened I lost all sense of being, and I couldn't afford to do that now. Not when I was about to become a new mom, with a demanding job, and the responsibilities which came with being a wife and a stepmom.

"What you did makes sense. I think it's the surprise that you could do all this without my knowing, which made me fret. Thank you for that, and for keeping everything out of the public eye."

"I would do anything for you. Now, are you ready for that massage?"

"You have no idea," I said as we got up and walked into the great room. The fastidious me would never leave dirty dishes in the kitchen sink, but tonight was different. *I must be very tired.*

I walked towards the large, curved sectional, Maxie's and my favourite reading spot. Before we sat down, I felt the warmth and the wet run down my legs, and heard it splutter. Within seconds, it had pooled onto the hardwood floor.

"Okay, calm down, Cara, don't panic. This is how it works when the baby is ready to come. Take a deep breath. Sit down. I'll go upstairs, get you a change of clothes. I'll call Clay and the photographer. I need to tell Michael I won't be at work. Where's Maxie? Is the baby's room really ready? I should dry the floor, you might slip. Do we need snacks? I think the baby is early. Do we need to call anyone else? You must be in pain, can I get you something for it? Did we ever get the correct diaper size? We haven't brought someone in to change the open risers on the stairs. He might fall through them when he's walking."

I had never met this version of an out-of-control Miles. It was refreshing. Despite who he was and all his experiences, he was another nervous new dad – I had met plenty of those.

"Miles, look at me. You need to calm down and have the breath you're asking me to take." I spoke softly but firmly.

"How are you calm? I'm losing my mind," he spoke in a high-pitched voice, notes I never imagined he could hit.

"I see that. Do everything I tell you, and you'll be just fine. Do you trust me?" I reassured him, as he had reassured me plenty of times before.

"I've just realised you're your mother's daughter. Tell me what I need to do, but I can't deliver him," he said, still in a panic.

"You're not delivering anything or anyone. You might pass out, or something equally dramatic." During it all, I couldn't help the chuckle. "I have a change of clothes in your office closet, can you put that in the downstairs bathroom for me? I packed the black Goyard bowling bag a few weeks ago. It has the correct size diapers and everything else the three of us will need." I didn't recognise the control which I heard in my voice as the pain zapped through my lower back. I drew a deep breath and exhaled through the pain.

"Right. Is there anything else? You have it all under control." He was wide-eyed as he took in my composure, now that he was over his initial panic.

"As soon as you've taken that breath and you've calmed down, then you will drive us to the hospital, and I will have our son."

"How did I get so lucky?" He exhaled as he kissed me, and hurriedly made his way to his office.

The End

Acknowledgements

Thank you dear reader for choosing this book out of the million other choices you had. I can't wait for you to read the next one. Don't forget to leave a review wherever you bought the book from.

Although writing is a solitary pursuit, I've had beautiful souls – both book professionals and otherwise in my orbit at every turn.

The Edit team at Represent Publishing – Who always go above and beyond.

Christin at Giessel Design – You understood everything, and executed precisely.

Christina at Bookescapes – Thank you for giving your valuable time freely and generously.

My sister who takes it upon herself to psychoanalyse the characters – I enjoy your hilarious take on all of them.

My mother who taught me to read, write, speak and treasure words in all the languages we speak.

My husband and children – you complete me...

The brave and beautiful survivors who shared their stories with me when I was researching and writing this book – You're all warriors!